THE LOST STARS

IMPERFECT SWORD

ACE BOOKS BY JACK CAMPBELL

THE LOST FLEET

The Lost Fleet: Dauntless
The Lost Fleet: Fearless
The Lost Fleet: Courageous
The Lost Fleet: Valiant
The Lost Fleet: Relentless
The Lost Fleet: Victorious
The Lost Fleet: Beyond the Frontier: Dreadnaught
The Lost Fleet: Beyond the Frontier: Invincible
The Lost Fleet: Beyond the Frontier: Guardian
The Lost Fleet: Beyond the Frontier: Steadfast

THE LOST STARS

The Lost Stars: Tarnished Knight
The Lost Stars: Perilous Shield
The Lost Stars: Imperfect Sword

WRITTEN AS JOHN G. HEMRY

STARK'S WAR

Stark's War
Stark's Command
Stark's Crusade

PAUL SINCLAIR

A Just Determination
Burden of Proof
Rule of Evidence
Against All Enemies

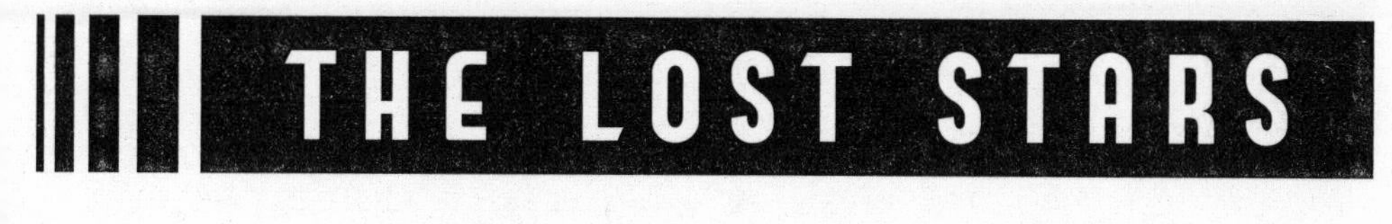

IMPERFECT SWORD

JACK CAMPBELL

THE BERKLEY PUBLISHING GROUP
Published by the Penguin Group
Penguin Group (USA) LLC
375 Hudson Street, New York, New York 10014

USA • Canada • UK • Ireland • Australia • New Zealand • India • South Africa • China

penguin.com

A Penguin Random House Company

This book is an original publication of The Berkley Publishing Group.

Library of Congress Cataloging-in-Publication Data

Campbell, Jack (Naval officer)
The lost stars : imperfect sword / Jack Campbell. — First edition.
pages cm. — (The lost stars ; 3)
ISBN 978-0-425-27225-1 (hardback)
1. Space warfare—Fiction. 2. Imaginary wars and battles—Fiction.
I. Title. II. Title: Imperfect sword.
PS3553.A4637L677 2013
813'.54—dc23
2014029829

FIRST EDITION: October 2014

PRINTED IN THE UNITED STATES OF AMERICA

10 9 8 7 6 5 4 3 2 1

Cover illustration © Craig White.
Cover photographs © Mr Twister / Shutterstock; © Eky Studio / Shutterstock.
Cover design by Judith Lagerman.
Interior text design by Laura K. Corless.

To Daniel V. Bearss,
faithful once and future friend, the ghost of Midway.
Excelsior!

For S., as always.

ACKNOWLEDGMENTS

I remain indebted to my agent, Joshua Bilmes, for his ever-inspired suggestions and assistance, and to my editor, Anne Sowards, for her support and editing. Thanks also to Catherine Asaro, Robert Chase, Carolyn Ives Gilman, J. G. (Huck) Huckenpohler, Simcha Kuritzky, Michael LaViolette, Aly Parsons, Bud Sparhawk, and Constance A. Warner for their suggestions, comments, and recommendations. Thanks also to Charles Petit for his suggestions about space engagements.

THE MIDWAY FLOTILLA

Kommodor Asima Marphissa, commanding
(all ships are former Syndicate Worlds mobile forces units)

ONE BATTLESHIP
Midway (not yet operational)

ONE BATTLE CRUISER
Pele

FOUR HEAVY CRUISERS
Manticore, *Gryphon*, *Basilisk*, and *Kraken*

SIX LIGHT CRUISERS
Falcon, *Osprey*, *Hawk*, *Harrier*, *Kite*, and *Eagle*

TWELVE HUNTER-KILLERS
Sentry, *Sentinel*, *Scout*, *Defender*, *Guardian*, *Pathfinder*, *Protector*, *Patrol*, *Guide*, *Vanguard*, *Picket*, and *Watch*

Ranks in the Midway Flotilla (in descending order), as established by President Iceni

Kommodor
Kapitan First Rank
Kapitan Second Rank
Kapitan Third Rank

Kapitan-Leytenant
Leytenant
Leytenant Second Rank
Ships Officer

CHAPTER ONE

LIKE a pack of immense sharks, warships of the rebellious Free and Independent Midway Star System roamed the dark emptiness of space, patrolling against any threats. At other stars, the crumbling but still-powerful and predacious empire of the Syndicate Worlds gathered forces and tried to stamp out revolution wherever it flared into existence. Midway, strategically positioned and a leader among the rebel star systems, knew it was only a matter of time until the Syndicate attacked again.

"I almost wish something would ha—"

"*Don't* say it."

"I'm sorry, Kommodor. It's just that there are few tasks more boring than standing sentry," Kapitan Diaz said. "Especially deep in space far from any planet or orbiting facility."

"And few things more dangerous than becoming bored or distracted as a sentry," Kommodor Marphissa reminded him, her voice sharp. "Let alone jinxing us with careless wishes!"

"I was about to say how important it was to stay alert," Diaz added quickly. He raised his voice for the benefit of the specialists on the bridge of the heavy cruiser *Manticore*. "If you're on sentry and not paying attention, some enemy might sneak up and stick a knife in you."

"Or one of your superiors might catch you napping," Marphissa said. "If that happens, you'll probably wish an enemy had killed you quickly instead."

"That's the Syndicate way," Diaz agreed. "But we rebelled against the Syndicate."

"And that's why we're on sentry duty," Marphissa said. "The Syndicate wants this star system back under their control." Her gaze shifted to the display before her command seat. The huge hypernet gate that helped make Midway Star System very important hung in space only ten light-minutes away, the massive structure seeming small and insignificant against a backdrop of endless stars. Space had a tendency to dwarf the mightiest human creations. The nearest ship traffic was almost a light-hour distant, a boxy freighter plodding steadily along toward the inner star system. President Iceni, the only one whose orders Marphissa would respect, was four light-hours away, on a planet orbiting only several light-minutes from the star. Marphissa's warships were on their own out here, as was she.

"How long do you think it will be before they attack again?" Diaz wondered.

Marphissa shifted irritably in her own seat. How many times had they had this conversation? "Maybe next week, maybe next month, maybe in the next minute. The only thing we know for certain is that the Syndicate will be back, and they will be bringing a large enough flotilla to make us fight for our lives."

"The battle cruiser should be operational again soon."

"It needs to be operational *now*, along with our battleship," Marphissa grumbled, lowering her voice so only Diaz could hear.

There were some things the specialists should not listen to. "We'll be sitting ducks if the Syndicate returns with a battleship of their own, and all we still have in fighting condition are these cruisers and Hunter-Killers—"

An alert blared, causing everyone on the bridge to jerk to full alertness and frantically focus on their displays as a new symbol sprang to life near the hypernet gate. Ten minutes ago, something had arrived at the gate, the light from that event one hundred eighty million kilometers away only now reaching Marphissa's own flotilla. Boredom and irritation vanished in a flare of excitement and fear as Marphissa waited for *Manticore*'s combat systems to identify the new arrival.

"We're getting a Syndicate ID on it," the senior watch specialist reported, drawing a curse from Kapitan Diaz.

Marphissa had once envied those who commanded flotillas, imagining them free of the day-to-day responsibilities that kept lesser souls in constant labor and worry. But she had already learned that the burdens of being in charge, of having no one else to turn to for orders and guidance, were as heavy as a neutron star and as unforgiving as the pull of gravity from a black hole.

And Marphissa would have to make all of the decisions. It would be almost four more hours before President Iceni even saw that a new Syndicate ship had arrived in this star system.

THERE were times when President Gwen Iceni regretted having learned that not every problem could be solved by ordering someone to be killed.

This was one of those times.

Because at this moment she really, really wanted to kill someone.

"We know that the next Syndicate attack could come at any time," she told General Artur Drakon in what Iceni thought a remarkably well-controlled voice. The way his defensive glower deepened at her words led her to suspect that her voice might not be as controlled as she thought. "There are unknown forces moving against us within this star system, though we've managed to keep the citizens quiet for now by giving them some voice in their own affairs. Supreme CEO Haris at Ulindi might try attacking us again. And, of course, we never know when the enigmas might return and wipe us all out. Did I forget any problems we currently face?"

He met her eyes, defiant despite the obvious guilt he felt. "We can't entirely trust each other." Drakon paused, then added more in even darker tones. "We can't entirely trust our own closest subordinates."

"Then you agree we had more than enough things to worry about before this." Gwen sat back, sighing heavily. "Why do I trust you at all, Artur Drakon?"

"Because you have to. The same reason that's always been there."

"No. I could have tried to have you killed. Where is she now?"

"Colonel Morgan? In her quarters."

"Her quarters." Iceni let the two words hang for a long moment. "After she exploited her position as one of your closest aides to betray you, that's all you're going to do?"

Drakon ran one hand through his hair, looking away. "I haven't decided. I told you. There are complications—"

Whatever Drakon had been about to say was interrupted by a high-priority alarm. Iceni tapped acknowledge, hoping her jerk of surprise hadn't been apparent to Drakon. "What is it?" she snapped as the image of her personal aide/bodyguard/assassin Mehmet Togo appeared beside her desk.

"A ship has arrived at the hypernet gate—" Togo began, his voice and expression both as placid as if nothing could ever unnerve or even annoy him.

"One ship? Why is that so critical?"

"A Syndicate ship."

Iceni felt a chill at odds with the earlier heat of her anger at Drakon and Morgan. "Just one? Did the Syndicate send an unescorted battleship to attack us this time?"

"The ship is a courier vessel," Togo continued. "It informs us that it carries one passenger, CEO Jason Boyens. The courier ship is en route this planet. Even though it is identifying itself as under official Syndicate control, it claims to be operating independently."

"Boyens? Alone?" She looked at Drakon, who frowned again.

"What the hell does he want?" Drakon growled. Boyens was known to both of them from his long service with the old Reserve Flotilla, but after going to the Syndicate supposedly to negotiate an end of hostilities, he had instead returned to Midway in command of a Syndicate flotilla attacking this star system. Timely assistance to Midway from Black Jack's Alliance fleet had forced Boyens to flee that time, but now he was back without any warships.

"Whatever it is, he's putting himself into our hands." She sat back, pushing aside her anger at Morgan and at Drakon, letting Boyens's sudden reappearance filter through the Machiavellian paths that experience in the Syndicate system had worn in her mind.

"Do you want to kill him?" Drakon asked.

"Do you?"

Drakon grinned ferociously. "Not right away."

"Agreed. Let's see what he can tell us, first," Iceni said. She didn't want to pursue further the topic of Morgan's treachery at this moment, so did not object when Drakon made a quick departure to make his own preparations for dealing with whatever news Boyens was bringing.

FIVE minutes after Drakon returned to his headquarters, Iceni forwarded a message from Boyens that she had just received.

Colonel Bran Malin began backing out of Drakon's private office. "I will leave you to discuss the matter with President Iceni, General."

"Hold it."

"General," Malin said, "I fully understand that your confidence in me has been damaged and that I cannot expect to be given the same access to critical issues until your concerns regarding me have been resolved."

"You're right that I'm going to be watching you more in days to come," Drakon said. "But recent revelations about you and Morgan do not alter the fact that I have come to value your insight and opinions. Let's both see what Boyens has to say."

Even Malin could not help a very brief smile at Drakon's words, but all he said was, "Yes, sir. You won't regret it, sir."

The image of CEO Jason Boyens appeared, looking confident but also regretful. "I won't insult you," Boyens began, "by pretending I don't realize that I am now the one who needs to make a deal for my own survival. I want you to realize how much I can do for you. The last time I was in this star system, I may have looked like I was in charge of that Syndicate flotilla, but I wasn't. There was a snake CEO at my back, literally at my back, almost every moment. The slightest misstep would have resulted in my death, and you at the mercy of a snake CEO instead of a friend like me."

A friend? Drakon thought. *Does he expect me to believe that he's now a friend?*

"I have information that you need," Boyens continued. "I could have gone to a lot of different places when I escaped from Prime. I came here. Give me a chance to show you how I can help you. Boyens, out."

Drakon glanced at Malin. "Well?"

Malin considered the question, his head tilted slightly to one side. "His story is plausible, General. Having a senior Internal Security Service agent monitoring his every move would have been a reasonable precaution for the current Syndicate government."

"Because they couldn't trust Boyens, either."

"Yes, sir. But he may know some very important things if he has been at all aware of what the Syndicate is planning." Malin nodded toward where Boyens's image had been. "He appears to have intended that message solely for President Iceni."

"I noticed." Iceni was clearly telling him that they remained allies despite recent discoveries about problems among Drakon's closest aides. "All right. We've seen that message and talked about it. Now, let's talk about you."

Drakon drummed the fingers of his left hand on his desk as he eyed Malin. He had been granted very little time to absorb the news of Malin's true relationship to Morgan, the huge secret Malin had kept from him and everyone else. *On the other hand, if my mother was Roh Morgan, I doubt that I would want anyone knowing, either.* "Never mind CEO Boyens. Can I still trust *you*?"

Malin usually struck people as reserved to the point of coldness, but now he seemed frozen inside at the question. "I . . . General, I will not betray you. I never have."

"Are there any more secrets that I should know?"

"No, sir."

The multitude of hidden sensors focused on Malin provided their verdict on the surface of Drakon's desk, the words polarized so as to be invisible to Malin himself. *No deception noted.* But Malin was as well trained as anyone could be in fooling the sensors that measured signs of dishonesty. "I want the simple truth out of you, Colonel. Where does your loyalty lie?"

The question puzzled Malin. "With you, General. I am loyal to you above all others."

No deception noted. "Have you been working with Colonel Morgan in any way I am not aware of? Engaged in any projects I did not order you to pursue?"

"No, sir."

No deception noted. "Any other person in my position would have you shot. You know that, don't you?" Drakon demanded. "You've been one of my closest assistants, you know just about everything about my forces and contingency plans, and you kept that kind of secret from me. You know too much for someone who misled me."

"The same could be said of Colonel Morgan, sir," Malin said, his words coming out as carefully as if they were footsteps through a minefield.

"I agree. Why shouldn't I have *both* of you shot?"

Malin gazed at him, his face rigid. "You have always been able to count on me, sir. Give me any task, and it will be done."

"That much is true," Drakon admitted. "And I will admit that is also one of the reasons I'm wondering if I can afford to trust you any longer. You're too damned good at getting things done. I need to be sure you're only acting for me."

"I am, General. At this moment, you have a very important task facing you. If you are going to let Morgan live, then you need me to protect you from her."

"You're no match for Morgan. You couldn't stop her if she tried to kill me."

Malin made a self-deprecating gesture. "Not if it was a direct attack, no. But she won't do that, General. She is intensely loyal to you even though that loyalty is warped. Morgan won't try to physically harm you, but that doesn't mean she won't do other things. I can monitor her, watch for schemes, plots, and unauthorized activities. I can identify anyone who contacts her, no matter the means."

Drakon considered the alternatives, then nodded. Until he knew more about what Morgan was up to, there was no one better suited for discovering her secrets than Malin. "Do not make me sorry for giving you another chance," Drakon said, his own words as cold as Malin's eyes. "There will not be any more chances after this."

"I understand, sir. Thank you for the opportunity to prove my continued loyalty to you." Malin saluted, then left.

Drakon sat watching the sealed door after Malin had departed, wondering if he had just made a deal with one devil in order to frustrate the plans of another. But Malin had been invaluable in the past and, aside from the secret regarding his real mother, had never shown any signs of disloyalty or unreliability. In all ways, Malin had always appeared to be bedrock stable and unflappable, which, given that his mother was Roh Morgan, was an impressive achievement.

He called Iceni. "I recommend that we tell Boyens to prove his good faith by telling us everything he knows about the next Syndicate attack. When it will get here, what forces it will consist of, who will be in command, and anything else that can help us prepare to defeat it."

Iceni nodded, her eyes hooded. "I agree. I will inform Boyens that he must provide that information right now, before any negotiations begin, to ensure his own safety. Kommodor Marphissa has detached *Falcon* to 'escort' the courier ship carrying Boyens to this planet. If Boyens betrays us again, or tries to flee, even a courier ship won't be able to outrun a light cruiser quickly enough to avoid being destroyed."

"Boyens will know that," Drakon said.

"I have had the transmissions from CEO Boyens during his last visit to this star system analyzed," Iceni added. An image popped up next to her own, showing Boyens on the bridge of a Syndicate battleship. The image zoomed in on a woman standing a few feet behind Boyens. "She can be seen in the same place relative to Boyens in every transmission. Do you recognize her?"

Drakon studied the broad, cheerful face of the woman, trying to remember if he had ever seen her. A chill ran down his back as her possible identity came to him. "Happy Hua? Is that her?"

"Have you met her?"

"No. I've just heard about her." Drakon gazed at the woman again. "Or rather, I was warned about her. Before her reputation became known, she fooled an awful lot of victims with that façade of hers."

"Hua is a CEO in the Internal Security Service, now," Iceni said.

"She has climbed high on the ladder formed by the bodies of the victims who mistakenly thought her external appearance was a reflection of internal goodwill. If that is the minder that Boyens had at his back, then I am inclined to believe that his words and actions were seriously constrained."

"We don't know how much, though," Drakon argued. "Boyens may have wanted to do some of the same things that Hua was insisting upon. And, for all we know, he didn't really escape to come here but was sent as a double agent."

"General Drakon, I have no intention of trusting the man." Iceni leveled a stern look at him. "I sometimes wonder if any man can be counted upon."

He suppressed the surge of anger those words created because he knew it was a guilty reaction. "I didn't try to hide anything from you, Madam President. Can you say the same?"

She laughed. "Oh, General, you will never know how many things I have kept hidden from you."

Her image disappeared, leaving Drakon gazing at nothing.

EVEN a courier ship boosting in-system at point two light speed required twenty hours to cover the billions of kilometers between the hypernet gate and the world where Iceni and Drakon waited. But at least it covered the distance fairly rapidly, constantly shrinking the time required for a message to travel between the ship and the planet at the speed of light.

Boyens did not look as confident in this message as he had in the last. "I'll tell you what I know about the impending Syndicate attack, just to show my good faith," he said, as if Iceni had not demanded the information of him. "I estimate you have about a week before it gets here. They could be delayed past that, but I don't think they can possibly arrive in less than five days at the earliest. The flotilla is supposed to once again include a battleship, as well as two heavy cruisers, six light cruisers, and ten Hunter-Killers."

He hesitated. "Here are the important parts. I am certain that command of the flotilla will be given to CEO Hua Boucher. If you don't know the name, she's a snake, and a particularly deadly one. I have no idea how good a mobile forces commander she is. From what I saw, she has no real experience at it, but she will be ruthless. Except in one way. I know the Syndicate government won't permit her to bombard Midway. They need everything here, all of the facilities, intact. But that won't stop Hua Boucher from killing by any other means at her disposal if she gets the chance.

"That's all I know. But I gave it to you freely! And there are other things, information that you need to have. If we work together, if you are willing to deal, you can have what you need, and I can get what I want. Boyens, out."

A snake in command. Iceni rubbed her eyes as she thought, then called Togo. "What do you know about CEO Hua Boucher?"

Togo's expression did not change, but thoughts could be seen moving behind his eyes. "She is Internal Security Service. Very dangerous, Madam President. I met CEO Boucher when she was an executive."

"Oh?"

"My training unit was interrogated regarding some shortfalls in food supplies at the unit cafeteria. I was the only member not arrested."

Iceni raised an appreciative eyebrow. "The others were taken in by Hua's happy appearance?"

"As if she were friendly, sympathetic, yes, Madam President," Togo said.

"How did you know better? You must have been pretty young and inexperienced at that point."

Togo paused, and for one of the few times in Iceni's experience, he gave the appearance of being upset. "I was emboldened by her pleasant appearance, so I stole a look into her eyes."

Iceni leaned forward, intrigued. “What did you see there?”

“Nothing, Madam President.” Togo gazed steadily back at her, now betraying no emotion, his words flat. “There was nothing in her eyes. It was as if I were gazing into a patch of space devoid of stars; no light, no life, nothing but cold and emptiness.”

“I see.” Iceni sat back, eyeing Togo. “What are her vulnerabilities?”

“She . . . is very confident in herself. I remember that. It did not bother her that I had looked directly in the eyes of a supervisor.”

“Can you tell me anything else about her?”

Togo made a throwing-away gesture with one hand. “She will show no mercy at all to you and honor no agreement.”

Iceni smiled. “I assumed both of those were true. Thank you.”

Despite the dismissal, Togo paused. “Madam President, I have heard rumors concerning General Drakon’s staff.”

“Yes,” Iceni said, still smiling. “You missed some very important information about Colonel Morgan.”

Togo hesitated, thrown off by that announcement. “I have been told that Morgan is under arrest.”

“Not technically correct. She remains off-limits. Do you understand?”

“She is a threat,” Togo said. Did she only imagine a tinge of weariness in his voice as he repeated that warning for perhaps the twentieth time? “Eliminating her would remove a serious danger to you and send a powerful message.”

“It would send the wrong message.” Iceni waved one flattened hand in a cutting motion to signify the subject was closed. “Have you learned anything else about whoever is trying to stir up trouble among the citizens of this star system?”

“No, Madam President. But I will find them.”

She waved again, this time in clear dismissal, and Togo left.

Iceni sighed, wishing again that her problems could be solved by simply having Morgan killed. But she had seen too many CEOs fall because they had thought they could kill their way out of any difficulty. It was a simple solution that rarely solved the problem, instead usually generating new enemies faster than they could be killed.

She faced a bigger and more urgent problem at the moment, anyway.

Iceni called up a display above her desk, one centered on the star Midway. Planets and numerous other objects whirled slowly about the star. Bright symbols indicated the warships she had to defend everything here. Four heavy cruisers, six light cruisers, twelve Hunter-Killers. A dangerous force in areas where Syndicate authority had collapsed or was tottering, but not adequate to defend against the battleship that CEO Boucher would be bringing. Iceni didn't trust Boyens, but she had no doubt he was telling the truth about that.

In order to defend this star system, Iceni needed her own battleship, but newly constructed *Midway* still had a lot of work that needed to be done before she could engage in combat. The battle cruiser recently acquired from Ulindi was much closer to being ready to fight, once the damage inflicted on the renamed *Pele* when it was captured from so-called Supreme CEO Haris's forces was repaired. *Pele* might be ready before CEO Hua Boucher arrived here. But what could a single battle cruiser do to stop a battleship?

I have no idea how to do that. But I know someone who can do it if anyone can.

This only involved mobile forces, so it wasn't a matter that required consultations with Drakon even if she wasn't still more than annoyed at him. Iceni checked her appearance, sat up straight, composed her expression with the ease of long practice in looking like she was in charge and able to handle anything that came at her, then tapped the control to send a message. "Kommodor Marphissa, there is another Syndicate flotilla en route here, one equivalent in strength to the previous attack. I have been told that it could arrive as soon as five days from now, but you should assume it could show up in only four days. We have strong reason to believe the flotilla will be commanded by a snake CEO named Hua Boucher who lacks experience in commanding mobile forces but is certain to be intensely loyal to the Syndicate. She may be overconfident, she will not care about losses among her workers, but it is likely she will have orders to minimize damage to her warships while trying to retake this star system. She will also have orders not to bombard this star system.

"You have proven your skill at command. I give you no specific orders beyond what you know, that you must defend this star system. We must prevent the Syndicate warships from succeeding in their mission and do so while protecting the people of this star system to the maximum extent possible. I trust in your skill and your judgment to deal with this threat as effectively as you have done in the past."

This was the point at which traditional Syndicate communications would add some motivational threats about the consequences of failure. But Iceni had already dispensed with another time-honored Syndicate practice (detailed orders spelling out exactly what Marphissa should do, since micromanagement was as much a part of the Syndicate way of doing things as paranoia, corruption, and backstabbing) and had found that she got much better results.

"There are a few other matters," Iceni continued. "I will be sending orders to Kapitan Kontos to assume command of *Pele* and make every effort to make her ready to fight within the next few days. I am sending *Falcon* back to you along with Captain Bradamont. Place Captain Bradamont wherever you want to make use of her abilities, but you are to remain aboard *Manticore* as your flagship. I don't want you and Kontos both on *Pele* because I can't afford to lose both of you if the worst happens.

"Good luck, Kommodor.

"For the people, Iceni, out."

Iceni sighed, then sent a message to Kapitan Kontos, conveying her orders for him to leave command of the *Midway* and move to the *Pele*. She grimaced before sending a third message, to Kapitan Freya Mercia, ordering her to take command of the battleship *Midway* in place of Kontos. That left only the need to copy Drakon on her last three messages, then inform him that Captain Bradamont needed to be lifted up to *Falcon* as soon as possible.

And that was pretty much all she would be able to do to prepare the defense of Midway against the latest Syndicate attack. No one in their right mind tried to dictate the details of time-critical activity across four light-hours' distance, though Iceni had known (and a few times had to work for) people who thought such a thing could work. Everything else would now be up to Marphissa, Kontos, the workers trying to get *Pele* ready for battle, and Captain Bradamont. Twice before, Admiral Geary's Alliance fleet had saved Midway Star System, an odd thing given the only recently concluded and century-long war that had nurtured generations of hatred between the Syndicate Worlds and the Alliance. But Midway was no longer Syndicate, Black Jack Geary was no average officer of the Alliance, and now perhaps Captain Bradamont, left here by Black Jack as an adviser and liaison officer, could help Midway's warships save this star system a third time.

Iceni gazed morosely at her calendar, knowing that the next few days would pass very slowly as everyone waited for the axe to fall.

At least the prospect of interrogating CEO Jason Boyens offered the promise of some distraction during that time.

CHAPTER TWO

DRAKON met Colonel Rogero as he reentered the ground forces headquarters complex. "Did you see off Captain Bradamont?"

Rogero nodded, looking unhappy as he did so. "It would be easier for me to be going off to face a tough fight than to see her doing it."

"You know the same is true for her if she had to watch you go. I've just informed Colonels Gaiene and Kai of something, and I need to tell you in person as well." Drakon did his best to keep his voice level. "Effective immediately, neither you nor anyone else is to follow orders from Colonel Morgan, even if she says those orders are coming from me."

To his credit, Rogero managed not to show any reaction to the statement. "I understand, General. May I ask why—"

"No. Colonel Morgan is going on special detached duty, so you won't be seeing her. But if she does contact you, follow the orders I just gave you."

Rogero nodded. "Yes, sir. Given the . . . change in policy contained in your orders, may I ask if the status of Colonel Malin has changed in any way?"

Drakon took a few seconds to think that through before answering. For the last few years, Morgan and Malin had been his right and left hands. Losing one hand was bad enough, and too difficult to explain at this time. Cutting off the other might well hurt him more than it did any hypothetical plots that Malin might be working on. "No. Except in one respect. If Colonel Malin conveys orders to you that he says are from me, follow your instincts. If anything about those orders smells wrong to you, check with me directly before you carry them out."

"Understood, General."

"Good," Drakon said, knowing just how many questions were boiling under Rogero's impassive surface. But he wasn't ready to answer any of those questions yet, so he shifted topics to another issue of concern. "How is your brigade doing?" He had asked that question many times before, so Rogero would know that Drakon was asking not about readiness statistics but about the mental and emotional state of his soldiers.

"No significant problems," Rogero replied. "But when I talked to my senior specialists this morning, they said they are noticing an increase in the number of odd rumors making the rounds that they believe are being fed to our ground forces."

"Odd rumors?" Drakon pressed. "Anything new?"

"Just in the specifics." Rogero frowned outward toward the rest of the city as he thought. "They fall into three broad categories. One set argues that you and President Iceni are only doing what you are in order to stay in control of this star system, that you remain Syndicate CEOs in all but name. That one isn't gaining much traction since our men and women know you by your actions and know that President Iceni has banned labor camps. The second set of rumors is that you and the president intend betraying this star system and the people in it by using it as a base to establish your own Syndicate successor empire. I'll be frank in saying that the soldiers are worrying about that more than I'm comfortable with. And the third set of rumors are variations on claims that President Iceni is planning on assassinating you and wiping out your ground forces to ensure her own place as ruler of this star system."

Drakon laughed sharply. "How is Iceni supposed to accomplish that? With planetary militia?"

"No, sir. That's one of the devious things about that set of rumors. It claims that some of our own ground forces, whole units or just officers, will betray the rest and help Iceni." Rogero twisted his lips in a crooked grin. "So the rumors foster distrust of President Iceni *and* of their fellow soldiers."

"Clever," Drakon admitted. "I don't believe for a moment that President Iceni is plotting that, but it's a well-crafted set of rumors to generate fear and suspicion."

Rogero inhaled deeply, blew out again, then fixed a keen look on Drakon. "You are certain the president will not try to kill you? There have been some attempts on you and on me."

"I know." It was Drakon's turn to smile without humor. "But if President Iceni were really the one plotting to kill me, we wouldn't hear any rumors of it. I'd just be dead whenever she gave the order. She's that good. Besides, I know I can trust you and that you'd spot any real plotting by some of the soldiers in your brigade."

"Thank you, General," Rogero said. "You know you can trust Colonel Gaiene as well. He may not keep track of affairs inside his brigade as closely as he should, but his executive officer is making up for that."

"And Colonel Kai has always been loyal," Drakon noted.

Rogero grinned hugely. "You can count on Kai, sir. For him to betray you would require Kai to act quickly and recklessly. When has Kai ever been quick or reckless?"

This time Drakon laughed. "He's like a rock, for better and for worse. No one's going to move him. Try to counter the rumors, keep me informed of them, and see if your senior specialists can trace the rumors to any sources. I would really like to speak to whoever is introducing those rumors into the ranks."

"Yes, sir. So would I."

"And, Donal, if anyone can handle that Syndicate attack force on the way, it's Captain Bradamont and that Kommodor."

It was easy to tell that Rogero forced his answering smile. "Yes, sir. If anyone can."

THIS time, the alert resounding through *Manticore*'s bridge did not warn of anything as easy to handle as a courier ship.

"One battleship," the senior watch specialist announced. "Three heavy cruisers. Five light cruisers. Ten Hunter-Killers. All are broadcasting Syndicate identification. They are arranged in Standard Box Formation One."

Kommodor Marphissa nodded, keeping her eyes on her display. Standard Box Formation One was as frequently used by Syndicate mobile forces as its name implied. The battleship occupied the center of a box formed by the smaller units with it, the three heavy cruisers holding three of the front corners along with one light cruiser at the fourth, while the other light cruisers held the back four corners and the small, expendable Hunter-Killers were evenly arrayed in the region between the cruisers and the battleship. "Is it the same battleship that was here last time?"

"Yes, Kommodor," the watch specialist said. "It is broadcasting BB-57E unit identification code, the same unit as was in the last Syndicate flotilla."

Kapitan Diaz turned a disapproving eye on the specialist. "Just because it is broadcasting that code does not mean it is the real code for that ship. See if you can spot the hull features that will confirm the battleship's identity."

"Yes, Kapitan," the specialist said, looking worried at his mistake. Things had changed on these warships since the revolt against the Syndicate, but no one could forget the experiences they had under the old system. Not answering a supervisor's question accurately, even for the best of reasons, often produced tongue-lashings or worse punishment.

But, having been on the receiving end of plenty of those tongue-lashings herself, Marphissa had vowed to reserve them for real, serious screwups. All she did was grimace, wondering what tricks the Syndicate flotilla might have up its sleeve. "At least the information from CEO Boyens was mostly correct. Let us see who is in command of this flotilla."

Kapitan Diaz glanced over at her. "Do you want me to—"

"No maneuvers, yet, Kapitan. They're ten light-minutes away. I want to watch what they do before I decide what we should do."

Captain Honore Bradamont came onto the bridge, moving fast. "It's them?"

The spectacle of an Alliance officer on the bridge of a former Syndicate warship was strange enough. Even stranger was that the specialists and officers on the bridge greeted her arrival with relieved smiles. Bradamont might be an officer of the hated Alliance, but she was also one of Black Jack's officers, and one who had played a critical role in ensuring the success of some recent operations by Marphissa's warships. To the crew of *Manticore*, she was no longer an enemy officer but one of theirs.

"It's them," Marphissa confirmed, turning a brief smile of her own on Bradamont. "They've got a battleship, all right."

"Damn." Bradamont came up next to her seat and squinted at Marphissa's display. "Where's *Pele*?"

"Still twenty light-minutes away." The battle cruiser had been charging toward the hypernet gate for the last several hours, accompanied by the heavy cruisers *Basilisk* and *Gryphon*. Far behind them, lumbering along its orbit as it had for countless years, was the gas giant planet near which Midway's main ship-repair facility hung in space, looking oddly forlorn now that *Pele*, the heavy cruisers, and the battleship *Midway* had left it.

Unlike the battle cruiser, though, *Midway* was slowly heading away from the other warships. Her projected path formed a huge arc through space, finally merging with the orbit of the main inhabited world where most of the humans in this star system lived and worked. At the sluggish rate she was accelerating, it would take *Midway* a week to cover the distance to that world.

Bradamont bent close to Marphissa's ear. "Is *Pele* really that ready for battle? Her shields and weaponry look in great shape."

"Kontos wouldn't fake the readiness of that ship," Marphissa said. "Not to us. I've known many an executive and CEO who would, to curry temporary favor, but not Kontos. He's too honest." She smiled again, bitterly this time. "He wouldn't have lasted another year under the Syndicate. Speaking truth to CEOs is a deadly habit."

"He's not being too honest about the status of *Midway*," Bradamont noted, nodding toward the depiction of the battleship on Marphissa's display. "It looks like the ship has suffered a recent major propulsion casualty rather than having full capability as it really does."

"That's some impressive camouflage, isn't it?" Marphissa said. "It looks just like more than half of the main propulsion units blew up. But that's misleading the enemy, not his own superiors. I'm perfectly fine with that. If *Midway* looks like a bird with a broken wing, the Syndicate flotilla should leave her alone and plan to nail her after they've gained control of the star system."

"Or they might try something foolish, thinking she's an easy target. You're keeping this formation?" Bradamont asked, phrasing the loaded question diplomatically. Marphissa had arranged her own warships in Standard Box Formation One as well, though in this case the two heavy cruisers with her, *Manticore* and *Kraken*, occupied the center, with the light cruisers *Falcon*, *Osprey*, *Hawk*, *Harrier*, *Kite*, and *Eagle* at six of the eight corners of the box, and her twelve Hunter-Killers at the other two corners and positioned inside the box.

"For now," Marphissa replied. "I know it's not the best formation to engage that Syndicate flotilla, but I want the Syndicate commander to think I'm still following Syndicate doctrine."

"Good idea," Bradamont approved. "The longer they believe you're going to fight a predictable battle, the better."

"Kommodor," the communications specialist announced, "we have just received a transmission from the Syndicate flotilla. It is addressed to the commander of our force."

"Bounce it to me," Marphissa said.

The window that appeared before her showed a woman whose wide mouth and cheekbones appeared to be set in a perpetual state of kind merriment. She would have seemed the personification of a warm, happy grandmother except for the jarring juxtaposition of the finely tailored Syndicate CEO suit that she was wearing.

"Happy Hua," Kapitan Diaz murmured, horrified. "That's really her, isn't it?"

"Speaking of false appearances," Marphissa said. "Even though I've heard of her, I still have trouble believing someone who looks like that is the most ruthless bitch in the Internal Security Service."

Hua began speaking. Her voice would have been pleasant enough, but the words she was speaking destroyed any illusion of congeniality. "To the commander of the rebellious mobile forces in this star system. You have two choices. Surrender your mobile forces to me, and be allowed the opportunity to prove your usefulness to the Syndicate Worlds once again, or die. I expect an immediate response. For the people, Boucher, out." As usual in Syndicate communications, the CEO droned out the "for the people" phrase in a quick slur of rote words that her delivery made clear were meaningless.

"That was clumsy," Bradamont snorted. "She should have tried to fool you into letting her get a lot closer before she issued that ultimatum."

"She's a snake," Diaz said. "She's not used to negotiating with her victims. I guess their offers to *surrender or confess and you might live* must fool some people because they always say that, but no one who was really guilty would be dumb enough to believe it."

Marphissa nodded. "That offer only catches the innocent who think their innocence will protect them. That CEO threatened me right off, Honore, because she doesn't realize how hard it will be to catch our ships with her battleship. Unless you've done space operations, it's hard to grasp just how huge the battlefield is. I bet she's thinking in planetary surface terms. Like, she can see us, so we can't be all that far away." She paused to think. "Comms. Give me a broadcast to every ship in the Syndicate flotilla."

"You have it, Kommodor. Key Two."

"Also prepare a copy of the record we have of the destruction of that Syndicate light cruiser the last time they were here. The one that mutinied."

"In a moment, Kommodor. One moment. Ready. Attachment Alpha."

Marphissa gestured Bradamont away from her seat, so that the Alliance officer would not show in the transmission, then took a deep breath and tapped the control. "To the people in the crews of the mobile forces still under control of the Syndicate, this is Kommodor Asima Marphissa of the free and independent star system of Midway. We are no longer slaves of the Syndicate. We rule ourselves. Every snake in this star system is dead, so we do not serve the whims of internal security or fear for the safety of our families and loved ones.

We are free, and you can be as well! Do not serve those who see you and treat you as cattle! Rise and slay the snakes among you, then join us, or return to your own homes to help them gain the freedom we have fought for. But beware of snake tricks. They will slay you without warning or cause, as they did the crew of this unfortunate light cruiser which belonged to the last Syndicate flotilla to come here. Join us, who value and respect all, workers and supervisors alike. For the people!" she ended, emphasizing and giving power to each word. "Marphissa, out."

She tapped the attachment control, sending the image of the light cruiser being blown to fragments by its own power core. Did the crews of the other Syndicate vessels know that light cruiser had been destroyed to prevent its crew from taking the ship? They would now.

"Those ships must be crawling with snakes," Diaz muttered. "What chance of successful mutiny do any of the crews have?"

"Probably none," Marphissa admitted. "But all of those snakes will be redoubling their watching of the crews of their own ships, worried about them, instead of watching and worrying about what we'll do. The snakes will question everything anyone in the crews does, slowing their actions and making them hesitate. You've been there, just like me. You know what it's like."

"Don't remind me! There were times I was afraid I might breathe wrong."

It would take ten minutes for the defiant reply to reach the Syndicate flotilla, but only three minutes later the operations specialist reported movement. "The Syndicate mobile forces are accelerating and coming onto an intercept vector with our formation, Kommodor."

"Standard acceleration profile for a battleship formation," Diaz noted. "Happy Hua is doing everything by the book."

Marphissa nodded again, her eyes once more on her display. "What are you thinking?" she asked Bradamont.

"If this CEO is inexperienced in space combat," Bradamont replied, "then, if it were me, I wouldn't merge this formation with Kapitan Kontos's when *Pele* gets close enough. I'd have Kontos operate separately. That CEO will have a lot more trouble grasping the situation and deciding what to do if she has two attacking formations to deal with instead of one."

"She's going to use the automated systems," Diaz said. "Don't you think? Hua Boucher won't trust the supervisors or workers in the crews, but she will trust the software because people that high up always believe their own propaganda about how perfect the automated systems are."

Marphissa nodded, chewing her lower lip as she thought. "Yes. Kapitan, you are right. And so are you, Captain Bradamont."

"Are your automated systems that bad?" Bradamont asked.

"It's not that they're so bad, though they're far from perfect; it's that we know them. We've got older versions of whatever CEO Boucher has, so we will know pretty much what those automated systems will tell her to do."

"Taking down a battleship is still going to be tremendously difficult with the forces you've got," Bradamont cautioned. "The ideas we discussed before are still your best options. Peel away the escorts, destroy them during repeated attacks, and leave the battleship alone so you can keep pounding it. They'll probably still be able to get away if they run, but if they stay to fight, you can eventually do enough damage to knock it out. It'll very likely cost you, though, and if you push the attacks too close, too early, your ships will get torn apart by that battleship's firepower."

"I have to be aggressive," Marphissa insisted.

"Yes. *And* patient. It's a tough combination. Syndic . . . I mean Syndicate battleships of that model are best hit on their stern flanks. That's where their shields and armor are weakest. You face more firepower than if you hit them dead astern, but their shields facing directly aft are a lot stronger."

Diaz gave Bradamont a troubled look, which Marphissa understood. The Alliance captain had gained her knowledge through experience, through battles against Syndicate warships like that battleship, and like the heavy cruiser which she now rode. It was jarring to be reminded of that, of how many times Bradamont had fought and killed their own comrades, while their comrades had done their best to fight and kill her. Only months, not years, separated those times from now. "Those were Syndicate," Marphissa murmured. "We are not."

Diaz bit his lip and nodded, while Bradamont looked away, understanding their discomfort. "Who is in command of *Midway* now?" she asked, deliberately changing the subject.

"Kapitan Freya Mercia," Marphissa said. "One of the Reserve Flotilla survivors we brought back. President Iceni was very impressed by her."

Bradamont looked away again. That hadn't been a safe topic after all. She had been in command of an Alliance battle cruiser, the *Dragon*, when Black Jack's fleet had destroyed the Syndicate Worlds' Reserve Flotilla. "I met her, too. If she is half as capable as she seems, Kapitan Mercia will do a good job in that command."

"But *Midway* is not in this fight," Marphissa said as she took another glance at her display. "And Kapitan Mercia can do little without weapons no matter how capable she is. We will reposition and begin making things as difficult as we can for CEO Boucher."

For all their mutual hostility, the Alliance and the Syndicate Worlds had retained the same simplified conventions for determining directions in the vast reaches of space that otherwise had no defined directions. Every star system had a plane in which its planets orbited. Humans designated one side of that plane as up, and the other as down, anything toward the sun was starboard or starward, and anything away from the sun was port. It wasn't precise, but it got the job done, where otherwise a command to "turn left" might find ships turning in every conceivable direction.

The Syndicate flotilla had finished turning their way, but would still require more than an hour and a half to intercept Marphissa's ships because of the battleship that was the enemy flotilla's greatest strength but also a drag on the flotilla's ability to accelerate. Because they were on a direct intercept, constantly closing the range, the Syndicate warships remained just off to the left of Marphissa's formation and slightly above it. They would stay in that aspect, getting closer and closer, unless and until Marphissa maneuvered her own ships.

Pele was way behind Marphissa, below and about fifteen degrees to the right relative to her. At least, that's where she had been twenty minutes ago. *Midway* was much farther away, nearly three light-hours, below and twenty degrees to the right relative to Marphissa's warships. "We will drop back toward *Pele*, so we can conduct simultaneous attacks with Kapitan Kontos. I want a vector that brings us within two light-minutes of an intercept with *Pele*, and maintains four light-minutes' distance from the Syndicate flotilla until then. Work it up."

Diaz gestured to his specialists, who began calculating the maneuvers. It wasn't hard, given the assistance of the automated systems. Input the variables, tell the systems where you wanted to go, and the answer would display itself in less than a second. It was just physics and complex math, measured against the exact capabilities of the warships under Marphissa's control, all of which automated systems were very good at. "Four light-minutes?" he asked Marphissa.

"It's not too close," she told him. "I don't want to end up within reach of that battleship's firepower unless it's on my terms. Four light-minutes gives us time to see what the Syndicate ships are doing and counter it. But it should also be close enough to make CEO Boucher very frustrated as she tries to close that gap and can't come to grips with us."

"So near, yet so far?" Diaz said with a grin.

"Exactly. She's a senior snake. She's used to the universe bending over backward at her command. *No one* defies her orders. But we will."

"We have the maneuver prepared, Kommodor," the senior watch specialist reported.

Marphissa squinted a bit as she studied the plan on her display. It showed her formation swinging into a wide arc up and to the right that steadied out onto a flattened curve reaching to meet the projected course of *Pele* and the two heavy cruisers with her. Next to the lines were time marks, indicating when to initiate each stage of the maneuver. With systems like that to produce solutions, it was easy for someone lacking experience (like CEO Hua Boucher) to think that they didn't need such experience to match those with a lot of time driving ships in space.

"The maneuver is acceptable," Marphissa said. Nothing fancy, nothing to cause Hua to worry about the skills or predictability of her opponent. "We'll let CEO Boucher think that's how we'll maneuver when we fight."

"She must know you're better than that," Diaz said. "The Syndicate has seen you command in fights here and at Indras."

"If reports of those fights have made it to the right people rather than being buried in the databases," Marphissa replied. "And if anyone who read them paid attention to them. I'll hope for anonymity born of ignorance or arrogance when it comes to what CEO Boucher may know about me."

After that, it was just a matter of waiting. Warships could boost to awesome velocities when measured in planetary terms. *Pele* was now coming toward Marphissa's formation at point two five light speed, Kontos having increased velocity once he saw the arrival of the Syndicate flotilla. Point two five light speed was the equivalent of seventy-five thousand kilometers per second. The human mind couldn't really grasp such distances or such velocities. Even the universe itself partially rejected them. By the time a spacecraft reached point two light speed, its vision of the universe outside it had begun stretching and distorting. Human equipment could compensate for that, could provide a "true" image of the outside, but once beyond those velocities, once a ship reached for point three or even point four light speed, human ingenuity could not prevail against the relativistic distortion that made the universe appear to be stretched and bunched like loose, elastic fabric. And the ship itself grew heavier, its mass increasing, making it ever harder to increase velocity. The cost and complications made such velocities much more expensive for trade than the extra days needed for travel cost. In practice, only warships boosted to point one and point two light speed, and didn't try to fight at higher speeds than that because of the impossibility of scoring hits on one another when their view of the universe was warped too badly.

Despite the obstacles facing them, humans had found the means to travel to different stars. Jump drives that pushed ships into a different place where distances were much shorter and the rules of this universe did not apply. The hypernet that used quantum entanglement to transport ships between stars without, technically, ever moving them. Humans had used those to settle the worlds orbiting other stars, trade between those worlds, and fight wars spanning the stars.

Wars like that of the last century, started by the Syndicate Worlds and sustained by the refusal of the Alliance to surrender and the refusal of the Syndicate to stop fighting. In the end, with both sides tottering on the brink of collapse, a man who had supposedly died a century before, the legendary Black Jack Geary, had reappeared just in time to save the Alliance fleet. Geary had annihilated the Syndicate forces sent to catch him and forced an end to the war. Defeated, with its mobile forces decimated and economy reeling from the costs of the long war, the iron grip of the Syndicate government finally slipped, and star systems began breaking free.

Star systems like this one.

"Five minutes to maneuver time," the senior watch specialist announced.

Marphissa shook herself out of her reverie. "Execute maneuver on time using automated controls. Link all ships in this formation." The precision with which the maneuver would be executed would make it clear to outside observers that they were using the systems to control the ships. That should further lull CEO Boucher into complacency.

"Link all ships and execute maneuver using automated controls," the watch specialist repeated to ensure that he had heard the order properly. "I understand and will comply."

At the mark, every ship in Marphissa's formation swung up and to the side, coming around under the push of thrusters and main propulsion units. The turn-together maneuver meant that every ship remained in the same spot relative to the other ships in the formation. They changed their facing and accelerated toward a meeting with *Pele*, but the box formation had not altered.

"You know," Captain Bradamont commented, "if Admiral Geary had required his ships to maneuver on automated controls, he would have had to fend off scores of complaints from his ship captains."

Kapitan Diaz gave her a skeptical look. "They only would have complained once, though. Right? Then he would have replaced them."

"No. It took him a while to assert authority over his ships, and even now his decisions get questioned at times."

Marphissa shot Bradamont an irritated glance. "Seriously? Before Black Jack came back, we saw the Alliance ships attack us in swarms rather than rigid formations, but we thought that was doctrine."

"In a way, it was." Bradamont sounded angry herself. "We'd forgotten that courage needs to be paired with discipline, individual initiative with support to your comrades. Admiral Geary reminded us that fighting as a team is much better than a bunch of ships battling individually. You've loosened a lot of the controls the Syndic government put on you, Asima. Be careful you don't let too much freedom into your military forces."

"But this is better," Diaz argued.

"It is. Just remember the need for balance, for tying everything into the goal of creating an effective military team that makes as much use as possible of the individual skills of your people."

"You always make things complicated," Marphissa grumbled. Her ships had steadied out on their new vectors, but were still accelerating, aiming to match the velocity of the oncoming Syndicate flotilla. "I was thinking, you said *Pele* should operate separately from my own formation, and I still agree that is a good idea. But if I timed *Pele*'s attacks to match my own, we would present CEO Boucher with a complication, but still she would be dealing with one set of attacks at once, then have time to recover while we repositioned for our next attack."

"That's true," Bradamont agreed.

"But if I just cut Kontos loose, tell him to hit the escorts and keep hitting them, and conduct my own attacks independent of him, then CEO Boucher will face more frequent attacks, from different angles. It will be harder for her to keep track of things and decide which recommendation to accept from her automated combat systems. And Kontos," Marphissa added with a sly smile, "is likely to do something unexpected, something that the combat systems on the Syndicate ship do not anticipate."

"Kontos still doesn't have a lot of experience himself," Bradamont reminded her. "He's good. Hell, he's brilliant at times. But he's young, and he hasn't been doing this long. A miscalculation on his part, a risk whose magnitude he doesn't fully appreciate because of a lack of experience, could be disastrous when we're facing a battleship."

"True." Marphissa pondered the matter as her ships finally matched the velocity of the Syndicate flotilla. The two formations were now tearing through space, separated by four light-minutes, heading toward a much faster intercept with *Pele*. "I believe that Kontos can do this, Honore. President Iceni moved him to command of *Pele* because she has confidence in him. President Iceni is a good judge of character. You know as well as I do that we need something extra. Something big extra. We might be able to destroy every escort that Syndicate battleship has got, but stopping the battleship itself with what we've got is going to take a miracle."

"It's your call, Kommodor," Bradamont said. "You are right about how hard it will be to hurt that thing without losing all of our own ships in the effort."

Marphissa tapped her comm controls. "Kapitan Kontos, I want you to use your three ships to conduct attacks on the enemy independently of my formation. We want to eliminate the battleship's escorts, confuse and frustrate the Syndicate commander, and ultimately wear down the battleship's defenses. Keep me informed as necessary of your intentions and planned actions. For the people, Marphissa, out."

"Syndicate flotilla is accelerating," the combat watch specialist reported.

"Match their acceleration using automated controls," Marphissa ordered the maneuvering watch specialist. "Maintain four light-minutes' distance between us."

"You could let CEO Boucher get closer," Bradamont murmured to Marphissa. "Let her think she's slowly gaining on you."

"I'm not trying to lead her anywhere," Marphissa said. "I want to taunt her and frustrate her, like a cat on a fence, just out of reach of the dog trying to get it."

"Kommodor," the senior watch specialist said, "our systems assess that the battleship is exceeding safe limits on main propulsion. If they continue to push their acceleration at the current rate, the chances of catastrophic component failure will rise rapidly."

"How long?" Marphissa demanded. "Do we have an estimate of how much longer they can accelerate at current rates?"

"There are some uncertainties, Kommodor. But they cannot sustain their current effort for more than another sixteen minutes at the most."

Marphissa stared intently at her display, imagining the scene on the bridge of the battleship. She had been in such situations before, the workers or junior executives warning of danger, a clueless CEO insisting that the current effort be continued, the sub-CEOs and most of the senior executives seeking foremost to avoid confronting the CEO and thus refusing to back up their juniors as danger readings crept closer toward disaster. More often than not, automatic safety routines had finally activated while senior ranks still denied or debated.

It was one area where automated systems had saved a lot of Syndicate ships.

Sure enough, the entire Syndicate flotilla kept accelerating at a rate that was unsustainable for the battleship. Kept accelerating for another twelve minutes, at which point the main propulsion on the battleship abruptly cut back.

"Syndicate battleship is now accelerating at eighty percent of capacity," the senior watch specialist said. "That is the standard recovery rate for overstressed systems."

"Reduce our acceleration to match," Marphissa ordered.

"Kommodor, the Syndicate flotilla has ceased accelerating and is changing course slightly."

On her display, Marphissa watched the long curve of the Syndicate flotilla's projected path shift. Four minutes ago, the enemy had bent their path a few degrees to port. "CEO Boucher is trying to position herself between us and *Pele*."

"She wants to prevent *Pele* from joining our formation?" Kapitan Diaz asked.

"Syndicate doctrine," Marphissa replied. "Concentrate forces. We still look Syndicate because we use Syndicate equipment, so Boucher is assuming we'll still fight like the Syndicate. She will soon learn otherwise."

Marphissa knew that she had to sound confident even though she still had no specific idea how to stop that Syndicate battleship. Any hint of uncertainty, of fear, in her voice and attitude would be scented by the specialists on the bridge and race through this ship and the rest of flotilla like a plague moving at the speed of light. She could lose this battle before a single shot was fired if her crews lost confidence in her.

At least her next move was fairly simple. Both her formation and the Syndicate formation were now racing through space along almost the same path at point two light speed, which meant their relative velocity was zero, the two groups of ships staying the exact same distance apart even though both were moving very quickly. It reminded Marphissa of two ground vehicles on a highway, both moving fast in the same direction at the same speed.

Her formation, in front, would need to slow down to get within weapons range of the Syndicate formation. "We'll need to brake down to point one light," she told Diaz as she set up the maneuver. "The timing is right for us to hit the Syndicate flotilla just as *Pele* is about to get there. Hua is going to have to watch both of our formations and decide what to do."

Marphissa considered options, then decided to stick with automated control of the maneuver one more time. "All units in Midway flotilla primary formation, I have sent the command for our ships to pivot one hundred eighty degrees and begin braking."

Thrusters on *Manticore* and the other ships pushed their bows up and over, so that the ships were now moving stern first through space, their bows facing the oncoming Syndicate flotilla. To an observer on a planet, their feet firmly planted in a place with an up and down, Marphissa's ships would have appeared to have looped onto their backs, the crews now upside down compared to their previous alignment. But to the crews, nothing felt different or looked different except that they were now facing the opposite direction. As the pivots ended, main propulsion lit off on all the ships, braking their velocity so that the pursuing Syndicate warships could finally begin to catch up.

"This is pretty simple," Diaz commented. "We've already got our bows with our strongest shields and armaments pointed at the enemy. All we have to do is slide over a little at the last minute to avoid going head-to-head with that battleship."

Marphissa nodded, then noticed the frown on Bradamont. "What's wrong?"

"I don't know," Bradamont said. "I just don't trust situations that seem too simple and too easy."

"We've got over an hour before we get within range of them," Marphissa said. "I expect they'll start braking soon, too, now that they see we're ready to fight."

But as the minutes crawled by, the Syndicate flotilla kept charging onward at point two light speed. "We're getting down toward point one light," Diaz reported, "but the Syndicate is still moving at point two light speed along the same vector as us. If they don't brake, we'll meet them at a relative velocity of point one light."

"That's not good," Marphissa said. Human fire control systems could do a decent job of scoring hits at velocities of up to point two light speed. Higher speeds than that caused accuracy to fall off fast. But slower speeds caused accuracy to increase just as rapidly. "They've got too much of a firepower advantage for us to meet them at point one light. We could get badly chewed up passing through them. Why aren't they braking? Is CEO Boucher smart enough to realize how that complicates our attack?"

"How could she be?" Diaz protested. "Happy Hua doesn't know enough— Oh, hell. That's why."

"What?"

Diaz waved an angry hand at his display. "You and I look at the situation and say, all right, we're still forty minutes from contact.

Plenty of time to pivot the ships and prepare for the engagement. But Hua Boucher is looking at it and sees us getting closer to her. She is told that to brake she must turn her ships so that their sterns face us, the most vulnerable parts of the ships where the least firepower can be brought to bear. And because she can see us coming and doesn't really understand how great the distance is between us, she won't do that. To her, it's too close to a fight for her to allow her ships to present their sterns to us."

Bradamont slapped her forehead. "Damn. Kapitan Diaz is right. Boucher is making this a lot harder for us because she doesn't know what she's doing."

"Great," Marphissa said. "That's great." She ran both hands through her hair, thinking. "We have to brake our own velocity down more."

"How much more?" Diaz asked.

"They're coming at us at point two light and not slowing down, and we want to engage them at a relative velocity of point two light! We have to get as close to zero absolute velocity as we can, maybe point zero one or point zero two light."

"That's very slow for a battle situation," Bradamont cautioned.

"I know! But what happens if they can target us too well when we get near that battleship? The slower we're going, the harder it will be for them to hit us, right?"

"Right," Bradamont agreed. "And Boucher is certain not to understand that, since it's so counterintuitive for someone thinking in planetary terms. For what it is worth, Kommodor, I concur in your assessment of the necessary tactics here."

Marphissa's hands moved rapidly as she set up the next maneuver. "We keep braking at a rate that will bring us down to point zero one light when we meet the Syndicate flotilla. I'll let all of my ships maneuver on their own during the attack run because that will mess up enemy firing solutions assuming our movements will be perfectly coordinated by the automated systems, but I'll also have an order already in the ships' systems to begin accelerating again the moment after we pass through the Syndicate formation. The Syndicate ships will be moving so fast they won't be able to turn back and hit us before we get our velocity up again."

"Looks good," Bradamont said, then shook her head. "Warn Kontos on *Pele*."

"Warn him?"

"He's also assuming that the Syndicate flotilla will brake before the encounter. That will throw off his own approach. I've noticed that you young officers tend to push your ships to the limits of their capabilities on your maneuvers, so if Kontos misjudges what the enemy is doing here, *Pele* won't physically be able to compensate. Kontos will overshoot the encounter and miss his firing run."

"Ah! Thank you for that warning!" Marphissa called Kontos, explaining what she thought CEO Boucher was thinking and planning, then sat back, rubbing her forehead. "I have so much left to learn."

Marphissa's formation continued braking, going slower and slower, though only their instruments told them that. Just as it was hard in the immensity of space, without nearby references, to tell when you were going very fast, it was equally difficult to know when you were dropping your speed to what amounted to a crawl for warships. It all felt the same.

"Ten minutes to engagement range," the senior watch specialist announced.

"All units," Marphissa ordered, "we will hit the upper, port edge of the Syndicate formation. I want fire concentrated on the two light cruisers holding the corners of that edge. Enemy Hunter-Killers are secondary targets if you can't get a good shot at one of the light cruisers. Don't waste any fire on the battleship even if it looks like a hit is possible. It'll just bounce off his shields. For the people, Marphissa, out."

At the velocities of space combat, enemy ships went from being way out there to *there* in what seemed the blink of an eye. If you were following standard Syndicate tactics, that wasn't much of a problem because you were headed straight for the enemy and hopefully your automated maneuvering systems, operating far faster than a human could react, would avoid collisions as the two forces went directly head-to-head. But standard tactics led to bloody encounters as the two sides slugged away at each other.

Black Jack had shown them a different way to fight. The trick was to make tiny changes in your vectors at a time when they could take effect but not so soon that the enemy could see it and counter your moves. If done right, it allowed your full force to hit a small portion of the enemy, inflicting a lot of damage but not suffering much in return. If done wrong, by only a tiny amount compared to the distances around them, it could result in your completely missing the enemy, or running head-on into them.

Simple. But very complicated.

Marphissa waited, intent on her display, as the remaining distance shrank rapidly. At two minutes before contact, she gave the order. "All units, execute maneuver using local controls. Come port zero one degrees, up point five degrees."

Only five seconds before contact, Marphissa sent the maneuvering order she had already prepared. "All units, full acceleration." By the time that order was received and the ships responded, they would be past the enemy.

In those last moments, Marphissa realized that she had miscalculated slightly. In her eagerness to ensure the firing run was not wasted, she had underestimated the final maneuver. Or perhaps Hua had slid her own formation in the same directions as Marphissa, by sheer luck doing just the right thing. Marphissa's formation would slide through the port side of the Syndicate formation closer than Marphissa had intended, and not as high. Not a direct head-to-head encounter, but far too close to that. It gave her warships better shots at the Syndicate ships, but also gave the Syndicate more chances to hit her. *Too late. Damn. Too late.*

The instant of combat came and went too fast for human senses to register, automated systems pumping out hell lances and grapeshot at targets whipping past at immense velocities.

Manticore jolted heavily several times. The lights flickered, Marphissa's display wavering in and out before steadying again. She waited for the surge of acceleration as the main propulsion units cut in, but felt nothing.

"The battleship targeted us. Our shields got knocked down, and we took several hits," Kapitan Diaz was reporting, his expression grim. "We have only partial thruster capability for maneuvering. All main propulsion is off-line."

No main propulsion. *Manticore* was nearly motionless in space and unable to change that.

Marphissa stared at her display. The firing run had done damage to the Syndicate forces. One of the Syndicate light cruisers was drifting out of formation, powerless and heavily damaged. A spreading ball of gas and debris marked where the second targeted Syndicate light cruiser had been. In addition, one of the small Syndicate Hunter-Killers had broken in half under the impacts of several hits.

But the Midway warships had been close enough to the Syndicate battleship for its firepower to be felt, and they had paid a price for that.

Marphissa's display showed red damage markers on many of her ships. The Syndicate had not concentrated their fire, so none of Midway's ships had been knocked out completely or destroyed. But few had come through the encounter unscathed. And, in addition to *Manticore*, the light cruiser *Harrier* had lost main propulsion and was also hanging helplessly in space not far distant. The other warships were accelerating away, only just realizing that their stricken comrades had been left behind.

The Syndicate formation had seen the same things. It was beginning to bend upward in as tight a turn as the battleship could manage, a vast curve through space that Marphissa knew would come nearly full circle. It would take more than half an hour for the enemy warships to finish that turn, but when they came back, *Manticore* and *Harrier* would be sitting ducks.

CHAPTER THREE

"CAN you fix your main propulsion?" Bradamont demanded of both Marphissa and Diaz.

"The answer is probably not," Marphissa murmured.

Diaz was speaking on an internal comm circuit, and now ended the call with a curse. "Leytenant Gavros is dead. Senior Specialists Kalil and Sasaki say the control circuits are shot to hell."

"But the main propulsion units themselves are fine? You can't replace or fix the control circuits?" Bradamont asked again.

"This is a Syndicate-designed ship!" Diaz erupted in frustration. "It is efficiently designed! Crew size is optimized for efficiency! Significant repairs are to be carried out at leased maintenance facilities!"

"Can't your senior specialists—"

"The senior specialists aren't trained to make repairs and aren't supposed to make repairs! The circuits are black boxes! They're not supposed to be fixed! All you're supposed to do is take out the broken one and put in a working one. We have a few black box spares aboard, but we don't have any working black boxes of the exact type we need to replace those broken black boxes."

Marphissa glared at Diaz. "Tell them to try! Tell Kalil and Sasaki and the other specialists in engineering that the old Syndicate rules against unauthorized repairs no longer apply. Tell them to break into those boxes and see what they can do. Break into every circuit they need to. Jury-rig, improvise, cross-connect, anything. If we are still sitting here in half an hour, this ship will be blown to hell!"

Diaz took a deep breath. "Yes. Why not try? What's the worst that can happen? A big explosion? We'll die anyway if we don't try." He called engineering, passing on the orders. "Kommodor, I want to go down there personally. I will be back within twenty minutes, before any Syndicate ship can get to us."

"Permission granted. Go." As Diaz bolted off the bridge, Marphissa glowered at her display, one hand moving as she set up another maneuver for the formation under her command that was speeding away from her. The display froze in midsolution, causing Marphissa's guts to tighten, but then jerked back into motion.

Pele, *Gryphon*, and *Basilisk* had finally reached the area, catching the lower edge of the opposite side of the Syndicate formation from the one Marphissa's formation had hit. Kontos had more luck or judged the approach better, *Pele* hammering the Syndicate heavy cruiser on that corner until it exploded, while *Gryphon* and *Basilisk* knocked out another light cruiser.

CEO Boucher ignored the blow, though, the Syndicate formation continuing on its path to come back to finish off *Manticore* and *Harrier. Maybe,* Marphissa thought, *I shouldn't have personally taunted Happy Hua the way I did. She sure wants me dead. But then this is Hua Boucher. She would probably want me dead regardless.* "All units," she transmitted. "Continue accelerating to point zero eight light speed, turn port zero two degrees, turn up one four seven degrees at time five zero."

The Syndicate formation was looping up and over, the formation inverting as it went through the circle formed by its path through space. Marphissa's ships could turn faster, even though that was a relative term. Planetary observers would doubtless describe the turn radius as huge, but what mattered was that it was less huge than that of the Syndicate formation encumbered by a battleship. This new maneuver would bring the remaining ships in Marphissa's flotilla back and across to sweep over the top of the Syndicate formation as it neared the summit of its loop.

"Good thing that CEO is inexperienced," Bradamont muttered. "With us sitting nearly dead in space, if she had simply braked and come back, that Syndicate formation would have gotten back here quicker. But instead, she's going through that turn."

"It's only buying us a few minutes," Marphissa pointed out. "Getting that battleship stopped and going again in the opposite direction isn't easy." She sent a separate transmission to *Kraken*, the remaining heavy cruiser in her formation. "Kapitan Seney, you are to assume command of the formation as it engages the Syndicate flotilla again. I'll be too far away to make any necessary last-moment adjustments in the attack. Don't get too close. We can't afford to lose *Kraken*."

Seney looked back at her, his eyes worried. "I understand and will comply, Kommodor. We can't afford to lose *Manticore*, either."

"Maybe we won't," she said, not believing it herself. "There's nothing you can do to stop the Syndicate flotilla from reaching us, though. If *Manticore* is destroyed, place yourself and the other warships under the control of Kapitan Kontos. He will be acting Kommodor, by my command, until confirmed by President Iceni."

"Kontos is young," Seney said carefully.

"We all are young, Kapitan, for what we must do. Will you comply?"

"Yes, Kommodor. I will acknowledge Kapitan Kontos as acting Kommodor should you be unable to fill the role." Seney brought his right fist around to tap his left breast in the Syndicate salute they still used. "For the people."

She straightened and returned the salute. "For the people."

Another call, to Kontos. "Kapitan, if *Manticore* is destroyed, you are to assume command of Midway's warships as acting Kommodor until confirmed by President Iceni. Don't waste your time worrying about us. There's nothing you can do to stop the Syndicate flotilla in time. Continue to focus your efforts on knocking out the battleship's escorts, then wearing down the battleship."

Pele was far enough away that Kontos's reply took several seconds. The youthful Kapitan looked stricken but determined. "I understand and will comply, Kommodor. I will not fail you or President Iceni. For the people, Kontos, out."

As the image of Kapitan Kontos vanished, Marphissa sighed heavily, slumping back as she stared at her display. There was nothing else that she could do right now. "What would Black Jack do, Captain Bradamont?"

"I don't know," Bradamont answered, her voice low. "He did abandon ship when the situation at Grendel was hopeless."

"Grendel? When was that?"

"A century ago."

"Hah!" It struck her as funny. "A century ago? Did they take prisoners then? I guess people did. Do you think CEO Boucher is going to? What do you think her ships will do to any escape pods they see? Escape pods full of men and women whom they consider to be traitors and rebels?" Marphissa snorted and gestured angrily. "Besides, there are only enough escape pods aboard for sixty percent of the crew."

"Sixty—?" Bradamont gave her a horrified look. "Why?"

"Because the Syndicate accountants crunched the numbers. On average, a ship too badly damaged to continue to fight, one that must be abandoned, will have lost forty percent of its crew. Therefore, they only need escape pods for the surviving sixty percent."

"Ancestors preserve us."

"Well, even dead ancestors probably care more than the corporate accountants trying to save a little money when they build ships," Marphissa said, her tone acidic. "The CEOs approved because they didn't want workers abandoning ships that could maybe still fight. Dammit, Honore. If I had managed that firing run right—"

"You handled that run as well as anyone," Bradamont said. "The Syndicate formation jigged slightly in the same direction you did, probably because its automated controls were trying to center their run on you. The enemy doesn't always do exactly what you want, and there are always uncertainties. Sometimes, you can do everything right and still get blown to hell. Sometimes, the biggest idiot survives and the smartest professional is in the wrong place when a hell lance comes through. There's nothing we can do about that firing run now. What *can* we do?"

Marphissa shook her head. "Go down fighting. That's all that's left to do if those specialists can't figure out in the next few minutes how to do something that they've been forbidden from trying in the past." She turned her head toward the back of the bridge. "Senior watch specialist, ensure all weapons stations remain at full readiness. We'll see who we can take down with us."

"Yes, Kommodor." The senior watch specialist bent his head for a moment, then raised it to look at her. "Kommodor, my name is Pyotor Czilla. I never wanted the CEOs to know my name. It was dangerous for them to know who you were. But I want you to know, because you were a good supervisor. The best."

The other watch specialists murmured agreement, causing Marphissa to wonder if she was blushing with embarrassment. "We're not dead yet," she reminded them all. "You might have to live with me awhile longer."

"Living awhile longer would not be a bad thing, Kommodor," Czilla said. His smile was tense. "All weapons report full readiness except for hell-lance battery 2, which sustained a direct hit and was destroyed."

"Very well. I will designate a single target when the Syndicate flotilla gets close enough," Marphissa told him. She finally made another call, one she had been dreading, to *Harrier*. "How does it look, Kapitan-Leytenant Steinhilber?"

Kapitan-Leytenant Steinhilber was in a sealed survival suit, as were the others who could be seen on the bridge of the light cruiser. *Harrier* must have lost internal atmosphere.

Steinhilber shrugged. "Main propulsion is gone, Kommodor. Shot to pieces. We've got the power core still running at thirty percent capacity, but it's shaky. Half our weapons are out, life support gone, half the crew dead or wounded. We'll hold for another twenty minutes though, enough time for the Syndicate to get back here, and we'll go down fighting."

"Glenn, I—"

He shook his head. "It is. That's all. It is. I'm sort of surprised I lasted this long. I should be grateful, right? I'm sorry I can't save the crew, though. They're a good crew, Kommodor. This is a hero ship. They should be remembered that way." Steinhilber sounded both earnest and oddly numb, as if his emotions were so tightly controlled that all the edges were being worn off before they could be felt.

Marphissa understood that. She herself could feel fear, anger, despair, but these were distant things, somehow separated from her by a barrier formed of resolve and a desire to not let down her comrades in these last moments. "*Harrier* is a hero ship," Marphissa said. "You will be remembered."

"Does *Manticore* have any chance?"

"We're trying to get main propulsion going. I don't know if we can."

"If you can," Steinhilber said with sudden intensity, "then go. Do not stay with us. Go. Honor *Harrier*'s sacrifice by continuing the fight when you have a chance to survive and to win."

Marphissa nodded, blinking back tears. "We will, Kapitan-Leytenant Steinhilber. But if that does not happen, if *Manticore* and *Harrier* fight our last fight together, then we will die in good company. The best company." She saluted with slow solemnity. "For the people."

"For the people," Steinhilber echoed, returning the salute.

That transmission over, Marphissa sat, feeling impotent in her command seat, wondering how Diaz and the specialists were doing on repairing the main propulsion controls, watching the incredibly fast movements of the nearest warships as they seemed to crawl through the immensity of space, thinking about those on *Harrier* who did not have even the slim hope of those aboard *Manticore*, and contemplating other issues that she usually tried to avoid thinking about. "Honore?"

"Yes." Bradamont's reply was a hushed as Marphissa's question.

"Do you think there is something on the other side? After death, I mean. The Syndicate always said no, that all we had was here and now, and so we'd better do as we were told because if we spent this life being punished, or had it cut short for committing crimes against the state, that was all there was."

"I don't know for certain," Bradamont said. "I believe there is something more. No one really knows, of course. No one has ever come back after having gone all the way."

"What about Black Jack? He came back, didn't he? After a hundred years?"

"Admiral Geary insists that he didn't die," Bradamont said, "and that he remembers nothing from his time frozen in survival sleep."

"Would he tell us the truth? If he knew?"

Bradamont paused, frowning slightly. "I think he would. He's said the same thing to Tanya Desjani, his wife."

"She was a battle cruiser commander, too, right?"

"Still is," Bradamont said. "Commanding officer of *Dauntless*. I don't think even the living stars themselves could convince Admiral

Geary to lie to her." She sighed. "Popular belief in the Alliance is that Admiral Geary did die, that he was in the lights in jump space, among his ancestors, until the time was right. But if he doesn't remember that, and there's no way to prove or disprove, it comes down to whether or not you believe."

Marphissa nodded. The Syndicate flotilla was almost near the crest of its turn, the remaining ships of the Midway flotilla moving fast to meet it. It felt very odd to sit here watching that happen, unable to take part, knowing that the turns being made by the other ships were so huge that the light from the images she was seeing was over two minutes old. The latest exchange of fire had already taken place, but the light seeing images from the battle was still on its way here. "Is it a good place? Among the ancestors and with those stars?"

"It's supposed to be," Bradamont said. "It's supposed to be better than we can imagine. Peaceful, happy, no pain or loss."

"Hmm. I guess if Black Jack had been there, they might have made him forget, right? When he came back? Because otherwise, what would it be like, remembering this really great place you got kicked out of to come back here and fight and struggle and hurt again?"

"There's that," Bradamont conceded. "How long do we have left before we find out for sure the hard way?"

Marphissa pointed to her display. "This is the time until we're in range of the Syndicate weapons. This other one is really the number that matters. If we can't get moving by then, twelve minutes from now, we won't be able to accelerate fast enough to avoid being caught by the Syndicate flotilla. We'll manage to string out the time a little until they hit us, but that's all. A moment like this is when we're supposed to pray, right? When we really need help?"

"Yes, and to give thanks if the help comes," Bradamont said.

"If you know anyone to pray to, feel free. Kapitan Diaz knows how to pray, his parents taught him in secret, but I've never learned." She wondered if Diaz was praying right now as he and the specialists struggled to get *Manticore* in motion before it was too late.

The light from the most recent engagement had finally gotten here. On her display, she watched the Midway flotilla and the Syndicate flotilla rip past each other so fast the event itself could not be seen.

Kapitan Seney had done a good job. Another Syndicate light cruiser had spun away helplessly from the enemy formation, maneuvering control lost, and two more Syndicate Hunter-Killers had been knocked out. In return, Midway's light cruiser *Osprey* and Hunter-Killer *Patrol* had taken enough additional hits themselves that they broke away from what was now Seney's formation, both ships staggering out of the fight, unfit for further combat until their damage could be repaired, but still able to maneuver.

She could see that Seney had begun swinging about again, looping toward the star and down to set up another intercept of the Syndicate flotilla, and realized that she had to make clear to him that the remaining ships in *Kraken*'s formation were his to command until further notice.

"Kapitan Seney," Marphissa sent, "retain control of the formation and continue to hit the Syndicate flotilla. Wear them down. I will notify you when—" She had been about to say *when I am able to resume command*, but realized how insanely optimistic that would sound. "When the situation calls for it. Marphissa, out."

Several more minutes crept by, Marphissa repeatedly fighting off urges to call engineering and demand updates that would only distract and delay whatever Diaz and the others were doing.

Diaz came back onto the bridge and sat down heavily. "I don't know," he said before Marphissa could ask. "I needed to get back up here, and I was really just watching, not contributing to the repair effort."

"Do you think there's a chance they'll succeed?" Marphissa asked, surprised at how calm the question sounded.

"I have no idea, Kommodor. Neither do they. But they are trying." He squinted at his display. "The Syndicate is still coming for us, I see. How long—? Is this figure right?" Diaz asked. "Senior watch specialist, do we have only three minutes left in which to start accelerating?"

"Kapitan," Czilla began with obvious reluctance, "that is probably a slightly optimistic projection. I would say it is closer to only two minutes—"

Manticore lurched into motion with a sudden shock of acceleration so strong that some of it leaked past the inertial dampers, shoving everyone against their seat harnesses and making Bradamont hastily grab on to Marphissa's seat for support.

Marphissa held a hand up toward Bradamont. "Did you pray?"

"Yes."

"All right. I believe."

"Kapitan?" A call came in for Diaz on the internal comms. "This is Senior Specialist Kalil. We got the main propulsion units going."

"I noticed!" Diaz said, as everybody else on the bridge broke into relieved gasps of laughter. "Are my controls working? I'm not seeing them active."

"Uh, Kapitan," Kalil said, "you are talking to the controls. Me and Senior Specialist Sasaki. We're opening and closing the circuits manually."

"Manually? By hand?"

"Yes, Kapitan. Right now we only have two settings for the propulsion units, completely off, or fully on."

Diaz shook his head, looking toward Marphissa with a wondering expression. "I can live with that."

"You may live because of that," Marphissa said. "Tell your specialists to keep the propulsion units on full."

"Did you hear, Senior Specialist Kalil? Keep the units on full."

"Yes, Kapitan. Uh, there is something else I should tell you. We don't know how long this will last."

"What?" Diaz asked, his relieved smile fading.

"Me and Senior Specialist Sasaki had to do some, uh, creative rewiring of circuits. You saw. She and I are not, um, entirely certain what all we rerouted. Because we were in a big rush, Kapitan, because you said—"

"Yes, yes! I know what I said!"

"—and so we don't know if something might happen because we did all that changing and cross-connecting of circuits."

Marphissa closed her eyes and gritted her teeth.

"Senior Specialist Kalil," Diaz said with great care, "when you say something might happen, are you talking about something like the freezer's shorting out and the ice cream melting, or something like the ship's blowing up?"

"Uh, Kapitan, me and Senior Specialist Sasaki think it will be something between those two things. But we don't really know. You told us—"

"Do it as fast as possible, I know." Diaz spread his hands toward Marphissa in a helpless gesture. "Keep the main propulsion units going, Kalil. Let me know if the ship is about to blow up."

"Yes, Kapitan, we will tell you if that is about to happen. If we know that is about to happen."

"Keep praying," Marphissa muttered to Bradamont.

"Already on it," she replied. "There's nothing we can do for *Harrier*?"

"Nothing. No, wait. The Syndicate flotilla has seen that we started moving again. How far off are they? Only thirty light-seconds and still closing. But their vector is altering." Everyone studied their displays as the Syndicate warships continued changing their paths through space. "CEO Boucher is altering course to stay on an intercept with us as we move away," Marphissa said as the reason became apparent. "If they change track enough—"

"They might pass by out of range of *Harrier*?" Diaz asked. "They might, Kommodor. *Harrier* is obviously out of commission. They might think they can leave her to finish off later."

Minutes ticked by, then dawning hope shattered as Marphissa saw that the last two Syndicate heavy cruisers had veered off slightly from their formation. "They're going to hit *Harrier*, then rejoin. Damn Boucher!"

"One and a half minutes until they get within range of *Harrier*," Diaz noted, anger straining his voice.

"Kommodor," Bradamont said, "you're too narrowly focused."

"What? What the hell are you talking—"

Marphissa stopped speaking abruptly as Bradamont's meaning became clear. She and the others had been watching only *Harrier* and the movements of the Syndicate ships. Perhaps the Syndicate ships and CEO Boucher had also been narrowly focused, locked onto both *Harrier* and *Manticore* as targets.

All of them had forgotten about *Pele*.

Kontos's battle cruiser, still accompanied by *Gryphon* and *Basilisk*, zipped upward close by the two Syndicate heavy cruisers which had left the protection of the battleship. A battle cruiser might not be a match for a battleship, but at close range one could do an awful lot of damage to a heavy cruiser.

One of the Syndicate heavy cruisers, the one targeted by *Gryphon* and *Basilisk*, must have seen the danger at the last moment, making a sudden evasive maneuver that threw off many of the shots by the Midway cruisers. But the other Syndicate heavy cruiser caught the full force of *Pele*'s armament.

A barrage of hell lances and grapeshot slammed into the heavy cruiser, knocking down its shields and going on to smash into the hull. The heavy cruiser jerked sideways under the impacts, then broke into several pieces that tumbled away.

The other heavy cruiser kept going, though, as *Pele*, *Gryphon*, and

Basilisk went onward out of range, unable to check their velocity or turn fast enough to quickly engage the Syndicate warship again.

But the Syndicate heavy cruiser must have been spooked by the unexpected attack and by the loss of its partner. As *Harrier* threw out a last volley from her remaining weaponry, the heavy cruiser twisted down and away instead of closing to hell-lance range. Instead, it pumped out two missiles, then a third, all aimed at the crippled *Harrier.*

Harrier's two remaining hell lances hurled out shots aimed at the oncoming missiles, but the defensive fire faltered as the hell lances overheated.

The first two missiles struck aft, detonating simultaneously and blowing apart the after half of *Harrier.* The third missile hit forward, and shattered on impact, cratering the surviving half of the light cruiser but leaving it still shakily intact.

"A dud!" Diaz breathed. "I've never been so happy to see a warhead fail."

"That wasn't a dud," Marphissa objected. "The warhead on a dud would still have detonated on impact. That was a practice missile. Some poor fool accidentally loaded a practice missile instead of a warshot."

Bradamont looked around at the faces of the others on *Manticore*'s bridge. "What is it you all expect to happen to that person?"

"Summary execution, if they're lucky," Diaz said, his voice harsh, "which would have been already carried out, or if they're not lucky, prolonged interrogation by the snakes on that unit to determine if that person deliberately sabotaged the attack. Once they get the confession, and snakes always get a confession regardless of whether or not their victim did anything, the person's family will be punished as well."

"Hell of a price for a mistake," Bradamont muttered.

"High-profile mistakes are often lethal in the Syndicate," Marphissa said. She pointed to her display. "Thanks to that failed missile hit, the forward portion of *Harrier* is still intact. Some of her crew may still be alive."

"They'll fort up in any remaining escape pods until the fight is over," Diaz speculated. "Not launching, because that would make them targets again, but using the life support in the pods."

"It's not like we can go back for them now, so I hope you're right," Marphissa said with a scowl. She started to say something else, then paused. There was an odd stutter in *Manticore* as the heavy cruiser roared at full acceleration. "Something's off," she said. "Feel that?"

"Now that you mention it, yes, I feel it, too," Diaz said, studying his readouts. "Engineering watch specialist, do you know the cause?"

The specialist, an older woman who looked near retirement age, was squinting at her own display. "Kapitan, it appears that number two main propulsion unit was damaged. Its output is fluctuating."

"Is there danger?"

"No, Kapitan. Stress and temperature readings are within safe parameters. But that unit is not putting out full thrust. Its output is varying from fifty to eighty percent of maximum."

"Let's hope that's enough," Marphissa said, her eyes locked on her display. The Syndicate flotilla was flattening out from its turn, charging toward the fleeing *Manticore* as the surviving Syndicate heavy cruiser scrambled to rejoin its companions before *Pele* could return. The rate of closure of the Syndicate flotilla on *Manticore* was dropping fast as the heavy cruiser strained to pull away and escape intercept. But that rate had to hit zero, then hopefully turn negative as the range began widening again, or else *Manticore* would still be doomed.

Kontos had brought *Pele* back again, too late to catch the heavy cruiser alone, swinging in from above to strike the rear of the Syndicate formation. The remaining Syndicate light cruiser blew apart as it tried to evade fire from the battle cruiser as well as *Gryphon* and *Basilisk*. The rest of the Midway flotilla, still in a separate formation under

Kapitan Seney on *Kraken*, had bent down and back, and was coming in a flat curve at the Syndicate formation from behind and below.

But CEO Boucher plowed on, closing the distance to *Manticore* with increasing slowness as the heavy cruiser kept increasing speed. "She knows this is the flagship," Marphissa said. "CEO Boucher has been analyzing our comm patterns, and she knows I'm aboard *Manticore*."

Diaz nodded. "And she wants to make an example of you. Kill the leader, and the rest will submit. Snakes always try that even though it rarely works. There's always another leader."

"I don't think her intentions matter any longer," Bradamont said, eyeing the display. "I think we're clear. We're going fast enough that the battleship will take about a week to catch us at this rate."

The words had barely cleared her throat before *Manticore* shuddered throughout her length.

The lights went out, the life-support fans stopped, and the displays vanished.

Marphissa waited in the hushed darkness for the second it took for the emergency lighting to come on. "Something happened," she observed to Diaz, who was fruitlessly pounding the internal comm controls on the arm of his seat.

"Engineering watch specialist!" Diaz said, his voice reverberating in the strange silence on the bridge. He lowered his voice before speaking again. "Get down to engineering and find out what's going on. We need power back. We need *everything* back."

Marphissa was gazing at where her display had been. Now, nothing but the blank, armored forward bulkhead of the bridge could be seen. The entire compartment felt strangely smaller with the equipment offline and life support not offering the constant, reassuring background noise of fans and ducts and circulating fluids. The bridge was buried deep in the ship, as safe as possible from enemy fire or other threats, which normally brought a sense of reassurance. At the moment, it was creating a feeling of literally being buried.

Senior Watch Specialist Czilla propped open a device pulled out of the emergency locker near his station. It lit, showing a series of readings. "We are still all right for oxygen and CO_2 concentration, Kommodor. Estimated time to dangerous reduction in O_2 and dangerous density of CO_2 is twenty-five minutes."

"We'll hold off sealing our survival suits to conserve their life support for when we need it," Marphissa said. "Damn! What is going on outside?"

"We're still moving," Diaz said. "We've stopped accelerating, but the Syndicate flotilla is still in a long stern chase. Those surviving Hunter-Killers with the battleship have been burning a lot of their fuel cells. Unless CEO Boucher provides new cells from the battleship's stockpile, those Hunter-Killers will be in trouble before the Syndicate ships can catch us."

"At the moment," Marphissa grumbled in a very low voice, "I'm worried about our own people catching us. We had made it back up past point one five light speed when the power cut out, and now we're racing outward at that velocity. If we get too far out before they can send someone to intercept us . . ."

"We could open some exterior fittings to vent atmosphere," Diaz said. "Pivot the ship using that method, then figure out how to light off main propulsion without power—"

"That's impossible. It would just blow up if the regulators didn't have power." Marphissa breathed a sigh of relief as the displays flickered to life again. "Progress. Maybe there is still hope." She peered at the display, which continued to waver in intensity from bright to dim. "There's nothing on it except a static view of what was last known. This is useless."

"Kapitan?" someone called.

Diaz hit his comm controls. "Yes! Senior Specialist Sasaki?"

"Yes, Kapitan. The power core did an emergency shutdown. We're not sure why, so we've isolated it and will do a restart."

"I need comms and sensors back online fast!"

"I understand and will comply, Kapitan. Two minutes."

But two minutes, then four minutes, then ten went past. Diaz's attempts to call engineering again failed as the comm circuit went dead once more.

The engineering watch specialist dashed back onto the bridge, gasping for breath. "Kapitan, the power core—"

"I know," Diaz growled.

"They are rewiring again, Kapitan. They found that just doing a restart would probably trigger another threatened overload and shutdown, so they've been pulling things out and redoing them."

"Why did I lose comms with engineering?" Diaz demanded.

The woman looked off to one side, groping for words. "They . . . needed a certain black box . . . Junction Model 74A5F Mod 12 . . . and the only one available was in the internal comms, so . . ."

"My ship is being torn apart from the inside out," Diaz said. "Those senior specialists are doing as much damage to my ship as the Syndicate did!"

Marphissa nodded. "If we survive, *Manticore* is going to need some extensive internal repairs. And we'll have to reward those senior specialists who are tearing your ship apart because otherwise we'd already be dead."

The displays vanished again, then reappeared before anyone could even curse their disappearance. "Kommodor, we have updated external information! External comm links and sensors are active again," Senior Watch Specialist Czilla reported.

Marphissa had been able to deaden her worries a bit when she literally could not see anything about events outside of *Manticore*, but now they sprang to full life again as Marphissa bent close to study her display.

The Syndicate flotilla was still in pursuit, still slowly closing the gap to *Manticore*, but the battleship now was accompanied by only the single heavy cruiser and three surviving Hunter-Killers. Kontos and Seney must have hit CEO Boucher's formation again. Both the *Pele* formation and the one now centered on *Kraken* were coming around for two more attacks.

"Look at that!" Diaz said in amazement. "*Midway*! The battleship, I mean."

Marphissa tore her attention away from the nearest ships, trying to figure out what Diaz was talking about. Then she saw it. The battleship *Midway*, light-hours away, had come around, accelerating at full capacity on a route that would place her between the Syndicate formation and the hypernet gate. "What is Kapitan Mercia doing? She's revealed for everyone to see that the *Midway* actually has full propulsion capability!"

Bradamont was staring, too, but suddenly gave out a burst of laughter. "She's a genius!"

"A genius? Mercia just let the Syndicate flotilla know—"

"That's why it's genius," Bradamont exulted, seeing the looks of incomprehension on the faces of both Diaz and Marphissa. "Don't you see? *Midway* appeared to have severely damaged main propulsion. But now she has revealed that her main propulsion is fully functional. *Midway* also looks to have only a few weapons operational."

Marphissa suddenly understood. "But now the Syndicate flotilla will think that is also a ruse? They will think maybe *Midway* is fully combat capable? And rushing to join the fight as soon as she saw an opening?"

"Yes! Rushing to block the retreat of the Syndicate formation so it can't escape. It's a deception inside a deception, using one deception to make outside observers believe that the real things they are seeing are also a deception."

"What will CEO Boucher do?" Marphissa wondered.

A few minutes later, the answer became clear as the Syndicate flotilla veered down and thirty degrees to port. "They're heading for the jump point for Kane," Diaz said. "Why? *Midway* won't be in position to block them from reaching the hypernet gate for nearly nine hours."

"Boucher is panicking," Marphissa said, hearing the satisfaction in her voice. "Nothing has gone right for her, she's getting hit again and again, nearly all of her escorts have been destroyed, and now her battleship is threatened. She's bolting along the nearest path to safety."

Bradamont nodded. "I think you're right. And it appears that CEO Boyens was accurate in saying that Boucher would have orders not to bombard this star system. Otherwise, she would probably be launching a vindictive bombardment right now. The Syndicate Worlds does want this star system back intact."

"They won't get it, intact or otherwise," Marphissa vowed.

The life-support fans came back to life.

"Damn," Diaz said, looking around as if he didn't believe what he was seeing and hearing. "We won. And we're still alive."

"Yes," Marphissa agreed. "Now get back down to engineering and make sure your senior specialists in their enthusiasm to conduct quick repairs don't blow us up now that the battle is won."

IT had been nerve-wracking watching the battle play out, light-hours distant, unable to intervene and knowing that whatever she saw had long since happened. President Iceni poured out two drinks and offered one to General Drakon. They were alone in her office. "We should drink a toast to another victory over the Syndicate, General."

"You have some disturbingly competent subordinates," Drakon observed.

"My warship commanders are good, aren't they?" Iceni asked, raising her glass in triumph. "We will live another day, General."

"Does it worry you?" he asked, looking down at his own drink.

"Their competence? No. Both Marphissa and Kontos are very loyal to me."

He made a sharp noise, halfway between a snort and a grunt. "Don't assume that their loyalty will necessarily lead them to the actions you want them to do."

"Point taken," Iceni said. "But let's not talk about *your* subordinates unless you want me to handle that situation."

Drakon frowned at her. "Don't touch Colonel Morgan. If anything is done to her, the child dies."

"The child is a ways from being born yet," Iceni pointed out. "And the child was only conceived because Morgan deceived you."

"She's still my daughter." Drakon met Iceni's eyes. "I've spent a lifetime at war, destroying things and killing people. In all my life, I've only had a part in creating one single thing. So, yes, the child matters to me."

Iceni sighed again, loud enough for Drakon to hear her frustration. "I can understand your feelings, but do you want *that* daughter to be born? She will also be Colonel Morgan's daughter. What would a child of *hers* be like?"

"I've thought about that," Drakon said in a low voice.

"Have you? Are you thinking about your little girl bringing you crayon drawings of unicorns playing with children under rainbows to hang on your walls? Because if that little girl is anything like her mother, she is more likely to be using her crayons to draw images of wolves tearing apart helpless travelers during thunderstorms. Have you really thought about what a child of Colonel Morgan's would be like? How could you know?"

He hesitated long enough for Gwen to worry, then shook his head and spoke as if bewildered. "I know what a child of hers would be like. I know her son."

"Her *son*? Morgan has a son?" She was torn between incredulity at the news and anger that her aide Togo had not caught such an important fact when he had supposedly chased down all that could be known about Morgan. "Where is—?"

"He's here," Drakon interrupted. "Colonel Malin. He's her son."

Iceni only gradually realized that she had slumped backward, her mouth hanging open in shock. *That's why Malin refused to kill Morgan for me? He's—?* "But they're almost the same age. How— That mission. When she was frozen in survival sleep."

"For about twenty years," Drakon said. "The baby, Malin, was removed from Morgan before the mission. Syndicate policy. Morgan never knew. She still doesn't know." The words came out quickly, followed by an abrupt silence as Drakon stared at Iceni.

You just figured out how powerful a weapon you blurted out to me? Iceni thought. *If Morgan doesn't know, and I threatened to tell her . . . hell hath no fury seems an apt description of what would happen next.* "How are you intending to handle that situation?"

He actually smiled, though the smile held no humor at all. "I'm torn between denial and just shooting both of them."

"I favor the second option, followed by denial."

"If anything happens to Morgan—" Drakon began.

"Yes, yes. She's set up mechanisms to ensure that the child dies. And if we try to find the surrogate carrying the child, that alone might trigger the child's death. Very clever, very devious, very ruthless." Iceni rested her chin on one hand as she gazed at him. "Have you considered the possibility that she also has backups?"

"Backups?"

"Clones. Morgan could have cloned the embryo and had the clones implanted in multiple surrogates."

Drakon considered that, frowning deeply. "Full human cloning is so heavily regulated, and forbidden under almost all circumstances, that she would have had to have found a doctor willing to risk the consequences."

"The CEOs running the Syndicate have no desire for identical copies of themselves to exist," Iceni said. "All of those old stories about identical twins taking over from the originals are regarded as cautionary tales for modern-day CEOs. But you know how Syndicate society works just as well as I do. If there is a product, and any demand at all, there will be suppliers. And because parts can legally be cloned to ensure a sufficient supply of spare human organs, the expertise already openly exists."

"And Morgan could have found people who could handle full human cloning if anyone could." Drakon sat straighter, meeting her eyes defiantly. "I want it understood that this is my situation to deal with."

Iceni waved an aggravated gesture toward him. "As long as it does not threaten me, you can play whatever games you like. I may control the warships, but you control the ground forces. I insist, however, that Colonel Morgan never be seen or heard by me again. Do whatever you have to in order to control her and protect your precious offspring, but if I personally see Morgan again, I will order my bodyguards to act."

He nodded heavily. "What about Colonel Malin?"

That forced her to pause and think. *Malin's hatred for Morgan has never seemed feigned, but if he is truly Morgan's son, that hate could either be real or faked for his advantage. But I can't afford to have Malin's access limited. Drakon apparently still doesn't know that Malin has been feeding me inside information about him for some time. Not that Malin has ever given me anything negative about Drakon.* "I have no quarrel with Colonel Malin," Iceni finally said. "If he had not identified Executive Ito as a snake agent and stopped her moments before she poisoned you, you would already be dead, and this star system would be coming down around my ears."

Drakon nodded, took a drink, then focused back on her. "If we're done talking about my subordinates, there's another situation I want to discuss. We've just repelled another Syndicate attack, this one with a bloody nose. We're going to have a little while to work with before the Syndicate can manage another attack."

"What is it you want to work on?" Iceni asked.

"We have to deal with so-called Supreme CEO Haris at Ulindi. He's already attacked us once. We pulled his teeth, but he could hit us again, or go for some other nearby star system like Taroa."

Iceni shook her head slowly as she thought. "I imagine that CEO Haris, excuse me, *Supreme* CEO Haris, would wait for the Taroans to get much closer to finishing their battleship before he moved in to take it and their star system. The Taroans haven't even got the hull exterior on their battleship finished yet. But Haris might hit someone else in the meantime, as you say. What does he have available to do that?"

"Right now?" Drakon asked. "And as far as we know, not much. Which is why we should hit him now, before he acquires more, just as we've acquired more. And some of his neighboring star systems don't have the means to defend themselves against very much in the way of threats."

"Overextending ourselves won't help anyone," Iceni said. She called up the data she had on Ulindi Star System and frowned. "But this is more persuasive for me. It appears that Haris is maintaining the full Syndicate security structure, with his snakes running everything at Ulindi. If someone on the inside took care of Haris, they would inherit everything they needed to immediately turn Ulindi back into a base for the Syndicate."

"That's right," Drakon said. "But if we can knock out Haris before he can build up his ground forces and add more warships to his assets, then we can replace his regime with someone more sympathetic to us, or at worst someone open to bribery or able to be swayed by our threats. We'll have reinforced the defenses of this region against further attacks from Haris or the Syndicate and made it more stable all around."

"You make a reasonable case," Iceni conceded. "Both for acting at Ulindi and for acting quickly rather than waiting to see what either the Syndicate or Haris do next. What were you planning on doing?"

He shrugged. "I can't do much planning yet because there's too much I don't know. I need more inside information about the situation at Ulindi. We need to confirm how many warships Haris has, and confirm the number of ground forces available to him, how loyal they are to him, and how well equipped they are. It's vitally important to be certain that we aren't sticking our heads into a hornets' nest. We also need to know if there are any alternative leaders to Haris still at Ulindi, or if Haris managed to eliminate the competition. I want to send one of my best . . . hell, my best, into Ulindi to find out the answers to those questions and prepare the ground for our move if the information confirms Haris's weakness and only if it confirms his weakness."

Iceni nodded again, her eyes on the display. "You want to send Colonel Malin? Into a star system controlled by a snake CEO? I'm surprised you're willing to risk him on what sounds like something very close to a suicide mission."

"Colonel Malin isn't my best," Drakon said, his voice growing rougher. "Not for a mission like this."

"Then who—?" Iceni shot a glance at Drakon, both of her eyebrows rising. "Colonel Morgan? You want to send Colonel Morgan?"

"Yes."

Iceni hesitated, wondering why she was feeling a mix of approval and disappointment. Sending Morgan on what was very likely to be a one-way trip to Ulindi was a cold-bloodedly brilliant solution to the problem she posed, particularly since Drakon was being absolutely honest in saying Morgan was the best person he had for the job. But such a callous and calculated act of self-interest wasn't what she expected of Drakon.

She gave Drakon a sharp look. "I agreed to let you handle that situation, but I admit to being surprised that you are proposing that course of action."

"It's the best course of action," he growled, avoiding her gaze.

"I agree. But, as I said, I am surprised that *you* are proposing it."

Drakon met her eyes with his own, his expression defiant. "I had to ask myself who I would send if this had happened a month ago. If it was purely about who was best for the job, who was most likely to succeed, and to survive. And the answer was Colonel Morgan. I'm not proposing to send her because of recent events. I'm proposing to send her despite those things."

"I see. But I still have one question."

"What's that?" Drakon asked.

"Why didn't you kill her immediately when you found out? You've made me desperate enough for an answer to ask you openly."

Drakon's face tightened with anger, but Iceni could tell the rage wasn't directed at her. "I was strongly tempted."

"What stayed your hand?" Iceni asked.

"I— All right. I didn't kill her at that moment because I didn't want the unborn child to be killed. And because I don't fly off the handle." His eyes met hers, stubborn and challenging. "I survived in the Syndicate because I didn't act without thinking. I evaluate things. I decide what to do, and I plan how to do it."

"And this is your plan for dealing with Morgan? What if something happens to not only Colonel Morgan but also that incipient child of yours as well?" Iceni asked.

He paused, looking angrier, though this time it was impossible to tell where that emotion was directed. "I am not sending her in the hopes that she dies. If she dies, that means she's failed. But I don't think she'll fail. She's best for the mission. Most likely to succeed. If Morgan succeeds, the risk to my soldiers will be greatly lessened. I can't risk their deaths in an attempt to shield my own from harm."

Iceni laughed. "Damn. You really are an ethical son of a bitch, aren't you?"

"What the hell is that supposed to mean?"

This time she was the one who had to pause to think through her reply. "It means that not every surprise you toss my way is an unwelcome one. I am perhaps too willing to be pragmatic about some issues.

We were all taught to do that, weren't we? To become the perfect Syndicate CEO, unentangled by sentiment and any concern other than self-interest. It is reassuring to me to see that you failed to take some of that teaching to heart."

He made a face, frowning at the floor. "Don't go assuming everything I do isn't pragmatic."

"Oh? Would you have me killed if that seemed to be your best, pragmatic, course of action, General Drakon?" Iceni asked, eyeing him with a cool smile on her lips. *How will you answer me, Artur? With evasion, or vagueness, or a direct reply?*

His frown deepened, his gaze staying on the floor. "I doubt that could ever be a good, pragmatic course of action, Madam President. This star system needs you."

"This . . . star system . . . needs me?" she pressed.

Drakon looked up again. "You know what I mean."

"No. I don't." Iceni wondered exactly what emotions were roiling behind those eyes of his. Unfortunately, rising executives in the Syndicate had to learn to hide their feelings well, and a survival tactic like that wasn't going to be abandoned by anyone who had mastered it.

"I can't run this star system without you."

"Oh," she said. "So it is simple pragmatism again?"

"Dammit, Gwen. I don't want to work with anyone else and I don't want to see you hurt. Is that clear enough?" He glared at her, obviously awaiting another sally from her side.

Instead, she smiled briefly at him. "Thank you." Not wanting to press him further at this time, Iceni shifted topics. "How are you planning to get Morgan into Ulindi?"

"According to the last information we have from various star systems in this neighborhood, Ulindi has recruiters out trying to convince skilled workers to come there for jobs. Morgan will be sent to one of those star systems and mix in with a batch of workers headed for Ulindi."

"She can make that work?" Iceni asked, letting skepticism show. "Colonel Morgan has a rather prominent physical presence."

"She can make it work," Drakon confirmed. "I've seen her do it. When Morgan wants to, she can damn near shapeshift to disguise herself."

"Are you sure that she's human?" Iceni asked dryly.

It wasn't until his face tightened with anger again that she realized how he would know for certain the answer to her attempted joke. "Yes. Physically, she's human."

Iceni looked away, annoyed that she had upset both Drakon and herself by getting on the topic of Morgan's body. "Very well. I agree with your proposed course of action." It was past time to get off this subject completely. "As for me, now that the Syndicate has been repulsed again, I'm going to have some more chats with our special guest."

Drakon made a face. "At least some of what Boyens told us was accurate."

"I'm wondering what else he might tell us." Iceni cocked her head slightly toward Drakon. "Do you want to participate in the questioning?"

"No, thanks. I don't enjoy interrogations. If you have no objection, though, I'd like Colonel Malin to sit in on them."

"Colonel Malin?" Iceni pretended reluctance, then nodded. "All right. Is he good at interrogations?"

"He's very good at them," Drakon said. "That's one of the things *he's* best at." He walked toward the door. "I'll notify Colonel Morgan of her new mission."

MORGAN grinned at General Drakon when he entered her quarters. She was lounging in a chair, cocky and confident as ever. "When do you want me to leave?"

"Leave?" he asked, feeling renewed anger at the sight of her and anger with himself at how he couldn't help noticing how good she looked and the memories that brought to life.

"For Ulindi." Morgan stretched like a panther, lithe and dangerous, as she stood up. "That's where I'm going, right?"

"You sound happy to be going," Drakon said, eyeing her. Despite being confined to her quarters, Morgan not only had means of keeping track of what was going on, but she was letting him know that. Was she simply flaunting her abilities, or sending a message about the futility of trying to outmaneuver her? Most likely both.

"Ulindi sounds like fun." She smiled again. "If you're going to fulfill your destiny, you need me to help lead the way. That's my destiny. I was getting bored sitting around here anyway."

"It's a dangerous assignment," Drakon said.

"Hell, I know that."

"What about—" He found himself floundering, unable to think how to ask the question.

Morgan cocked a serious gaze his way. "She'll be fine if anything that happens to me occurs in the line of duty. I do things right, General. The only thing that might cause problems is if that worm Malin tries to sabotage me."

"Why do you spend so much time worrying about Malin?" Drakon asked, deliberately goading her even though he kept his voice dispassionate.

"I . . . don't. He's not important. But he is a threat, so I watch him."

"I'm watching both of you," Drakon said. He wondered again if Morgan did subconsciously realize that Malin was her son. She had disliked Malin intensely from the moment they first met, but Drakon hadn't suspected the real reason until Malin had recently confessed it to him.

Morgan shook off the momentary uncertainty that the topic of

Malin had generated. "You don't need to worry about my doing my job, General. We need to take down Ulindi, and I'm just the girl for taking down a star system." She checked her sidearm, which Drakon had let her keep, knowing that Morgan didn't need a weapon to be deadly. "Tell me how you want me to break some stuff, General."

CHAPTER FOUR

KANE Star System had been through a lot in the past year. The CEOs representing the Syndicate Worlds had done their best to tamp down rising rebellion, which had meant thousands of victims rounded up and summarily executed or shoved into rapidly expanded labor camps, where many died after months of deprivation. The final collapse of Syndicate authority had been marked by mass demonstrations that had too often turned into mass riots, inflicting considerable destruction on the cities of Kane's main inhabited world. The ship repair and construction facility which had once orbited a gas giant world had been destroyed by the retreating Syndicate forces. And, once the hated Syndicate overlords were gone, there had been too many others competing to rule Kane, none strong enough to prevail and none willing to compromise enough to ally with other factions. Debate and argument had led to open fighting, inflicting further misery on the people of Kane and further destruction on their cities.

Given all of that, it was understandable that more than a few inhabitants of Kane Star System saw the arrival of a Syndicate battleship, accompanied by a curiously small number of escort ships, with anticipation as well as concern. Kane had no warships and no surviving orbital weaponry, no means of defending itself from space attack, so not even a futile gesture of resistance was possible. There were quite a few people who hoped the Syndicate would come in, wipe out those who had been fighting to rule the star system, then leave again, allowing saner heads to finally prevail in Kane. There were plenty of people who would have welcomed a return to Syndicate control if it brought stability. That had always been one of the Syndicate's biggest arguments for legitimacy, that it provided peace and security for those under its rule. The price for those benefits was a steep one, but after the last year of death and disorder, the trade-off seemed a lot more worthwhile to some. As a result, this was one of the few times many of the residents of a star system greeted the appearance of Syndicate warships with any semblance of hope.

Kane's orbital sensors had also long since been destroyed in revolt and infighting, and many ground-based sensors had also been lost. The first warning people received of the actions of the Syndicate warships came when fiery streaks appeared in the sky, marking the paths of bombardment projectiles tearing through atmosphere on their way to their targets.

Few had time to seek any cover or shelter before the bombardment began hitting, the falling projectiles producing massive explosions that gutted cities and shattered any industries that had survived until now. In a matter of minutes, more than half of those still surviving at Kane died, their bodies buried in the ruins of their cities and large towns.

The dazed survivors gathered what weapons remained to them and waited for the Syndicate warships' next move, for further attacks or demands for surrender. But, after watching the results of their attack, the Syndicate vessels departed without any other actions and without transmitting any messages. They had, after all, already sent a message about the price of rebellion and had also ensured that nothing remained in Kane worth conquering.

GWEN Iceni sat watching the transmission with her expression schooled into stony impassiveness. It was hard, very hard, to watch the devastation that had been inflicted at Kane without revealing the revulsion she felt at those who had ordered such an action. "Where did we get this?"

"A freighter arriving from a Syndicate-controlled star system," Togo answered, his voice betraying no more emotion than Iceni's face did. "They were told the same information was being sent to all star systems in this region."

"At least we know what CEO Hua Boucher did after we chased her out of this star system." Iceni closed her eyes as the video continued to play, revealing the results of the bombardment of Kane in carefully composed and edited scenes designed to emphasize the resulting death and destruction. The images formed an incongruous counterpoint to the quiet and comfort of Iceni's private office. "Didn't another freighter just arrive here after passing through Kane?"

"Yes, Madam President. Their observations confirm that the bombardment shown actually took place."

"Can they tell us anything else?"

Togo nodded, the placid gesture at odds with the ugly subject of their conversation. "There was no demand for surrender before the bombardment. No communications at all before the bombardment began striking. Afterward, messages asking for help were directed to the freighter from those on the surface."

"What could a freighter do to help?" Iceni muttered angrily.

"Nothing," Togo answered. "But the freighter did promise to bring word of what had happened at Kane to us here."

"Why bother?" Iceni said, frustrated. "What can we do? Poor, damned Kane didn't have anything left that the Syndicate wanted, so they turned that star system into an object lesson of the costs of revolt. It would take twenty star systems, twenty *wealthy* star systems, to be able to muster the resources to help Kane! I want to know how this transmission is playing with the citizens here, Togo. After seeing it, are they worried, scared, defiant, angry, or what?" She knew they would see it, no matter what efforts were bent toward preventing anyone from viewing the images. Those who had lived under the Syndicate knew how to pass information to each other by means even the once all-powerful snakes of the Internal Security Service could never completely shut off.

"I will have that matter investigated, Madam President," Togo said with another deferential nod.

"And I want word spread around through our agents among the citizens," Iceni added. "What happened at Kane *didn't* happen here. No rioting, no fighting among factions for power, no bombardment by the Syndicate. Make sure the citizens are thinking about the fact that having me in power has prevented all of those things from occurring at Midway."

"Yes, Madam President. Our agents will remind the citizens that they owe their lives and their security to you."

She gestured for him to leave, a sharp flip of one hand, and Togo slipped out the door silently. Iceni waited until the door had sealed, waited to run a status check on her security systems and see the green status reports that claimed all was well, then called Drakon. "General, have you seen the images from Kane?"

The question had really been unnecessary. Drakon looked considerably grimmer than usual. "I've seen them."

"Kane has asked us for help."

Drakon grimaced, looking to the side. "Anything we can do is a drop in the bucket compared to what Kane needs."

"I know. But . . . dammit, Artur, I wish we could have destroyed Happy Hua's battleship and her with it."

Drakon shrugged. "If wishes were warships," he said, repeating the first half of the old saying. "Look, we can make a . . . symbolic gesture. That's all it would be. It would save a few lives."

Iceni gave him a keen glance. "I didn't think we could even manage a symbolic gesture."

"Sure. The Syndicate intended that Midway serve as a forward base if they deployed other forces here against the enigmas. We've got a fair amount of equipment stockpiled that would have been used by those forces." Drakon was squinting as he read something off his own screen. "Yeah. We can break out of the warehouses two field hospitals and a deployable water purification/reclamation plant. One big freighter can carry all of that. I can send some of the local troops along to get the stuff set up and give a little assistance. Like I said, it's a drop in the bucket, but it's something."

"We don't need those hospitals and the water plant?" Iceni asked.

"We don't need them now," Drakon said. "Maybe someday we might, but we've already got a lot more junk in the buried warehouses here and on other planets in this star system than we can use."

"What is it worth?" Iceni said, wincing inside at the need to consider cost.

"Worth? If we needed it, it would be priceless. But we don't need it. Kane does, though."

"Kane does," Iceni agreed. "Artur, I am incredibly grateful for this. It may be a very small thing measured against Kane's need, but Kane will remember this, that we helped them when they needed it."

Drakon paused, studying her. "Is that what this is all about? Political maneuvering? Getting someone else to feel in our debt?"

"No! I—" *Why am I objecting? Of course, I should be doing this to get Kane in our debt. That's just a smart way of doing business. So what?* "Is there some other reason?"

He shrugged again. "Just checking."

"Listen, General, it doesn't matter what our motivations are. Kane will be grateful."

"And . . . ?"

"And *what*?"

Drakon gave her a serious look. "I was wondering if our motivations do matter. We started doing all this in order to survive. Is that still our reason for what we're doing?"

Iceni leaned back, letting a small smile play on her lips, giving the outward image she had learned to project as a Syndicate CEO. "Isn't that enough of a reason?"

"I don't know," Drakon replied, sounding thoughtful. "Survival can lead to a lot of short-term solutions that blow up in your face over the long run."

"That's not exactly breaking news," Iceni said, wondering what Drakon was driving at.

"What do we want at Kane? There's a lot of potential there, and the Syndicate just pretty much wiped out all the different people who were fighting to be in charge. It will be a decade before Kane can rebuild much, but if you and I are still around then, what do we want Kane to be? And what about Ulindi? If we take that star system, do we let them set up some government we can live with, or do we install a puppet, or do we make Ulindi part of our . . . what? Empire?"

She paused to think that through while Drakon waited with stolid patience. "Empire" sounded nice. But . . . "Could we even hold an empire? Defend it against external attacks and maintain internal order?"

"I don't think so. We don't have enough ground forces or warships for that job. Not even close." Drakon waved one hand upward. "We've got enough firepower to do what the Syndicate just did at Kane, but I don't mind admitting that I don't have the stomach for that."

"Nor do I. We're trying to tie Taroa tightly to us. Why not do the same at Ulindi?"

Another shrug. "If we can, sure. What is it we're building here, Gwen? Not another Syndicate, right? But what is it, then?"

"The Syndicate was never big on teaching about alternate forms of governance." Iceni rested her chin on one hand, gazing into the distance. "We sure as hell can't call it an Alliance. That name is poison here after the war. Partnership? Consortium?"

"Those sound pretty Syndicate," Drakon said.

"They do, don't they? But we're talking about an agreement, shared among several parties. A treaty?"

"Maybe."

"Or compact? A cooperative? There's no rush coming up with a name, is there?"

"There might be." Drakon frowned at her. "What we call it, what we propose to call it, will send a message to everyone else. Anyone we want to be part of it will be looking to see if the name implies anything Syndicate. Anyone outside it will be looking for signs it is a nickname for empire. When someone wants to know what Midway represents, what message do we send them? Survival and power for you and me? That probably won't be too persuasive for other star systems. It might also create internal problems. Labeling ourselves rulers of something that sounds Syndicate would make our own citizens wonder if some of the rumors making the rounds are true."

"If we present a name that sounds too weak," Iceni objected, "it will make us look like an easy target. You're right. We do have to think about this. It's a marketing problem, isn't it? We have to look strong but not threatening to those outside, and like a source of internal stability and protection but not Syndicate-level repression to those inside. We need to sell this to star systems that we want to join up, and present the right image to those we want to keep at arm's length."

"It's not just marketing," Drakon said, with an open disdain that made it clear what he thought of marketing as a profession. "Not just propaganda. It's also about what form this grouping of stars takes, how much control we have or want."

Iceni sighed, pressing one hand over her eyes. "We're still working out how *this* star system will be governed. The details of that, anyway. Will what we decide to do here even work in other places, like Taroa, even if we can impose it on them?"

"We don't necessarily have to impose it," Drakon pointed out. "I talked to Captain Bradamont about how the Alliance worked. She said there's a set of principles the member star systems agree to, that they can't be like the Syndicate, for example, but beyond that individual star systems get to run themselves any way they want as long as it doesn't conflict with the principles."

"Hmmm." Iceni lowered her hand and gazed at the nearest star display. "That's not just Alliance propaganda, then? They do allow more . . . autonomy . . . for individual star systems?"

"That's what Bradamont said. She admitted that under the pressure of the war, the Alliance central government gained a lot more power but insists that power is still limited." He must have seen Iceni's skepticism because Drakon added more. "And she is Alliance. You know how their officers are about that honor stuff and not lying."

Iceni laughed. "I know how they go on about how honor is so important to them. I'm certain that some Alliance officers shade the truth a lot more than they admit to. But Bradamont does not seem to be one of those. She's annoyingly honest in all matters. Well, if we're not capable of enforcing some way of governing on other star systems, letting them do what they want as long as it doesn't harm us or help the Syndicate might be a smart way to go. Most importantly, it is so different from Syndicate practice that it will defuse claims we're trying to set ourselves up as a mini-Syndicate out here. Would you be upset if I expressed surprise that you thought of all this before I did?"

He smiled. "No. You're a better CEO than I was in the sense of running a business. I didn't think of it. Colonel Malin suggested we needed to think about it."

"Colonel Malin?" She kept her tone of voice neutral as a welter of thoughts responded to that identification. "Colonel Malin appears to have many ideas."

"He says he's been thinking about things like this for a while," Drakon said. "He didn't think there would ever be a chance to do anything as long as the Syndicate remained too strong and the Alliance remained at war with us, but things happened."

"Things happened," Iceni agreed. "The old order has crashed and burned, and now . . ." Her voice trailed off as a memory fought to become clear.

Drakon waited, eyeing her, smart enough not to interrupt and chase away the image that Iceni was trying to recall. He did have some very good qualities even though sometimes their arguments were heated enough to start fires.

Fires. There it was. "A phoenix."

"A what?"

"A phoenix," Iceni said. "You said we need an image. I thought of this a while ago, that the phoenix might be useful. That's why I didn't name one of our heavy cruisers *Phoenix*. Do you know what a phoenix is?"

"Something that doesn't actually exist," Drakon said. "Wait a minute. Isn't there a creature called a phoenix on a planet in Gladias Star System?"

"Don't know, don't care," Iceni replied. "I'm talking about the real thing, which isn't real." He grinned at the joke as she continued. "It is very long-lived, a fire bird. Like a star. But that's not all. When the phoenix is hurt, it regenerates. It can't be defeated, you see? And when it dies, it burns up, then rises again from its own ashes. It can't be beaten, it can't be destroyed, but it's not a monster."

Drakon sat back, nodding. "Damn. That's one hell of a strong symbol."

"One hell of a strong symbol for whatever we're building," Iceni said. "Right? Something that will endure, something that will recover from any injury, something as powerful as the stars our worlds orbit."

"The Phoenix Stars?" Drakon asked. "Rising from the ashes of the Syndicate?"

"Maybe." Iceni nodded as well, to herself as well as in response to Drakon. "That leaves the exact nature of the association vague but projects a strong image, an image that has nothing in common with the Syndicate. But we don't just need an abstract symbol. When were you planning on asking about the other thing?"

"The other thing?" Drakon shook his head. "What would that be?"

"The public face of our not-the-Syndicate-or-the-Alliance group of stars. You? Or me? Or both of us? What is the face of the Phoenix?"

He smiled slightly. "I was assuming both of us. Me to frighten people, and you to project that image of indestructible protection."

She spent a long moment eyeing him, trying to figure out if Drakon had made a sarcastic jab at her. "Protection? That's my image?"

"That's what our citizens want from their president," Drakon said. "And that's how we want them to think, right? Protection from the sort of things that happened at Kane."

That certainly sounded like a compliment, but Iceni still felt an odd irritation at the image. "Fine. But do you think I need you beside me to look frightening to our enemies?"

His smile grew but stayed enigmatic. "No. Your wrath can inspire plenty of fear, and for good reason."

"I'm glad you realize that." Her eyes narrowed as she thought. "There are advantages to being able to employ the old good cop/bad cop routine. I have no idea how long that tactic has been around, but I do know that it has endured because it works so often. I don't want either of us locked into one of those roles, though. It might inspire someone to think knocking off one of us would cripple the other. We need to both look strong, but not menacing, to those inside our realm of control. We need to look strong *and* menacing to those outside."

"Agreed." Drakon gestured in the direction of the confinement cells. "Speaking of those inside and outside, Colonel Malin says CEO Boyens hasn't been able to tell us much more."

"No." Iceni flipped her hand in the same direction, giving the gesture equal measures of disdain and aggression. "Boyens is spending his time trying to get information out of us instead of answering our questions. I think he's trying to build the best picture he can of conditions here so he can decide which way to commit."

"That doesn't make much sense," Drakon said. "If he's already on the run from the Syndicate, he can't just jump back into their laps."

"That's the question. Is he on the run from the Syndicate? Was he sent here with information we would consider valuable but that the Syndicate didn't think would enable us to stop their flotilla?"

Drakon thought about that, his brow lowering. "Which would potentially give him a chance to get inside our operations again. Is Boyens their fail-safe if that flotilla didn't succeed?"

"I asked you first." Iceni glared at the interruption as an urgent tone sounded to indicate someone wanted to come into her office. "What is it?"

"An urgent communication," Togo's image replied without visible emotion.

Something he didn't want anyone but her hearing, apparently. But Drakon had already heard the exchange and was watching her. "Come in," she told Togo.

Togo entered, walking to stand beside Iceni's desk, then waited until the door had once again sealed before replying. "It is Kahiki, Madam President."

"Kahiki? It's been quiet there."

"It is quiet again if this communication is truthful," Togo said. "Kahiki has overthrown Syndicate authority and requests our protection."

"Kahiki," Drakon muttered. "Have you been there?" he asked Iceni.

"No. There isn't much there there, is there?"

"Depends what you're talking about. There's a lot of rocks and a lot of bugs. I was sent to inspect the ground defenses, remember? About six months before our revolt. There's not a lot of good real estate at Kahiki. The only habitable world is a bit too close to the star, so it's livable but hot, mostly desert with some decent-sized seas. At each pole there are swampy jungle areas that are cool enough for humans to manage though they're not comfortable by any means." He paused. "Let's see. The total system population was about two hundred thousand. Two cities, one at each polar area, and a scattering of towns, including orbital installations at that planet and a couple of others. One brigade of regular Syndicate ground forces."

"Jump points allowing access to only one other star system besides Midway," Togo added, his voice actually sounding stiff at Drakon's having provided some information to Iceni first.

Iceni glanced at Drakon to see if he had noticed and saw him looking back at her with a bland expression but sardonic amusement in his eyes. "Most importantly," Drakon said, "Kahiki has some major research and development labs intended to support the Syndicate war effort and exploit anything that was ever recovered from the enigmas."

"Ah, yes," Iceni said. "I remember that now. Planet of the nerds, my predecessor called it. Supposedly analyzing everything known about the enigmas to determine what they were really like and how to beat them."

"Yeah. They'd been working on that for forty years or so before Black Jack came back and found the real answers in a few months. I imagine they're kind of sore about that."

"I imagine that Syndicate CEOs were dictating the researchers' every *creative* thought," Iceni said dryly. "You know what a handicap that can be to actually discovering anything. So, a star system set up for research. They would be a liability at the moment if they want us to protect them, but a very valuable ally to have in the long run. How many snakes were at Kahiki?"

"Not too many," Drakon said. "There was a satellite headquarters rather than a full system headquarters for the snakes."

"Two hundred twenty ISS agents are listed as having been present at Kahiki according to captured records," Togo added quickly.

"That is minimal," Iceni said. "Or rather, was minimal. I doubt there are still two hundred twenty snakes alive there. What did Kahiki do with its snakes?" she asked Togo.

"Their message did not say."

Iceni switched her attention back to Drakon. "Who was in charge of that brigade of ground forces?"

He frowned in thought again. "Sub-CEO . . . Santori. She struck me as very by-the-book, very cautious. It was easy to see that she browbeat her staff. They were scared of her but also sabotaging her in subtle ways."

"Which came first? Santori's treatment of them, or the sabotage?"

"I don't know, but Santori didn't impress me." Drakon looked at Togo. "I'd like to see this message from Kahiki."

Iceni nodded to Togo, who nodded back, then touched a control on his data pad.

The virtual window that appeared next to him showed a half dozen men and women seated at a conference table. Iceni watched and listened, paying less attention to the words than to the tones of voices and the body language of the six people who said they now ruled Kahiki. "What do you think?" she asked Drakon when it finished.

"The woman on the far left wasn't Sub-CEO Santori. She was

Santori's executive officer." Drakon rubbed his chin. "From what I remember, she struck me as unhappy but professional, trying to keep things running despite Santori's lack of leadership. It looks like she's in charge of the ground forces at Kahiki now."

"We lost some sub-CEOs when we revolted," Iceni commented.

"I imagine Santori took a short trip out of a high window courtesy of the executives she had been abusing. Commanders don't need their troops to like them, but they'd damned well better give the troops grounds to respect them, or sooner or later those troops will find a way to even the score. Those guys who say they're running Kahiki are definitely scared," Drakon added.

"Yes. Either that, or they are very good actors." Iceni tapped her lips with her forefinger as she studied the last image. "They said that what happened at Kane motivated them to revolt. CEO Boucher's attempt at intimidation appears to be backfiring."

"It's plausible," Drakon said. "But only because we're here. You heard them. They've learned that we now have a battleship and a battle cruiser, and that we've repulsed more than one Syndicate attack, so they think we offer potential protection against the Syndicate's doing to Kahiki what it did to Kane."

She gave him a significant glance. "But can we offer protection? We barely managed to repel that last Syndicate attack on us."

"Like you said, at the moment, they're a liability." Drakon gestured toward the star display. "But a limited liability. As your aide said, there's only one other jump point to Kahiki besides us, and that's to Tuvalu. There's nothing at Tuvalu except a lot of space rocks and an automated emergency station in case anyone passing through needs help. There isn't any simple way for the Syndicate to get an attack force to Kahiki. More importantly, the normal path for communications from Kahiki to Syndicate authorities was right here, through Midway. It's going to take a while for the Syndicate to even learn that anything has happened at Kahiki."

"You're sure?" Iceni asked. "The Syndicate didn't have alternate communications paths in use?"

"I inspected the defenses," Drakon reminded her. "That included reviewing comm paths and contingency plans. In an emergency, if Midway fell to the enigmas, Kahiki was to hunker down and use any available spacecraft to send word through Tuvalu. With the lack of a dedicated courier ship or other interstellar craft, and the time involved in getting word out through Tuvalu, everybody at Kahiki knew what that really meant. *You're on your own, and don't forget to kiss your butts good-bye.*"

Iceni smiled, though the expression had more ferocity than humor to it. "How many times during the war with the Alliance was that the only contingency plan? More than I care to think about. But it's true that if Midway had fallen to the enigmas, Kahiki would have been indefensible. The Syndicate would have had a lot of trouble doing anything to save or evacuate Kahiki even before Black Jack annihilated so many of the Syndicate's mobile forces. All right. I am in favor of extending our protection to Kahiki, of inviting them to ally with us."

Drakon sat hunched over slightly, his eyes looking off into the distance, then finally nodded. "I agree. But let's keep the agreement secret for now, along with the fact that Kahiki has revolted. The longer it is before the Syndicate finds out, the longer it will be before they try to come up with a counterattack."

"I'll send a senior official to negotiate the deal. Something along the lines of what we agreed to with Taroa. Is that acceptable? Let me know which representative you want to send for the negotiations."

Once again, Drakon spent a while thinking before answering. "Gwen, as long as the agreement is along the same framework as we used with Taroa, there's no reason for me to insist on having someone looking over the shoulder of your representative."

Iceni raised her eyebrows at him, surprised that Drakon had openly expressed that degree of trust in her. Out of the corner of her eye, she caught a glimpse of Togo reacting before he could cover it. Oddly enough, he had reacted at the start of Drakon's statement, not at the end.

Togo had reacted when Drakon called her Gwen.

What had she seen in Togo in that brief, unguarded moment? Surprise? Worry? Anger? It was impossible to tell. "That is all," she told Togo.

She waited until he had left, then pointed to Ulindi on the star display. "Have you heard anything more about that situation?"

"No," Drakon said.

"Has . . . your agent . . . arrived there yet?"

"She should be getting there anytime now," Drakon said. "But I don't know exactly how she was planning on sneaking into Ulindi, so I don't know exactly when she'll be there."

"You obviously still trust Colonel Morgan a great deal," Iceni said, hearing the coldness entering her voice.

Drakon, judging from the grimace he made, heard it, too. "In certain matters, I still do. She's very skilled at this sort of thing."

"I have heard frequent references to her skills," Iceni said, wondering if frost was forming on her words. "But in most cases only the vaguest references to where and how she acquired such skills."

"I don't know all of the particulars," Drakon said, meeting her iciness with a steady gaze. "She had many of those skills when I first met her, so she gained them young. There are things none of us who grew up in the Syndicate system talk about. Colonel Morgan has her share of those."

"Colonel Morgan has too many secrets."

"We're in agreement on that. I'm using her skills to help us with Ulindi. Don't think that means I still trust her in other matters."

After Drakon had left, Iceni scowled at the star display. It would simplify things immensely if Morgan died on Ulindi, no matter how that might complicate Drakon's task. *When it comes to double-dealing and death, I have no trouble believing that witch started learning her trade young. I wonder just how young she was.*

Sometime in the past . . .

Executive Fifth Class Roh Morgan, eighteen years old and recently promoted from Line Worker Fourth Class, leaned back and smiled at the man in the pilot's seat. She slowly extended one leg toward Executive First Class Jonis, showing off not only the leg itself but also the boot she was wearing.

Jonis smiled, too, but at the boot, not at her. "Nice work, Roh."

"I got everything you wanted," Morgan said. "Her boots, some skin flakes, a few other subtle pieces of evidence to salt the crime scene."

"Excellent." Putting the aircraft on autopilot, he extended a hand toward Morgan. "The stealth gear."

She straightened a bit, reaching into a large pocket in her vest, and brought out an assortment of bracelets, earrings, and rings. "This is the latest gear in the Internal Security Service's inventory? You'd think the ISS would be prepared to spot its being used."

"I told you they wouldn't." He held the hand out again, this time demandingly. "There's always a slight lag between new stealth gear being introduced and defensive sensors being reprogrammed to spot signs of the new gear."

Morgan dropped the jewelry into Jonis's hand. "So it will be useless soon."

"Not useless." Jonis, at least two decades older than Morgan, took on the lecturing tone he enjoyed using with her. "It is still effective. But a smart agent never depends on equipment that can be detected or found, no matter how well disguised it is. If you get caught with gear of this nature, it's very hard to claim you're not guilty of something.

The lessons I gave you on avoiding attention from my fellow agents are far more valuable in the long run than toys like this. And unlike technical devices, other methods to avoid being noticed don't become obsolete or need upgrades." He leered at her. "Once we finish planting this evidence, and Sub-CEO Tarranavi gets nailed for crimes against the Syndicate, I can give you a lot of other lessons of a more personal nature. You know, a lot of other men wouldn't have waited until now for that kind of payoff in exchange for their . . . guidance."

Morgan smiled. "You know the wait will be worth it."

"Yes. I think it will." He laughed again. "After that, as my protégé, you can do a lot of good service as an undercover agent for the ISS and earn the rewards that come with that."

"It sounds like I'll be getting lots of . . . rewards as your protégé," Morgan purred. "Why do you hate Tarranavi so much? Why do you want her arrested?"

"Arrested? That's the least of it. She'll be executed for sure. But I don't hate her. I don't care about her at all. She's in the way," Jonis explained matter-of-factly. "I want her job, Tarranavi shows no signs of leaving it or making the kind of real mistake I could exploit, so I'm giving her a nudge off the edge of the cliff, so I can continue on my own way upward. Speaking of mistakes, it's never a good idea to ask why you're carrying out a mission. Just do it and let your bosses worry about the reasons." He laughed as if he had just said something funny.

Morgan laughed, too. She had no trouble putting real amusement into the laugh despite the loathing that filled her as she looked at Jonis. She resisted glancing toward the control panel, knowing that any second now . . .

A warning light began blinking on the control console, accompanied by an urgent beeping tone. Startled, Executive Jonis turned his head to look at it.

Roh had already stiffened her hand. Her shoulder pivoted as her arm shot out and drove the hand with deadly accuracy into just the right spot on Jonis's neck. His spine cracked, then his head slammed into the side of the cockpit under the force of the blow.

Sighing, Roh massaged her hand, smiling at the blank expression fixed on Jonis's dead face. "Did you really think I was that young and naïve? That I didn't know that after you'd had all the fun with me you wanted, you were going to kill me so I couldn't betray you for setting up Tarranavi? Did you really believe that I wanted to be a snake like you, you scum? Did you forget I'd had commando training and knew how to kill with my bare hands? I guess you did, on all counts. Too bad for you."

Dropping the aircraft low, she set it on course toward the nearby mountains, carefully sprinkling the skin flakes from Tarranavi in the cockpit. "I already planted some other evidence of Tarranavi's involvement in the sabotage I did to this aircraft's safety systems," she told Jonis. "That sabotage is what set off the alarm that distracted you for the second I needed. What? Aren't you pleased at how well I learned your lessons? Oh, that's right, you're dead. But it will look like you died when this aircraft hits those mountains and the collision-protection equipment fails to deploy. Poor little snake, his neck broken in the impact! And all the evidence will point to another snake's being responsible."

Hauling out the low-altitude parachute she had brought along, Roh Morgan cast a regretful eye on the stealth gear she had returned to Jonis, the jewelry having fallen from his limp hand to lie sparkling on the floor of the cockpit. "Thanks for warning me how your fellow snakes can trace that stuff," she told Jonis cheerfully. "Otherwise, I probably would have tried to take it. Hey, did you notice that I'm wearing skin gloves so none of my skin flakes or prints will show up on that gear or in this aircraft? No? Too bad. Good-bye, snake."

She popped the side door, slid out of the cockpit, felt the chute deploy in the moments before reaching the ground, then rolled into a landing.

A powder sprinkled onto the chute caused it to shrivel into fragments. The snakes would find those fragments, of course, but the only evidence they would have as to who had used the chute would be the footprints from Sub-CEO Tarranavi's boots, which were on Morgan's feet.

Morgan disposed of the boots at her first stop, changing into other boots. Over the next twenty kilometers, she changed footwear several more times, using a dozen different methods to throw off any possible tracking or pursuit through open country, then the city. By the time she reached the military barracks where she was stuck, waiting for someone to accept her into a unit, she had thoroughly muddled her trail.

The sub-CEO running the barracks had made no secret of her own eagerness to see Morgan shunted off to some cannon-fodder unit where the combat life expectation of an Executive Fifth Class would be measured in minutes. But Morgan had managed to throw up a series of obstacles that had so far prevented her assignment to that kind of unit. Increasingly, Morgan realized her delaying tactics were only postponing the inevitable. No other kind of unit wanted her. No one else wanted her for any other purpose. No one had ever wanted her. So such a suicidal assignment would probably be her fate despite the medical assessment that had cleared her for duty. Morgan smiled at the sub-CEO's office as she passed it, thinking that she had already survived one suicide mission and wondering if she could eliminate any more snakes or equally poisonous executives and CEOs before being shipped out.

Not that she would die even then, despite every attempt to kill her. Morgan somehow knew that she was destined for something big, some greatness, even though everyone was against her. She hadn't died on that suicide mission into enigma space. She knew that the person who had come back wasn't the Roh Morgan who had been sent on the mission. She had changed, become much more than before. She felt that.

And the proof of her belief was that no one had ever come back from enigma-occupied space. Except her. That meant there must be a reason, a big reason, why she hadn't died. She was learning more every day, gaining the knowledge of her victims before sending them to the fates they deserved, preparing herself for whatever came next.

Her comm pad buzzed urgently. Morgan checked it, read the message, then had to pause to read it again.

Someone had agreed to take her as a junior executive in their combat unit. Someone had believed in her, despite her youth and her brief, checkered past. CEO Artur Drakon. *"This officer deserves a chance,"* Drakon had written.

Morgan didn't know who Drakon was. But as she looked at the message, a totally unexpected event, she knew he must be the one person in this dark, vicious universe who was on Morgan's side, who might not only deserve her loyalty but be the one worthy of helping her fulfill her own still-dimly-seen destiny.

Sometime now . . .

Colonel Roh Morgan, part of the crowd of rumpled and weary travelers leaving the tramp freighter which had brought them to Ulindi Star System, approached the security checkpoint at the docking facility orbiting Ulindi's primary world.

The checkpoint was an impressive one, with at least twenty snakes scrutinizing every person going through the checkpoint and ten ground forces soldiers in full battle armor backing them up. Clearly visible automated sensors and weaponry tracked the movements of those approaching the checkpoint, and it was a given that more sensors and weaponry were concealed in the walls and ceiling. Not just a security checkpoint, it was a strongpoint, well defended enough to hold off a serious attack.

A young man next to Morgan in the crowd muttered to himself as he stared aghast at the menacing snakes. "I wish I had one of those gadgets that make you invisible."

Idiot, she thought. Idiot to say that out loud, where snake sensors would pick it up, pinpoint the source, and ensure that the young worker received extra attention during the security screening. And idiot to think any piece of equipment could make you invisible in this kind of setting, where the snakes were searching with all of their equipment and skill for enemy agents and threats.

Searching for someone pretty much like Roh Morgan, when you got right down to it.

Morgan walked with the crowd toward the checkpoint.

CHAPTER FIVE

MORGAN had no equipment with her to help evade detection or attention by the snakes running the checkpoint and everything else in this star system. No one would be able to spot stealth equipment on her which no innocent civilian traveler should be carrying. Knowing how the snakes operated, what they looked for and what they didn't think of, made it a lot easier to know what not to do. Thanks to experience and study of the enemy's methods and tactics, Morgan also knew what she should do.

She wore slightly baggy, shapeless worker clothes in neutral colors, the clothes neither old nor new, neither fashionable nor unfashionable. Morgan had tinted her hair into a shade so bland that it was hard to find a descriptive word for it, and had cut it into a style matching that of countless other workers. Her skin had been similarly tinted, neither light nor dark nor shiny nor flat, but just there. Contacts shaded her eyes to an unremarkable color. She walked with a loose, slightly slouching posture, shoulders rounded a bit, matching the speed of the others around her. On her face, Morgan kept an expression of vague concentration, as if even routine actions required a little extra mental effort. She did not look scared or nervous or confident or any other emotion that might attract any attention. It wasn't easy to project a blank presence without its becoming apparent that you were being blank, but it could be done, like a magic trick in which the observers did not even realize their attention had been distracted.

The gazes of her fellow travelers and those of the snakes at the security checkpoint slid over Morgan, finding nothing to hold their attention or attract interest or rest in their memory. Even when Morgan handed her forged documents to the snake at the screening station, his attention barely rested on her for a moment before looking beyond in search of something worth seeing. "Purpose of travel to Ulindi?" the snake asked her in a bored monotone, his gaze wandering over the other passengers.

"Looking for work," Morgan said, her voice pitched so it could be easily heard but not any louder, her accent as generic to this region of space as possible.

"Register with neighborhood safety officials when you get accommodations." The snake droned the standard phrase, tossing the documents back at Morgan.

Feeling slightly miffed that her excellent forging job on the documents had been wasted on a snake too dumb to really examine them, Morgan merged with the flow of workers heading for the general seating cabin of the shuttle. Once inside, she wormed her way against a bulkhead, not apparently watching anyone as she slumped in a bare metal seat. Syndicate shuttles didn't waste money on worker comforts. Morgan did her best to continue looking unremarkable, knowing that the snakes would have sensors monitoring this cabin just as they did nearly every public place.

Without any first-class passengers aboard in the special, luxurious cabin reserved for them, the shuttle didn't bother with gentle maneuvering. The entry into atmosphere was even more uncomfortable than a combat drop. When the shuttle had finally grounded and dropped its ramp, Morgan once again merged with the crowd. There was another security checkpoint before the terminal, naturally, and another snake who smiled unpleasantly at an attractive worker in the throng as he waved Morgan through without a glance. She passed down a long hallway, pretending she wasn't aware of the many sensors scanning her and her bag as she walked.

Once outside of the terminal, Morgan adjusted her gait to a purposeful but not hurried walk. She looked like someone who had somewhere to go, a worker on assignment or heading to her job. Not enthusiastically. Not reluctantly. Just going. None of the police or other security personnel she passed gave her a second look.

Morgan had once thought about the irony that it took a tremendous amount of effort and concentration to look like someone who was completely uninteresting, but when actually doing that, she could not afford the distraction of extraneous thoughts. Any focus not directed at personal monotony was aimed outward at those around her. Morgan remained aware of every cop and every possible snake near her. She didn't give the slightest sign of that awareness, but every time one of those people twitched, Morgan knew it.

She didn't worry about looking much at the buildings, though. Syndicate cities, following central planning guidelines and approved architecture, tended to a drab sameness except for the occasional grandiose civic folly commissioned by a CEO who wanted a personal monument. After a while, even the undisciplined and erratic architecture of Alliance cities started to look the same. To Morgan, after her years of combat, all that mattered was that some buildings and some cities were broken and burning as you fought through them, and some weren't. This city wasn't broken or burning (yet), which made traveling through it a bit easier.

Morgan chose a hotel suitable for a worker with just enough funds to afford a private room. Inside, she found and "accidentally" blocked a hidden surveillance unit, then underwent a swift transformation using supplies and one of the two spare outfits in her bag. Within a short time, she had changed into nice clothes that emphasized her figure, washed out the drab hair tint and washed in a subtle glow effect for her hair, recombed it to look slightly exotic, scrubbed her face free of the first tinting and replaced it with a shade darker than her natural one, and popped the contacts in favor of another set that gave her green eyes. A small prosthesis at the bridge of her nose and two more on her cheekbones, blending invisibly into her real features, would totally throw off facial-recognition software trying to identify her. Every time she varied the undetectable facial camouflage, she would appear to be a totally different person to the artificial-intelligence routines trying to get facial matches.

Leaving nothing in the room, Morgan walked again, this time a little more briskly, her shoulders back, one hip popped out whenever she paused at a crossing signal, a slight smile on her lips, pretending not to notice the occasional looks that lingered on her new appearance. It didn't take her long to spot the sort of bar that snakes frequented. Snakes didn't have official hangouts, but they tended to lay claim to certain places for as long as it amused them, driving away other patrons who didn't want to risk being noticed by security personnel with a few drinks under their belts. Such places were easy to spot because of the way citizens familiar with the area avoided even looking at them as they walked past.

Morgan strolled inside, gazing around with feigned uncertainty, looking every inch like someone unfamiliar with the neighborhood who was just searching for a place to get a drink. In a minute, she was at the bar, where the tender served her with a warning glance around the room that Morgan ignored.

Two minutes after that, a male snake slid onto the seat next to hers, the ISS agent smiling in welcome. "New in town?"

Morgan nodded, smiling back. "I just came in from Gosport," she said, naming another, smaller, city on the planet. "New assignment."

"You must be lonely, then."

Morgan smiled wider. "Yes. I am."

Ten minutes afterward, they were entering a hastily rented room at a much better hotel than Morgan had visited earlier. She pointed around with a worried expression as the door closed. "I . . . don't want anybody knowing about this."

The snake laughed and brought out a palm-sized device. "Me, neither. There. It's on. All surveillance sensors in this room are blocked. Nothing can see or hear what we—"

Morgan caught his body before it hit the floor and lowered it gently the rest of the way. She shook her hand, wincing at a mild twinge. "I must be getting old," she told the dead snake as she knelt beside his body. "Death strokes aren't as easy as they used to be."

She checked him over carefully for other security gear or protective devices before pulling out his data pad. Her own data pad, outwardly an old, barely functional model, concealed an inner heart of the latest hacking and cracking software as well as the fastest hardware available.

Linking the two, Morgan swiftly broke into the ISS planetary central file system using the dead snake's pad as a Trojan horse. She went to internal files first, locating and downloading files on every citizen tagged as a likely security risk. Four times her data pad blurped as it ate and discarded security programs from the snake systems that were trying to infect Morgan's gear. Three other times the data pad bleeped to report it had blocked covert downloads of pigeon programs that would have secretly reported back her exact position to the snakes at every opportunity.

She checked the time. Six minutes elapsed since the snake had died. It would be another twenty minutes before ISS security systems would begin wondering why his remote monitors weren't updating his physical location and status.

Morgan switched to another section of the database and began downloading the ISS records on Supreme CEO Haris's armed forces. Since the ISS regarded the military as just another form of potential internal security threat, they always kept detailed files on local forces. Information on every weapon, man, woman, ship, and shuttle available to Haris poured into Morgan's data pad. She tapped in another command, sending back her own malware to infect the ISS systems. Most of the malware would probably be spotted and eliminated, but anything that survived would be very useful in the future.

A different alert sounded from her data pad. Morgan eyed the warning that system security sharks were closing in on her tap, checked the status of the armed forces information download and malware uploads, waited another ten seconds for those to complete, then broke the connection.

She knelt again, pulled out the hand weapon the snake agent had concealed under his coat, hacked the settings to cause it to catastrophically overheat, then laid it carefully on top of the snake's data pad, where it now rested on the floor next to the body. After rolling the dead snake on top of both, she picked up her bag, hid away her data pad, then strode out of the room with a satisfied smile on her face, ensuring the door was firmly closed behind her. The security cams in the hotel would notice nothing unexpected as she left. By the time fire alarms sounded, Morgan would be blocks away. The overheating weapon would reduce the snake's data pad to slag and do enough damage to the snake's body to make it unclear what had killed him, while that body blocked evidence of heat and smoke long enough for the destruction to be far along before any alarms tripped.

It took another change of appearance using the last set of clothes and cosmetics in the bag and another relocation before Morgan was able to check over some of the files she had pilfered. Drakon wanted her to get in touch with and organize any possible sources of resistance to Haris on this planet. If such people existed, the snakes were probably already watching them. All she had to do was evaluate the snake files to see which ones under suspicion were probably actually disloyal to Haris.

She frowned as she scanned the data. Over a week ago, the snakes had started hauling in a lot of the people whose files she had downloaded. The usual suspects were being rounded up, along with many others. Something must have triggered that, but there was no hint of what that something might be in any of the files.

Morgan checked the time, annoyed by what she saw. She had been on the ground for three hours, and aside from successfully infiltrating the planet, breaking into the ISS files, downloading everything she needed, uploading various malware that might escape the notice of the ISS, and killing one snake, she had hardly accomplished anything yet.

Still, as the old underground joke went, what did you call one dead snake?

A good start.

GWEN Iceni stood in her office, facing the grand virtual window that dominated one wall. Once, the window had shown a cityscape, as if looking out upon a large metropolis from a vantage point in a high building, the image changing in real time as each day wore on. A real window in that wall would have shown only rock, or perhaps armor, since her entire office was buried and well fortified against attack.

She had never really worried about whether the city in the false window was real, and if so where it was really located, or whether it was just some computer-generated fantasy. It still represented her reality in a way, that what lay outside her office was not terribly important.

It was just one more planet, one more place to work in before she moved on to somewhere else. Perhaps even to wherever that city was.

But, soon after the revolt against the Syndicate, Iceni had changed the view to show a beach here on Midway. A beach she knew really existed, one in the same latitude and not too far north of here, so the sunrises and sunsets and weather were the same as on the surface of the planet outside her office. She had kept the view there, and now stood watching the small waves roll in over the white beach, no two moving exactly the same or reaching the exact same height up the beach before falling back into the mass of the sea.

Like human lives, perhaps, reaching out of the universe's mass of . . . something . . . to reach for . . . something . . . before their brief span was done, no two the same, most of them causing only the smallest changes, though every once in a while great waves driven by the storm would change the beach in a way that endured for some time. And then they were gone.

Hell, aren't I the moody one today? Iceni thought. *Maybe I feel another storm coming.*

A voice spoke out of the air around her. "Madam President, Captain Bradamont has arrived."

"Send her in." As Bradamont entered, Iceni kept her eyes on the waves, then finally turned and faced the Alliance officer. "Good afternoon, Captain."

"Good afternoon, Madam President." Bradamont, looking as out of place as ever in her Alliance fleet uniform, also revealed some curiosity. "You requested that I come to see you?"

"Yes." Iceni walked back to her desk and sat down, waving Bradamont to a chair as well. "Do you realize the level of irony that you encapsulate, Captain?"

"Probably not." Bradamont took her seat, then gave Iceni a speculative look. "Do you mean the fact that I'm helping a former Syndicate star system fight off its enemies?"

"That's just part of it." Iceni waved again, and the star display sprang to life, many stars hanging in silent splendor in the air to one side of her desk. "The biggest part is this. You are an officer of the enemy, the Alliance, the force that the Syndicate, that people like me, fought and hated and killed and were killed by, for the last century. And you are also the only person in this star system that I can completely trust."

"Surely—"

"No, not General Drakon or my closest aides or anyone else in this star system can have my full trust. In fact, all of my training and experience cautions me that the less trust I place in them the better." Iceni leaned back. "I suppose that feels very alien to you."

Bradamont crooked a smile. "Not compared to the enigmas. Madam President, I have worked for or with more than one person in Alliance circles who seemed to personify the same concepts of not trusting anyone. I do have trouble grasping the idea of an entire society organized along those lines."

"Even after being here awhile?" Iceni gestured toward the door. "You left your bodyguards outside. You've become accustomed to having bodyguards accompany you whenever you leave the ground forces headquarters complex, and you didn't question that those bodyguards did not come in here." She touched a control on her desk and a slight rumbling transmitted through the walls and doors. "At a single command, I can turn this office into the equivalent of a citadel on one of our battleships. There is that much armor, that many active and passive defenses, built into it. Right now, it would take an immense amount of effort to break into here."

Bradamont looked around, impressed. "It's amazingly well concealed. You have those defenses because of the enigma threat?"

"Every star system CEO has an office like this, Captain. Because we fear our own citizens, the people, more than we fear the Alliance or the enigmas." Iceni touched the control again, deactivating the defenses. "That's what I want to talk to you about. Not my warships, but the people."

"Your people?"

Iceni hesitated, then nodded. "Yes. My people. That's hard to say. I'm not supposed to care about the workers. They're just another form of spare part. When one breaks, you throw it away and get another, and the fewer resources you invest in them, the better." She made a face. "It's *supposed* to be efficient, but as far as I can tell, it leads to immense inefficiencies. That's a problem I'm trying to correct."

"General Drakon shares your assessment of that problem," Bradamont said.

"Yes. That is one of the factors that led me to first reach out to him as a potential ally." Iceni rested her elbows on her desk and clasped her hands in front of her, looking at Bradamont over them. "Here's the core of my problem, one that I can only talk about to you. Any government rests on certain legs. The more legs, the more stable it is. A traditional Syndicate star-system government depends on four legs for stability. One is the CEOs, another is the Internal Security Service, the third is the mobile forces, and the fourth is the ground forces. If one of those legs falters, the other three keep the government stable, keep the citizens in line through fear and coercion, although frankly the snakes don't falter very often."

Bradamont nodded, her eyes intent with thought. "In the Alliance, our star-system governments depend upon support from the people, the different branches of the government itself, the business community, out of self-interest, and backup from the Alliance government if they need assistance. I guess that adds up to a lot more than three legs."

"When it works as intended?" Iceni pressed.

After a moment's hesitation, Bradamont nodded again. "When it works as intended. I'm going to be honest with you. There are some in the Alliance who believe that things like secrecy and strong internal security are the most important pillar of the government."

Iceni laughed. "If secrecy and strong internal security were the answers to stability, then the Syndicate Worlds would have been the most stable government in the history of humanity. Haven't you learned anything from us?"

"Perhaps we've learned the wrong things," Bradamont said. "Some of us, that is."

"You wouldn't be the first." Iceni traced an idle pattern on the surface of her desk with one finger. "Now, we have Midway Star System. How many legs support this government?"

Bradamont frowned. "Four?"

"Two."

"But . . . I was thinking the leaders, you and the general, the people, the ground forces, and the warships."

"No." Iceni shook her head to emphasize the word. "There are only two legs. One is me, and one is General Drakon. The people do not yet form a supporting leg. It's not a role they are used to, they do not trust General Drakon or me because they have spent their entire lives not trusting their leaders, and such lessons are hard to overcome, and they lack experience in guiding their own affairs. My warships will not act against the people on my orders. I could tell Kommodor Marphissa to bombard a city, and she would not do it."

"You're right," Bradamont said. "If she did pass on the order, her crews would rebel rather than carry it out."

"And what does Colonel Rogero tell you about the state of the ground forces?" Iceni asked.

Bradamont smiled sardonically. "I know you've been informed of that. They are loyal and will support you, but they won't fire on the citizens. Not anymore."

"Exactly. The citizens are not a leg. They are a club that could knock our legs out from under us." Iceni brooded for a moment before saying more. "So we depend on two legs. What if something happens to Drakon or me? Then we're trying to balance the government on one leg. It can be done, by balancing opposing forces and doing whatever is necessary, but it is a constant struggle and requires a cold-blooded willingness to betray, murder, and subvert in any way necessary to keep the government standing on that one leg. If you misjudge, if something happens to you, it topples."

"You want something better than that?" Bradamont asked.

"I want . . ." Iceni spent a few more moments in thought. This wasn't something she could risk saying to anyone other than Bradamont. "I would like to create something that depends for stability on many legs, none of which are fear of our own or of others or of the unknown. I would like to spend days coming up with new things to do, new horizons to explore, not putting out fires and plotting and trying to keep the whole mess from toppling into ruin. I would like to know that I can someday retire and not worry about being put on trial or murdered by my successor. I want to build something that endures. Something that people don't dread but truly do see as their protector. I want the sort of thing I have never seen. And, yes, I want people to remember that I built it."

"If you do build something like that," Bradamont said, "you will be remembered. Why are you telling me this?"

"Because you're not one of us, you haven't been poisoned by the experiences we have had, and because I am worried, Captain Bradamont. I am worried about external enemies. But I am also worried about the mood of the people of this star system, who have this bright, shiny new toy offering them more freedom, more power, and more responsibility than they have ever been allowed in Syndicate space. You know what has happened in many other star systems as Syndicate control weakened or collapsed. Fragmentation of authority, internal fighting, endless argument and warfare over who gets to control things. I sense this star system tottering on the edge of such a cliff precisely because I have allowed the people here more right to decide and to rule themselves, and they simply lack the experience to do so without repeating the mistakes of the only form of government they really know—the Syndicate form of government. Moreover, there are agents among them, enemy agents, snakes and possibly others, who are trying to create trouble, feeding fears, trying to get our people to do things that will knock the legs out from under this government."

"Does General Drakon share those fears?" Bradamont asked.

"No. Or, at least, he hasn't expressed them in any form I can see." Iceni waved toward the star display again. "General Drakon is focused on external threats, on building . . . well, defensive walls. And he's not wrong that we need to deal with Ulindi. He wasn't wrong that intervening in Taroa was in our best interest. He was willing to spend precious resources to let the people of Kane, those who still survive, know that we want to help them and that we are nothing like the Syndicate. However, the walls won't do us any good if the people inside them go on a rampage."

"But you're focused on internal stability," Bradamont said. "In a good way, from all I am hearing. Is that a bad division of labor? General Drakon looking toward external threats and you to internal stability?"

"Not if you put it that way," Iceni conceded. "You have to understand that neither General Drakon nor I have much experience with actually working together with other CEOs. What seems to you a reasonable division of labor seems to us to be a dangerous ceding of authority to someone else."

"Or, ceding some authority to the people?" Bradamont suggested. "That's the same thing to you, isn't it? Something dangerous?"

"It is. I'll tell you frankly," Iceni added, "that it's easier to trust Drakon than it is to trust the people, but neither comes easily. What do you know about the situation regarding Colonel Morgan?" It was strange how hard it was to say that woman's name without putting her feelings into her tone of voice.

Bradamont made a face. "Only what Colonel Rogero was told, that Colonel Morgan no longer speaks for General Drakon and no longer has command authority. I understand she has also been sent on a special assignment."

"What is your impression of Colonel Morgan?" Iceni asked.

"She scares the hell out of me," Bradamont admitted.

"That makes two of us. Why do you suppose General Drakon placed so much trust in her for so long?"

Bradamont hesitated. "I am reluctant to betray confidences . . ." she began in more formal tones.

"If you don't want to talk about what Colonel Rogero has told you, just share your own impressions."

"Then I would say that General Drakon trusted her because Colonel Morgan has a fanatical level of loyalty to him. He could tell that. Maybe he was flattered by that, especially coming from a woman like Colonel Morgan. But I don't think General Drakon was manipulated by her. I think he believed her and believed in her."

"Men." Iceni put a world of meaning into the single word.

Bradamont smiled. "They all need some work, don't they?"

"As do all of us," Iceni said. "I would welcome your suggestions, Captain Bradamont, on handling the people in this star system."

"I think you're doing a good job," Bradamont said. "But you are, I believe, absolutely right that the people need to become a stable leg of the government. That means they need to see the government as their government. They need to see you not just as the leader but as *their* leader. Whatever you do has to reinforce the idea that you and the people are the same. Words won't matter, not among people who are used to their government's lying to them. What will make a difference is what you do. The steps you have taken to reform the legal system for example, to make it a system actually interested in justice, are very important. The changes to the legal system are a bit disruptive, but you can't afford to halt them because simply halting forward progress would be seen as backsliding."

"Very true, but if the citizens begin rioting, if they are provoked into rioting, my options will be limited," Iceni said moodily.

"I understand. One thing Admiral Geary always emphasized to us was to think in terms of what the enemy wanted us to do, what the enemy expected us to do, and not to do those things. If agents hostile to you are trying to stir up your people, then they want you to do certain things in response to that."

Iceni nodded, impressed that Black Jack had known that. But of course he knew that. Based on what he had accomplished, Black Jack was twice the political schemer that anyone else could ever be. "Yes. War and Syndicate politics have a lot in common. One of my own early mentors gave me the same advice. Never let the wolves herd you in the direction they want you to go, is what he said."

"Do you have any idea what direction the wolves want you to go, Madam President?"

"I can only speculate," Iceni said. "But my best guess is that they will want me to do things that foster an image contrary to what you suggested. They want to push me to act not as the leader of the people but in a typical Syndicate CEO manner, arrogant and dictatorial."

Bradamont looked around the office. "A short time ago, you showed me how easily you can turn this office into a fortress, because Syndicate CEOs fear their own people. Is it possible your enemies will want you to act in that way as well, as someone who fears and distrusts the citizens rather than someone who is their leader? Something as simple as holing up in here would convey a powerful message. The citizens won't believe that the government is their government if it is hiding behind walls and armed guards."

"That would be the wrong kind of message," Iceni agreed. "If I look fearful, I look weak, and if I am fearful of my own citizens, that means I don't trust them, or that I am doing things that I don't want them to know about. I would look very much like a Syndicate CEO and not like a president. Yes. Thank you for pointing that out. Distrust of the people, fear of the people we rule, is so much a part of the way I have been trained to think that I could easily have fallen into such displays without even realizing what I was doing."

"How serious are your concerns at this moment?"

Iceni rested her head on one hand as she looked at Bradamont. "Captain, can you walk through a ship and feel the state of the crew? Their mood and their morale?"

"Yes," Bradamont said.

"I can do the same with the citizens. Yes, I sometimes disguise myself and go out alone to walk among them. There's no better way to get a sense of how they really feel, and there is an instability there that worries me. The citizens are the Achilles' heel of this star system. Our opponents know that."

"Can I speak of this to Colonel Rogero?"

Iceni considered the question before answering it. Anything Bradamont told Rogero would surely be passed to Drakon. "No." She laughed. "My pardon, Madam Military Emissary of the Alliance. I can't order you around. It is my wish that you not discuss the matter with Colonel Rogero as of yet."

"I will respect your wishes in the matter, Madam President," Bradamont replied. "But I will say that I do not believe that you have any grounds to fear General Drakon. He has given explicit orders to his commanders not to move against you."

"Unless the orders to move against me come from him," Iceni said wryly.

"He didn't caveat the instructions at all, Madam President. He said do not move against the president. Period."

Iceni looked at Bradamont, sitting with a straight-backed military posture, her uniform adorned with rank insignia and the ribbons representing medals and commendations won in long years of fighting against the Syndicate. It was hard to believe that a woman who had been through so much could be so naïve. *Drakon knew that Rogero would tell you and that you were likely to tell me. So this reassurance means nothing. But you, with your honor, can't even see that.* "Thank you. Have you seen anything else that you believe I should be aware of?"

"I assume that you've been getting reports on the progress of fitting out *Midway* and getting her ready for battle."

"Yes." Iceni leaned forward a bit. "The reports say that everything is going well. In fact, if I didn't trust Kommodor Marphissa as much as I do, I'd be inclined to think they were exaggerating the amount of progress."

"They're not," Bradamont said. "The crew is working very hard, and Kapitan Mercia has come up with a number of improvements to procedures that are allowing much more rapid progress than would have been possible under the old system."

"The Syndicate system, you mean." Iceni remembered references to that. Mercia had conceived of the improvements years ago, but of course the Syndicate bureaucracy hadn't been interested in changes suggested by some mobile forces executive. "The vast majority of *Midway*'s crew is made up of survivors from the Reserve Flotilla. What is your impression of them?"

Bradamont sketched a brief smile. "They know their business. They are also highly motivated. There is a pervasive sense among the crew that they were dishonored by the actions of Executive Ito."

"Dishonored?" Iceni asked, making clear her mockery of the term.

"I'm sorry, Madam President, but I don't know any other term that fits. Perhaps none of them understand what the Alliance fleet calls *honor*, but I feel that they understand *dishonor*, even if they could not place that name on it. They are determined to make up for what Ito tried to do. And they all know that *you* saved them. Kommodor Marphissa never hesitates to remind them that the flotilla that picked them up from Varandal, that escorted them safely here past the Syndicate, was ordered to do that by you despite the risks." Bradamont smiled again, her eyes challenging Iceni. "They don't want to let you down, after you have done so much for them."

Iceni made a snort of combined disbelief and derision to cover up her internal confusion. Bradamont couldn't be right. Workers didn't think like that.

But suppose they could think like that if motivated by things other than fear? She had considered the idea before, but time and again it had been shoved into the background by the need to deal with emergencies and unforeseen developments.

For a long time after Bradamont had left, Iceni sat gazing into the distance, thinking about things she had been told were true, had seen were true, but that might not be true.

MORGAN nodded to the man who had been designated in snake files as a potential security threat. Not a serious potential threat. Those had all been arrested or had simply disappeared before she had even reached Ulindi. The accelerated rate and number of arrests argued that Supreme CEO Haris was planning something in the near future, but every check Morgan had made revealed nothing in snake files about any impending activity.

Dark walls loomed around them, most of the light provided by the devices in Morgan's hand which were blocking any hidden surveillance system. Two more snakes had died to provide her with the right equipment.

The man stared back at her, one eye twitching nervously. "I don't know what you want."

"The same things that Citizen Torres wants," Morgan said smoothly.

"Wanted. Past tense. Torres is dead. If you think you're going to lure me into saying or doing anything disloyal, you're wrong."

Torres was also dead? The snakes had been two steps ahead of her on that one. "Haris's time is limited," Morgan said. "If you choose the right option, you can help bring about his downfall."

The man shook his head rapidly, gazing around as if trying to meet the eyes of unseen observers. "I have no interest in that. I am loyal. I will report you, though."

"Is that what started the snakes hauling in so many citizens? You reported on people?"

"No! The dragnet just began, out of nowhere! No one had done anything! I hadn't done anything!"

Morgan let a moment of silence build fear in the man while she thought about means to make him blurt something useful. "What about Citizen Galanos?" she finally asked. "What would he think of what you're saying?"

"Galanos? I . . . I don't know any Galanos."

"Don't be a fool," Morgan said. "The snakes know you've met with Galanos."

"That's not true! If it were, I'd be—" The man stopped, swallowing before he could speak again. "I am loyal," he protested weakly.

Morgan would have taken the man's denials a little easier if he wasn't the fifth contact who had refused to even begin working with her. Four others she had tried making contact with had either disappeared or died before she could reach them. She was feeling frustrated and more than a little upset.

Before she could say anything else, though, a small alarm chirped in her left ear, followed by a blinking light on the masking equipment she was carrying.

Snarling, Morgan slammed her palm against the man's forehead hard enough to launch him backward into the wall behind him. The impact could be clearly heard, doubtless alerting whoever was sneaking toward her from the left, but Morgan still paused long enough to run her gear over the man's body. Sure enough, he had been wired. The snakes had been a step ahead on him as well.

She yanked out the memory clip on the wire and ensured the man was dead, then thumbed the timer on an improvised explosive that she had concocted, setting the device in the dark shadows near the wall opposite the man's body. Drawing the weapon she had taken off a dead snake, Morgan faded back to her right, moving quickly and surely along the escape path she had worked out before setting up the meeting. There had been another path available to the left if the snakes had come from the other direction.

Not that this one was safe after all. Morgan froze, scanning the darkness for another sign of whatever trace of movement or sound had registered on her subconscious. There. And there. She waited patiently, counting silently to herself, weapon lined up on one of the almost-impossible-to-spot figures.

Morgan pulled the trigger a second before the improvised explosive detonated in the alley behind her. Without waiting to see the result of her shot, Morgan jumped sideways, firing twice more at the second figure who had become visible in the momentary light of the explosion, the sound of her shots masked by the echoes of the blast.

As the light faded, and darkness fell again, Morgan raced down the alley past the two dead or wounded snake sentries. Shots rang out behind her, and some to the side, but she was moving too fast along her preplanned route.

As she cut through a segment of an underground utility tunnel, a figure appeared to one side. Morgan didn't wait to identify the person or see if they posed a threat, one hand flashing out to inflict what could have been a killing blow. She didn't pause to find out if the strike had been lethal, continuing onward without pause.

Every plan had to be modified when necessary. The idea of getting armed resistance cells going here had seemed a good one but was proving to be way too hazardous and lacking in any actual recruits for the cells.

Morgan finally stopped in a carefully prepared hiding place, going to work to change her appearance again and dispose of anything that could be used to identify or track her.

She had to wait for daylight to move again without attracting all the wrong kinds of attention, so Morgan sat back and thought.

There had been a lot of arrests in this city and elsewhere on the planet in the last month, beginning a couple of weeks prior to her arrival. A lot of arrests. The bugged citizen who had died tonight had been near the bottom of the sort of long list of usual suspects that snakes routinely maintained. No one on a Syndicate world publicized arrest statistics, but from what Morgan had been able to put together by listening to murmured comments on the street and scanning the want ads for suddenly available job positions, there had been thousands of arrests recently.

Was Supreme CEO Haris that scared? Good. He should be.

Where were the snakes keeping all the citizens they were rounding up?

That might be an important thing to learn though Morgan suspected the answer would be an unpleasant one.

She hoped the information she had already smuggled out to General Drakon would be enough for him to achieve another overwhelming victory. Not that the general needed much help in winning battles. Strategic vision, that was another matter, but the general had her to keep that firmly targeted.

Morgan twisted her head up and to the side so she could peer up into a crack of night sky visible from her hiding place. Dawn was beginning to pale the darkness above, but the brightest stars were still visible.

Our daughter will rule those stars.

Despite the discomfort of the position, Morgan held it, watching until the last star's glow was lost in the spreading light of the new day.

GENERAL Drakon leaned back, indicating the display. His office was smaller than Iceni's, and more Spartan than luxurious, but those were as much lingering manifestations of what the Syndicate demanded of different levels of CEOs as they were reflections of Drakon's preferences. The exact size of a ground forces CEO office in any star system was laid out in detail in Syndicate regulations. A CEO could exceed the limits of office size for his or her position, but only at the cost of advertising ambition and risking preemptive actions by superiors. Since the revolt, Drakon could have expanded his office to match Iceni's, but he hadn't seen the point. As far as he was concerned, the size of a man's office didn't matter as long as there was enough room for a desk and a trash can, and bigger offices didn't make bigger men or women. "Did you go over the information Colonel Morgan sent?" he asked Colonel Malin.

"Yes, sir. It's very complete." Malin called up an image of Ulindi Star System. "It confirms some of our other information. Supreme CEO Haris was badly hurt by his failed attempt to seize our battleship. He lost his battle cruiser and four Hunter-Killers, leaving him with only one heavy cruiser that we knew of. Morgan's information tells us that Haris also has a single light cruiser at his disposal. Our prisoners from Haris's former battle cruiser suspected that he had the light cruiser but also thought it might have defected from Haris."

"And no warships under construction or repair," Drakon said. "Two cruisers can't stop us from landing troops wherever we want in Ulindi."

"Not if President Iceni sends along a sufficiently strong flotilla as escort," Malin agreed. "I would recommend asking for two heavy cruisers and two or more light cruisers. If either Kommodor Marphissa or Kapitan Kontos commands the flotilla, two-to-one superiority will be more than enough to ensure the neutralization of Haris's warships."

"That's about half of our warships. I think President Iceni will agree to a flotilla of that size. Why not ask to bring the battle cruiser as well?"

"There's no need for the battle cruiser, General," Malin said. "Unless Haris suddenly produces a much more serious warship threat. But if we arrive at Ulindi and see such a threat, we can cancel the landing operation and withdraw."

"I expect that President Iceni would say the same thing if I asked for the battle cruiser as well as half of her other warships," Drakon conceded. "I understand why she would want to keep *Pele* protecting Midway. If we don't keep our base here safe, taking Ulindi won't do us any good."

Malin gestured toward the display. "The data on the ground forces also matches what we knew, with only one brigade of regular Syndicate forces assigned. That brigade lost some of its soldiers, who were added to the battle cruiser's crew to assist in capturing our battleship. All of those died when we took the battle cruiser." Malin paused, eyeing the display. "And then there are a couple of battalions of planetary militia which are considered unreliable, and the snakes loyal to CEO Haris. Some of the ground forces and some of the snakes are deployed to orbital bases and locations around the star system. From the records Morgan procured, I estimate the actual ground strength of the opposition will be about sixty percent of officially authorized personnel for the Syndicate brigade."

"One brigade of regular forces at sixty percent strength," Drakon repeated, "and a couple of battalions of planetary military that have no heavy weapons because the snakes don't trust them. What do you make of the arrests that started before Morgan got there?"

Malin smiled without visible humor. "Haris is worried. He is seeing more enemies everywhere and striking out at everyone. The sort of mass arrests that Colonel Morgan reported will further turn the population and the ground forces against him." The smile went away. "However, it means that Colonel Morgan's attempts to form resistance cells may be limited in success."

"Through no fault of hers," Drakon said, frowning. "Haris must be smart enough to know that mass arrests are going to destabilize the populace. It's the fear of arrest that keeps most Syndicate citizens in line. If the arrests become so common that no one appears safe, they become counterproductive. Haris is courting serious trouble in the long run."

"Perhaps he is not smart enough to know that, General."

Drakon eyed Malin. "Colonel, I know you want this operation to be carried out. You want Ulindi turned from threat to ally. Maybe we can achieve that. But I don't want eagerness to cause anyone to turn a blind eye to potential difficulties." He was feeling the lack of Morgan here. She would have been challenging Malin's assumptions, keeping him honest, and pointing out alternatives. And Malin, anticipating her jabs, would have taken extra effort to double-check his own plans.

As mother/son relationships went, it was sort of messed up, but then Morgan didn't know it was a mother/son relationship, and it had worked pretty well for military planning as far as Drakon was concerned.

"Sir, I am considering all possibilities," Malin said.

And, to be honest, Drakon couldn't see any significant problems with what Malin was presenting. "Even if the military in Ulindi stays loyal to Haris," Drakon said, "we should still be able to take them with no trouble with two brigades of our own supported by warships in low orbit. Captain Bradamont says it should be simple to take down the few antiorbital defenses that Ulindi has."

"I agree with her assessment," Malin said. "Morgan also included her assessment that morale is low among the ground forces in Ulindi. It looks . . . almost easy."

Drakon nodded, twisting his mouth as he gazed at the display, glad that Malin had brought that up. "Too easy. What are we missing?"

"I can't find anything, sir. Morgan's information is very complete, and no matter her other . . . activities . . . Colonel Morgan is very good at this sort of thing. Supreme CEO Haris's recent actions, the surge of arrests and executions, do not suggest confidence or a feeling of strength on Haris's part."

"He's acting scared, isn't he? But it still looks pretty easy."

"We could bring three brigades," Malin suggested. "There should no longer be a requirement to stiffen the locals—"

"No." Drakon smiled briefly to soften the firm rejection of Malin's suggestion. "Two brigades won't short this effort. Haris is not acting like someone with a hidden trump card ready to play, and Morgan would have spotted any hidden trumps. If everything were quiet here, and we had the necessary lift on hand, I'd take all three of our brigades, but President Iceni needs backup, and getting enough lift for two brigades is going to be hard enough. What's your assessment of the security situation here?"

Malin paused before answering. "General, there is no doubt that someone is working to create problems with the citizens. My sources have yet to identify who that someone is, but with the changes that President Iceni has made, it will be much harder for them to cause civil unrest. The local forces under her control should be more than sufficient—"

"I think President Iceni requires one of our brigades," Drakon said in a way that made it clear the matter was closed. "Your last guess was that snakes weren't actually involved," Drakon pressed. "Do you still believe that?"

"No, sir," Malin admitted. "Midway needs the commerce that passes through this star system, but that commerce can easily mask the movements of Syndicate agents. I suspect that has happened. There are also very likely more snakes among the personnel from the Reserve Flotilla. I have cautioned against crewing the battleship almost exclusively with them, and against giving command of the battleship to a Reserve Flotilla veteran as well. I still believe that is a mistake we may all regret."

Drakon made a casting-away gesture with one hand. "That's a lost battle, Colonel. President Iceni has the utmost faith in Kapitan Mercia. I understand that Captain Bradamont also believes the crew of the *Midway* are overwhelmingly loyal."

"How many snakes does it take to bite?" Malin asked. He always projected a cool demeanor, one that many thought actually cold, but now the heat behind his question came through. "If we lose that battleship, then nothing else can possibly make up for it."

"It's pretty hard to destroy a battleship," Drakon said, leaning forward and placing his elbows on his desk. "You're not really worried about *Midway*, are you?"

"Sir?" Malin gazed back with an uncomprehending expression.

"You're worried about Colonel Morgan. You want to ensure that we can take Ulindi so she can be safely recovered."

"General, with all due respect," Malin said, his voice stiff, "that is not my primary concern."

"I didn't say it was. But you've already admitted that you've been protecting her for years, without her knowledge."

"Only when absolutely necessary. She has been sent on a hazardous mission," Malin said, speaking with extreme care. He had gone cool again, betraying no feeling. "I would be concerned about any officer under those circumstances. But the mission always comes first."

"Of course," Drakon agreed, sure that Malin believed what he was saying, but also pretty certain that it wasn't true. There had been too many incidents in the past which had only become understandable after Malin's relationship with Morgan had been revealed.

"Sir, all three brigades—" Malin tried again.

"Are not going." He didn't know why he felt a growing certainty that a brigade had to be left here. It was like that sixth sense that warned that someone was aiming a shot at him. What it meant, he didn't know, but Drakon had learned to pay attention to those kinds of intangible premonitions. In this case, though, he had some very tangible reasons as well. "Apart from other considerations, having to arrange transport for and load a third brigade will add significantly to our preparation time for this operation. I won't waste weeks of time in order to pad our margin of victory, which seems very comfortable already. Do you believe that is a misperception, Colonel?" Drakon asked.

Malin shook his head, poker-faced. "No, sir, I do not. Two brigades of our soldiers, supported by orbital bombardment from our warships, should easily succeed. Which brigade will be left behind, General?"

"I'll talk to President Iceni about that."

"Colonel Kai—"

"I'll talk to President Iceni," Drakon said, emphasizing the words this time to ensure that Malin knew he was pushing it.

After Malin had left, Drakon hunched over his desk, trying to grasp what was bothering him. Part of it was Malin himself. After years of feeling that he knew everything important about Bran Malin, feeling that Malin could be counted on, he now found himself questioning Malin's actions and motivations.

Morgan, of course, always questioned Malin's actions and motivations. That had left little need for Drakon to do it. But without Morgan, the dynamic had changed abruptly.

Perhaps I've grown too dependent on Malin and Morgan. As a team, they were often a pain, but they were also very, very capable. That made it too easy to lean on them and take their support for granted.

That's gone, though, and it can't return.

Is there anything else that could be giving me subconscious worries?

Things were quiet here, despite the impossible-to-eliminate rumors among the military and the civilians. Morgan had confirmed the state of Haris's forces, so they knew exactly what they would be facing in Ulindi. And Ulindi did have to be dealt with, despite the inevitable risks of any military operations, and despite the problems they would face rounding up enough freighters modified for carrying troops and attaching temporary air locks and shuttle clamps to them so that the two brigades could get to Ulindi and hit the ground hard and fast.

It all seemed pretty simple.

He had to be missing something.

CHAPTER SIX

"WHO are you planning on leaving here?" Iceni asked. She had that look she got when she was facing a necessary choice that she would prefer not to have to deal with.

"Colonel Rogero," Drakon replied, having learned not to string out answers when Iceni felt that way. This being a meeting at which critical decisions were being made, it was being carried out in person to avoid the chance of someone's tapping in to any comm link. He had come to her office for that meeting, as he usually did, and wondered if she was even noticing that concession to her. Not that he was going to bring that up. With Gwen Iceni sitting less than three meters away, he had no interest in antagonizing her.

"Rogero?" She paused, thinking, then gave him a keen look. "People are going to think he's my favorite."

"He is, isn't he?"

"As ground forces brigade commanders of yours go, yes," Iceni said enigmatically. "Is that why you chose him to remain?"

"Partly." Drakon nodded toward the star display. "Colonel Kai is as steady as a rock and absolutely dependable."

"That sounds like he would be the best choice to leave here," Iceni commented.

"Yes, but he's deliberate."

"Slow, you mean," Iceni said.

"He can be," Drakon conceded. "You can count on him absolutely, but he might take a while to act when quick action is necessary. I can get him moving faster, but you might not be able to."

"You think quick action might be necessary?" Iceni sat back, her gaze on him intent.

"I don't know." Drakon made an irritated chopping motion with one hand. "I don't know of any threat. But if something did happen, if Colonel Kai were the ground forces commander here, he might take too long to react. His temperament is best suited to being along on this operation."

Iceni watched him for several seconds, then nodded. "So, not Kai."

"That leaves Colonel Gaiene. I know your opinion of him, but if I thought he was best for this, I'd be urging you to accept his remaining behind. He's not the best, though. He raises hell anywhere he is, which is good on a battlefield and not so good in garrison."

"None of our subordinates are perfect," Iceni said, looking off to one side as she spoke. "But I would prefer not having to depend on a ground forces commander who might be drunk and in the wrong bed when he is needed."

"Which leaves Rogero, who would be a damned good choice regardless."

"And," Iceni added dryly, "if you leave Colonel Rogero behind, you won't have Captain Bradamont upset at you."

"She's among those I wouldn't want upset at me," Drakon agreed, giving Iceni a look that drew a small smile from her. "I was uncertain whether you'd want her to accompany the flotilla going to Ulindi, though."

"No," Iceni said. "I sounded out Bradamont on the matter. She was concerned that her participation in an offensive operation by us might violate her orders. I think she would do it if I said pretty please, because taking out Haris is really a defensive offensive operation, but this is something Kommodor Marphissa should be able to handle easily, and with her gone from Midway, I'd like Bradamont here backstopping Kapitans Kontos and Mercia."

"That seems prudent," Drakon agreed.

"I'm glad you approve."

"Gwen, are you unhappy with this operation? I've done planning, but that's it. I can write that off to contingency thinking. We can postpone hitting Ulindi or call it off completely. Haris is a problem, but he's not an imminent threat."

She made a face, looking downward. "I suppose I'm not hiding it very well. Yes, I'm unhappy with this operation, but if you asked me to list reasons not to go ahead with it, I would be hard-pressed to give you any, and I agree with the reasons why we need to eliminate the threat posed by Haris without waiting for things to get worse. I also agree that the level of arrests and executions at Ulindi indicate that Haris feels weak and is taking desperate measures to shore up his position. What happens to your Colonel Morgan if we called it off?"

"I can get word to Morgan to get herself out of Ulindi. She'll be able to do it."

"Unfortunately, you're probably right." Iceni sighed, running one hand through her hair.

"There is also the consideration," Drakon said, "of what happens to Ulindi if we don't go ahead with this, but Haris gets downsized by local opposition and someone loyal to the Syndicate hands Ulindi back to the CEOs on Prime."

"Too many worries. There are always too many. We never have

time to lay one completely to rest before others occupy our attention." She took a deep breath and looked at him, her expression hardening. "If this operation goes well, and if your Colonel Morgan survives, we will need to talk once you return."

"About Colonel Morgan?" He watched her nod, then nodded in reply. "I understand."

"Do you? She betrayed you, Artur. She used her position close to you to exploit you when you were at your most vulnerable in order to further her own plans. I happen to agree with you that Colonel Morgan is a tremendously capable individual. She's also crazier than a loon. That's a very dangerous combination."

"Believe me, I know."

"Then why—" She bit off the question before saying it.

But he knew what it would have been. "Because I was drunk and depressed and stupid."

His candor didn't seem to mollify Iceni. "I hope the experience was worth the trouble it has caused us."

"To be perfectly honest," Drakon said, "though when the hell are people like you and me perfectly honest? But the truth is I don't really remember it. I was seriously drunk."

"You slept with Colonel Morgan and you don't remember any of it?" For the first time during this conversation, Iceni seemed genuinely amused. "Maybe there is some form of cosmic justice."

Drakon felt some irritation at that. "I hope you realize by now that it never would have happened if I hadn't been that drunk."

"Is that an excuse?" Iceni asked.

"No. I don't have any excuse. It was a terrible personal and professional failure on my part."

Something, either the words or the way he said them, finally made Iceni show some limited signs of relenting. "All right. We will talk more about her, about what to do about her, if she gets back. I already told you I was going to send Kommodor Marphissa to command the warships. I'm going to give her two heavy cruisers, two light cruisers, and four Hunter-Killers. That will leave a decent though still-inadequate force to defend this star system, and should offer you a very comfortable margin of superiority over Haris's mobile forces, as well as a small but adequate bombardment capability to support your landing."

Drakon nodded. "I won't deny that I'd love to have the battle cruiser as well."

"Oh? Are you regretting that gift to me already?"

It took him a moment to realize that Iceni was teasing him. She must be feeling better. "No. You know how to use it a lot better than I do, and I know that Midway needs to be protected while the other warships are gone. Then we're agreed? We're going to get the ball rolling?"

Iceni once more took a few seconds to answer, gazing at the star display, unreadable thoughts moving behind her eyes. "Do you remember when this started? When the primary thing worrying you and me at this point would be the fear that when one of us was out of the star system the other would stab them in the back?"

"That's not what's worrying you?" he asked.

She paused again, for a long time, then spoke in a rush. "No. What's worrying me is not having you here."

Drakon gave her a puzzled frown. "You're worried about what I'll do while I'm not here?"

"No! I— Forget it! Forget I said anything until we resolve the issue of that colonel. Yes. Let's get the ball rolling. The sooner we get rid of Supreme CEO Haris, the better."

TOGO, as deferential and discreet as ever, waited for her to take notice of him.

Iceni closed out the document she was reviewing and looked at him. "Is there a problem?"

"I was asked to ensure that you were aware of the costs involved in the freighter modifications requested by the ground forces," Togo said.

"I have seen the estimates and approved them. This is an assault operation. The ground forces have to bring a lot of shuttles along and have the means to quickly load the soldiers from the freighters into the shuttles."

"I understand, Madam President, but the finance directorate—"

"Why am I explaining and justifying my decisions to you or to the finance directorate?" Iceni snapped. She didn't have to feign being unhappy to give more force to her words. "I'm aware of our current financial situation. The finance directorate should be aware that a defense support payment from Taroa is scheduled to arrive this month."

"The cost of the mobile forces continues to escalate—" Togo began.

"If you know a way to keep the Syndicate from reconquering this star system without us maintaining a strong force of warships, I would be very pleased to hear it." Iceni rested her chin on one fist as she glared at Togo. "Mehmet, you have been a valuable assistant. A very valuable assistant, who as far as I can tell has been happy in his job. But I have a growing sense that you are unhappy with your current situation."

Even Togo couldn't hear that question from her without revealing some surprise and worry. Questions from CEOs about whether you were happy with your current situation were, in the Syndicate, often precursors to suggestions that your resignation would be a smart move, suggestions that were in fact orders. "Madam President, I have no complaints. I have been honored to serve you and wish to continue doing so."

"And I wish that you would continue to serve as my special

assistant," Iceni said. "But I must be confident that you are committed to that job."

"I could not be more strongly committed," Togo said.

Iceni didn't bother checking the readouts on her desk that would tell her whether or not Togo was lying. She knew that he could defeat the sensors designed to detect such things. Such talents, among others, made him extremely valuable, but they also made him a source for worry. "I am pleased to hear that," she said. "Have you been able to identify any previously undetected snake agents, or sources for the rumors that continue to keep the citizens on edge?"

"No, Madam President. I will find them."

Iceni paused, frowning, then looked at Togo again. "Could you take Colonel Morgan if you were ordered to dispose of her? I don't want boasting or overconfidence. I want the most accurate estimate you can give me."

It was hard to tell which emotion Togo was suppressing this time. A smile? Maybe.

"Madam President," Togo said, pronouncing each word with slow precision, "if I am allowed to choose the time, place, and circumstances, there would be no doubt of the outcome. If any variables are introduced, they would reduce my chances, but I cannot conceive of any scenario in which my odds of success would not be at least two to one. You need only give me the order—"

"I am *not* giving you such an order. Is that clear? I am considering contingencies." Iceni leaned forward, arms on her desk, emphasizing each word. "What I need most at this moment is to know who is trying to stir up the citizens. I want names, and I want to know who they are working for. Get that for me, and get it as soon as possible."

Togo nodded, not revealing his feelings about the assignment. "It will be done, Madam President."

"What about that mob operation diverting manufacturing output to the black market? Are we ready to shut that down?"

"Whenever you give the order, Madam President. However," Togo added in his most diplomatic tone of voice, "recent changes to the legal system will complicate inflicting the appropriate punishments for all guilty parties."

Iceni felt her lips twist into a darkly amused smile as she gazed back at Togo. "I have developed an interest in wanting only those parties actually guilty of something to be punished."

"They are all certainly guilty of something," Togo argued.

"Then there should not be too much difficulty in ensuring they are found guilty and punished," Iceni said. "The changes to our legal system are, so far, fairly minor compared to those that have existed elsewhere and currently exist in the Alliance. Have you ever wondered why the Syndicate suffers from such high levels of corruption and crime when it assigns such strong penalties and guarantees convictions of anyone even suspected of wrongdoing?"

"People are inherently corrupt," Togo said, both face and voice impassive.

"Are they? I used to be as certain as you are. Now I want to know more." She leaned forward again, eyes on Togo. "Because if that's wrong, then any actions based on an erroneous assessment are likely to be wrong as well, or at least far less efficient than they should be. I don't want anyone making the mistake of assuming that I am going soft. My goal is to make certain that the right people are caught, and that the right people are punished in ways that reinforce my authority. In the past, my enemies could be fairly confident that they knew what I would do and how I would do it. Now they cannot be confident of what I will do or what methods I will employ."

Togo blinked. "I . . . understand, Madam President. My apologies for underestimating your subtlety and cunning."

"You're a lucky man," Iceni told him. "Most of the people who learned not to underestimate me found out their error too late to save themselves. Tell the police to move ahead on busting the black-market operation. I want to see how that is handled under the changes to the legal system. After that, stop by the finance directorate and inform them that, if there is any further delay in approving payments for those freighter modifications, I will choose some executives from the directorate at random to accompany General Drakon's ground forces during their assault. I'm sure the general can use a few special volunteers to spearhead his attacks."

COLONEL Roh Morgan, wearing the suit of a junior executive fifth class in the Syndicate ground forces, sat nursing a drink in one of the Junior Executive Break Networking Universal Training Personal Improvement Limited Refreshment Facilities inside the primary ground forces base on Ulindi. Like any Syndicate-designed military base, it was heavily fortified, prepared to withstand attack not only from the Alliance but also from the citizens of the planet if those citizens should be so foolish as to stage a rebellion. That had made it a little harder for Morgan to infiltrate, but with the snakes and other security forces combing the city itself for her, no one had spent much time checking the identification documents of a nondescript junior executive who was entering the base.

While Syndicate bureaucrats had over the decades added on one after another officially approved descriptive terms for what was essentially a blandly decorated bar that could also be used as a meeting room, those bureaucrats had adamantly refused to add on a single comma to the name. Since no one who actually used the facilities used the official name, instead just calling it the Jebnut, nobody actually worried about the odd lack of commas.

Jebnuts tended to be inadequately lighted, because the Syndicate used the terms "efficiently" and "cost-effective" where others might have thought "insufficiently" and "least-expensive" were the more appropriate words. However, the dim lighting suited junior executives who wanted to nap during mandatory "voluntary," "informal" training sessions, and now suited Morgan well as she did her best to fade into the background. No one was likely to take notice of one more junior executive of the lowest salary grade who had no visible distinguishing characteristics. Morgan had taken a table against a wall and was once again wearing a combination of makeup and small facial prosthetics that combined with a slightly-too-large version of the standard junior executive fifth class suit rendered her appearance completely unremarkable. Having dealt with countless come-ons in bars and restaurants, Morgan had also perfected the ability to generate a "leave me alone" aura that effectively repelled any mammalian lifeform except cats.

A booth a few tables down from her was occupied by several ground forces executives on lunch break from their duties at headquarters. Morgan didn't expect to hear any major secrets because no one with any brains spilled major secrets in a Syndicate facility that was surely being monitored by the snakes, but a lot could be learned from routine talk among people who dealt with so many classified items that they no longer could tell what really mattered.

"It's off-limits," one of them was telling the others. "Sealed off."

"Any idea why? We don't have people deployed to that training area," another asked.

"Maybe the . . . you know . . . security. Maybe they're using it."

"The Supreme CEO's people? Maybe."

"Then maybe we better talk about something else."

There was a pause, then someone else started talking. "Did you hear about the comm stand-down? If you've got anything that needs to go out, better get it sent."

"Stand-down? What are they standing down?"

"Everything. There's some check of systems going to be carried out looking for unauthorized taps and security effectiveness and all that junk. It's no secret. But everything will be silenced for seventy-two hours. Landlines, networks, over-the-air junk, everything."

"How the hell are we supposed to get anything done during those seventy-two hours?"

"Does this mean I'll have to talk to the people at the desks near me? I hope not."

"They're probably hoping the same thing."

"Seriously, this isn't some investigation? It's just a complete comm-system check?"

"That's the official word. They wanted a period of time when everything was quiet before they ran the check, so this means they're not expecting any trouble during those seventy-two hours."

"They better get all of those shuttle drills done by then."

"Those still going on?"

"Yeah. Every shuttle is out at dispersed landing locations doing recertification drills. They got them going up into low orbit and down again all night long."

"Maybe they're running them that hard to get the drills done before the comm stand-down."

"Yeah."

Another pause, then a voice pitched lower than before. "My boss said to be ready for some deployments."

"Deployments? Where? I thought CEO— I mean, the Supreme CEO only controlled this star system."

"For now."

"Could that be what the shuttle drills are about? Getting ready for combat drops?"

"Guys, shut the hell up. If it is, we shouldn't be talking."

"Yeah, especially now, what with . . ."

Another pause.

"It's always been bad, but—"

"Shut up."

"You must have heard about Jarulzki—"

"Shut up!"

Silence fell, a quiet that Morgan knew would last this time. She wondered what, if anything, the unfortunate Jarulzki had done. If the high rate of arrests among the citizens was any indicator, the snakes would also have been raking in for questioning higher than usual numbers of military personnel.

But the talk of a sealed-off training area was something new. And an upcoming comm moratorium. And intense shuttle training. Was Haris getting ready to launch an attack on another star system, or was this entirely related to internal security at Ulindi?

There was only one way to find out.

Given the time since she had left Midway, and the time required to assemble an assault force, Morgan guessed that General Drakon and his forces should arrive in Ulindi within the next few days. That left time to check on this information and ensure that it wasn't anything the general would need to worry about during his conquest of Ulindi.

As Morgan made her way back out of the base, she spent some time considering who Drakon would be bringing. The entire division? Maybe. That would give her a chance to check on what Rogero was up to. Why Drakon had kept him and Gaiene in their command positions baffled her. Gaiene was bad enough, half-drunk half the time, but at least (unlike Rogero) his sleeping partners were harmless. Rogero, though, with his Alliance girlfriend, was another matter. He had also shown far too much interest in working closely with that Iceni woman. Was Rogero selling out to the Alliance, or to Iceni, or playing both to see who coughed up the best deal?

And Malin. That little slime would be up to something, too. Maybe here at Ulindi, his luck would finally run out. If there was only some way to nail him herself in such a manner that the general couldn't possibly trace it back to her. But she had far too much respect for Drakon to assume he would not be able to track an assassination of Malin to its source.

Well, Haris's forces might do the job for her.

The only thing she couldn't understand, given the loathing she had felt for Malin since first meeting him, was why the thought of him dead caused any kind of mixed emotions in her.

MARPHISSA waited for the drop out of jump space. The only good part of the mental jolt that left humans unable to think or focus clearly for up to half a minute after leaving jump space was that no one was immune. Unlike most ailments in which some people were never affected, such as motion sickness, the jump-space jolt was endured by everyone. Nobody got a free ride by virtue of genetics or experience or training. The universe might be fundamentally unfair, but at least in this one way all humans operated on a level playing field.

All humans. Did the enigmas, the Kicks, or the Dancers suffer the same way? She wished that Bradamont was here to ask. *Hell. I wish Honore was here for a lot of reasons. She has so much more experience than I do in just about everything.*

"Departing jump in fifteen seconds," Senior Watch Specialist Czilla warned.

Marphissa braced herself for the exit from jump space. Everyone did that, everyone always did that, even though it didn't make any difference at all.

Manticore fell out of jump space.

A moment before, the heavy cruiser had been apparently alone except for the occasional inexplicable lights that were the only relief from the dull grayness of jump space. Abruptly, *Manticore* was surrounded by the other ships of the flotilla, while the stars once again looked down upon them all from the endless dark of the universe.

Manticore and the other warships, the heavy cruiser *Gryphon*, light cruisers *Hawk* and *Eagle*, and the small, swift Hunter-Killers *Sentry*, *Sentinel*, *Scout*, and *Defender*, all of them shepherding the twenty large, clumsy freighters carrying the two brigades of ground forces. The freighters normally looked awkward, but more so now with dozens of aerospace shuttles fastened to their exteriors like remoras clinging to whales.

Marphissa kept her eyes locked on her display, waiting for it to update with information on what was in Ulindi Star System. Certain things would definitely be here and unchanged, the things that had existed at Ulindi for untold years before humans came and gave the star a name, and would continue to be here when the last trace of humanity's presence had crumbled into ancient dust. A star a bit cooler and a bit larger than Mother Sol, the standard against which all stars continued to be measured by humans. Ten orbiting objects large enough to qualify as planets, two of them swinging around less than two light-minutes from the star, far too close to it and far too hot by human standards. Another a bit farther out at four light-minutes, but still too close, so that its oceans had long since formed a permanent hothouse. Six more planets whose orbits ranged from ten light-minutes to nearly five light-hours from the star, too far out and too cold to be suitable for humans to walk around freely, getting progressively more frigid the farther they were from the sun, the middle three of them gas giants.

And one planet swinging around its star at seven and a half light-minutes' distance. As planets went, it was just the sort of place humanity wanted. About sixty percent of the surface covered with water, a minor axial tilt so seasonal variations weren't too extreme, and plenty of native vegetation and other forms of life that over millions of years had transformed a world of raw rock, water, and a heavily carbon dioxide atmosphere into a place of oxygen, dirt, and trees.

About a million humans made their homes at Ulindi, most of them on that planet. Some of the rest were in space, and some of those were on warships. "There's the heavy cruiser and the light cruiser," Kapitan Diaz said as the symbols appeared on his display. Both were orbiting the habitable planet, nearly six light-hours away from where the ships from Midway had arrived. Haris's two warships would not know the attack on Ulindi had begun until they saw the light from the event reach them six hours from now.

The few other defenses that were visible at Ulindi all matched the descriptions Marphissa's warships had received before leaving Midway. "That spy did good work," she commented. "There's nothing here that we didn't expect to find, and no threats anywhere near us. As long as we keep those two cruisers away from the freighters carrying the ground forces, this shouldn't be too hard."

"Not compared to fighting off Syndicate flotillas," Diaz agreed.

Marphissa gazed at the description of the habitable planet. "That's a nice little world," she said out loud.

Kapitan Diaz nodded and snorted at the same time. "Soon we'll be dropping bombardment projectiles on that nice little world."

"Not all that many compared to what a big flotilla could accomplish," Marphissa said. "We'll do some serious localized damage, but that's it. A lot of nice little worlds like this were bombarded to hell and back during the war."

"We're not going to do that," Diaz objected. "Like you said, just localized damage to military targets. And the snakes. We could never do what was done to Kane."

"No. I hope not." Marphissa looked over at Diaz. "I've talked to Honore Bradamont about that, about how horrified Black Jack was when he came back and found out the Alliance was bombarding cities and towns indiscriminately. Yes, that was true. Black Jack could not believe that his own people were doing that. Bradamont researched it afterward, trying to learn when the policy had changed, and found out there was never one big decision made. It was lots of little decisions, doing one thing, then another thing, each little thing justified when a big decision to just bombard cities never would have been approved. But before they knew it, there they were, and they didn't even realize what had happened, what they were doing that would have horrified those ancestors they care about so much."

"You believe her?" Diaz asked. "Maybe she was taught it happened that way, like we were taught that the Alliance started the war and everything else bad."

"Oh, she was taught it was all the Syndicate's fault," Marphissa agreed. "But she researched it, using classified access to learn for sure what happened. And that's important for us. For you and me. Between Black Jack's time and not so long ago, the Alliance fleet gradually started doing things they never would have done. That could happen to us. We have to make sure it never does, and pass on to those who come after us that it must never happen."

"We could never—" Diaz began, then stared at his display with a pained look. "I wonder how many people said that over the last century, then found themselves doing things. You're right, Kommodor. It has to be something stronger than a rule or law that can be changed or ignored. It has to be something that no one would even imagine changing."

"There, you see?" Marphissa said. "As long as you say *you're right, Kommodor*, everything is fine. Remember that."

Diaz grinned. "Yes, Kommodor. But what would be strong enough to ensure our people do not find themselves on such a road?"

"I don't know. Maybe show those vids from Kane. We could do that once a year, on the anniversary. Kane Day, to remember what separates us from the Syndicate." She could sense the reaction from the crew on the bridge, a feeling of approval, support, and determination. "But that is for the future. Now, let's get to that planet and get rid of Supreme CEO Haris."

Marphissa gave the orders that brought the warships and freighters around a bit and down, slowly accelerating. At an average velocity of point zero five light, which would push the lumbering freighters to the limits of their capabilities, it would take five days to reach the planet where Haris and his two warships awaited them. "All ships return to standard readiness conditions," Marphissa ordered.

"Kapitan?" the comms specialist said. "Something has happened with communications in this star system. They've stopped."

Diaz glanced back at her, frowning again. "Which comms have stopped? Why?"

"All of them, Kapitan. I'm not picking up anything. The last message we received was *commence stand-down*. That came from the inhabited world. Then everything went silent."

"A complete comm stand-down?" Diaz looked over at Marphissa. "That's unusual. But it can't be related to our arrival. That stand-down message was sent nearly six hours before we got here."

"Kapitan." The comm specialist spoke again. "We're continuing to analyze the comm traffic. Some of the last messages we picked up talked about an upcoming stand-down and suggested it was security-related."

Marphissa frowned, thinking as she looked at her display. "Maybe that spy who gave us the information about the defenses here tripped some alerts. If he or she was digging around in databases, it might have led Haris's snakes to order a stand-down to look for the access points and other vulnerabilities. You're right that it can't have been caused by our arrival here. The times don't line up. Let me know as soon as comms go active again," she ordered, then touched her own comm controls.

General Drakon responded within a few seconds. He must have been on the bridge of the freighter he was riding. He had that rumpled look that anyone acquired when riding freighters, an appearance born of not enough room for clothes, not enough opportunities to get clean, and not enough room of any kind. It brought to mind the old joke about *lots of small confined spaces inside a large confined space inside an infinity of empty space.* "How does it look, Kommodor?" he asked her.

Marphissa waved outward. "No surprises, General. Haris's two warships are orbiting the inhabited world. I'll notify you when they break orbit there. No other defenses aside from the minor ones identified by our agent."

"Good. How long until we reach our objective?"

"Five days, General. I should mentioned that there's some unusual comm activity, or rather lack of comm activity. It looks like a total comm stand-down that began six hours before we arrived here. There are some indications that it might be security-related."

Drakon nodded. "They've probably been dealing with a lot of intrusions lately," he commented. "Let me know how long it lasts."

Marphissa, expecting Drakon to demand from her a detailed description of her plans for dealing with Haris's cruisers, was no longer sure what to say. "We'll get the freighters safely to the inhabited world, General."

"I never doubted that, Kommodor. Give me a heads-up if anything changes. Otherwise, we'll plan for the drop one hundred twenty hours from now."

She eyed the place where Drakon's image had been, trying to sort out her feelings. Marphissa still had vague suspicions about the general. She had heard rumors that he was plotting against the president, but never any details. And Honore Bradamont trusted General Drakon, said he was loyal to President Iceni, as hard as that was to believe. After all, Drakon had been a Syndicate CEO.

But then, so had President Iceni.

And, for whatever reasons, General Drakon was giving every indication of trusting Marphissa to do her job well.

Despite her earlier ambivalence, Marphissa found herself wanting to make sure that she did not let the general down.

GWEN Iceni, irritable with General Drakon and worried about having two-thirds of his soldiers and half of her operational warships gone from Midway, decided to question CEO Jason Boyens again. If he didn't reveal anything worthwhile this time, she might authorize some coercive measures on him just to make herself feel better.

Unfortunately, she knew that authorizing coercive measures wouldn't make her feel better, and in fact would make her feel worse, which only made her more irritable.

She took a seat in front of the wall-sized virtual window that gave a clear view of the cell Boyens occupied. As cells went, it wasn't bad, with halfway-comfortable furnishings. Boyens, having been told that Iceni was coming to speak with him, was already seated in a chair facing her. There were several rooms and armored walls between where the two sat, but they appeared to be facing each other separated by only a couple of meters. "To what do I owe the honor of your visit?" Boyens asked in a cheery voice.

"I'm trying to decide how to kill you," Iceni said flatly, "and was hoping to get some inspiration from conversing with you."

He grinned. "Gwen, if you were going to kill me, I'd be dead before I knew what you were intending."

"Then you should be aware how close you are to that," Iceni said. "Your failure to provide us with any more useful information is leading me to conclude that you are actually here as a Syndicate agent. Tell me why I shouldn't have you disposed of simply to eliminate that possibility."

Boyens sobered and sighed heavily. "The only thing keeping me alive is what I know. Once you have it, how do I know you won't dispose of me as no longer useful?"

"You claim to know me, and yet you say that?"

He watched her, then nodded with clear reluctance. "I know you well enough to know when you mean what you say. Does Drakon feel the same way?"

"He did when he left."

"Left?" Boyens looked startled. "He left this star system? With you in charge?"

She felt amused by that, by her ability to surprise someone used to the ways that Syndicate CEOs normally operated. "Yes."

"So it's just you now." Boyens made it a statement, not a question, then looked mildly surprised when she shook her head.

"General Drakon and I are partners," Iceni said.

"Oh."

The way Boyens said that one word, and the careful lack of visible reaction on his face, irritated her even more. "I'm not referring to any personal relationship," Iceni snapped at him. "It is purely professional, not that it is any business of yours. All you need to know is that both General Drakon and I know the other will not betray them." That was an overstatement, of course, and Boyens probably wouldn't believe a word of it. What surprised Iceni was discovering as she said it that the statement felt like the truth to her.

Boyens nodded apologetically. "It's your star system. You get to run it however you want. Can you . . . tell me where Drakon went?"

"If I do, I'd better get something extremely useful in exchange for the information."

Boyens hesitated, then nodded again. "Deal."

"He's gone to Ulindi."

Boyens stared at her, visibly rattled. "Ulindi? You're sending forces to Ulindi?"

"That's what I said."

"You— How many? How large a force?"

Iceni eyed him, wondering what Boyens was up to. "Why should I provide you with *that* information as well?"

He looked down, chewing his lip, and remained silent for several seconds. Finally, Boyens looked back at her and shrugged. "All right. I didn't want to play one of my last trump cards. You're going after Haris, right?"

"Supreme CEO Haris, yes," Iceni confirmed. "Why does that concern you so much? Is he a friend of yours?"

"Haris? The only friends Haris cultivates are those that can help him gain a promotion." Boyens grimaced, running one hand through his hair. "But he's not really Supreme CEO. I mean, he didn't come up with that title. The snakes did."

"The snakes?" Iceni felt a chill run down her spine. "Haris is acting under orders?"

"That's right. He didn't really claim any autonomy. It's all theater. Haris is just as much a part of the Syndicate ISS as he always was." Boyens leaned forward, his expression urgent. "The Syndicate has reinforcements ready to commit to Ulindi. I don't know what those reinforcements are or how many there are. It was all within snake channels, and I couldn't risk snooping into those very much. But Haris has more firepower than you think he does."

Iceni cupped her chin with one hand as she studied Boyens. All of the interrogation-cell indicators glowed green, so either Boyens was amazingly talented at fooling interrogation gear or he truly believed what he was telling her. "We had some very good preoperational surveillance," Iceni finally said. "It didn't spot those reinforcements that you are claiming exist."

"It wouldn't! Nothing at Ulindi has any records of that! There are total cutouts between Ulindi and the rest of the Syndicate, just as if Haris had really broken off from the Syndicate. But any ISS sources left at Midway who spotted any of your preparations to hit Ulindi would have passed information back to the snakes, and the snakes would have timed reinforcements to get to Ulindi and hammer whatever you sent. Given the time lag involved in passing information, your sources at Ulindi wouldn't have been able to get word back here of the reinforcements arriving at Ulindi before your attack force left."

Boyens held both of his hands before him, palms turned toward her, his voice pleading. "Look, I know you have reason to be skeptical of me. But I don't want you and Drakon to be crushed, and I know you guys can't afford to lose a big chunk of what forces you have. I'm telling you that whatever you sent to Ulindi isn't going to be enough. Your attack force is walking into a trap."

CHAPTER SEVEN

ICENI shook her head, maintaining an impassive expression despite the riot of emotions inside her. "Ulindi is a trap? Why should I believe you?"

"Because—" Boyens broke off and laughed in a sad way. "Because I want to work the angles, the options, Gwen. That's me, right? And I can't work options if there aren't any options. You see? Right now, and as far as I can tell, you and Artur Drakon are the only alternative to the Syndicate that has a chance out here. There are other star systems revolting against the Syndicate in other nearby regions, but I don't know the people or the exact situations in those places, and a lot of them are just going to hell as different factions fight for control. If the Syndicate regains enough strength, it will roll up each of those other star systems. If the Syndicate just keeps trying to regain control of them, the back-and-forth struggles are likely to devastate those places no matter who ultimately wins."

Boyens spread his hands and smiled ruefully. "I don't want to gain temporary power over ruins. Hell, I don't want ruins. I won't lie. I want power, I want a secure position of authority. Look around, Gwen. Where do you see security and stability? Here. Not on Prime, where the knives are out, the CEOs are busy stabbing their rivals, and the snakes are getting rid of anyone who looks strong enough to threaten them. Imagine having Happy Hua at your back, ready to strike if you fail too badly or if you succeed too well. I don't know how you and Artur figured out how to work together, but between that, breaking the snakes' power here, Black Jack's support, and the forces you've managed to accumulate, you've got a real chance."

"You're acting purely out of self-interest, then?" Iceni asked. "You believe that we represent your best chance to get what you want?"

"Damn right."

"*That* I can believe." Iceni paused to think through her options.

"You've got to send a ship after your attack force," Boyens urged. "Recall them before it's too late."

"It's already too late. By the time any warning I send could reach Ulindi, the ground forces will have already landed. I need to send some reinforcements to even the odds."

"Reinforcements?" Boyens looked around as if he could see through the walls confining him. "What have you got that could make a difference?"

"I'm going to find out," Iceni said, hoping that she could come up with something big enough to make a difference. "Damn you! If Artur Drakon dies because you withheld this information until now, I promise you that *you* will die as well, and it will *not* be an easy death!"

THE training area was well out in the country, far from the city, along routes normally traveled only by military vehicles. It had taken Roh Morgan far too long to cross that distance without being spotted, only to encounter a newly expanded and reinforced sensor field surrounding the training area. She was tempted to turn back at that point but realized that she had to know what all of those sensors were protecting. It had to be something significant.

The sensors were the latest models, the most sensitive yet created, but that was all to the good as far as Morgan was concerned. The more sensitive the sensor, the more it had to be adjusted and calibrated to ignore the presence and movements of native animals, birds, and insects as well as the movements of vegetation in the wind. With the right clothing and the right ways of moving, someone could mimic those native creatures and natural movements enough to keep the sensors from alerting.

The downside was that such travel was painstakingly slow, and this sensor field unusually wide.

By the time Morgan reached a vantage point looking down onto the training area, another several hours had been wasted. She raised the cam-nocs she had lifted from ground forces headquarters, using the same deliberate, careful movements that had brought her this far, zooming in the focus on the terrain below her.

The tents and equipment on the field were well camouflaged. Morgan knew she wouldn't have seen them if she hadn't known exactly what to look for.

Her curses stayed silent inside her, but didn't lack for force. There was a lot of equipment down there, equipment that couldn't be accounted for by the files that Haris's snakes had maintained.

A shuttle dropped down so quietly that she knew it must be a full-stealth model. As it came to rest, a woman came out of a tent and hurried to meet it. Morgan zoomed in closer, identifying the woman's suit as that of a sub-CEO. A sub-CEO implied this was a brigade-sized force . . .

The shuttle ramp dropped, and a man and woman came walking down it, the pair surrounded by several bodyguards. Morgan grimly focused on them, seeing what the presence of the bodyguards had already telegraphed.

A CEO, and another sub-CEO, both of their suits carrying the minor ornamentations that marked them as serving with ground forces.

That meant there could be an entire division of ground forces hidden here and in other training areas around the planet. A division that wasn't in any of the snake files. Morgan respected the snakes too much to think that this could have been done under their noses, especially in this star system, where the snakes had insinuated themselves even more deeply into the ground forces than usual.

Haris hadn't revolted. He hadn't unilaterally declared himself Supreme CEO of this star system. It had all been theater, a trick to make it seem that Haris was no longer loyal to the Syndicate and could no longer be sure of Syndicate backing.

The show had to have a purpose, and this was it. They must have learned an attack force was coming from Midway, they had brought in this division only a few days beforehand, using shuttle drills as a cover for landing all of the soldiers and equipment, and the comm silencing period was designed to ensure no possible hint of the extra troops' presence leaked out.

General Drakon must already be on the way. Must already be within a day or two of landing, expecting to encounter one understrength brigade of regular ground forces, not that brigade plus a division more. With the comm stand-down still in effect, trying to get a warning out would be a lot harder once she got to a transmitter, and just getting to a transmitter would take a while.

She felt a surge of fury, a desire to fling herself down the slope, to kill until she reached a transmitter. But she knew how likely that was to fail. If she died before she reached a means of sending a warning to General Drakon, then there would be no one to warn him at all.

And there was another mission that must be completed to ensure that Drakon survived. If she didn't ensure that some critical control lines remained disabled in ways that weren't apparent to the snakes,

General Drakon would not survive the victory that he might still be able to achieve despite the dramatic change in odds.

Morgan gritted her teeth, calmed herself with an effort of will that left her gasping, then began slowly, methodically sneaking back out of the sensor field.

LIFE on the crowded freighters was so unpleasant that Drakon found himself looking forward to combat as an alternative to staying in the cramped accommodations, breathing air fragrant with the smells of too many men and women who hadn't bathed in too long. Right now he was crammed into his grandly named stateroom, which in any surface dwelling would have been classified as a closet, along with Colonel Conner Gaiene. "What did you need to talk about?"

Gaiene made a face. "I've been thinking."

"Seriously?" Drakon asked.

Gaiene's expression shifted into a grin. "I still do that on occasion. Not every brain cell is dead, yet, and I have done this sort of thing a few times." The smile faded, replaced by that haunted look from eyes that had seen too much on too many battlefields. "The plan calls for using the warships to conduct a preliminary bombardment."

"Right," Drakon said. "The cruisers don't carry nearly as many bombardment projectiles as battleships or battle cruisers do, but they have enough to cause some real damage to one big target."

"So I see. We're going to turn snake headquarters on Ulindi into a big crater made up of a lot of little craters. But the snakes will have an alternate command post."

"Of course they will," Drakon agreed.

"How do we keep them from setting off the buried nukes? We are assuming that the snakes have buried nukes under the cities and big towns of this planet, aren't we?"

"Yes, we're assuming that," Drakon said. "Colonel Morgan will make sure the alternate command post can't send the detonation orders."

Gaiene bent a skeptical look on Drakon. "How is she going to do that all by herself? It would be a tough job for a company of special forces troops."

"You know Morgan."

"I certainly do," Gaiene said in a tone of voice that held great depths of meaning. "Though never in any physical sense, I assure you."

"Then you know that you don't ask her how and you don't tell her how," Drakon said. "You just tell her what you want done and pull the trigger."

"As smart weapons go, she is in a class by herself," Gaiene admitted. "But . . ."

"But, what? If you've got concerns, I want to hear them, Conner."

"There was that prolonged comm silence."

Drakon nodded, his expression grim. "The timing was suspicious, but it started well before we got here, and it ended yesterday. Now, of course, there's a lot of talk about our being here, but that's to be expected."

"We didn't catch any unguarded comms from before we arrived," Gaiene pointed out. "Those usually provide important information."

"I agree. And Colonel Kai has raised the same concern. Do you believe that period of comm silence justifies calling off the assault?" He waited for the answer, knowing that Gaiene would tell him whatever Gaiene believed and not what he thought Drakon might want to hear.

Gaiene paused for a long moment, his eyes averted, the pose almost that of a man listening to something he couldn't quite make out. "No. Based on what we know, I believe that we should go ahead with the assault."

"Is something else bothering you?"

Another pause, that same attitude of almost-listening, then Gaiene shrugged. "I don't know, General. Just a feeling. Have I ever thanked you? For overlooking my failings in the last few years?"

"You've earned your keep, Conner," Drakon said, eyeing Gaiene. He knew Gaiene could get moody at times, especially the last few years, but this felt different. "You're sure there's nothing specific bothering you?"

Gaiene smiled. "Just a feeling," he repeated. "I've been running away from the past for a long time. I . . . almost feel that it will catch up to me here." He laughed. "I'm sure Lara hasn't been happy with me."

Drakon didn't know what to say for a moment. "You haven't said Lara's name for a long time."

"She's been far away. She's closer now." Gaiene looked straight at Drakon, his eyes dark. "Thank you, General."

"Can you lead your troops into this fight?" Drakon asked. Gaiene had acted fey before, but not like this.

"Yes, sir. All the way. Not a problem." Gaiene smiled once more and suddenly seemed his usual self again. "I feel better than I have in a long time. Is drop time still in fourteen hours?"

"Yes. The Kommodor will let me know when we're exactly two hours out. I'll pass word to you and Kai then, so you can get your troops prepared for the assault. The shuttle pilots have already gone over their birds and can be ready to go in half an hour after I alert them. The bombardment will go out twenty minutes before we launch the first wave."

Gaiene looked at one bulkhead, his eyes obviously not seeing the bare metal but something from the past, his expression wistful and distressed in equal measure. "Do you remember how many times we've watched assault forces coming? Sitting there on the surface, you and me and the rest of us, seeing any friendly mobile forces around trying to fight off the attackers, watching the enemy assault transports get closer and closer as each day, then each hour goes by? Watching the bombardment launch and bracing ourselves for the impacts as the ground shook and shook and men and women died? And then the shuttles coming down through our defensive fire, dropping off loads of Alliance ground forces or maybe Alliance Marines, and the fights that took forever and no time at all and never seemed to stop. Or all the times we were the ones dropping into the fight, knowing that if we failed in the assault, no one might be able to get us out of there again. How many friends have we watched die, you and I?"

"I stopped thinking about that a long time ago," Drakon said, his voice soft.

"You only pretended to stop thinking about it," Gaiene corrected him.

"Yeah, I guess that's true. Conner, it's different now. We're not fighting for the Syndicate, we'll take as many prisoners as are willing to surrender, and when this is over, we'll go back to Midway and only fight to defend ourselves or to help others who need our assistance."

Gaiene nodded. "It's different. Yes. We know that. But the weapons we fire don't know that, General. All they know is how to kill, and they don't care why the triggers are pulled or what the target is." He saluted before leaving.

Drakon stared at the hatch after it closed, trying to remember if Conner Gaiene had ever before saluted him when they were in private.

ICENI was sitting in her office, clasped hands before her mouth, brooding, when an urgent alert sounded. Muttering a curse, Iceni spun to look at her display. What she saw made her anger change to a jolt of anxiety.

"An enigma ship arrived at the jump point from Pele," her watch-center supervisor reported anxiously.

She took a deep breath, calming herself and focusing her attention. "Only one? Is he a scout for a larger force?" The enigma had shown up more than four and a half hours ago. But watching its movements still created a sense of urgency in Iceni.

"Madam President, we cannot determine— He altered vector. A major change."

Iceni watched the movements of the enigma, movements made hours ago, the alien ship whipping around at an amazing rate. *If only our ships could move like that!* "He's . . . heading back," she said.

Then he was gone.

"The enigma ship has jumped back to Pele," the supervisor reported. "It must have been a surveillance mission, Madam President, taking a snapshot of everything here, then getting out before we could react."

"He could have hung around the jump point for hours and been safe from any reaction by us," Iceni said. "We don't have the luxury of stationing warships near that jump point."

The supervisor hesitated. "He very likely had firm orders to leave immediately."

"Why?" Iceni asked. She had learned the importance of encouraging her workers to share information instead of jumping down their throats whenever they volunteered something. That sort of thing was hard for the workers to get used to after their experience with the shut-up-and-do-it attitude of the Syndicate.

The watch-center supervisor spoke with care, feeling out each word. "We have seen numerous indications that the enigmas have a Syndicate-type level of discipline. The enigma commanders who sent this ship could not know whether we would have somebody stationed at the jump point, guarding it, so they may well have given that ship orders to return to Pele immediately after making their observations rather than giving its commander discretion on how long to stay and observe. It had plenty of time to see every ship here and what else was happening inside this star system."

"And so accomplished its mission with minimum risk of failure," Iceni said. "You are probably correct. Thank you."

She ended the call and stared glumly at the display, wishing that the enigmas had timed their reconnaissance mission for a different period. As it was, they would have seen precious few defensive assets in this star system, and the last extra thing she needed now was for the enigmas to launch another assault.

MORGAN had made a mistake, allowed herself to be spotted while killing that last sentry because she hadn't realized there would be a tertiary backup sensor monitoring the sentinel. Tertiary sensors were not standard in Syndicate practice for this layer of security in this kind of building, raising the question of just how many other additional security measures might be ahead of her. Alarm sirens split the predawn night as Morgan spent two seconds deciding whether to press on and try to reach the transmitter in this building. But, even if she managed to get past the alerted security, there did not seem any chance of having the time to get a warning message out to the general before the transmitter was disabled and overwhelming force cornered her.

Fading backward, Morgan moved like a ghost toward the access she had opened through the fences protecting the building. Extra lights were on, sweeping the cleared area between the building and the fences for anyone whose heat signature was blocked well enough to remain undetected by the infrared sensors. An aerospace craft swung into sight overhead, sliding over the building, weapons tracking in search of targets.

Someone had taken some very extensive extra measures to protect those comm terminals powerful enough to punch a signal through the wide-scale jamming that had replaced the comm stand-down. These extra security measures, too, had not been in the snake files. Someone had hidden them from not only spies like Morgan but from most of the snakes in Ulindi as well.

Morgan rarely felt any trace of uncertainty, but as she added things up, a very ugly picture had begun to appear. Ulindi had looked weak even when closely examined. An inviting target with, in Supreme CEO Haris, the sort of ruler who would motivate the leaders of Midway to strike at him.

But hidden beneath the surface had been another Ulindi, and what had been happening lately, the comm stand-down and the jamming and this extra security, implied that someone was trying to ensure that their prey did not see or hear anything before an ambush was sprung.

These thoughts ran through her mind as Morgan took careful aim on the hovering aerospace craft and put two shots into the spot where the lateral controls were least protected on the side facing her.

The warbird's weapons swung toward the place where the shots had been fired, but Morgan was no longer there. As the aerospace craft twisted in place to head for the spot, it lurched wildly as half of its lateral controls failed. At low altitude, the craft couldn't recover before sliding close enough to the building to clip it.

Morgan huddled against the building, just around the corner from where the aerospace craft was noisily self-destructing. The instant the wave of concussion, heat, and debris was past, Morgan ran, heading for the path she had cut through the fences. Behind her, part of the building's wall collapsed in a prolonged rumble punctuated by the thuds of large pieces of the warbird crashing into the soil all around.

She made it to the fence as shots finally erupted, tearing through the air around her while Morgan raced through the access path she had painstakingly created to get inside the complex. She had just cleared the last fence when a shot slammed into her right arm from close range. Morgan rolled with the blow, spinning to a halt on the ground with her pistol up and aimed at the guard who had waited to see if she was dead before he fired again. He never got the chance as Morgan put a shot between his eyes.

Forcing herself to her feet despite the pain of her wound, Morgan put away her pistol, grabbed the guard's body, and held it before her as she moved toward the perimeter road through the confusion.

Two more guards were standing by a vehicle, looking around anxiously, their weapons ready. "This guy got hit!" Morgan yelled at them as she carried the dead guard toward them at a trot.

"How bad?" one of guards asked, lowering his weapon and taking a step to meet her.

"Hey—!" the second guard started to say as he got a better look at her.

Morgan dropped her burden, yanking out the dead guard's own sidearm as the body fell, and shot both guards. It took only a couple of seconds to find the key fob in one of the guard's pockets, start the vehicle, and block the remote override routines in its control software. Morgan hauled one of the bodies into the vehicle and tore off down the road.

There was a checkpoint, of course, but once again Morgan yelled, "I got a wounded sentry here!" and raced through it.

That bought her enough time to clear the checkpoint, but shots pursued the vehicle as Morgan floored the accelerator.

She held on for about a kilometer, activating the vehicle's autodrive so she could apply a field bandage from the vehicle's first-aid kit to her arm. Morgan set the vehicle controls to continue at maximum safe speed down the road, then rolled out and down the embankment, slamming the door shut behind her as she dropped away.

It hurt all the way down the slope, especially every time she rolled over her wounded arm.

Morgan stayed in place just long enough to rebandage her injury to stop the bleeding. She headed off at right angles to the frenzy around the complex, knowing that sensors and searchers would be looking for someone heading directly away from it. By sunrise she was still moving but barely conscious as she stumbled through an alley in the town where she had prepared an emergency hidy-hole sometime before.

She found the hidden access, pulled aside the concealing cover, slid inside the cramped space, and barely managed to get the cover back into position. Her confused thoughts were working mainly on instinct at that point, unable to formulate any clear plans for what to do next. Morgan passed out to the rhythm of her mind repeating the same words. *Got to warn him . . . got to warn him . . . got to warn . . .*

"IN another fifteen minutes, there will be two hours' travel time remaining to the inhabited planet," Senior Watch Specialist Czilla reported.

Marphissa scowled at her display. The freighters were braking their velocity at the best rate they could manage, which didn't say much. The planet was only about four light-minutes away now, so close that the images she was seeing of Supreme CEO Haris's heavy cruiser and light cruiser were getting close to real time.

As of four minutes ago, neither cruiser had moved from its orbit about the planet.

Diaz knew what was bothering her. "Why don't they do something? Maybe they are planning to surrender to us."

"Half of their crews are probably snakes!" Marphissa objected. "They would have to be carrying out their orders from Haris right up until they mutinied, and why would Haris have them just sit in orbit instead of sending them to try to hit our freighters? They should have come after us days ago. It's almost time to notify General Drakon to prepare for his landings, and those damned cruisers are still just sitting there! I don't like this. It's like they're waiting for something."

"What could they be waiting for?"

"If I knew that—"

Urgent alerts blared, cutting off Marphissa's comment as she gazed at the warning symbols springing to life on her display.

"Kommodor!" Senior Watch Specialist Czilla called out, his voice shaking. "We have just seen more mobile forces, at the closest gas giant."

"They've been behind it since we got here," Diaz said, studying his display with an appalled expression. "They must have known we were coming and stayed positioned behind the gas giant to hide from us until now. How did they know and where did Haris get more ships?"

"Spies must be how. They knew not only that we were coming but about when we would get here. They must have a good inside source at Midway." Marphissa stared at her display as the sensors on her warships combined their readings and produced an assessment. One battleship. One heavy cruiser. Three Hunter-Killers. She didn't need the sensors to confirm the identity of the warships. "It's Happy Hua's flotilla. The one that escaped from Midway and bombarded Kane."

Kapitan Diaz shook his head, bewildered. "Happy Hua's flotilla? But they're Syndicate. They should have attacked Haris."

"They didn't." The only possible reason struck her. "Haris is still Syndicate. He must be. That's the only reason why CEO Boucher wouldn't have attacked him."

"But," Diaz gasped, still trying to recover from the surprise, "why hide out there? Why not hit us earlier? They're far enough away now that we can outrun them if they come after us."

"Not all of us can run fast enough," Marphissa said, her voice grim. "They waited until we were deep into this star system and a long ways from any of the jump points. Have your specialists run some vectors. Tell me if there is any way for us to get our freighters out of this star system before that battleship can catch them."

Diaz's eyes went from her to his display, his face stricken. He gave the order to his specialists, then leaned close to Marphissa so he could speak in a very low voice. "I don't need to run vectors. That battleship is in position to block any escape run by our freighters unless they head for the jump point for Kiribati."

"That's my assessment also," Marphissa said. "I was hoping I was wrong."

Less than a minute later, Czilla's report confirmed her fears. "The only route the freighters could take that would avoid the battleship is heading across the star system and taking the jump point to Kiribati in Syndicate-controlled space, Kommodor. Any attempt to return to Midway or reach the jump point for Maui has a one hundred percent chance of intercept by the Syndicate battleship."

"If only these freighters were faster!" Diaz snarled.

"They're not," Marphissa said. "You might as well wish that we had a couple of battleships of our own, or that Black Jack would show up in the nick of time again." She gestured toward the comms specialist. "I need to speak with General Drakon immediately."

It only took a few seconds for Drakon to reply. He did not look happy. "The crew of this freighter is really upset. Are they right? Is that a Syndicate battleship?"

"Yes. Commanded by the same snake CEO who attacked Midway and bombarded Kane." Marphissa wasn't about to sugarcoat the situation. "They were waiting for us."

"No matter what else happens, we need to make sure that information gets back to Midway so that President Iceni will know we have a serious internal security problem. What are our options?"

"Option one," Marphissa said, "the freighters continue on to the main inhabited world and drop you off before the battleship can get here to stop you. That gives you a fighting chance on the ground, but after that you'll have to worry about a battleship overhead. Option two, all of the freighters continue onward at the best acceleration they can manage, all the way to the jump point for Kiribati, and jump for that star, hoping that the Syndicate doesn't have anything waiting to ambush you at Kiribati."

Drakon shook his head. "These freighters have limited life support, food, and water for the numbers of soldiers they are carrying. We have enough to get back to Midway if the landing was aborted, but traveling across the rest of the width of this star system followed by a jump for Kiribati would put us close to exhaustion of everything, even if there weren't more Syndicate warships waiting there."

"You could try doubling back, jumping back for Ulindi right after arriving at Kiribati, hoping that all of the Syndicate warships followed you to Kiribati, and that they wouldn't get there until those clumsy freighters managed to get turned around. But you'd have to put your people on starvation rations starting right now, and even then you might not make it back before they were exhausted."

She hadn't worked much with Drakon in the past, and was impressed now when he accepted her assessment without demanding she come up with something easier even if it was also impossible. "What about heading back for Midway, or Maui?" Drakon asked.

"Neither of those are really an option. The battleship will catch you and blow those freighters apart. There's no uncertainty. The freighters can't outrun the battleship if they head for those jump points, and my ships cannot stop the battleship from destroying them."

"All right." Drakon rubbed his chin, eyeing her. "It sounds to me, Kommodor, like our best option is going ahead with the landing. As you said, that gives us a fighting chance, which we will not have otherwise."

"That would be my recommendation, General. You may have to hold guns on the freighter crews to keep them from running before all of your forces are off-loaded. My ships will carry out the planned bombardment of targets on the surface, but after that you will be on your own. I will do everything I can to distract and engage and maybe even damage that battleship, but I cannot promise anything."

Drakon smiled dourly, his lips pressed into a thin line. "We had a lot more warships available when that battleship attacked Midway, and they couldn't stop it. Kommodor, from what I have seen of you, and from what both President Iceni and Captain Bradamont have said, we couldn't ask for a better mobile forces officer to guard our backs against that battleship. I know that you will do everything possible with the forces available to you."

"Th-thank you, sir." It was not the response she had expected when she had called Drakon with such horrible news.

"We'll get down to the surface, take out the Syndicate ground forces, then scatter," Drakon continued. "If you can keep that battleship occupied for a little while, we'll get dispersed enough that it will have to worry about bombarding every square meter of that planet in order to get us."

"Yes, sir. We'll keep it busy for as long as possible. My flotilla will escort the freighters until we are close enough to the planet to be sure you can off-load without Haris's warships getting to you. We will protect you to the utmost of our ability. For the people!" Marphissa sat rigidly straight and saluted Drakon.

Drakon smiled again, returning the salute. "For the people," he echoed. "If the worst happens here, don't get your forces wiped out fighting a hopeless battle. Get back to Midway and help President Iceni. She can hold out, Midway can hold out, even if we lose all the ground forces here. As long as people like you stick by her."

He ended the transmission, leaving Marphissa gazing at nothing and blinking away tears. *Damn. And to think I didn't trust him.* "Kapitan Diaz."

"Yes, Kommodor?"

"Let's put our heads together. If there is any way to slow down that battleship with what we've got, we need to figure it out. We have to give those ground forces all the time we can."

"Kommodor . . ." Diaz didn't look at her as he spoke again in a barely audible voice. "There's no possible way. They're doomed."

"No," Marphissa said, surprised by the fierceness in her voice. "We were doomed when *Manticore*'s propulsion controls were shot out. Have you forgotten already? But we found a way, and they may find a way. We do not quit, we do not give up, we give them everything that we can, so if they do die on that planet, it will not be because we did not do everything that human skill and courage and effort can achieve. Do you hear me?" She had raised her voice so that it rang across the bridge. "Everyone. Do you hear me? We do not give up, we do not falter, while one of our soldiers still lives and fights on the surface of that planet!"

A ragged chorus of agreement and cheers answered her words, Diaz also raising his head and nodding to her firmly. "Comm specialist," he said, "send a vid of the Kommodor's last statement to the other units. Your orders, Kommodor?"

What were her orders? Marphissa wondered. It was one thing to make a sweeping statement about giving the effort her all, but another thing to figure out what specific steps to take.

Marphissa focused on the nearest enemies, those on the planet and those in Haris's two cruisers. "Since we're going ahead with the assault on the planet, we'll accompany the freighters for another half hour. At that point, our warships will break away from the freighters earlier than planned and move to engage Haris's heavy cruiser and light cruiser. We'll launch the bombardment as scheduled, but from farther out than planned."

"We'll get scatter," Diaz warned. "It's not just the greater distance from the planet when we launch. We'll also be dropping the projectiles at a lower angle through the atmosphere. We can't have pinpoint precision under those circumstances."

Marphissa scowled, studying the bombardment plan. It did call for aiming at specific portions of the snake headquarters complex, but Diaz was right that the odds of a perfect hit were low when they had to launch under difficult circumstances. Under the Syndicate, no one would have been allowed to worry about rounds that missed the target and struck in the surrounding city, but she did not want to take even one step back onto that road. "There might be an answer. Show me a circular error probable for a bombardment round aimed at the center of the snake complex under the new range and atmospheric entry angle we'll be using."

Diaz gestured to his weapons specialist, who worked frantically for a few moments.

A circle appeared on Marphissa's image of the bombardment targets. A circle centered on the snake headquarters complex and extending about four meters beyond its boundaries into the wide-open area that surrounded the complex. "There's our answer. It's not perfect, but it will have to do."

"Kommodor," a puzzled Diaz asked, "I'm sorry, but I do not—"

"We aim every round at the center of the complex! Most will hit near there. The rest should scatter randomly within this error circle, meaning they will hit everywhere inside the complex."

"But we can't be sure they'll hit everywhere," Diaz objected. "It's statistical and random. One little patch may take a dozen hits, and another nearby area might be untouched."

"I know that." Marphissa kept her voice level with effort. "It's still our best option because aiming for specific points will face the same circular error probable for every shot, only centered wherever that particular projectile was aimed. And any spot that doesn't take a direct hit but sustains a lot of near misses is still going to take some damage."

Diaz grimaced, rubbed the back of his neck with one hand, then nodded. "Yes, Kommodor. It is our best option if we want to do as much damage to the complex as possible under the launch conditions we will face."

"I want to hold back two projectiles on each heavy cruiser and one on each light cruiser. The ground forces might need a few more rounds dropped in their support. Everything else will go into the bombardment. Have your specialists modify it and let me know as soon as the revised plan is ready."

"Yes, Kommodor."

Marphissa looked to Haris's cruisers next. She had been expecting them to finally strike at the freighters just before the ground forces began landing, but that had been before the Syndicate flotilla appeared. It was now clear that the cruisers had been kept on a short leash to avoid scaring off the Midway flotilla before it was too deeply committed to the operation to be able to get the ground forces and freighters out of this star system safely.

If she went after them once the ground forces were down, they would run. She could chase them all over this star system, driving down the fuel reserves on all of her ships, and have no hope of catching them. But if she didn't go after them . . . "Do you know what they're planning on doing?" she asked Diaz, then answered her own question. "They're going to wait to see if we go after them. If we do, they'll run and frustrate us while forcing us to use up our fuel cells. If we don't, they'll charge through our formation just as the freighters are dropping shuttles, creating an awful mess and potentially taking out a lot of ground forces while they are helpless."

Diaz looked from her to his display, then made a helpless gesture. "I agree with your assessment, Kommodor. What will you do, then?"

"I'm going to do neither, Kapitan," Marphissa announced. "I'm not going to chase them all over this star system, and I'm not going to sit here waiting for them."

"But . . ."

"We're going to lunge at them as if beginning an all-out pursuit, then, after they take off to avoid us, brake to stay near the freighters." Marphissa shook her head. "No. Not all of us. We're going to need all of our fuel reserves. I'm going to leave the Hunter-Killers positioned above the ground forces' landing site. They can't do much there, but they'll be able to provide some close support, and they'll be conserving their fuel cells."

"Then what?" Diaz asked. "After we abort our pursuit of Haris's cruisers?"

"I expect the freighters to scatter once the last ground forces have left them. At that point, *Manticore* and *Gryphon* will shadow Haris's heavy cruiser, which I expect will try to pick off the scattered freighters one by one. *Hawk* and *Eagle* will shadow Haris's light cruiser. Maybe one of Haris's ships will make a mistake."

Diaz grimaced. "What about the Syndicate flotilla? What about the battleship?"

Marphissa blew out a long breath before replying. "I am hoping that, as we screen the freighters and try to take out Haris's cruisers, one of us will come up with some brilliant and effective means of dealing with that battleship."

"Kommodor—"

"Dammit, I know! Unless we come up with some other ideas, the only thing we can do is stay out of the engagement envelopes of the weapons on that battleship. CEO Boucher is not going to cut loose her remaining escorts. Syndicate regulations call for battleships to have escorts. She won't go against Syndicate policy."

Diaz gave her a grim look. "If she decides it is necessary, Happy Hua *will* bombard the hell out of that planet in order to get as many of our ground forces as possible."

"I know." Marphissa left it at that. She had nothing else to offer, no ideas to present. Instead, she touched her comm controls. "*Sentry*, *Sentinel*, *Scout*, *Defender*, you are designated flotilla three. *Sentinel* is senior ship for flotilla three. Proceed to a position in low orbit above the ground forces' landing area and provide close support."

She reached out to her display, designating Haris's heavy cruiser and light cruiser as the objectives for intercept, then waited the fraction of a second for the *Manticore*'s automated systems to come up with the necessary maneuvers. "*Manticore*, *Gryphon*, *Hawk*, *Eagle*, immediate execute come port two three degrees, down zero two degrees, accelerate to point two light speed."

The four Midway cruisers slewed about under the push of their maneuvering thrusters, their bows swinging past the vector that would have brought them into position above the planet. As they steadied out on the new course their main propulsion units lit off, pushing the warships onto a path that would bring them into firing range of Haris's warships in twenty minutes.

Marphissa tapped her display a few more times, confirming that the weapons specialists on *Manticore* had adapted the bombardment plan to the new positions and vectors from which it would be fired. "*Manticore*, *Gryphon*, *Hawk*, *Eagle*. Launch bombardment using modified plan echo as your ships cross the firing point on your vectors."

For better or for worse, the battle for Ulindi had begun.

CHAPTER EIGHT

THE bombardment projectiles fell for kilometer after kilometer, picking up energy as they plummeted toward the surface, tracing streaks of fire across the planet's sky as they dropped through atmosphere that grew thicker with every meter. Rocks had been among the first weapons that humans employed against each other, and these projectiles were really just refined versions of rocks, projectiles of solid metal that depended on mass and accumulated energy to inflict damage on their targets. But where humanity's first ancestors had lobbed rocks with uncertain aim, human technology and ingenuity had advanced to the point where these projectiles could be dropped from great distances with incredible accuracy against targets that had no ability to dodge.

Targets like buildings on the surface of a planet.

Targets like the snake headquarters complex, heavily protected by walls and barriers, fences and mines, guard towers at frequent intervals, many portions of the headquarters buried under armor and layers of rock proof against most weapons.

The projectiles fell to earth, and the earth and the works of humanity broke beneath them.

MORGAN woke to the shuddering of the building she was in. She knew that sensation and, in the instant of waking, unsure where she was or why, wondered if she was one of the targets of the attack. A moment later, as memory returned, she felt a lilt of savage joy at knowing it represented an orbital bombardment falling on her enemies some distance from where she was.

The joy lasted just long enough for her to recall the events of last night and for her to start feeling the stiffness and pain of her body. Morgan took several deep breaths, willing away the pain, putting herself once again in that state where mere physical limitations could not stop her. Going to a medical clinic to get her wounded arm looked at was out of the question. The snakes would have every clinic and hospital within a hundred kilometers of the transmitter site staked out, waiting for someone to show up with wounds from gunfire.

She twisted, pulling out the first-aid kit from the vehicle as well as some emergency medical supplies she had earlier stolen and stashed here in case they were needed. It took some awkward maneuvering in the limited space available to do what needed to be done to her arm to stop the pain and allow it to function again. There would be a price to pay later on for pushing the limb into use despite the injury, but there was always a price to pay no matter what. She took meds to clear her mind as well, and to compensate for the blood loss she had endured, then wolfed down special rations designed to boost healing and blood regeneration.

Having done what she could without access to medical care, the pain blocked, her right arm almost fully useful again, Morgan paused to think through the situation. The bombardment meant that General

Drakon was here. He must be very close to the planet or already in orbit. Assault doctrine called for launching the landing as soon as possible after the preliminary bombardment to take advantage of the disruption and damage caused. The shuttles would be starting their drops soon.

It was too late to warn the general. She could not get to a sufficiently powerful transmitter in time even though the snakes who had been hunting her would now have a lot of other things to worry them as the attack went down.

But she had a major assignment yet to complete. Making sure that the snakes could not use their alternate command complex to detonate their hidden nukes on this planet. Morgan had done the preliminary work, but she needed to finish the job so that the codes would go nowhere even though the snake systems would think everything was working perfectly.

If she failed at this, the general would die, and she would as well.

DRAKON paused before entering the shuttle he would ride down to the surface. It was already full of soldiers, inhuman in their battle armor, their armored faceplates offering no clues to the feelings of those inside. "Colonel Malin, how does it look on your ship?"

Malin, occupying a different freighter, answered immediately. "The troops are fine, General. I can't say the same for the freighter crews. General, Haris has been waiting for us. There may be more surprises on the surface."

"I'm aware of that, Colonel." He managed not to snap the reply. Malin looked and sounded as if he were reciting an assessment of an issue in which he had no previous involvement. It would be very easy to lash out at Malin, to blame him for championing this operation, but that not only wouldn't accomplish anything, it also wouldn't be fair. The reasons for coming to Ulindi had appeared to everyone to be good ones. "I'm also aware that we have no alternative but to get down there and win."

"General, have there been any messages directly to you from Colonel Morgan?"

"No. Either she hasn't spotted anything unexpected on the surface, or she hasn't been able to get to a transmitter." The possible reasons why Morgan would not have been able to achieve that task, the sort of obstacles that could stop even her, worried Geary at the moment more than the Syndicate battleship light-hours distant.

"Sir, if Morgan hasn't taken out the links from the snake alternate command center—"

"I know. But her report indicated she had already done the work on that and only needed to activate the bypasses. We have to assume she succeeded. Once you get down, take charge of sending scouts out to check buildings outside of our perimeter. The ground forces down there have had plenty of warning that we were coming, and plenty of time to dig in at their base, but they might have left teams outside it to harass us."

"Yes, sir. I regret that I proposed this operation, General. There were obviously aspects to the situation that I was not sufficiently aware of."

So Malin did feel some guilt, though even now expressing it with cold formality rather than a heated statement of regret. "That's not important at the moment. What matters is frustrating whatever plans Haris has and finding out whatever other surprises exist before they find us. Focus on that."

"Yes, sir." This time Malin's voice clearly conveyed a determination to make up for his error.

Drakon ended the call to Malin, then took one more long look at his display before issuing the next order. He checked the consolidated status reports of the shuttles and the companies making up the two brigades. "Colonel Gaiene, Colonel Kai. Are you ready to go?"

"Yes, sir," both replied.

He called the aerospace commander of the shuttles. "Major Barnes, are all shuttles ready to land the first wave?"

"Ready, sir," she said.

"Kommodor Marphissa, I'm beginning the assault. Good luck."

"Good luck to you, General," the Kommodor answered. "We are unable to precisely evaluate the results of the bombardment of the snake headquarters complex due to the dust and debris masking our sensors, but the complex is assessed to have been totally destroyed." She was young enough and inexperienced enough for her worries to sound in her voice but had spent enough time in command not to extend the farewell with platitudes or meaningless promises.

"Thanks," Drakon said. "We'll finish the job."

He switched from the external command circuit for talking to the warships and back to the internal circuit tying together every unit under his command. "All units," Drakon said. "Commence assault."

He boarded the shuttle, locked one armored fist onto the brace that would hold him in place, watched the ramp seal, then felt the shuttle lurch and fall. All around, other shuttles dropped off from the freighters carrying them and dove toward the surface, firing chaff barrages ahead of them as they fell.

Any landing operation against opposition was a matter of tight guts, pounding hearts, and hope. Hope that your shuttle would make it to the surface without being hit, hope that you would get off the shuttle without being hit, hope that you would find cover without being hit, hope that the shuttle had dropped you in the right place and you weren't surrounded by enemies, hope that somehow you would survive this whole mess and come out in one piece on the winning side.

Drakon felt the shuttle he was riding rock several times from near misses as it dropped. He called up a display showing the faces of all the soldiers in the shuttle with him, stacked across his helmet's faceplate like figures on playing cards. "They're lousy shots," he told the soldiers, trying to put the best face he could on the situation.

Most of the soldiers smiled, though nerves made a lot of the smiles resemble grimaces. "It's pretty hot down there, General," one offered.

"Not nearly as hot as some places I've been," Drakon said. He steadied himself as the shuttle jolted again. The pilots driving these birds were veterans of the aerospace forces, and despite the hideous losses often sustained in landings against opposition, a fair number of the pilots had made drops in the face of determined enemy fire more than once. They were pushing their experience and their birds to the limits.

Drakon's shuttle was coming down so quickly that his armored boots threatened to rise off the deck of the troop compartment. Another small virtual window on his helmet display showed the view outside, which right now consisted of sky littered with all of the active and passive countermeasures, collectively called chaff, that the shuttles had fired down into the atmosphere before descending. Mixed in with the chaff was the dust and fine debris that had in some cases risen high in the atmosphere from the recent bombardment of the snake headquarters complex only thirty kilometers from where Drakon's troops were landing. All of that junk did a pretty decent job of confusing and blinding sensors on the ground, which was the only reason any of the shuttles had survived even this far into their drops to the surface. The surface defenses were probably firing on manual aiming, drastically reducing their chances of a hit, but some of their shots were coming uncomfortably close. "Remember the drill when we hit dirt. Most of you have done this before. Anyone who hasn't, you're just going to have to trust me."

That got some laughs, even from the newer soldiers who had joined Drakon's division after the exile to Midway. Joking with the troops wasn't something the average Syndicate CEO did, but Drakon believed that the fact that he had rarely acted like the average Syndicate CEO had been one of the things that had earned the loyalty of these soldiers. The average Syndicate CEO wouldn't have been riding in this shuttle, going down with the troops charged with carrying out his plan, sharing their fate.

Of course, he hadn't had much real choice. The freighters would be sitting ducks for the Syndicate warships unless that Kommodor could pull off a miracle. At least on the surface, he would have a chance to shoot back at the Syndicate.

The red lights on their helmet displays changed to yellow, warning that the ground was coming up fast. "Brace yourselves!" Drakon ordered. "They're going to brake hard!"

The words had barely left his mouth before g-forces slammed his armored boots flat to the deck. Drakon grunted as his body tried to compact onto the lower portions of his armor, painfully emphasizing that Syndicate armor designs did not incorporate nearly enough cushioning. His internal organs felt like they were compressing into his waist and legs, too, but he endured it, knowing it would not last.

After so many years of war and so many years laboring under the arbitrary, cruel, and profit-driven Syndicate, Drakon believed that was half the trick to remaining sane. Knowing that nothing would last, that no matter how bad things got, sooner or later they would either get better or possibly worse, but at least different.

The shuttle grounded hard enough to jar Drakon's teeth even through the armor, the ramp dropping at almost the same instant. "Out!" he yelled, leaping out onto the surface of Ulindi's primary inhabited world.

He let one foot land, using it to propel himself forward and down toward a building that loomed close by. The door was locked, but Drakon in his heavy battle armor smashed through it as if it were made of tinfoil. That had been a safe bet since the Syndicate Internal Security Service forbade nonofficial buildings from having doors strong enough to withstand forced entry. The rule made it a lot easier for the snakes to get into places, but also for attacking soldiers. Drakon rolled onto the floor inside, barely noting the office furnishings being hurled aside by the impacts with his armor, then came to his feet, weapon questing for targets.

Other soldiers from the shuttle came diving through the door, others through two nearby windows, and several more through the wall. Drakon knew the building could handle the abuse. Like most modern structures, it was built with a strong frame that could flex under stress and curtain walls over and inside the frame that also had some ability to absorb stress and vibration. Punching holes in the curtain walls didn't weaken the structure much.

The sergeant in charge of this unit ordered the soldiers to take up firing positions and told off several to scout around and ensure no defenders were elsewhere inside this structure. Confident that nearby security was being competently handled, Drakon knelt to study his helmet display.

Shuttles were grounding in a roughly rectangular pattern defined by streets facing the last row of buildings before the open area surrounding the main base of Haris's ground forces. The buildings offered protection against aimed fire from the base as the shuttles came down. Drakon could see the symbols for soldiers spilling out of each shuttle as it landed, then scattering into the buildings for cover as the shuttles leaped skyward again to rendezvous with the freighters and pick up another load of soldiers. There were few reports of contact with enemy forces to be seen, and those individual enemy soldiers encountered had either faded back toward their base or vanished into the buildings on the other side of the street from those occupied by Drakon's troops.

As the first wave of ground forces consolidated their positions, Drakon could see his square perimeter taking shape, the enemy ground forces base in the center and the rest of the city outside.

Like many Syndicate ground fortifications, the base had been deliberately constructed inside a dense section of a city, ruthlessly maintaining a clear security area around the base but leaving the buildings beyond that in place. Drakon had been told that the original designs had been intended to prevent ground forces mutinies by keeping them in areas easy for the snakes to monitor, to allow easy use of ground forces to suppress demonstrations or riots by citizens in the cities, and had also been constructed amid cities because the Alliance had once shied away from bombardments of civilian targets. That last piece of logic had lost any meaning as the war went on for decade after decade, and the Alliance began bombing as indiscriminately as the Syndicate mobile forces, but the Syndicate had never made a habit of changing any of its practices just because they no longer offered any benefits.

One significant negative of his forces' current position was that this first line of buildings facing the base consisted of fairly low structures to avoid blocking lines of sight against targets in the air. At only three or four stories tall, these buildings were overlooked by the taller structures across the street. But since Drakon didn't intend staying in these buildings, that shouldn't be a problem for very long.

He had dropped with Gaiene's brigade, which was forming into a half square centered on the hexagonal shape of the Syndicate ground forces base. Warning symbols glowed all around the outside of the Syndicate fort, cautioning of active defenses as well as mines and other hazards. Having watched the Midway attack force approaching for days, the Syndicate forces had received enough warning to concentrate inside the fort and ensure all of the base's defenses were prepared.

On the other side of the Syndicate base, Kai's brigade was dropping and forming into another half square, linking up with Gaiene's to completely surround the Syndicate soldiers. Under cover inside the buildings just beyond the base's cleared security perimeter, the vast majority of Drakon's forces were facing inward, preparing to assault the base, only a few watching their backs for threats coming from outside the circle. With the Syndicate ground forces trapped inside that base, there shouldn't be—

Alerts appeared on Drakon's helmet display as a chorus of shouts and warnings cut across the comm circuits. He forced himself to study the information carefully instead of barking out orders before understanding what was happening. Threat symbols flickered in and out as momentary detections registered on the sensors of battle armor worn by the scouts conducting reconnaissance of the buildings outside the perimeter.

"What have we got?" Drakon asked.

"General," Colonel Kai said, sounding annoyed the way he usually did when something interfered with the smooth progression of a plan. "The squads I sent to search the buildings outside our perimeter are spotting indications of enemy ground forces."

"How many? I'm seeing contacts fade in and out."

"My scouts are estimating the enemy in that area at about platoon strength. It's hard to tell, though, because the enemy ground forces are avoiding contact."

"Avoiding contact?" Drakon questioned. "Are they running?"

"No," Kai said. "They are remaining in the area but evading contact whenever my scouts try to close. I have ordered my scouts to cease pursuit because it looked very much like they were being drawn into an ambush."

There were times when Kai's caution paid off, and this was such a time, Drakon thought. "Good move. You're right. If they are staying close but just out of contact, they must want us to pursue."

"Should I reinforce my scouts, have them hold position, or withdraw?"

Drakon frowned, one part of his attention watching as the shuttles kept rising to pick up the next wave of soldiers from the freighters. Any of the three options could be justified based on what was known. "What does the senior soldier on the scene think?"

"I will link them in and ask. Sergeant Gavigan, what is your feel for the situation?"

Gavigan's voice was steady, but her words carried uncertainty. "Everything our sensors can see feels fine, Colonel. But there's something about this that doesn't feel fine. I've got my scouts widely dispersed, and they've all got that crawly feeling like people are infiltrating around them. We're not getting new detections right now. Just that feeling. We sent out gnats, those are what picked up most of the unknowns we spotted earlier, but the enemy must have deployed wasps because our gnats have been dying fast."

If the gnats, tiny robotic scouts which could not do very much or for very long distances but were very hard for enemies to spot, were being taken out by wasps, slightly larger robotic hunters whose sole function was to spot and destroy gnats, then whoever was hiding from his scouts wasn't just a patrol caught outside the base. They were equipped to deal with Drakon's scouts and capable enough to employ concealment and countermeasures to remain almost entirely hidden.

Drakon glanced around at the fine dust in the air from the recent bombardments and the damage to the buildings. "Do you have enough dust floating where you are to spot stealth suits in motion, Sergeant Gavigan?" Even the best stealth suits could not avoid revealing their presence amid smoke, mist, or dust.

"Yes, sir, General. There's enough dust. We can't see anything moving . . ."

"But . . ." Drakon prompted.

"I'd really like to fall back and concentrate my forces a little, General. If it was up to me. But we'll push on and see what we can find if those are our orders."

"Colonel Kai?" Drakon asked.

"We are still pretty thin on the ground," Kai pointed out. "If I reinforce the scouts, it will have to come from forces preparing to assault the base."

That decided Drakon. "Bring your scouts back in, to the near side of the buildings across the street from our perimeter, and have them maintain a close watch. Leave snoops behind. I want to see what follows the scouts when they pull back. Have your other forces continue their assigned tasks."

"Yes, sir."

Kai had scarcely signed off before more alerts sounded. "We've got something out there," Gaiene reported. "Unknown strength, avoiding contact."

"Are your scouts pursuing?" Drakon demanded.

"With extreme caution."

"Pull them back. Near side of the buildings across the street from your half of the perimeter. Leave snoops when they fall back. Did your scouts send out gnats?"

"Yes, sir," Gaiene said. He might be a frequent drunk in garrison, but in a fight he was on top of every detail. "But the gnats are getting eaten."

"Colonel Kai's troops ran into someone with wasps on his side, too. We can't divert forces from preps for the assault on the base, so have your scouts do their best to find out what they're facing but do not let them stick their necks out."

"Yes, sir, yes, sir, three bags full."

Drakon had barely ended that conversation when more alerts sounded, and his display lit with new threat symbols. "Warbirds!" someone called across the comm circuit.

"Engage when they reach effective range—" Colonel Kai began.

"Sir, they're not heading for ground attack. They're climbing to intercept the shuttles."

Damn. Drakon glared at the symbols representing the enemy aerospace craft. His forces didn't have any antiair weapons with enough range to hit the warbirds if they stayed high, and they were going for the most vulnerable part of his forces.

"Did that charming Kommodor leave anything in orbit to help deal with these fellows?" Gaiene asked Drakon.

Had she? That had been the plan, before the Syndicate flotilla had shown up. "I—" More symbols on his display. Particle-beam fire, coming down from above, spearing four of the warbirds climbing toward the shuttles. "Yes, she did."

The remaining warbirds scattered, some attempting to continue toward the once-more-descending shuttles. But it was very hard for anything moving at atmospheric speeds to evade a weapon moving at the velocity of a warship's hell lance. Four more warbirds were stricken by a second volley from high above, some spiraling off like lifeless, falling leaves and others exploding as the weapons they carried detonated.

Protected by the fire of the warships in near orbit as well as by a fresh barrage of chaff, the shuttles started down with the second wave of assault troops. They would land in the same areas as the first wave, on the streets just outside the current perimeter of Drakon's forces.

And there were unknown forces lurking inside the buildings on the other sides of those streets.

"Screen the drop zones," Drakon ordered. "Colonel Kai, Colonel Gaiene, pull half the first wave forces prepping for assault and send them to reinforce the units around the shuttle drop zones so the next wave can get down."

"Are you noticing the curious lack of artillery and missile fire on our positions?" Gaiene asked.

"Yes." They had assumed the landing areas and the occupied buildings would be getting hit by this far into the operation. "Haris doesn't have that much long-range bombardment capability. Maybe he moved it out of range of this location and is having to get it back into place."

"Or," Gaiene said, "maybe they're worried about rounds hitting whoever is in the buildings across the street?"

"The snoops my scouts planted are being taken out," Kai reported. "Someone is neutralizing them before they can provide detections."

Someone was a lot more capable than the single brigade of professional ground forces on this planet was supposed to be. "Each of you get a company set up in defensive positions across the street."

"They'll have to come from—" Kai began to object.

"I realize that," Drakon said, studying his display. "I've got a bad feeling. If we don't cover those landing zones and protect our rear, our assault could be defeated before it begins."

"Do we abort further landings?" Kai asked.

"No! Anyone we left on the freighters would be sitting ducks. We need to get them all down here so we can move in on that Syndicate base. The sooner we take it down, the sooner we can move out from it to eliminate any remaining enemy ground forces."

Shuttles once more began landing in the streets outside, their exhaust pushing abandoned ground vehicles around and stirring up clouds of dust. Soldiers raced out of them as the ramps dropped, fanning out and diving into the already-occupied buildings facing the enemy base.

Threat symbols appeared on Drakon's display again, multiplying rapidly in the buildings across the street all around the perimeter. This time the contacts stayed solid, and red markers indicated combat under way.

"My forces across the street are coming under pressure," Kai remarked laconically. "Estimated enemy strength of at least a company."

"Here, too!" Gaiene announced. "We're holding."

Shuttles were leaping upward again to pick up the third and last wave of ground forces from the freighters. Drakon tried calling the warships in orbit but could not get through the jamming that Haris's forces were employing. He switched to the circuit for the shuttle wing commander. "Major Barnes, what can you and your pilots see of the situation on the ground?"

Barnes, understandably, sounded distracted as she answered. "We're not too focused on that, General. There's still a lot of fire coming at us. Damn! Wait." A pause, then Barnes came back on. "My bird took a hit. Nothing serious. General, I can't make out details, but some of my pilots have spotted something unusual. Normally, we come in like this, and we see people fleeing the city. People in vehicles, on foot, whatever. Can't see that here. Wait." Another pause. "My bird is going to need some work when this is over, General. What we're seeing is stuff coming in. Vehicles, groups of people on foot, but not crowds."

"Not crowds?" Drakon pressed. "People on foot coming into the city. But spread out and not crowded together?"

"Yes, sir. Coming in from all sides near as I can tell. Looks like ground forces to me from the way they're moving."

"When you get high enough, ask whatever warships are up there to see if they can knock down bridges and interdict other routes into the city."

"Yes, sir. Got it. I think you've got four HuKs still in close support. Before our last dive, I saw all of the cruisers heading off after Haris's cruisers."

Four HuKs wasn't much, but it was a lot better than nothing.

Drakon pulled out the scale on his helmet display. The enemy base, and Drakon's troops, were located a little way from the city center. Reinforcements coming in would not all arrive at once as those with more distance to travel took more time to get here.

Reinforcements. Was the enemy base nearly empty and being defended mostly by automated weapons?

Or did Haris have on the ground the same sort of surprise that the Syndicate battleship had provided in space?

Why hadn't Morgan made contact yet? How could she have missed substantial additional ground forces?

"General, something is wrong—" Colonel Malin began. He was over on the opposite side of the perimeter from Drakon.

"I already know that. Listen up, all three of you," Drakon said, linking in Kai and Gaiene as well. "The birds have spotted ground forces coming into the city and no citizens fleeing it. We need to know how well defended that base actually is."

"They have been throwing out shots whenever they get a glimpse of our soldiers," Kai said.

"I've seen that. But it's apparent that we're going to be facing a much more serious threat outside our perimeter than we anticipated. We may have to assault sooner and with fewer troops. Try probing the base's defenses to see how much fire you draw."

"I would caution against a premature attack," Kai said. "We need enough troops on the ground to not only penetrate the base's defenses but also hold their gains and expand them. We do not have those forces available yet."

"I believe that Colonel Kai is right," Malin said.

"Test the defenses," Drakon repeated. "Let's make sure that base is as strongly held as our plans assumed." He was seriously second-guessing his own decision not to ask the warships to bombard part of the base's defenses as well as annihilate the snake headquarters. Given the limited bombardment capability of the few Midway cruisers, it had seemed much better to ensure the total destruction of the snake complex and to capture the base intact, along with the weapons and supplies within it. But that decision could not be revisited now. If the Midway cruisers had followed the plan, they had expended all of their bombardment projectiles.

"General?" Drakon instinctively looked up as he once more heard the voice of his shuttle commander, Major Barnes, through a hiss of static and wavering jamming tones. "Sir, we're loading up now. We've lost two birds, several others have hits but are still flyable. What do we do after we drop the last load?"

The plan had been for the shuttles to return to the freighters and await further developments in orbit. But that plan hadn't anticipated having an enemy battleship bearing down on them. "How long do we have left before the battleship gets here?"

"Twelve hours. The freighter crews are acting like it's already coming within weapons range, though. They'll run as soon as we leave with this last wave of the assault, General. I guarantee it. There won't be any freighters in orbit for us to link up with after the last drop."

Drakon exhaled heavily, glaring at his helmet display. "I hate to give this order, Pancho, but after your last drops, have the shuttles scatter. Stay real low to avoid any warbirds that Haris still has operational. Tell your people to find spots to land and hide until they get word to lift and rejoin us inside the base."

"Yes, sir. General, it's pretty hard to hide something the size of a shuttle."

"It'll be easier to hide on the ground than if you're in the air or in orbit. We've taken out Haris's orbital sensors. We'll have to hope that Haris's warships stay focused on our warships and the freighters and don't do orbital searches for you. Odds are the attention of Haris's ground forces is going to stay focused on us right here."

"All that's true, General. Good luck."

"Same to you. Tell all of your pilots that they did a fine job, and I'll stand them all for drinks when this is over."

"We'll hold you to that, General. All of my birds are loose and starting the last drop. And . . . the freighters are scattering. Looks like they're going to hug the curvature of the planet to hide themselves from the battleship for a little while, then head off in different directions."

"Understood." Drakon clenched one fist, wondering if his next sight of one of those freighters would be a ball of fire blossoming high overhead as the Syndicate warships closed in on them. He had no idea where Haris's two cruisers were right now or what Kommodor Marphissa was doing with her cruisers.

"The pressure on our perimeter is increasing," Gaiene reported. "I've got at least two companies of ground forces pressing on my people holding the far side of the street."

"Pull another company out of the perimeter to reinforce your people in those buildings," Drakon ordered. "Colonel Kai, you do the same."

"General," Kai began, "we're not yet under the same strain as—" He paused, then spoke again. "They just began hitting us harder. These are not just probes of our own defenses, General."

"No. Assume we're facing significant forces outside our perimeter. Once the third wave lands and the shuttles clear the landing areas, I want you to pull everyone back inside this ring of buildings. We need to do it fast and clean, so no one is caught trying to cross the street."

"Yes, sir."

"General?" Malin called. "I've been monitoring our testing of the base's defenses. I have no doubt that the base is strongly held."

"What are we facing here, Bran? Any ideas?"

"They were waiting for us in space, and they were waiting on the ground. If they have additional ground forces on the same scale to us as that battleship is to the Midway warships, then we could be facing at least a division."

"How could Morgan have missed that?" Drakon demanded.

"I don't know, General. My best bet is that the additional forces arrived too late in the game for Morgan to get word to us."

Drakon glared at his display, where enemy symbols continued to proliferate as the pressure on his outer perimeter intensified. "They must have had some pretty precise information about our plans."

"Yes, sir. Very precise. Someone close to you, or to the president, must have provided them with good enough information for them to plan this."

"I already discussed that with the Kommodor. We'll deal with that issue when we get back." He refused to say *if we get back*. "Another half hour, and we'll have everyone down here. We need to hit that base with everything we can as soon as we can. Help get that set up."

"Incoming!" someone shouted across the comm circuit.

More alerts pulsed on Drakon's helmet display, warning of a barrage of long-range missiles on its way. "They're timed to hit when the shuttles are dropping the last load. Pancho, delay the drop."

"Got it," Major Barnes said, her breathing coming fast. "Braking hard. We can't delay too much at the rate we're coming down. We'll reach the landing zones on the heels of the missiles and hopefully miss any shrapnel."

"Ladies and Gentlemen," Colonel Gaiene called over his brigade's comm circuit. "Get your butts under cover or kiss them good-bye." He switched to speak only to Drakon. "This could be a little ugly if some of those missiles hit the buildings we're in."

"I know."

"The enemy forces engaging me are pulling back," Kai reported.

"Smart of them," Gaiene said.

"Yeah," Drakon agreed. "They don't want to get hit by their own missile bombardment." He frowned as one of the missile tracks vanished from his display. "What—?" Another disappeared. "The warships. They're nailing the missiles with their hell lances."

"Too bad there are only four up there at the moment," Gaiene said. "They got another. This might not be too bad."

"Their hell lances can't fire continuously for long," Malin cautioned. "They'll overheat."

A detection hovered at the edge of Drakon's sensor picture. He stared in disbelief. "One of those HuKs is coming really low. He's getting into real atmosphere."

A half dozen more missiles vanished, but more warnings sprang to life as other missiles and surviving warbirds bolted upward after the Hunter-Killer that had come perilously low to support the ground forces.

"Get clear!" Drakon shouted at the Hunter-Killer, wondering if they would pick up his message through the jamming.

Whether the crew of the Hunter-Killer heard or not, the warship pivoted on end and shot back toward space, tracing a fiery path through atmosphere as its tortured hull overheated. The pursuing missiles and warbirds dropped back, unable to match the velocity of a spacecraft's main propulsion.

"She took some damage doing that," Kai remarked in an admiring voice. "And she attracted a lot of the defenders' attention by coming down that low."

"We owe her and her crew," Drakon agreed.

The blare of the *incoming barrage imminent* alarms in their battle armor caused them all to hit the floor wherever they were and wait for the few remaining seconds before the surviving missiles released multiple warheads that began slamming into the street outside. Drakon felt the floor of the building he was in flexing wildly, but, fortunately, earthquake proofing also helped structures survive the effects of nearby large explosions. Any windows still intact shattered as designed into clear gravel that fell like hail through the buildings. The street outside was obscured from view as the missile warheads filled the air with smoke and debris. As the thunder of detonations eased, he heard shattered walls of other buildings collapsing. Somewhere nearby, a fire alarm stuttered forlornly amid the wreckage.

"Coming in!" Major Barnes cried as the shuttles dropped, chasing the falling debris back to the ground. "We have no interest in staying any longer than necessary!"

The shuttles landed all around the perimeter, many making last-minute lurches to avoid new craters in the street as they dropped the last few meters. Once more, soldiers came out the ramps and scattered into the buildings, but this time as the shuttles lifted they bent into tight arcs that kept them low as they raced away across the city, dodging ground fire as they went.

Yells resounded in the street near Drakon. He glanced out the blown-out window nearest to him and caught a glimpse of a crippled shuttle cartwheeling across the sky, trailing smoke and fire. The shuttle clipped the top of a building, spun wildly, then crashed into another building farther on. Drakon couldn't see it as the shuttle exploded, throwing pieces of itself and the building in all directions, but his armor's sensors dutifully reported the burst of heat, pressure, and debris that marked the death of the shuttle's flight crew.

He made another check of all comms and sensors for information on the situation above the atmosphere. But with the defender's jammers still active, Drakon's surviving shuttles racing away at very low altitude seeking hiding places, and the freighters running for their lives, there was no longer any means of relaying data about events in space.

"All right, you apes," Drakon called over his command circuit to every one of his soldiers on the ground, all of whom either knew or suspected that this assault was not going as well as planned. "Stand by for assault on the Syndicate base in five minutes."

"Hey—!" An exclamation was cut off as a lieutenant died.

The soldiers defending the buildings across the street had followed orders, withdrawing as soon as the last shuttles lifted. Most of them had made it across safely, but Drakon saw threat markers multiplying rapidly as the sensors on his soldiers' battle armor reported a swiftly increasing barrage of enemy fire from the vacated buildings. "General," Colonel Kai said, "from the volume of enemy fire, I would estimate there is at least a full brigade facing me."

"Same here," Colonel Gaiene reported. "General, the pressure on our outer perimeter is rising fast. They're sending out thrusts across the street at us. If I don't shift a lot more troops to defending against attacks from the outside, we'll get overrun."

"I concur," Colonel Kai said.

"Shift troops as necessary," Drakon said. He knew that would leave too few soldiers available for the attack. "Delay the assault on the fort until we've stabilized the security of our outer perimeter."

Neither colonel asked how long the delay would be. They were both busy shifting their brigades to defend against the counterattacks, and they both knew that Drakon didn't have any answer for how much time it would take before they could launch the postponed attack.

With the pressure on his forces from outside the perimeter, attacking the enemy base might no longer be an option. The victory they had planned for, and had thought would be fairly easy, now seemed impossible.

Drakon looked at his display, hearing the thunder of battle increase on all sides, and wondered whether surviving would be possible.

CHAPTER NINE

THE freighters were heading off in all directions, doing what freighters always did, seeking individual safety, even though under most circumstances the only way to stay safe was to stay together where friendly warships could protect them.

But these weren't normal circumstances.

The Syndicate battleship had veered slightly off the vector that would have brought its flotilla to the inhabited planet. It was now heading for one of the fleeing freighters. Battleships were slow and cumbersome for warships, which meant they were vastly faster and more agile than freighters. Freighters were designed for economy, to haul large cargos across long distances by the most efficient means. Warships were designed to catch and destroy other ships as quickly and effectively as possible. All of the inefficiencies of their design, the extra crews, the extra propulsion, the weapons, combined to produce a platform that could easily annihilate efficient spacecraft.

Kommodor Marphissa glowered at her display as if her displeasure could somehow change the laws governing acceleration and momentum and mass. "He can't get away."

"No," Kapitan Diaz agreed. "The freighter's only chance would be if we caused the Syndicate flotilla to divert its path."

"Can we offer it bait? Do you think CEO Boucher would take bait? A cruiser with its main propulsion out?"

"Hua saw that at Midway," Diaz pointed out. "*Manticore* was truly disabled in that fight, and we still got away from her. She's not going to abandon destroying that freighter to chase us. She's going to destroy that freighter, then probably veer port to hit this second one, then swing from there—"

"I can see the path," Marphissa snapped. Only those freighters fleeing all out for the jump point for Kiribati had any chance of escaping, and even a single, small Syndicate warship waiting at Kiribati would catch them there.

Diaz looked away. "Your orders, Kommodor?"

Instead of answering him directly, Marphissa hit her comm controls. "*Sentry*, *Sentinel*, *Scout*, *Defender*, remain above the ground forces providing what support you can, but take any necessary evasive action to avoid enemy warships. Your priority—" This was so hard to say, so hard to get the words out past something in her throat that wanted to block them. "Your priority is to avoid enemy attacks. If you must abandon support positions above the ground forces to do so, then take that action." The small Hunter-Killers would not stand a chance against Haris's cruisers or the Syndicate flotilla, and *Scout* had already taken damage from an heroic but reckless dive into the atmosphere to support the ground forces.

"Kommodor," *Sentry* protested. "If we abandon the ground forces—"

"If you are destroyed, you will not be able to support anyone. Do not hold your ground support positions if that will result in your destruction by enemy warships." She wanted to spit once she had said those words. Anything to get the awful taste of them out of her mouth.

"We understand, Kommodor. We will comply." The answer came reluctantly. *Sentry* did not sound any happier than Marphissa did, but they could not argue the ugly logic that drove the order.

"*Hawk* and *Eagle*," Marphissa told the light cruisers, "you will be flotilla two. Your mission is to shadow and attempt to engage Haris's light cruiser. It will probably try to hit one of the freighters that the battleship cannot reach. *Hawk* is senior ship in your flotilla. *Gryphon* and *Manticore* are now flotilla one. We will shadow Haris's heavy cruiser and attempt to bring it to battle. Everyone, do your best. For the people, Marphissa, out."

She ended the call and slumped in her seat, gazing despairingly at her display. This is what her brave words had come to. Nothing. All her warships could do was try to keep Haris's two cruisers from doing damage to the freighters, while the Syndicate battleship flotilla went where it would and did what it would.

She would keep her warships here as long as possible and try to support the ground troops if possible, but Marphissa knew that her ability to influence the outcome of events at Ulindi was almost nonexistent. She felt the bitterness of defeat even as she ordered *Manticore* and *Gryphon* into another hopeless charge toward Haris's heavy cruiser to force it to veer away.

PRESIDENT Gwen Iceni stood in her office with her arms crossed, looking steadily at the man about a meter in front of her. "Colonel Rogero, you have had more than one opportunity to kill me under circumstances that could have been labeled an accident. Instead, you have used those opportunities to save me."

Rogero frowned. "Madam President—"

"I am not done." Iceni studied him as she spoke. "You became emotionally involved with an Alliance officer, placing your loyalty to her above your own safety, and have since her arrival here not attempted to hide your relationship. Those are not the acts of a snake."

"I should hope not," Rogero said.

"And, Captain Bradamont, who seems to have an exceptionally good head on her shoulders, trusts you." Iceni raised one hand to point at him. "As does General Drakon. I am going to tell you something, Colonel, something that no Syndicate CEO in her right mind would share with someone like you. I do not entirely trust my own closest staff. I do trust you. I also trust General Drakon, though I often find him frustrating."

Rogero gazed at her silently for almost a full minute before replying. "Thank you for your trust, Madam President. Do you believe that your safety is endangered here?"

"I'm not sure how to answer that, Colonel Rogero, but I do want you to know that you have my confidence. If for some reason we cannot communicate, I will be certain that you are acting in the best interests of myself and General Drakon. Do not hesitate to take actions you consider vital even if you cannot contact me to receive authorization from me. You understand why I had to convey these instructions face-to-face."

"Thank you, Madam President," Rogero said, staggered inside at the enormity of such an order. Coming from anyone trained and experienced in the Syndicate system, it represented a tremendous placement of trust in him and a repudiation of much of that training and experience. Of course Iceni had no choice but to give such orders in person. If they had come over any sort of comm link, he (and anyone else) would have assumed a transmission with such instructions had been fabricated. And if anyone had intercepted such a transmission, they would have gained very valuable information about the extent of Rogero's freedom to act. "I will not fail you."

"I needed you to know that I believe you when you say that," Iceni said, waving a dismissive hand and turning to face her virtual window, where the waves came and went heedless of human concerns. Still facing away from him, she asked a question. "What do you think General Drakon's chances are?"

"I am . . . concerned," Rogero said. "The Syndicate is playing the sort of underhanded game it knows very well. But, I am comforted by the fact that General Drakon is the one they are trying to trap. If anyone can frustrate their trap, it is General Drakon."

"Are you whistling past the graveyard, Colonel?" Iceni asked.

"No, Madam President. General Drakon was exiled here because the snakes suspected him of frustrating one of their operations, but also because the Syndicate did not want him dead. They wanted him available if they needed him. They knew how good he was."

Iceni lowered her head, speaking in a quieter voice. "If they know that, then they will have planned their trap accordingly, Colonel. Return to your headquarters and prepare for the worst."

Fifteen minutes later, Rogero glared out the window of the government VIP limo carrying him back to the ground forces headquarters complex after the personal meeting with Iceni. He was not happy. Bad enough that Honore Bradamont had been sent off as part of a desperate rescue mission. Bad enough that, with General Drakon gone, he was senior ground forces officer in the entire Midway Star System, with all the extra responsibilities that role carried with it. Bad enough that President Iceni had made no secret of her worries that General Drakon might be facing very serious trouble at Ulindi, because people trained as Syndicate CEOs did not reveal worries like that unless the worries were extremely severe.

On top of that, his instructions from President Iceni were deeply disturbing. What level of concern would force a former CEO to grant a subordinate that much discretion to act?

He sat back, wishing the vehicle could get him to ground forces headquarters faster. Built to Syndicate standards, the VIP limo had equal measures of lavish comfort and hidden protection. Many armored fighting vehicles carried less protection than the limo. But it could not fly above the traffic in the streets, which, though clearing a path for the official vehicle, took time to do so in a crowded city.

In front of and behind him, two other limos moved as escorts, all three vehicles having been insisted upon by Iceni. Given what CEO Boyens had finally admitted knowing, it was understandable why Iceni was worried about Drakon's safety, but why was the president so worried about security here as well? The rumors among the citizenry were still a concern, and the danger of individual assassins could never be discounted, but this kind of protection for Rogero, on top of her orders, implied that Iceni either knew of or suspected a much more serious threat currently out there on the streets of this city.

Rogero suppressed his annoyance with the flamboyant security measures and his anger that Iceni might know something important about dangers here that she was not sharing, and focused instead on the situation. He was a soldier, after all. He should be analyzing this situation to determine whether this security was being used effectively, and the best way to do that was to look at it from the perspective of an attacker. If he wanted to kill someone, and that someone was in a VIP limo escorted by two security limos, how would he go about it?

"Driver," Rogero called, hitting the intercom control.

"Yes, sir?" the reply came almost instantly. The driver was concealed from Rogero's direct view behind thick layers of internal armor that separated the driving seat area from the VIP compartment, but Rogero could see the driver's image on the virtual window that covered the armor and projected a forward view as if nothing lay between them.

"What route are we taking back to the headquarters complex? Display it for me."

"Yes, sir."

A map appeared in the air before Rogero, showing a three-dimensional image of this part of the city, the limo they were riding in clearly indicated, a path snaking from it toward the ground forces headquarters.

The city had been designed so that the roads leading toward the ground forces headquarters, like those leading to other important locations such as the former snake headquarters and President Iceni's offices, funneled down into a few wide boulevards that could be easily secured with security checkpoints. That made a great deal of sense if you were already inside the complex and worried about what might be coming your way, but if you were outside the complex and wanting to get in, it meant there were only a few paths you could take for the last stages of the trip. Even though VIP caravans routinely varied their routes to avoid providing predictable targets, there wasn't much variation possible as the available roads necked down before reaching the complex.

Rogero looked at the map and realized what he was really unhappy about. If someone dangerous enough to warrant limo-procession-level security was out to get him, that someone would be dangerous enough to figure out how to get him despite the protection afforded by the limo. "Driver, alter our path. I want to turn right up ahead, proceed for half a kilometer, then follow the route I will show you. Tell the escort vehicles."

"Sir, that will take us around the complex instead of toward it. President Iceni ordered that you be taken back to your headquarters. I am not authorized—"

"I am giving you an order! *Comply!*"

Syndicate training insisted on obedience, backing up that insistence with vicious penalties for failure, but Rogero, like all Syndicate executives and CEOs, had long ago learned the problems that created when contradictory commands existed. Untrained at resolving issues for themselves, inexperienced with making their own decisions, and above all afraid to comply with the wrong order, workers often simply locked up like a machine told to both open and close a door at the same time.

The resulting delays could be fatal.

"Comply!" Rogero yelled again, as the limo went past the turn he had indicated and into the multipronged intersection leading into the nearest one of the main approaches to the ground forces headquarters complex.

The driver finally acted, jerking the limo to a halt in a vain attempt to back toward the missed turn. The security limo behind braked frantically, slewing to one side and narrowly missing the limo carrying Rogero, while the lead limo went onward several more meters before realizing that anything was happening.

Rogero, cursing the confusion, reached for the door release.

His hand had not touched it when the lead limo slid onward another meter as it began braking, and tripped a hidden sensor in the roadway. Massive shaped-charge explosions erupted from the roadway beneath and from locations on the façades of the buildings on either side.

IT had taken far too long to get to this point. First, Morgan had been forced to infiltrate the outer areas of the snake alternate command center, following a route she had previously used, until she could activate the necessary loops on the taps in certain control circuits heading out from the command center. Having neutralized the snakes' ability to set off their buried nukes, Morgan had then worked her way out past snake security, through more security checkpoints and columns of enemy vehicles, to where she could waylay a laggard soldier and use his gear to tap into the enemy tactical display.

Colonel Roh Morgan could finally see what was happening.

General Drakon was trapped, an entire Syndicate division of ground troops consolidating to form a solid ring around his perimeter, the enemy brigade occupying the base dug in and well supplied, lots of newly arrived artillery being moved into position to turn the unfortified buildings holding Drakon's troops into masses of rubble before the enemy ground forces launched an all-out attack.

She had failed him. There was no way to stop this, no way for her, alone, to do enough damage in a short enough time to an entire division of enemy troops and all of their supporting weapons to make any difference in the outcome. Even if her arm hadn't been injured and she had been at full physical capability, it simply wasn't possible. The snake nukes had been neutralized, but that didn't matter. The enemy didn't need the nukes.

Morgan fought off tears, shaking her head with growing rage. *No. No. Even if he dies here, even if I die here, our daughter will live. Our daughter will avenge us.*

But all vengeance will not wait for her.

One more snake has to die this day, the snake who set this up, the snake who tricked me, and who is not going to live to enjoy his victory. Don't worry, General. I failed you in everything else here, but I won't fail in this. I'm going to make sure that snake dies.

She took the dead enemy soldier's sidearm and eased onto the nearest street, heading back toward the snake alternate command center.

THE echoes from the explosions near Midway's ground forces headquarters were still resounding through the city when crowds of agitated citizens began pouring into the streets, blocking traffic and filling every public square.

Iceni looked from one virtual window before her desk to the next, at dozens of tiled scenes of embryonic mobs. Part of her had to admire whoever had set this up, priming the citizens with anxiety and fears that would burst into hazardous motion when a fuse like the explosions went off.

Only part of her, because the other parts of her were busy.

"Find out what Colonel Rogero's status is!" she demanded of the senior police officer at the scene of the explosion. "I want to know the instant you find out, and I want you to find out immediately!"

Another virtual window was displaying messages flooding through social media, news, and other citizen communication feeds.

General Drakon has been killed by Iceni.

President Iceni seriously injured in assassination attempt by Drakon.

Ground forces soldiers forced to take new oath of loyalty to the Syndicate.

Iceni has invited Syndicate to return to Midway to restore order.

Drakon has smuggled large numbers of snakes into star system and given them back control of their headquarters.

Open fighting in city as forces of Iceni and Drakon battle for control.

Iceni declares herself sole CEO at Midway.

Drakon has drawn up plans for mass arrests.

Iceni to reopen labor camps.

All elections canceled, all elected officials ordered arrested.

Mobile forces ordered to bombard planet.

Mobile forces mutiny.

Ground forces mutiny.

Iceni sells out Midway to the Alliance.

Drakon a traitor, deliberately lost battles to Alliance, say ground forces.

Midway to be surrendered to enigmas.

Enigma attack imminent, most defenders away by order of Iceni.

Enigma attack imminent, most defenders away by order of Drakon.

She slammed a comm control hard enough to wonder if it was possible to physically damage a virtual control. "Why aren't these messages being stopped? Why are they getting sent all around the planet?"

A senior aide, looking terrified, shook his head. "We don't know, Madam President. You have loosened restrictions on content—"

"And we have retained full control of every mechanism for distributing messages like these! Why haven't we shut them down?"

A grim-faced woman answered. "Someone sabotaged the control software. We can't activate any of the censor overrides. They're letting through everything. Our software people—"

"To hell with the software people! Shut everything down! Kill the power!"

The woman blinked in surprise. "Oh. That's a hardware solution. I'll need to contact—"

"Do it! Pull the plugs!"

"Yes, Madam President!"

"Get everything except security comm channels off-line," Iceni directed. "Then power it back up piece by piece with reloaded software. Start it happening now! We need those media channels back so we can start sending out our own messages to calm this mess!"

She could see the crowds reacting to the messages, see waves of growing anger and fear rippling through the masses of citizens, each wave reinforcing the others. It didn't matter if the fears contradicted each other. It didn't matter if the fears made sense. The citizens were moving past the point where logic, reason, common sense, and even their own safety and security had any restraining influence.

Everywhere in the cities on this planet, crowds were on the verge of becoming mobs.

Iceni hit another control. "Mobilize every police officer and order them to assemble at local stations. Call all government employees into their offices with orders to report immediately. Lock down all government buildings, security status one alpha. Get me someone at ground forces headquarters. Who is in charge there until we find Colonel Rogero?"

A wide-eyed woman stared back at Iceni. "We're . . . going to use the ground forces, Madam President?"

Everyone raised in the Syndicate knew what that meant. Compliance measures using live ammunition and killing as many citizens as necessary to make the survivors submit to authority. If word started going around that Iceni was planning such an action, every crowd would explode into violence. "No! We need the soldiers to protect the citizens! Tell everyone that! Someone is trying to make the people riot, someone wants them to cause deaths and destruction! The soldiers will protect the people and their property! Now get me someone at ground forces headquarters!"

Brave words. Idealistic words. But if the mobs erupted into full-scale rioting, would she be able to abide by those words? Or would she have to order the actions necessary to stop the rioting?

Iceni paused, all of the comm links off so that for a moment no one could see her, and leaned heavily on her desk, her arms locked, head lowered, trying to find the strength inside not to give in to despair. She had to look strong, be strong, and, most important of all, be smart. Her enemies had clearly outthought her, and outthought Artur Drakon as well. A long, carefully thought-out chess game had reached a climax with both the queen and the king under threat of check.

But the queen was still the most powerful piece on the board.

Iceni hit another control with vicious force. "Togo! Where the hell are you?"

No response. She tried two more circuits, including the emergency circuit, then hit another control. "Where is Mehmet Togo?" she demanded of her chief of staff.

"I—I do not know, Madam President." The chief of staff didn't bother trying to hide his bewilderment since Togo always came and went purely by Iceni's orders. No one was supposed to question or hinder Togo's movements.

"When was the last time he was seen?"

The chief of staff barked an order to an underling, then waited nervously until the answer came. "His last sighting was thirteen hours ago, on a security camera."

"Thirteen hours. Wait. He wasn't seen by someone? He was recorded on a security camera?"

"Yes, Madam President."

Iceni ended the call, staring at the top of her desk. *Togo has the equipment to blind security cameras and knows where they all are. He never lets his movement be tracked by routine security equipment. Why would he let himself be seen by one?*

The star display next to her desk, almost forgotten as she concentrated on the situation on this planet, suddenly showed a bright warning symbol near the hypernet gate as an alarm blared for her attention.

Iceni raised her head and looked at the display.

A lot of warships had arrived at Midway's hypernet gate about four hours ago. A lot of large warships. Midway's sensors were busy evaluating the new arrivals, trying to identify who they were.

Iceni realized that she was smiling, her lips tight in a snarl of defiance, as she gazed at the display. *You think this is checkmate, don't you?* she mentally asked her faceless enemies.

You're wrong.

"WHAT'S your assessment?" Drakon asked. The building he was in shuddered as part of it collapsed.

"As the workers say, it's root hog, or die." Gaiene sounded happy, as if he were reporting good news. The origin of the phrase had long been lost in the mists of time, but everyone knew what "root hog, or die" meant. *You're on your own, to fail or succeed, and if you fail, you're finished.*

"Colonel Gaiene is correct," Kai said impassively. "They're not trying to punch through at a few points to split us up, General. I'm seeing even pressure all around the portion of the outer perimeter that my troops are defending."

"They want to ensure our total annihilation," Malin said, "by forcing our perimeter back upon the Syndicate forces holding their base. Right now, they are just maintaining pressure until their full force arrives and is in position. At that point, we can expect a barrage using all of their available artillery and surface-to-surface rockets, followed by all-out assault. It is already apparent that the Syndicate forces have significantly more artillery than expected."

"They've got significantly more of everything than expected," Gaiene pointed out.

"Recommendations?" Drakon said.

"We can't hold very long," Gaiene observed nonchalantly. "Even if we ride out the bombardments and hunker down in the rubble well enough to fight off assaults, we'll only have a couple of days at the most before we run out of energy and ammo. Getting lifted out is impossible. The only available landing areas are covered by either the base's weapons or the enemy troops now occupying the buildings across the street. Our shuttles wouldn't last thirty seconds against the amount of fire those Syndicate troops can bring to bear."

"With the Syndicate battleship here, going back to the freighters would just trade one trap for another even if we could do it," Kai added.

"The freighters aren't in orbit here anymore," Malin said. "The shuttles could only move some of our troops to another location on the surface before the rest got overrun, but as Colonel Gaiene says, the shuttles would not survive any attempt to land."

"On the other hand," Gaiene said, "if we try to retreat on the surface, there's only one way we can go, and that's inward. We'll run right into the defenses around that base."

Drakon felt himself smiling though he felt no trace of humor within. "I know what you're driving at, Conner. We can't hold, and we can't retreat. That only leaves one option."

"Yes, General," Gaiene agreed. "It does. We need to attack."

"Attack?" Kai asked. "A breakout?"

"Hell, no," Gaiene protested. "We're outnumbered two to one on the outer perimeter. I always prefer the path of least resistance."

"Attack inward?" Malin said. "It's true that the least reliable troops that Haris has are those holding that base against us, and we outnumber them. But they are dug in at the base, behind their fixed weapons and fortifications."

"We can't abandon the outer perimeter," Kai said as if discussing a difficult simulation whose results would have no personal impact on him. "And as soon as the forces outside the perimeter realize we are attacking inward, they will redouble their attack on us."

Drakon studied his display, letting options run through his mind. "If we can gain control of that base, we'll be behind their fortifications and have access to their supplies. We'll have protection against artillery bombardment. But there's no way to hold the outer perimeter and attack inward with sufficient force to overwhelm the defenses of the base. Half measures will leave us using too few troops to take the base and too few troops defending the outer perimeter."

"Use them all," Malin said suddenly. "Every soldier on the attack. Completely abandon the outer defenses and shove everything at the base, all-out attack."

Gaiene smiled broadly. "I knew you had promise, young fella."

"It risks everything on one throw of the die," Kai argued. "Can we afford to do that?"

"Can we afford not to?" Malin asked.

"We have to act fast," Drakon said. "We're taking more losses every minute, and we have no idea how much time we have left before the troops outside the perimeter launch their assault. We'll go in simultaneously from all sides, using every surface chaff round we have to provide cover. We can't afford to have the attack falter or hesitate, so we'll personally have to lead it and keep everyone moving." He moved his finger around the virtual display before his face, knowing that the motion would be seen by the others even though they were at different places around the perimeter. "I'll lead the attack from this quarter, you from here, Conner, you from here, Bran, and you from this quarter, Hector. Have some weapons set up on the outer defensive line to fire on auto controls to make it look like the perimeter is still being defended. The moment I give the attack order, we completely abandon the outer lines. Everyone is to charge inward at the base."

"Win or die," Kai remarked with resignation. "It beats hiding in a hole until they come to kill us, I suppose."

Malin spoke to Drakon on a private channel that neither Kai nor Gaiene could hear. "This is insane, General. I'm sure that Colonel Morgan would approve."

"She'd be surprised that you came up with it," Drakon replied on the same channel. "But, yeah, it's the sort of thing she would do. Morgan is probably dead, you know."

"Yes, General, I realize that." It was impossible to tell Malin's feelings about Morgan likely having died already. He ended the conversation without saying anything more.

But Gaiene came on next. "General, this is going to be a rough one."

"We'll get through it," Drakon said. "You three, you and Kai and Rogero, have been my invincible trio through a lot of fights. This is just one more, right?"

"Invincible doesn't mean indestructible," Gaiene said, sounding wistful. "Since there is a more than reasonable chance that we won't be able to talk after this is over, I want you to know that Lieutenant-Colonel Safir has my strongest recommendation to become commander of my brigade should there be an opening for that position in the near future. She is highly competent, respected by the troops for all the right reasons, and has been pretty much running the brigade anyway."

"I'll remember that," Drakon said. "But you and me, we've got to make it, right? These kids wouldn't know what to do without us."

"Ah, yes, these kids." Gaiene paused for a moment. "I should have had kids. But they would have been so ashamed of me the last several years. It's better this way."

"Conner—"

"Do not worry, General. I won't let you down. My soldiers won't let you down. We'll take that damned base."

"I never doubted that, Conner."

Gaiene looked back at him with those dark eyes, and his mouth bent into that old grin. "I'll see you later, General."

"Yeah. See you later."

"IT'S Black Jack? You're certain?"

"They are Alliance battle cruisers and escorts, Madam President," the command center supervisor said. "We have positively identified several hulls so far, and one of them is *Dauntless*, Black Jack's flagship. They are accompanied by the Dancer ships, but those have headed for the jump point for Pele at a high rate of acceleration while the Alliance formation has remained near the hypernet gate."

Black Jack. Not the Syndicate. Not a coordinated attack, but a source of support. Iceni took a deep breath to steady herself, then froze again as the supervisor looked to one side with a startled expression. "What is it?"

"Colonel Rogero, Madam President. He's alive. He's trying to get through to you."

She started breathing once more. "Link him to me. Private circuit."

Iceni had been raised not to believe in higher powers that looked out for those who did the right things and punished those who did wrong. Most of what she had seen in the Syndicate, in which those who did wrong won higher promotions and gained higher salaries, and those who did right often ended up as victims, had done little to change her mind.

But at the moment, she was seriously considering offering any sacrifice demanded to whatever power was looking out for her.

The man whose image appeared before her wore a uniform torn and blackened by smoke, but his expression was strong and firm. "Madam President. If I couldn't have gotten through, I would have acted as you previously directed. But I was able to establish contact and await your orders."

Iceni gasped with relief before she could answer. "Colonel, I hope that Captain Bradamont will forgive me for saying that at the moment you are the most beautiful thing I have ever seen."

Rogero grinned through the smudges on his face. "I'm sure that Captain Bradamont will understand."

"How did you survive?"

"My vehicle halted just short of the weapons buried in the street, so none of the upward-focused explosions hit it. A blast from one side was absorbed by one of my escort vehicles that had came up on that side. The blow from the other side struck the forward portion of my vehicle, killing the driver and pinning me in the wreckage for a while. The doctors on the scene wanted to send me to the hospital, but with the help of some of my soldiers who arrived on the scene, I convinced the physicians that I had work to do. Do you have a plan?"

"I'm developing one. I need your ground forces," Iceni said, grateful again that Drakon had chosen to leave Rogero here. "All of the ground forces. The citizens are within a hairsbreadth of erupting into violence at locations all over this planet."

"Yes, Madam President, I agree. Request permission to speak freely."

"Colonel, don't bother with the formalities right now! We don't have time. Tell me what I need to know."

"Very well." Rogero gestured all around him. "I've already given orders for all ground forces to mobilize. They are gathering at mobilization sites as we speak, but I must to tell you that we have to handle them carefully. They are on edge. My soldiers trust me, but the local ground forces are less reliable."

"What has them on edge?" Iceni asked. "Anything specific, or the same sort of anything-that-could-possibly-be-wrong rumors running through the citizenry?"

"Something very specific concerns them," Rogero said, both voice and expression now grim. "They fear being ordered to undertake compliance actions against the people."

"And you believe they might refuse such orders?" Iceni said.

"Yes, I think the local ground forces will certainly refuse to obey those orders, and even my own soldiers probably will not obey."

"I want alternatives, Colonel," Iceni said. "All of my training tells me to send every soldier out with orders to open fire on any citizens who don't disperse and return to their homes. My instincts tell me that such actions would shatter, perhaps beyond repair, my efforts to create an alternative to the Syndicate way of governing."

"I concur, Madam President," Rogero said. "If we send armed troops out to confront the rioters, some of the soldiers might open fire, either out of obedience or out of fear if confronted by a dangerous mob."

"And there is this, Colonel," Iceni added. "Whoever stirred this up, whoever brought this planet to the brink of mass chaos, wants me to order compliance actions. They want me to kill large numbers of citizens. Do you agree?"

"Yes."

"Then give me options that don't involve mass murder."

Rogero inhaled deeply, looking away as he thought, then back at her. "There is one option that might work. It is a dangerous option, because if it fails, we won't have the ability to try anything else."

"Tell me."

"LISTEN up," Drakon said over the universal command circuit. "You've been told the plan. When I give the order to fire chaff, I want every round we've got dropped into the area in front of the enemy base. Ten seconds after the fire command, I'm going to order the assault, and at that point, everyone is to head all out for that base. Don't pause, don't delay, don't hesitate. Your colonels and I will be leading the assault. Once we get inside the base, some of you will be designated to occupy the base defenses and turn them against enemy troops from outside our perimeter who will be pursuing us once they realize what we're doing."

He didn't have to lay out the results of failure. The Syndicate, especially a Syndicate star system where the snakes had such a strong presence, would not offer any mercy to rebellious soldiers. Drakon's troops knew that they had to succeed in the assault if they wanted to live.

Drakon didn't think there was any chance of getting through to the warships that might or might not still be in orbit overhead, but it couldn't hurt to try. "This is General Drakon. Request that you immediately start hitting the buildings across the street from our perimeter with any weapons you've got. I say again, begin bombarding the buildings across the street from our positions. Do as much damage as you can as long as you can." Even if the bombardment with hell lances did not cause much damage, it might make the Syndicate ground forces believe that Drakon was about to launch a breakout attack.

He didn't think the Syndicate would expect a break-in attack.

Only a couple of minutes remained. He knelt near a ragged opening where a window had once been, letting the recon probe on his armor stick out enough to view the enemy base. The defensive fire coming from the base wasn't steady but frequent enough to make it clear that the defenders were not sitting passively. For the first time, Drakon wondered if those defenders knew about the trap. Were they aware of how many reinforcements were outside, pressing on Drakon's troops? Or did they think they were still facing a desperate fight?

Well, they were facing a desperate fight. In a few minutes, the defenders of that base were going to find out what a lot of desperate soldiers could do on the attack.

"Stand by," Drakon said.

"Good-bye, General," Gaiene answered on a private circuit. "And thank you again. I could not die under any conditions but the best, and you have given me that."

"Conner, what the hell—"

"I'll say hello to Lara for you. Take care of my soldiers, General."

And then it was time, with no room left to demand that Colonel Gaiene stop acting foredoomed. "Fire chaff!"

Scores of rounds arced into the area before the base, blossoming into fields of smoke, small strips of metal, heat decoys, noisemakers, and every other device known to humanity for blocking or confusing the sight and senses of any and all sensors and targeting devices.

"Go!" Drakon shouted. "Follow me!"

On the heels of the ancient exhortation, Drakon leaped to his feet, charging out the nearest gaping opening in the building and across the open area before the enemy base. On his display, he could see a mass of thousands of symbols doing the same, all suddenly in motion, all heading inward. Then he entered the chaff cloud, and all of the decoys and jammers and screens that blocked enemy sight and sensors also blocked his own. To either side and right behind, he could sense the movements of the soldiers closest to him, but his display could only show an estimate of what was happening, assuming the attack kept moving forward at the same rate.

It took a few seconds for the base to react to the sudden assault, then with a roar that filled the sky every defensive weapon opened up. Many of the defenders' weapons fired blindly into the chaff-created murk, hoping for lucky shots. Others exploded into spheres of shrapnel that did not need guidance to find anything unfortunate enough to be too close and in their paths.

The attackers didn't form a perfect square as they converged on the base, instead forming into four blunt angles whose points were centered on the enemy fortification. At the center of each point, leading the way, were Drakon and his three colonels.

Drakon didn't feel anything as he charged except a sense of dislocation, as if he were somewhere else watching himself running full tilt toward the enemy's fire. He saw the alerts on his display screaming of incoming fire that came close enough to be spotted through the chaff, he felt the force of nearby explosions and saw the track of shots passing very close by him, heard his breath rasping in and out, and it all felt unreal and a bit distant in time and space. How could it be real? Who in their right minds would be doing this?

As Drakon and the others leading the attack came through the final layers of chaff and out into the open near the base, a storm of defensive fire lashed at them. At the same time, their displays finally updated as the network between their battle armor automatically reestablished links. Markers sprang to life on the display, some of them almost immediately dimming to show soldiers who had been struck by the defenders' fire.

An energy pulse hit Drakon on his lower abdomen, his armor's outer surface ablating to absorb and dissipate the heat. A solid projectile clipped one of his shoulders, glancing off the armor and causing Drakon to stumble as he ran.

He saw one marker in particular flare to show a soldier had taken a solid hit, heard that soldier grunt with pain. Gaiene. He called up the window to show the view from Colonel Gaiene's armor, saw that view tilted in a way that meant Gaiene was on one knee, wavering a bit, red damage markers flaring on his battle armor's display. "Onward!" Gaiene yelled to his soldiers as they streamed past, his voice hoarse. "Take them, lads and ladies! Make me proud!"

The enemy sensors could spot comm nodes if they were close enough, and now they focused their fire on Gaiene, reducing the amount of shots aimed at the soldiers near him. The view from Gaiene's suit rocked as another round hit him, more danger markers flashing as his helmet display flickered.

Gaiene gasped from the pain of his second injury, then started laughing, sweeping his rifle slowly from one side to the other, firing continuously at the enemy fortifications as his soldiers began reaching them. "That's it! Onward! Onward!"

The view from Gaiene's armor went blank.

Drakon, still running toward the enemy, saw that the symbol for Colonel Conner Gaiene on his display had gone out.

He was suddenly here again, completely here, charging for the point where an engineering team had placed a breaching charge, following the charge through the enemy defenses right on its heels so that the blast and his entry were almost one event. He saw defenders frantically turning toward him, defenders wearing Syndicate battle armor, and he knew Syndicate battle armor, he knew its every weakness and every flaw, and he killed six of the defenders without pausing or thinking, barely aware of anything except that lack of a symbol on his display where Conner Gaiene should have been.

But something clicked inside him as the surviving defenders at this spot raised their hands or huddled on the floor, their weapons cast aside. Drakon's hands hurt from the pressure they were putting on his weapon, but he controlled them, he controlled himself. Because Conner Gaiene had not died so that Artur Drakon could massacre enemy soldiers who were trying to surrender, had not died so that Artur Drakon could forget his duties and his responsibilities to every other soldier in these two brigades.

He started directing the soldiers streaming into the breach behind him. Some to continue onward to roll up resistance inside the base. Others to take over the defenses and watch for the Syndicate soldiers who were surely pursuing them from the outside by now.

In the breaks between issuing orders he checked his display for updates, but it was full of gaps now, gaps created by the inability to get signals through the base and enemy jamming. But the gaps were shrinking rapidly, and he could see symbols marking his own units pouring through the base like water into a basin, scarcely pausing as they rolled over scattered resistance.

"General?"

"Yes, Colonel Malin."

"I'm near the base command center. Those inside are offering to surrender."

"Tell them they won't be harmed as long as they turn over the command center intact."

"Yes, sir."

Another call, this time a woman speaking with mixed anger and grief. "General Drakon, this is Lieutenant Colonel Safir, acting commander of the Second Brigade. We have taken every enemy position except those already occupied by units of the Third Brigade. I am reinforcing defenses along the base perimeter."

"Thank you," Drakon said, trying to accept the fact that he would never speak with Conner Gaiene again. "You are field promoted to colonel and are assigned command of Second Brigade, on the specific recommendation of Colonel Gaiene."

"I—Thank you, sir. I—Damn that man!"

"I know," Drakon said. "But he died the way he wanted to. You've got a lot to live up to."

"I will," Safir vowed. "General, my troops have spotted movement at our old positions."

The pursuit had taken longer than expected. The Syndicate division commander must have feared that Drakon's attack was a feint, a trick to lure the outer perimeter of Syndicate soldiers into the open, and thus advanced cautiously.

Colonel Kai sounded a bit out of breath, but otherwise unruffled. "Chaff rounds are being fired opposite sector three," he said.

Malin, in the base command center, had done his usual wizardry with the Syndicate operating systems. New lights glowed on Drakon's display as Malin's work provided all of Drakon's soldiers access to the base sensors, weapons systems, and plans. The sectors into which the base perimeter was divided were now references for Drakon's ground forces just as they had formerly been for the enemy.

"Contact at sector five!"

"Medics are receiving fire!"

"Cover them!"

Drakon pulled up the right views to see the areas outside the base where his force's medical personnel were still in the open, treating wounded from the attack where they lay and hauling inside those ready to move. Syndicate fire had begun reaching out from the buildings which Drakon's own forces had recently abandoned, threatening the medics who worked with their usual stubborn tenacity at trying to save every injured soldier that they could. "Get some troops out there," Drakon ordered. "Lay down heavy suppressive fire on the buildings to force the Syndicate soldiers to keep their heads down, and help bring in every casualty who is still outside the base."

"General, the medics say some of the casualties can't be moved—"

"Both medics and casualties will be moved!" Drakon said. "Anyone who doesn't move will die out there. Get it done!"

"Attack under way at sector one! Require reinforcements!"

"Handle that," Drakon ordered Safir. Despite the losses suffered in the assault, he still had twice as many soldiers as the understrength enemy brigade that had previously held this base. But he still had casualties being brought in, he had medics still working outside the base with total disregard for their own safety, and he had over a thousand prisoners inside the base to worry about, as well as the likelihood that snakes were hiding wherever they could within the base. "Malin, make sure the patrols looking for snakes inside the base check every possible hidy-hole."

"Yes, sir," Malin said, his voice rushed, some of the elation of an at least temporary victory uncharacteristically audible in his voice. "General, some of the surrendered soldiers are volunteering to assist in the search for snakes."

"Negative. Some of those volunteers might be snake agents. Until we can screen the prisoners, everyone is a potential snake. Understood?"

"Yes, sir. Base sensors are spotting heavy enemy forces massing opposite sector three."

Drakon moved as quickly as he could through the underground passageways of the former enemy base, the soldiers he encountered flattening themselves against the nearest wall to make room for him to pass. "I'll be at the command center in two minutes. Colonel Kai, what have you got available to reinforce sector three?"

"Nothing," Kai said. "All of the people I have are on the line, guarding prisoners, or searching the base. The final wounded are being brought in now. I will shift locally as necessary to deal with pressure at each point."

Hopefully, that would be good enough. "Colonel Safir, if the Syndicate troops follow doctrine, they'll be preparing to hit sector six on the opposite side of the base within a few minutes of the attack against sector three beginning. Be ready for it."

"Yes, sir. We're dragging in the last of the medics and the wounded. They'll be under cover within a minute, but we're going to lose some of the wounded."

Damn. "Getting them inside the base was their only chance," Drakon said.

"No argument there, General," Safir said. "Uh-oh. We've got incoming."

"I see it," Drakon said as his display lit with warnings. "How heavy is this barrage, Colonel Malin?"

"It looks like they're throwing everything they've got at us," Malin reported. "We're about to find out how well this base was constructed, General."

"Let's hope they did a good job," Drakon said, eyeing the massive artillery barrage that was seconds from impacting. "The ground attacks will come as soon as the barrage ends. Everyone on the outer fortifications get into the nearest blast bunker now!" If there were any snakes hiding in the base's surface structures, they were about to discover how big a mistake that had been.

He entered the command center as the barrage landed, and the world around him shook.

CHAPTER TEN

"WE have to do something," Kommodor Marphissa said. "Is there any way we can hit any of the escorts around Happy Hua's battleship and still screen the surviving freighters?"

Manticore's displays showed the expanding balls of wreckage that marked the ends of two of the freighters. As Marphissa had feared, Hua had let some of her escorts swing out far enough from the battleship to destroy the escape pods that the freighters' crews had used in futile attempts to escape.

And she could still do nothing.

"Kommodor," a message came in from *Defender*. "We have received a broken transmission from General Drakon. As best we can determine, he is asking us to immediately open fire on the enemy ground forces positions nearest his own soldiers. We have been holding back from firing our hell lances in order to save them for any further rocket barrages, aerospace craft attacks, or cruise missiles. Request instructions."

Marphissa checked the distance. *Manticore* and *Gryphon*, in their futile attempts to screen the freighters and inflict some damage on Haris's heavy cruiser, had moved about a light-minute sunward of the inhabited planet. *Defender*'s message was a minute old. The delay was bad, but not horrible.

She hit the reply command. "Follow General Drakon's request and open fire on those ground forces positions. Do so as soon as you receive this message. Hit the ground positions as many times as you can before your hell lances overheat."

Diaz was staring at his display. "Drakon must need that support very badly. But there's nothing else we can do."

"Maybe we should give up on trying to protect the freighters," Marphissa grumbled. "All that we are doing is delaying the inevitable. Maybe if we all head back to the inhabited world and concentrate our fire on the enemy ground forces, we can help General Drakon."

"But . . ." Diaz clenched his hands into two fists. "Maybe we should. We can't save the freighters."

Marphissa looked to where *Hawk* and *Eagle* were trying once more to come to grips with Haris's light cruiser, which was once again dancing out of reach.

She reached for her comm control, but paused, wincing, as another alert sounded.

Another ship had arrived at Ulindi hours ago. And she did not expect any reinforcements, so it was probably more bad news.

DRAKON glanced upward at the overhead that bounced and shuddered continuously. The base command center was buried under armor and rock, above it other subsurface rooms also protected by armor and rock, and above them the surface where a variety of buildings had once stood. Those buildings were now piles of rubble that splintered and flew under the hammerblows of the artillery barrage flaying the former enemy base.

Fine dust shifted down onto Drakon and the other soldiers in the command center. The emergency lighting didn't waver, though, and the displays remained bright and steady. The base's power plant was buried deeper than anything else, invulnerable to anything short of a massive orbital bombardment.

"They're not scoring many direct hits on the outer fortifications," Malin reported. "Their global-satellite positioning arrays were taken out by the Midway warships before we landed, and all of the chaff and dust in the atmosphere near here is interfering with direct targeting systems, so their accuracy is far from precise."

"They're getting some hits, though," Drakon said. Most of his soldiers were huddled in the blast bunkers near the outer defenses of the base, riding out the barrage in as much safety as possible. "If they were dropping rocks on us from orbit, we'd all be chewing dirt right now."

"The Kommodor must be keeping the enemy warships occupied."

"If she doesn't continue to keep that battleship occupied, it will drop a world of hurt on us. We can't disperse over the surface as I'd hoped while we're penned in here by those Syndicate ground forces out there." Drakon turned as a prisoner was escorted up to him.

The prisoner saluted in the Syndicate fashion, right fist coming across to rest on the left breast. "Sub-CEO Princip."

Drakon ran his gaze over the man's precisely tailored suit. "Why weren't you in battle armor when you were captured, Sub-CEO Princip?"

Princip gave Drakon a disdainful look even though he couldn't hide his nervousness as the ground shook from more impacts above them. "I am not a front-line worker. I am a high-level manager."

"No, you're a waste of resources," Drakon said, leaning closer, menacing in his own battle armor, his blank faceplate a few centimeters from Princip's sweating forehead. "I want a full accounting of snakes in this base, and I want it now, or I am going to give you an escort up to the surface, where you can personally evaluate the effectiveness of the artillery striking this base."

"I—I—I don't have—"

"Get rid of him," Drakon told Malin, turning away.

"Finley would know! Finley is the senior snake here! Get her!"

Malin nodded, smiling. "We have an Executive First Rank Finley among our prisoners. A logistics executive, she claimed."

"Get her and find out what she knows. We're getting hit hard from the outside, we're about to get hit harder, and we don't need any hits from the inside."

"What about the sub-CEO?"

A thought of Conner Gaiene crossed Drakon's mind, along with a temptation to order Sub-CEO Princip disposed of. But Conner hadn't liked that sort of thing, and neither had his much-longer-dead wife Lara. "Put him with the other prisoners."

"I am a sub-CEO!" Princip protested. "I should—"

"Shut up while you're ahead," the senior soldier among his guards cheerfully informed Princip. "General Drakon is already treating you a whole lot nicer than you deserve. Get going."

Cringing as well as outraged to be talked to that way by a mere worker, Princip left the command center under the prodding of the barrels of weapons. Drakon knew his soldiers would not disobey him by killing Princip, but he suspected that the sub-CEO would "accidentally fall down the stairs" at least once on the way back to the other prisoners.

A medic came into the command center, attention focused on her helmet display. "Who needs a patch and a pill? You."

She rapidly applied a combat wound patch to a soldier's arm, pushed three tablets into the soldier's mouth, then, with another look at her display, began to leave.

"Medical specialist," Drakon said.

"Do you need—?" Her eyes focused on him, and she went to attention, saluting. "I'm sorry, General, I didn't—"

"Never apologize for doing your job," Drakon said. "Were you one of those out in the open bringing in the casualties?"

"We all were, sir."

"Pass the word around that I told you how much I admire all of you medical personnel for doing your best to save our wounded while under enemy fire."

"Yes, sir." The medic sounded a bit confused as well as very tired. "That's our job, sir. Our responsibility."

"You do it well. All of you. Thank you. I'll make a formal announcement to everyone when this is all over."

"Uh . . . yes, sir." The medic left, heading for the next soldier who her display indicated needed help.

Drakon sensed the next event a second before his display alerted him. "The barrage is lifting."

Malin nodded, his hands moving rapidly over his display. "Colonels Kai and Safir are ordering their soldiers out of the blast bunkers and into the outer fortifications. Surviving base automated defenses are already engaging attackers."

"They sent the first wave in too close to the barrage," Drakon said with disgust. In an attempt to catch the defenders still in their blast bunkers, the initial attacks had gone in while the barrage was still under way. That was risky enough when precision guidance was ensuring the artillery fell pretty close to exactly where intended. With precision guidance on the artillery badly impaired, it was too risky for any commander who cared about their soldiers.

But, then, the commander of the Syndicate forces was a Syndicate CEO, and to him or her, the soldiers were workers, faceless creatures whose fates did not matter.

Heavy artillery or rocket rounds falling short of the base ravaged the front ranks of the attackers. As the survivors staggered out of the blasts, no longer screened by chaff clouds this close to the base, a wall of fire from the base's defenses and Drakon's soldiers hit them and wiped them out.

No one cheered. Like Drakon, many of them had been sent on similar attacks in the past while still under command of the Syndicate, lucky enough to survive and knowing too well how it felt.

Enemy warbirds darted closer through the skies overhead, continuously testing the base's antiair defenses and preventing any of those weapons from shifting to engage ground targets.

Another wave of enemy soldiers erupted out of the murk, going all out. "Colonel Safir is reinforcing sector six with her reserve company," Malin reported. A single drop of sweat trickled down his face, clearing a meandering path through the dust. "She's going to need more."

"We haven't got more," Drakon said, eyeing the disposition of his soldiers through the base. "They want us to short Kai's forces because they're going to hit there next."

Malin, his voice calm, pointed. "We have a lot of soldiers tied up watching the prisoners."

"No. I will not murder the prisoners to free up those soldiers."

"General, this is a matter of pragmatics," Malin argued. "If we do not survive, if *you* do not survive, all we have fought for will be lost."

Drakon shook his head. "You miss the point, Bran. If I start doing whatever I think needs to be done purely on a pragmatic basis, then I've already lost."

"I can give the order."

"Outsourcing murder doesn't outsource the responsibility," Drakon said. "I want you to evaluate each prisoner holding location and reduce the guards to the minimum number. If we can seal off the entrances to a location and just post guards on each entrance, that will do. See how many we can free up."

Malin hesitated, then nodded. "Yes, sir." He bent over the display, eyes intent, hands once more moving rapidly.

Drakon opened a window to see the view from Safir's armor, immediately giving him front-line perspective again. Safir was moving through the defensive strong points in her brigade's sectors, personally checking on the soldiers and bolstering their morale. As Drakon watched, Safir's weapon came up and she joined with a platoon pouring fire at a wedge of attackers charging one of the strongpoints. The wedge shattered under the blows, Syndicate soldiers falling back or going to ground, but another wave came through right behind them.

"How does it look?" Drakon asked Safir.

"Ugly, General," Safir replied, aiming and firing as she answered. "Wait one. Tanaka! Pull a squad from Badeu's platoon and shift it ten meters to the left! Here, where I'm designating. Got it? General, they're breaching the perimeter in spots. We're sealing every penetration so far, but I'm running out of assets, and ammunition is getting low in many units."

Drakon looked at Malin, who had straightened up. "Two platoons," he told Drakon.

"Load them up with ammo from the base stockpiles and send them to Safir. Colonel Safir, I've got two platoons with ammo resupply on the way to you. Put them where you need them."

"Thank you, sir!"

Malin was watching his display. "The Syndicate forces should hit Colonel Kai any second now."

"That's what I was thinking." Standard tactics, trying to get the opponent to shift forces to counter a major assault, then hitting the weakened areas with assaults at least as powerful. Alerts sounded at sector two. "There they are."

"Kai will hold them if anyone can," Malin said.

"I know. He's my rock." Others had complained about Kai's slowness, his careful evaluation of aspects before making decisions, his caution on the attack. But, on the defense, Kai would not be moved. "Colonel Kai, let me know if you need anything."

The view from Kai's armor showed a mass of Syndicate soldiers coming into view, the attack wide enough to cover most of the second sector's frontage. "We might need some more ammunition," Kai said judiciously. "This is a very target-rich environment, General. I'll let you know if any problems develop."

Kai's soldiers and the remaining base defensive weaponry in sector two opened up, tearing holes in the attacking ranks.

Malin was watching, too, and now shook his head. "We need to be prepared to fall back on inner defenses, General. Kai simply doesn't have the firepower to stop that heavy an assault. The Syndicate commander is sending them in without regard to losses."

Drakon checked Safir's status, seeing that her brigade was still being heavily pressed and that no forces could be shifted from her to help Kai. "Set up a plan for the fallback. What are our odds if we have to abandon the outer fortifications?"

"Poor," Malin said.

"Do the best you can." Drakon watched the wave of Syndicate troops lapping against Kai's positions, masses of more attackers crossing the open area behind, saw the ammo status of Kai's troops dropping far too rapidly, and knew the line would fall within minutes. "Get it done fast."

He barely had time to notice the alert on his display before several massive explosions erupted outside the base, tearing huge gaps in the forces attacking sector two. The entire base trembled as the shocks rolled through the planet's upper layers like minor earthquakes.

Malin's mouth had fallen open in surprise. He shut it with an audible snap. "Orbital bombardment. Kommodor Marphissa must have saved a few bombardment projectiles, General, and managed to get her ships back overhead despite the enemy warships."

The attack against Kai's brigade had been shattered, the Syndicate attackers closest to the base suddenly isolated and panicking, breaking off the fight and fleeing into the newly spawned craters where the bombardment projectiles had fallen. Kai's forces kept firing as long as they had targets, riddling the retreating enemy ranks.

Drakon checked with Safir, seeing the Syndicate attackers falling back there, as well. "I think they're worried there may be more rocks falling," Safir announced with glee.

"There probably aren't," Drakon said. "Our warships probably just shot their last load. But that one barrage hurt the Syndicate badly."

"Their CEO has been throwing their lives away to keep the pressure on us," Safir said. "Unless they've got another division in the rear, they're not going to be able to keep that up."

"Yeah," Drakon agreed. "It almost worked, but after the losses they sustained, they're going to have a hard time hitting us that hard at multiple points again."

Maybe, just maybe, the situation had swung from hopeless to not-quite-hopeless.

Assuming that Kommodor Marphissa had figured out how to handle that Syndicate battleship.

MARPHISSA felt a sudden surge of hope as she realized that the new ship had arrived at the jump point from Midway.

It was a big ship.

Pele. It must be the battle cruiser. *Pele* wouldn't even the odds, but it would give them more of a chance. "I don't believe it!" Marphissa cried out loud. "Thank you, Madam President! How could she have known?"

Kapitan Diaz was staring at his own display. "It's not *Pele*."

"What? How can it not be *Pele*? That's too big to be anything but—" Marphissa couldn't say anything else for a moment as *Manticore*'s sensors produced a unit identification for the new ship. "It's the *Midway*."

Marphissa could hear the bridge crew unsuccessfully trying to suppress cries of joy. Diaz was grinning like a fool. "Our battleship. This more than evens the odds!" Diaz said.

Had they forgotten that *Midway*'s weapons were still being fitted, activated, and integrated? Would a bluff work again, on the attack? Marphissa was about to dump cold water on the enthusiasm when *Midway*'s status feed arrived. "Do you see that?" she asked Diaz, amazed. "Look at her status!"

"They've got almost all the main armament operational," Diaz said, still grinning.

"How did they—? How did President Iceni know we would need her? Is it for real?"

Diaz indicated his display. "The weapon status is on the classified feed. Kapitan Mercia would try to fool the enemy with false appearances, but she wouldn't be sending us that information unless it was true."

"I knew they were getting close to integrating the weapons into the combat systems and bringing the whole thing online, but she must have really cracked the whip to get them that far that fast."

On the heels of the light showing the arrival of the *Midway* came a message addressed to Marphissa.

"Greetings, Kommodor," Freya Mercia said. She was seated on the expansive bridge of the battleship, looking gratifyingly confident and composed. "It appears that we got here in time. I will be proceeding at my best speed in-system toward the main inhabited world until I receive other instructions. President Iceni had concerns about our warships and about General Drakon's ground forces, and I can see those concerns were more than justified. I await your orders, and assure you that *Midway* is ready to strike the enemy and avenge the citizens of Kane."

The view of Kapitan Mercia panned slightly to one side, revealing another figure in the seat next to her, a woman wearing a very different uniform. "We have also brought Captain Bradamont along. She knows a few things about fighting Syndicate battleships, after all. Please inform CEO Boucher for me that this star system will be her graveyard. For the people, Mercia, out."

Marphissa pointed at Diaz. "Kapitan, give me a vector to get *Manticore* and *Gryphon* back to the planet and over General Drakon's troops again. I'll order *Hawk* and *Eagle* to join up with us there. If I know CEO Boucher, she's going to stop worrying about the freighters, collect Haris's two cruisers, and head for an intercept with the *Midway*." She straightened, adjusted her uniform, put on her best command face, then touched her comm controls. "Kapitan Mercia, Captain Bradamont, we are very happy to see you. Remain in your current vector. I expect CEO Boucher to alter vector to attack you. We will give the ground forces what remaining support we can, then head to meet up with *Midway* before you encounter the Syndicate flotilla. For the people, Marphissa, out."

"Kommodor," Diaz said after she ended the transmission, "Happy Hua might decide to strike at General Drakon before heading to attack the *Midway*."

"No, she will not." Marphissa turned a fierce look on Diaz. "The Syndicate was waiting for us here. They knew a lot about our plans and our forces. They will have told CEO Boucher that the *Midway*'s weapons are still not operational, and using Syndicate standards, Hua will feel safe in assuming those weapons could not possibly have been brought to operational status in this short a time. She will be furious that *Midway*'s bluff chased her from Midway Star System last time. She will want to counter what she believes to be another bluff. Happy

Hua's priority will be to catch and destroy *Midway* before she can escape from Ulindi."

Diaz smiled. "Hua is going to close her hand on a bear trap."

"And we're going to be there when she does. But first, we're going to give the ground forces what support we have left." Marphissa called up an image of the last-known status of the ground forces. "Are they still in the buildings or have they taken the base? We can't drop a bombardment if we don't know. Have your comm people try to get in contact with the ground forces."

"Get on it," Diaz ordered the bridge comm specialist. "Tell comms I want to punch through to the ground forces."

"Yes, Kapitan," she replied. "There is still a lot of jamming and other interference, and the ground forces' transmitters are relatively weak. But we will do it if it can be done."

Diaz leaned back, looking pensive as he gazed at his display. "I worked for a sub-CEO once who would have told me to do it even if it couldn't be done."

"I worked for one like that, too," Marphissa said. "Three like that. At least we're closing on the ground forces' locations. Maybe when we get close enough, we can talk to someone."

"Half an hour until we should be in orbit directly over the ground forces," Diaz said.

Marphissa stirred, touching a comm control. "*Sentinel*, have you or other Hunter-Killers been able to monitor activity on the surface?"

Sentinel's reply took almost six minutes. "Negative, Kommodor. We have seen fighting and figures moving, but our ability to see through all of the smoke and chaff is pretty low. All we can tell you for certain is that fighting is still under way around the base."

Marphissa waved away the virtual window showing *Sentinel*'s commanding officer. Asking the Hunter-Killers had been a long shot.

They were small, they had relatively limited and weak sensors compared to those on larger warships, and as *Sentinel* had said, there was so much junk in the atmosphere that seeing what was going on at the level of detail necessary to distinguish between Midway soldiers in Syndicate battle armor and Syndicate soldiers in Syndicate battle armor would have required a miraculous level of luck.

"Kommodor," Senior Specialist Czilla announced. "We have firm tracks on both of Haris's cruisers."

Marphissa checked that portion of her display, smiling as she saw that the vectors for both cruisers were heading to an intercept with the Syndicate flotilla. *We walked into your trap, Happy Hua. Now you are doing what we expect and what we want, and the trap will spring on you.*

"Kommodor," the comm specialist said, "we do not know whether any of our messages have reached General Drakon's forces, but we have just received a text-only message for you from the planet. Our ground forces must have gained access to a more powerful transmitter, but it appears text-only is all they can get through the jamming that Haris's forces are maintaining."

"What does it say?" Marphissa asked, resting her chin in one hand while she gazed at the old depiction of the ground situation.

"Have taken enemy base," the comm specialist recited. *"Drakon forces now inside base. Under heavy attack from estimated division-strength Syndicate ground forces outside base. Request any assistance possible."*

Diaz shook his head. "How can we believe that? Haris could have sent it, trying to fool us into bombarding Drakon. What if it is our own ground forces that are still outside, attacking Haris's forces inside the base?"

"That's a very good point," Marphissa said, frowning. "Every text message looks the same, no matter who sent it. How can we tell one side from the other when we're looking down at a ground battle from orbit, and both sides are wearing the same battle armor? Is that the entire message?" she demanded of the comm specialist. "Was there anything else?"

"Just a section at the end that must have gotten garbled, Kommodor," the comm specialist replied.

"What does it say?"

"It says . . . *wash your sins away in the tide.* That's what it says, Kommodor. It doesn't make any sense."

"Wash—?" Marphissa sat straight. "Show it to me. Show me the entire text message."

A window popped into existence next to her, the lines of text marching across it. There at the end was the phrase the comm specialist had repeated. "Wash your sins away in the tide," Marphissa repeated out loud, smiling with relief.

"Does that mean something?" Diaz asked. "What does that mean?"

"It means, Kapitan, that whoever sent that text message is a person entrusted by President Iceni with certain phrases that allow other trusted people to recognize them. President Iceni trusted the person who sent this text message enough to give them that phrase. I will believe that the message is true."

"But what if Haris learned the phrase?" Diaz objected.

"If that is true, if he knows that much, then we are lost," Marphissa said.

"But . . . the message claims they are under attack from an entire division of Syndicate ground forces that we didn't know were there? An entire division?" Diaz asked.

"You would make a very bad yes-man," Marphissa said. "That's one of the things I like about you as a Kapitan, but don't take it too far. Think about it, and it makes sense. That Syndicate division is the ground forces equivalent of the Syndicate battleship that was hidden, waiting for us in space. I don't know how they managed it, but it's a classic snake trick. Let someone think they have the upper hand, let someone believe that they are in control, and then when they have stuck their necks out, bring the axe down."

"That's right," Diaz said. "So we assume that General Drakon's forces are inside the base?"

"Yes." She turned to look at the comm specialist. "See if you can get a message back down to them. I want to—" The comm specialist got a look that caused Marphissa to stop speaking. "What is it?"

"Another text-only, Kommodor, but only partial. *Barrage incoming. Require assis*— And then nothing."

"Does that make sense?" Diaz asked Marphissa.

"Yes, it does," Marphissa replied. "I talked about this once with someone who had encountered it. Transmitters at fortified bases are buried beneath the surface so they won't be destroyed, but in order to send a message, they require antenna links leading up to the surface. Barrages that destroy objects on the surface will break the links, so that even though the transmitter still works, it cannot get a signal through the rock above it."

"Is that what happens?" Diaz asked. "I never thought about that."

"Of course not! Up here, we never have to deal with that problem unless we're trying to send a message straight through a planet, and how often does a planet block our line of sight to another ship or planet without any other ships or objects to relay the transmission?" Marphissa jerked her chin at her display. "That's how they tricked us here. We're used to seeing everything that's out there, being able to talk to anything. We don't think in terms of hidden enemies or obstacles, not unless we're really close to a planet."

"I can promise you," Diaz said, "that I will be thinking much more about those things from now on."

"You and me both." Marphissa switched her attention back to the image of the captured enemy base and the area around it. "As soon as we can spot targets, we'll plan the bombardment. We don't have many bombardment projectiles left, but maybe we'll find something worth taking a shot at."

They were five minutes out from the planet when the combined data from the sensors on the Hunter-Killers and Marphissa's cruisers finally produced a partial but ugly picture. "Lots of ground forces in the open, here and here," Diaz noted.

"Yes. It looks like a lot more on this side, though. All of the other areas around the base have some soldiers, but they're spread out." Marphissa reached out, touching several spots not far from the base where the masses of enemy soldiers were heading. *What if I am wrong? What if those are Drakon's soldiers, making a last-ditch attempt to take the base? But there are so many of them.*

Look how many are dying. I can see them, even from this far away, the masses surging against the obstacle of the fortifications and dying. Honore Bradamont told me that General Drakon doesn't do that. He doesn't waste the lives of his people in human-wave attacks.

It is a Syndicate mind that is ordering those attacks.

They are *the enemy.*

Marphissa touched the commands that turned her indicated points into targets for bombardment, using the six projectiles remaining. Only six, but they would cause tremendous damage where they hit. She paused, taking one last second to ensure she really wanted to do this, then touched the commands to authorize the bombardment and for it to launch automatically when her cruisers reached the right point. "Give me a vector to join up with *Midway*," she told Diaz. "We'll move onto it as soon as the bombardment launches."

Two more messages to send. "General Drakon, I don't know if you will hear this, but please accept this close-bombardment support with the compliments of the mobile forces."

And, finally, "*Sentry*, *Sentinel*, *Scout*, *Defender*, you are to join up with the main formation as we swing by the planet. Take up your assigned positions in box formation one.

"We have a battleship to destroy."

"WHAT the hell does that mean?" Iceni's tone could have sliced through solid diamond, but of course the image of Kapitan Kontos before her did not flinch. Kontos was light-hours distant and this message had been sent hours ago.

"Watch the different stars," Kontos repeated, as if he were responding to her question even though he couldn't have heard it for hours yet. He must have known that Iceni would want the message restated. "The Dancers sent us that message, marked for *the symmetries of this star system.* I believe that is intended to mean you and General Drakon, since you are the two governing leaders here. That was the entire message.

"We have not yet heard anything from Black Jack's force. I await your orders. For the people, Kontos, out."

As Kontos's image disappeared, Iceni looked at the virtual windows providing views of the many places where restive citizens were still gathered, waiting for either something that would calm them or the trigger that would cause them to explode. She had kept the police in their stations and their substations, guessing that with all forms of communication media shut down and no other stimuli provoking them, the citizens would mill about indecisively.

But that state of affairs could not last. She had to defuse the citizens. As soon as she heard from Colonel Rogero that his preparations were complete, she would find out whether or not Rogero's gamble would work. If it didn't work . . . well, Rogero had already said it. There wouldn't be any way to try anything else except huddling inside fortified areas and waiting for the rioting to burn itself out.

Gwen Iceni had a lot of practice at hiding her true feelings and projecting what her audience wanted to see. That was a necessary survival tool in the Syndicate, where most superiors did not care if they were being lied to as long as the lies were the ones those superiors wanted to see and hear. It was also a very important skill to use with the workers, who would believe the lies because the lies held the only hope the workers could have, and the workers needed hope, even false hope, to continue on day after day.

Now, despite the anxiety she felt and her anger at those who had engineered these crises facing her, despite her worries about the fate of the forces sent to Ulindi and in particular (*admit it to yourself, Gwen, even if you never will to him*) worries about the fate of Artur Drakon, Iceni presented an image of calm confidence as she touched the command to transmit a message to Black Jack. "Admiral Geary, my friend, I am hoping it is you who have returned to this star system." *Even though you haven't contacted* me *yet. Are you waiting to see what I do about the mobs?* "We are currently undergoing some minor domestic disturbances, which I regret to say are occupying my full attention. General Drakon is at Ulindi, assisting the people there in throwing off the chains of the Syndicate. You will be pleased to hear that your Captain Bradamont has proven to be an exceptionally valuable resource in our attempts to both defend this star system and to create a more stable system of governance for it. I regret that she is currently aboard our battleship *Midway*, which is also at Ulindi, and cannot speak to you directly. I assure you that she is both safe and highly respected by the officers and specialists of our military forces.

"From what I can see, it appears that the aliens called the Dancers are returning home. I would appreciate confirmation of this." *I hate begging. Why did you make me ask, Black Jack? I suppose you're just reminding me how much power you have compared to me.* "They sent us a message directly. *Watch the different stars.* We have no idea what that means." Would Black Jack? When last here, he had claimed to have only basic communication with the alien minds of the Dancers, but perhaps in the time since then, some breakthroughs had occurred.

"I am certain that our current domestic disturbances are the work of foreign agents." *And perhaps some local sources. But who are they?* "I will be focusing my efforts on calming the situation here without resorting to Syndicate methods." *Those methods are no longer available to me even if I wanted to use them, but I might as well present the whole mess in the best possible light.*

"Please advise me of your plans. I remain your friend and ally, President Iceni." *Don't make me crawl! You need me, too, whether you realize it or not!* "For the people. Out."

It would take nearly eight hours to receive a reply if Black Jack sent one. *Space is too damned big,* Iceni thought. *Where is—?*

A special tone sounded on her comm system. Iceni's hand darted out to touch the receive command and watched Colonel Rogero's image appear once more. He was in a clean uniform now, but his sidearm holster was empty. "The ground forces have been briefed and prepared, Madam President. Everyone fully understands what the risks are, what we are to do, and what must not be done. We are ready."

"Why are you unarmed, Colonel?" Iceni asked.

"I will go out there with my soldiers."

"There has already been one recent attempt to assassinate you, Colonel. Did something about the event cause it to not register on your mind? Were the explosions too small?"

Rogero smiled in the face of her wrath. "I understand the risk, Madam President. I do have a concealed weapon. But I believe it is critically important that I go out there with my men and women, and I cannot look as if I am threatening my own soldiers by being armed when they are not."

"Colonel Rogero," Iceni said in her most even voice, "you do realize that, if our fears regarding Ulindi come true, you may be the senior surviving ground forces officer? That the future security of Midway

Star System may already be dependent on your survival and your steady hand?"

This time, Rogero hesitated a moment before replying. "Madam President, I would not be going out there if I did not believe it was absolutely necessary to ensure that Midway has a future. There is an old saying that he who will not risk cannot win. I am certain that applies here."

"What about me?" Iceni asked. "Will there be a requirement for me to risk in a similar fashion? Do you believe I should expose myself as well?"

Another moment of hesitation, then Rogero shook his head. "Not immediately. I would recommend waiting to see how things go when the ground forces deploy. Most of the soldiers are workers in the eyes of the citizens, and our officers are relatively junior supervisors. We all take orders. You, on the other hand, give orders. That's how the citizens see it, so you represent the ultimate level of authority for them. If you decide that the situation remains in the balance despite our efforts, an open appearance from you at that time could make all the difference."

"I agree," Iceni said. "Make sure you do not die, Colonel Rogero. I shall be extremely upset with you if that happens."

He grinned, accidentally revealing his own tension in the quickness and tightness of the expression. "I will keep that in mind, Madam President. We will move out in five minutes."

"I will have media reactivated as you do so," Iceni said. "I am assured that the worms and bots that previously prevented us from controlling what went out along media channels have now been deactivated, and we once again control all media."

"Excellent," Rogero said. "If anything we don't want gets through despite that—"

"I don't think we have to worry about that, Colonel. I asked my techs how many software engineers it would take to deactivate a bomb in the same room with them, and none of them seemed eager to learn the answer through experimental trials."

"Well, that would be another hardware problem, wouldn't it?" Rogero saluted, then nodded to her. "I will report in after this is over, Madam President."

"See that you do."

She checked her clothing. A nice suit, not the standard Syndicate CEO suit, which she had grown to loathe, but rather something that had no trace of the Syndicate to its cut and color. A suit that projected authority and power but not ruthlessness. Iceni took a good look at her hair and face. Neither was perfect, but that was all to the good. If the citizens needed to see her, they needed to see her as human, as one of them in some ways. Being a president had proven to be much more of a challenge than being an autocratic CEO, but she had already learned a lot.

Then she waited, watching the many virtual windows.

"Madam President? Should we open media broadcasts as scheduled?"

"Yes. Do it."

She saw random patterns of reaction moving through the restive crowds as media access was restored, and citizens began searching for information.

The ground forces appeared. Not just Colonel Rogero's, but all of the local soldiers as well.

None of them wore armor. None of them carried weapons. They wore their uniforms neatly, proudly, and walked with slow, confident strides as they marched in many small formations along the streets and toward the plazas and parks where the crowds were massed.

Iceni zoomed in some views, knowing that every media channel would be showing similar images. The citizens nearest the soldiers were watching them, instinctive fear and hostility toward the traditional enforcers of Syndicate control shading into bafflement at the lack of riot-suppression equipment.

The soldiers smiled and waved as they marched, small clusters of uniforms isolated amid the mobs. If the mobs turned on them, they would be swamped in moments.

There was Colonel Rogero, walking with some of his soldiers, looking as if he had not a care in the world.

"Everything is fine," Iceni heard some of the soldiers saying.

"No problems," from others.

"Do you need anything?"

"Is everyone all right?"

Iceni eyed the scenes, listened to the voices, watched various media channels showing actions and reactions. She let her instincts evaluate all of those things, let her next action be dictated not by cold calculation but by processes operating below the level of conscious thought. She had risen through the Syndicate ranks by reading people, by sensing their moods and their attitudes, and at the moment that particular skill told her something very important.

The efforts of Rogero's ground forces weren't enough. The crowds were still wavering, still uncertain. They knew the ground forces would be following orders, *her* orders, and if she was following the old Syndicate ways, she would not be worried about what would happen to those soldiers if everything went bad.

The people needed another push, another demonstration, one dramatic enough to finally tip the balance.

Iceni looked down, closed her eyes, centered herself internally on the calm, cool place inside where her emotional core lay.

She got up and walked out of her office.

Her bodyguards leaped into position around her as she walked, but Iceni waved them back. "Stay here." She felt naked in her vulnerability, wondering once again what had happened to Togo, but kept walking with a firm, steady stride as the bodyguards stopped moving, obedient to her command but staring after her with uncomprehending eyes.

Iceni went up stairs and along passages until she reached the massive, formal front entrance to her governing complex, gesturing to the guards there to open the armored doors and stand aside.

There was a vast plaza before the building, and in that plaza a vast crowd.

She walked alone across the entry portico as media zoomed in on her, walked down the flight of granite stairs, and stood right before the edges of the crowd, only one step above their level, one woman facing a mass of humanity.

She wondered about assassins as she faced so many strangers with no bodyguards anywhere close to her. There had to be some trained killers on the planet, the same who had tried to murder Colonel Rogero. But such assassins were careful planners. They watched where their targets went and what their targets did, and they prepared with special diligence to kill under just the right circumstances, as they nearly had with Rogero.

Which assassin would have predicted this, that she would be here, in the open, where she never came?

For a while, at least, she must be safe from that threat, having done the unpredictable and the unthinkable.

All she had to worry about instead was the raw power of tens of thousands of citizens who could erupt at any moment.

Iceni smiled as the crowd fell silent. "Everything is all right," she said, her words amplified through the plaza. "I wanted to tell you that in person. There is no danger threatening us at this moment. As you have seen, Colonel Rogero is alive and well, and I am alive and well. The ground forces are not fighting, our mobile forces protect us, and your elected officials remain free and able to fulfill the roles you chose them for. There is no danger to you from any of your leaders. Most especially not from me. I am *your* president."

She waited. The thousands of people here stared at her in disbelief. Very few of them would have ever seen a star-system CEO in person, and if so then only through a screen of heavily armed bodyguards. Countless other citizens must be watching the media feeds with equal incredulity. Syndicate CEOs did not go out among their people, not openly, not without enough bodyguards to fight off a small army. Iceni had been a Syndicate CEO, and to many of the citizens, she had remained tainted by that.

One young woman, bolder than the others, finally found her voice. "Why are you here?" she called.

"Because," Iceni said, making sure her voice carried effortlessly across the crowd, knowing that her words would be picked up and transmitted everywhere on the planet, "I am not afraid of you. And I do not want you to be afraid of me."

It was perhaps the biggest lie she had ever spoken, and there had been some truly majestic lies spoken by her over time. Iceni was desperately afraid, her heart pounding as she smiled serenely at the huge mob almost within arm's reach of her. The words of every mentor, every superior, every teacher, every companion of equal rank came back to her. *They are dangerous, they must be kept leashed and controlled, you must never expose yourself to them, you must never appear vulnerable or small before them, you must beat and subdue and force them into submission because if they ever believe that they can change their fates or exact revenge, then you will be torn to pieces by them.*

A hand reached out of the crowd toward her and it took all of Iceni's discipline and strength to avoid flinching back from it. But the hand did not threaten, it just reached, and after a moment Iceni forced herself to reach back and gently grasp it. "Greetings, citizen," she said in the same placid-but-carrying tone of voice.

She felt it then, as if by touching that hand she had thrown a stone into a pond, the ripples spreading out from that gesture, the smiles appearing and the tension evaporating. That was how it was with mobs. When they tipped, they went all out, and this mob had tipped not into violence and rage but into reassurance and celebration. She felt it and she knew it and her fear was suddenly charged with a strange exhilaration. *"For the people!"* Iceni cried, raising her hands, and the words came repeated back to her by the mass of humanity in the plaza, a roar of support and approval that terrified her with the immensity and the force of it, the sound echoing back from the structure behind her with what felt like enough power to rock her on her feet.

Steeling herself, Iceni walked another step toward the crowd, citizens pushing to be closer to her, but still maintaining a slight distance through force of habit, touching, cheering, waving.

The tiny comm device in her right ear murmured with Colonel Rogero's voice. "Congratulations, Madam President. You did it. All areas are reporting that the crisis ended when media showed your appearance outside your residence. The crisis has turned into an enormous party. We're going to make sure all of the liquor outlets and drug outlets stay closed, so the partying doesn't get out of hand."

Iceni kept smiling even though she wanted to collapse with relief, tried to control the rapid beating of her heart, tried not to let her awe of the power of the mass of humanity before her show in her eyes, as she touched and smiled and waved back.

She had them, she suddenly realized. She had all of their strength in her hands at that moment. They would do whatever she asked, not reluctantly out of coercion, but enthusiastically out of belief in her, putting their hearts and souls into the task. This was the power that the Syndicate feared, this was the power that the Alliance claimed to wield, and it was hers. She had been afraid of these people before, afraid of the power of the mob, but now that she held their power to use or misuse, now that she finally held that which she had longed for, it scared the hell out of her.

CHAPTER ELEVEN

"HERE comes another barrage! Into the shelters!"

Drakon sat down, feeling clumsy and massive in his battle armor, the seat creaking beneath his weight. The command center had few soldiers in it besides him and Malin. He eyed the information on his display about the incoming barrage, judging it through his way-too-extensive experience with being bombarded by enemy artillery. "It's a little lighter than the first one. They must be running low on rockets."

"There is a higher proportion of gun artillery," Malin agreed. "Sir, we're going to have to employ chaff from the base stocks if they hit us again after this. Everything blocking precision weapon targeting and sensors out there is starting to get thin."

"This second Syndicate barrage will throw up more junk," Drakon said. "Colonel Kai, Colonel Safir, how are your troops doing for ammo?"

"Fully resupplied, General, with more stocks in ready resupply right behind the forward positions," Kai said.

"Same here, General," Safir reported. "The troops are tired, though. It's been a long day."

"Up patches are authorized for anyone who hasn't employed one yet," Drakon said. Using too many of the stimulant patches too fast was a recipe for psychotic episodes, which was a particularly bad thing when heavily armed soldiers were involved. But it was probably past time to give his soldiers a mental and physical boost after all they had already been through.

"Yes, sir. My people believe that they have spotted preliminary indications of Syndicate troops massing opposite sector four," Safir said.

Malin nodded in agreement. "From the small signs our sensors have picked up in the Syndicate positions, I estimate the next two attacks will come at sectors one and four."

"They'll do the same thing," Kai said. "Failure is no indication of a flaw in planning." Safir laughed sharply, drawing a puzzled look from Kai. "I was merely pointing out Syndicate tactical philosophy," he said. "Do you disagree?"

"No, Colonel. I was admiring the accuracy of your statement," Safir replied.

Drakon barely managed to hide his own smile. Safir, having served so long with Gaiene, had plenty of experience with comebacks. But the reminder of Conner made the smile vanish before it could form, then the bombardment arrived.

The sky fell on the base again, the overheads, the walls, and the floors trembling with the constant shock of explosions. But the Syndicate could build things well, and this base seemed to be lacking in the most common construction flaws and errors. Ground-penetrating artillery was being foiled by layers of special armor, surface fortifications were shrugging off armor-penetrating artillery, and the concussions of the high-explosive rounds were accomplishing little but to bounce around the increasingly fine gravel and dust which this morning had been the surface structures of the base.

Malin took a report, then shook his head at Drakon as more dust silted down from the ceiling. "Executive First Rank Finley, the supposed senior snake here, is dead. She was taken prisoner during our initial assault but was found dead among the prisoners, all of whom professed to know nothing about what happened to her."

"Funny how often snakes die during assaults or when captured and left among other prisoners," Drakon said, leaning back and looking up so he could see through his helmet's visual sensors a stream of dust falling toward him from a small crack in the ceiling.

"A lot of them died here," Malin agreed. "From what I have been able to piece together, that's what allowed us to seize the base so quickly once we penetrated the fortifications. The snakes stationed at the front lines began shooting soldiers who tried to retreat, and the other soldiers took that badly enough to start massacring the snakes among them. The brigade holding this base fell apart from the inside when we punched the outside hard enough."

"Morgan was right about that," Drakon said.

"Yes . . . she was."

Drakon gazed upward at the falling dust, wondering again what had happened to Morgan, and wishing as usual that he could leave whatever command center he was in and go to the front line. He had never liked the usual necessity of holding back from getting directly involved in the fighting, so he could focus on the big picture. It did not feel brave or right when his soldiers were fighting and dying as a result of the commands he issued. *But I know I have to do it that way. If I'm not looking out for the big picture, acting like the commanding officer should act, then I would be betraying them. Who would do my job if I weren't doing it?*

Who would care about these soldiers if I didn't?

"The barrage is ceasing," Malin cautioned. "Surviving surface sensors see no more inbound rounds after the next volley hits in thirty seconds."

Drakon sat up, stood up, and focused on his display. "All units, the latest barrage will cease after the next rounds land. Exit blast bunkers in forty seconds and reoccupy all outer fortifications."

The ground shook through a final spasm, then Drakon saw on the virtual windows before him Syndicate chaff rounds sprouting their clouds of confusion in the open area all around the base.

"Hold on," he heard Colonel Safir say to what was now her brigade. "Don't fire until you have targets. Wait for it."

"Stand by," Colonel Kai told his soldiers. "Ready."

The defenders had been able to rest during the barrage. They had been resupplied from the ample stockpiles of ammunition in the base and had eaten rations from the base supplies. Now they packed into the fortifications where many of the automated defenses had been destroyed by earlier fighting, their own weapons leveled toward the chaff clouds before them.

At both sector one and sector four, a mass of figures in battle armor burst through the murk and into full view less than twenty meters from the outer fortifications.

"Fire," Safir and Kai said simultaneously.

The front ranks of the assault evaporated under the defensive fire at both locations. Stubborn attackers kept coming, stumbling over the bodies of their comrades, facing a storm of fire that knocked them down mercilessly.

The attackers at sector one faltered, standing still for a few moments, leaning into the defensive fire as if it were a heavy wind. Then they broke, scrambling back into the chaff clouds.

But opposite sector four the attackers confronting Safir's soldiers kept coming, wave after wave, until their bodies began blocking the firing ports of the fortifications.

"Colonel! We can't cover the base of the wall anymore! Their breaching teams will have a free shot!"

"The hell they will!" Safir cried. "General, request permission to counterattack."

Malin cast a startled glance at Drakon, who had been watching the pressure build on Safir's troops. "General, that's—"

"A very good idea," Drakon said. "The Syndicate troops back at their lines won't be able to see our forces leave the base because of the chaff they laid to screen their own attack. Colonel Safir, permission granted. Sally your counterattack from sector five. Clear the base of the wall, then get your people back inside."

"You heard the man!" Safir called. "Third Battalion, go!"

Sally ports shot open in the base of the fortifications to one side of where the masses of attackers were piling up against the base's outer wall. The Third Battalion of the Second Brigade, with Colonel Safir in their midst, poured out, immediately pivoted ninety degrees, and hit the side of the Syndicate assault like a hammer.

The attack collapsed, many of the exhausted Syndicate soldiers simply dropping to their knees and throwing away their weapons as the rest of the assault force fled. Armored figures who must have been snakes or frustrated supervisors tried to shoot those surrendering, but Safir's troops targeted anyone still holding a weapon and wiped them out. "Round them up!" Safir ordered. "You!" she added, shifting to an external speaker that the microphones on the Syndicate battle armor would pick up. "If you want to live as prisoners, move! Anyone left out here when we get back inside is a target!"

"General," Malin said. "As soon as the Syndicate commanders realize we have soldiers outside the base fortifications—"

"They will order in a bombardment of that area," Drakon finished. "I worked in the Syndicate system long enough to know how much time it takes for that system to identify new information, make a decision, and get a sudden change implemented. We've got at least four minutes. Colonel Safir, get your people back inside in less than four minutes."

"Yes, General," she replied, sounding breathless. "They'll know better than to mess with Conner Gaiene's lads and ladies again."

Drakon realized that he was smiling. The Second Brigade was no longer commanded by Gaiene, but he had been in charge long enough to put his stamp on the unit, especially once Drakon's division had been exiled to Midway and thereby, ironically, given a bit more freedom from Syndicate micromanagement as a result of being punished. For a while longer at least the Second Brigade would still think of themselves as Gaiene's, and that was not a bad thing. Not a bad thing at all.

"I think Colonel Safir was around Colonel Gaiene a bit too long," Malin said.

"It looks to me like she was around Conner for just about the right amount of time," Drakon said.

The Third Battalion, showing little patience with laggards, hustled the disarmed prisoners inside the base and resealed the sally ports. "Well done, Colonel Safir," Drakon said. "Make sure the prisoners are under strong guard until they've been individually screened for any weapons we might have missed in the rush."

"Barrage inbound," Malin announced, then looked at Drakon again. "Four minutes, fifteen seconds."

Drakon grinned at him, feeling a rush of relief that the latest attacks had been repulsed. "Close enough for Syndicate work."

"A damned sight better than Syndicate work, sir." The ground trembled once more as the barrage struck outside of sector two. "The Syndicate soldiers surrounding us will know that barrage is hitting any of their wounded outside the base."

"We brought in every wounded soldier we could," Drakon said.

"We know that, but the Syndicate ground forces will assume those wounded are still out there and being killed by their own artillery."

Malin smiled that cold smile of his. "With that on top of the losses they've sustained in futile attacks today, the Syndicate forces are going to face some serious morale problems."

Drakon nodded, his eyes on his display, where the chaff clouds now drifted with no signs of the enemy visible behind them. "I'm going to need the Syndicate prisoners screened for potential recruits, Bran. The ones from the brigade that held this base and the ones we just picked up outside. We've taken way too many losses today. Maybe we can find some recruits with potential among our prisoners."

It took Drakon a moment to realize that he had just thought beyond the next hour, beyond today.

He might just have a future again.

But they were still surrounded; despite their losses, the Syndicate ground forces still had big advantages in supporting arms like artillery and aerospace warbirds, and above all else there was still that Syndicate battleship to worry about.

IN terms of numbers, the two flotillas rushing toward each other were closely matched. Each had a single battleship. Now that Haris's cruisers had joined it, the Syndicate flotilla also contained two heavy cruisers, one light cruiser, and three Hunter-Killers. Marphissa's ships had met up with the newly arrived *Midway*, giving her flotilla two heavy cruisers, two light cruisers, and four Hunter-Killers.

"I should switch flagships," Marphissa said reluctantly. She had gone to her stateroom to talk privately with Mercia and Bradamont, who were in one of the battleship's secure conference rooms, but thanks to the conferencing software appeared to be sitting right next to Marphissa's desk on *Manticore*. "I should be aboard *Midway*. There's plenty of time for a shuttle to come over to *Manticore* and transport me back to the battleship."

Kapitan Mercia looked over as Bradamont cleared her throat.

"Kommodor," Bradamont said, speaking formally, "I recommend that you stay on *Manticore.* Not because of any flaw with *Midway,*" she added with a gesture toward Mercia. "We all agree that the Syndicate believes the *Midway* is once more bluffing, that her weapons are still mostly not operational. If you switch flagships, the Syndicate will see the shuttle movement and know what the significance of that must be. It will cause them to wonder if the *Midway* is indeed bluffing. Why would you transfer to a ship without working weapons?"

Kapitan Mercia nodded. "So, if the Kommodor switches to *Midway,* it might well lead CEO Boucher to question whether *Midway* might be fully operational, or at least much more ready to fight than the Syndicate expects. I agree with Captain Bradamont."

"But," Bradamont continued, "if you stay on *Manticore* even though you have the opportunity to transfer to *Midway,* it will serve to confirm to the Syndics, excuse me, the Syndicate forces, their belief that *Midway* is not a functional warship."

Marphissa nodded as well. "That is an important consideration. I will be very close to *Midway* in any event, able to communicate with you with no meaningful delay. I will stay aboard *Manticore.* I want to take every measure to ensure that Happy Hua is badly surprised by our first engagement." No one had mentioned that as a heavy cruiser, *Manticore* was far more vulnerable than a battleship like *Midway.* This was not a matter in which personal safety of the flotilla commander should be deciding the course of action.

"Hua will be aiming for *Midway*'s propulsion," Bradamont added. "Above all, she wants to be sure that this battleship does not get away from her."

"And I will be aiming for her battleship's propulsion," Mercia said with a laugh. "We're both going to be chasing the other's backside."

"Both of you have a lot more experience with engaging battleships than I do," Marphissa said. "Is there any other way to quickly cripple Happy Hua's battleship? Besides trying to hit her main propulsion?"

Mercia shook her head. "In a one-on-one engagement? In one firing pass? Even if we had that Alliance fog weapon, we couldn't do it except by aiming for the main propulsion. But we'll never get a clean shot at her stern if both of us are trying to do that. Neither of us can outmaneuver the other. It will just be a succession of head-to-head firing passes, gradually wearing down both ships, and if Hua finds she is being worn down faster, she will have a chance to bolt and escape from us."

"What can we do then?" Marphissa demanded.

"You said," Bradamont commented to Mercia, "it couldn't work *if* both battleships were trying for each other's propulsion."

"Yes, I did." Mercia hunched forward, her hands moving to illustrate the movements of ships. "CEO Boucher thinks we're bluffing. She's coming toward us in what will be a head-to-head encounter. I can appear to fumble the angle of our bow at contact, which won't strike CEO Boucher as odd because I'm just some junior executive or even worker who killed her betters and got promoted immediately to command a warship, right? That will seem to allow the Syndicate battleship a partial shot at my stern. *Midway* herself only fires a few weapons on that pass, as if that's all we've got. We come out of it with some of our main propulsion apparently inoperative as a result of lucky hits. The external damage won't be there, but there are plenty of internal reasons why main propulsion units can go off-line after taking fire, so it will still look plausible. We turn away and loop back toward the jump point for Midway Star System. It looks like we're running. Our bluff has been called, and we've taken damage." One of her hands swung in a wide turn.

"But we've lost some main propulsion, so the arc of our turn is wider than what Happy Hua's ship can manage," Mercia continued, her other hand moving in a tighter arc inside that of the first. "It's hard to shift the vectors on so much mass. Happy Hua turns inside us and aims for our stern, coming in at about, hmmm, our stern quarter. Even if I try to turn bow on toward her, I'll just be pivoting my own stern along the same path that Hua is taking. She'd still be able to hit my stern quarter as she passes."

"That's your most vulnerable point," Bradamont said.

"Yes. This is all if we held our vector. But, we're on that arc. We have a lot of momentum along a wider angle that our main propulsion is fighting as it keeps pushing us through the turn." Mercia's hands moved again. "If I completely kill our main propulsion, we stop turning along that arc at that rate. My ship changes speed relative to Hua's ship, and immediately begins to swing out along a much wider arc. You see? Hua has set her firing pass to come close to our stern, but when I change my arc by killing my propulsion just before contact, it changes the situation. She will suddenly find her battleship passing," Mercia said with a grin, as her hands moved past each other, "just in front of my bow, angled away from me, giving me a perfect shot at *her* stern quarter."

Marphissa stared intently, running the maneuvers through her mind. "It could work."

"It *will* work," Mercia insisted. "We all deal with momentum. It's a major factor in how we maneuver. But battleships deal with it most of all because of our mass relative to our main propulsion. Hua can't appreciate that because she lacks the experience. Her automated maneuvering systems will provide a textbook-perfect firing run on my battleship, but because they deal only with what is, and not with all the possible options I might employ, they will not warn her what will happen if I make that change in my vector in the last minutes before contact, and, most importantly, they will not warn her that when she tries in those last moments to shift her own vector and her own battleship's facing to counter my actions, she will be fighting not just me, but also all of the mass and existing momentum of her own battleship. She won't be able to succeed."

"You're saying there's no risk?" Marphissa asked skeptically. "That this is a sure thing?"

"Of course there is risk!" Mercia replied. "This is war, not a game or simulation where we can order the umpire to make things come out as we please. Something could go wrong. *Midway* might take real, significant damage during the first engagement if the Syndicate gets lucky. Happy Hua could do something so stupid it is smart and totally messes up our plan. One of the sub-CEOs or executives on Happy Hua's ship might spot the risk and warn her, and Happy Hua might listen to them, as unlikely as that is. I might misjudge the exact second to kill my main propulsion and miss my shot at Happy Hua's battleship, or Worker Gilligan might short out all of my controls just as I need them."

"I actually had a worker named Gilligan once," Marphissa said. "He didn't cause any disasters, but that was probably because everyone watched him constantly, expecting him to do something like that. Honore? What do you think?"

"I think it's brilliant," Bradamont said. "What are your cruisers and HuKs going to do while the battleships smash at each other on that first pass?"

Marphissa pondered that for a few seconds. "Happy Hua will concentrate her fire on *Midway*. All of her ships will be told to target our battleship as well because she knows that is by far the most important target, and she wants to inflict as much damage as possible before *Midway* runs for safety as she expects her to. Agreed? That should give us shots at taking out some of her cruisers and HuKs while they are firing on *Midway*."

"*Midway* should fire back at the battleship on that first pass, though," Bradamont said. "Since you'll be using only the few weapons you intend to employ to further the impression that *Midway* is still barely operational. Seeing the few shots *Midway* fires bouncing off her battleship's shields will enhance CEO Boucher's feelings of her own invincibility this time around."

"Yes," Kapitan Mercia agreed, nodding. "That's a good idea."

"How did a sub-CEO with your kind of brains survive under the Syndicate?" Marphissa asked.

Mercia smiled. "There were a few times I nearly didn't. But the supervisors who were unhappy with me never got around to reporting it."

"Accidents?" Marphissa asked.

"Yes. It was sad."

Bradamont eyed the two of them. "I never know when you people are joking."

Marphissa didn't reply, not wanting to discuss realities of Syndicate life that Bradamont found either incomprehensible or abhorrent. Instead, she went back to discussing the upcoming engagement. "Happy Hua's flotilla is twenty-six light-minutes away and coming on fast on a direct intercept. We're both going about point two light, so that would be an hour's travel time left before contact. We'll start braking in fifteen minutes. I want us down to point zero eight light speed when we encounter the Syndicate flotilla."

"Point zero eight?" Mercia questioned. "You're assuming that Happy Hua won't brake?"

"I don't think she will brake *enough*," Marphissa said. "She gained some experience in our last fight. She knows she has to keep her relative velocity from being too fast when we meet or she won't be able to hit us, and Happy Hua wants to hit us. But she's also still inexperienced enough to think that going faster is better. So she'll compromise and do neither well enough. My guess is that in this encounter she will get down a lot closer to point one light, but not all the way."

"That's a reasonable guess," Bradamont said. "CEO Boucher probably also still underestimates how hard it is to make a battleship's mass do what you want in a hurry. The Alliance usually tries to assign battleship commands to officers with a lot of previous experience on battleships, but occasionally they get someone without that experience who tries to make a battleship dance like a battle cruiser. It's not pretty."

Mercia eyed her. "You're telling us about Alliance policies? How your fleet does things?"

"That's one of the reasons Admiral Geary assigned me to Midway Star System," Bradamont said.

"So I was told, but . . . yes, that's a valid observation. CEO Boucher probably will underestimate the difficulty of making rapid changes to her battleship's facing and vector. I saw that in a lot of new commanders."

"All right," Marphissa said, sensing the tension that had become apparent between Mercia and Bradamont. "Have we forgotten anything?"

"What will your formation be?" Bradamont asked.

"Standard box— Hell." Marphissa laughed at herself. "The problem with defaults is that they become habitual. I think . . . Modified Diamond. *Midway* at the point."

"At the point?" Mercia asked, surprised. "That is an unconventional arrangement. Probably not the best, either."

"I know," Marphissa said. "That's why I think it would work. The Syndicate thinks we're young fools, out of our depth. Why not look a little clumsy? It won't hurt us. It's not the best arrangement for protecting *Midway*, but since we're only facing one other battleship, it won't make any difference in terms of how much fire *Midway* takes."

"True," Mercia conceded, her eyes intent.

"Then we will prepare to execute the plan we discussed. I will call the vectors as we approach the Syndicate flotilla, but you, Kapitan Mercia, will independently adjust your final heading as you feel best to give the Syndicate what they think is a shot at your main propulsion. After the first engagement, I want a recommendation from you, Kapitan, on how wide to have *Midway* turn."

Mercia nodded. "You will get it."

"Are you comfortable with Captain Bradamont's offering advice when she feels appropriate? She is discreet."

"Then . . . yes, Kommodor."

"I may not have much to offer in this engagement," Bradamont said. "I have a lot less experience with battleship maneuvering than Kapitan Mercia, and that is what will count."

"But you have already helped us plan the engagement," Marphissa said. "Is there anything else?"

Mercia cleared her throat. "Kommodor, may I speak with you privately?"

Marphissa glanced at Bradamont, who nodded to her without any sign of discomfort, and left the conference room on the battleship.

Once they were alone, Freya Mercia gave Marphissa a serious look. "I wanted to be certain that something was out in the open. This is not a conversation that would have been held under the Syndicate, and so the matter might have festered and created problems."

"What matter is this we must discuss?" Marphissa asked, trying to mask her tension. Mercia was older than her, had more experience with mobile forces, and had more experience in command positions. Was the old veteran about to attempt to slap down the young pup?

"I have been around awhile longer than you," Mercia began, apparently oblivious to the way her words caused Marphissa to shift into a defensive posture. "That has the potential for problems which I know would concern me if I were in your place. However, I wanted you to know that I accept my role as your subordinate. I will not conspire against you in the Syndicate way because from all I have seen and heard, you are not operating in the Syndicate way. Just now, we discussed what to do, and you listened, and you asked questions, then you decided. I know I am respected. That will take some getting used to after my years with the Syndicate, but I am grateful for the chance to use my skills and experience for those who value what I can offer."

Mercia waved around her. "I have command of a battleship, and

I am fighting for a good cause. I have no complaints, Kommodor. I will support you and comply with your orders. I did not want you to have worries on those counts."

"Thank you," Marphissa said. "I did have some concerns. Was it obvious?"

"No. You actually hid it very well."

"Do you understand that you can trust Honore Bradamont? She is Alliance, but to her, we are no longer Syndicate."

"Syndics," Mercia said with a twist of her lips. "I admit I am having some trouble at times seeing an Alliance officer on my bridge. But, yes, her insights are useful, and she admits when she knows less on a matter than one of us. She does not act like a conqueror, which I had anticipated from an Alliance battle cruiser commander. Her lack of arrogance and superiority is unexpected and welcome."

"I trust Captain Bradamont," Marphissa said. "In time, I hope you will trust her as fully. How is your crew handling having her around?"

"Oh, that!" Mercia rolled her eyes. "It has been . . . interesting. But they understand that any display of hostility or aggression toward her will result in serious consequences. She has bodyguards as well, of course, to keep her safe from the crew."

"At first, it was like that on *Manticore*," Marphissa said. "Now Bradamont is seen by the specialists as one of us. She is Black Jack's."

"The one who destroyed my flotilla?" Mercia asked. "But also the one who captured us instead of destroying our escape pods."

"And it was Bradamont who suggested getting you all from the Alliance, bringing you back to us." Marphissa shook her head as memories rushed in. "We wouldn't have made it back, made it through Indras Star System, without her advice to me. I called all the maneuvers, but Bradamont told me how I should use the escorts to protect the freighters. I had never commanded such an operation."

Mercia raised both eyebrows. "I saw enough of the action there from the command deck of the freighter I was on to be very, very worried. One of the reasons I didn't object to your being my boss was knowing how you handled your ships at Indras. I hadn't heard about Bradamont's role, though."

"It was between her and me. She never undermines me in front of my crew when she offers advice."

"That's good." Mercia sighed, grimacing. "I haven't had much time to learn things about all of you. I've been so busy getting the weapons on this ship operational, it hasn't left much time for anything else. I admit I was surprised, and a bit resistant, when President Iceni insisted that Bradamont accompany *Midway* to Ulindi. But Kapitan Kontos thought it was a good thing, almost a natural thing, and I wasn't about to defy Iceni and have them thinking I might be like Ito, so I went along."

"If anyone thought you were like Executive Ito," Marphissa said, "you wouldn't have been given command of *Midway*."

"Thank you. Bradamont didn't mention it, but she is worried about the ground forces."

"So am I. I've done all we could up to this point. Once we take out CEO Boucher's flotilla, *Midway* should be able to offer major support for the ground forces." Marphissa looked down, then back at Mercia. "Hopefully, it won't be too late. Is there any other matter we should discuss?"

Mercia shook her head. "No, Kommodor."

"Good. I have full confidence in you. You've achieved a miracle by getting *Midway* ready to fight as fast as you did. I have no complaints."

"No complaints? What kind of supervisor are you? How am I supposed to be motivated unless you treat me like dirt?" Mercia laughed.

"You know what? If we destroy Happy Hua's battleship, I'll also praise you. Publicly praise you and give you your fair share of the credit. You'll just have to get used to that kind of thing."

THE Syndicate flotilla's warships remained in Standard Box Formation One as they rushed to intercept, rising a little and coming along a slightly curved path just off to port of the Midway flotilla. The center of the box was occupied by CEO Boucher's battleship, the two heavy cruisers at the upper front corners and the light cruiser at a lower front corner. One of the three enemy Hunter-Killers was at the other lower corner, and the other two at the back upper corners. The enemy ships had closed to within five light-minutes, and had braked down to point one three light speed.

"No imagination at all," Kapitan Diaz scoffed. "Except for the velocity being too high, she's doing it exactly by the book."

"Which is good for us. We should be able to do some damage to those escorts." Marphissa had arranged her ships in the Modified Diamond, which was not a by-the-book formation at all. She had kept the formation flat, all of the ships in the same plane, but had given it a three-dimensional quality by slightly canting the formation downward relative to the Syndicate ships, so it would pass through at an angle rather than evenly. *Midway* occupied the front and lowest point. *Gryphon*, one of her two heavy cruisers, was at the point behind and to the port side of the battleship. The light cruiser *Hawk* was on the point opposite *Gryphon*, while the light cruiser *Eagle* was at the highest and rear point. At the center of the diamond was *Manticore*. Spread out at equal points within the diamond were the four Hunter-Killers *Sentry*, *Sentinel*, *Scout*, and *Defender*.

"Are you sure?" Diaz had asked, puzzled, as he saw the formation.

"Yes," Marphissa said. "It's not aimed at the Syndicate battleship. I want *Midway* to be leading to ensure she draws their fire, leaving our escorts to hit some of the Syndicate escorts hard while ignoring the Syndicate battleship."

"Won't they expect that?" Diaz said. "It's what we did last time we encountered CEO Boucher."

"Yes, but last time we did not have a battleship with us. The forces were very lopsided. And Syndicate doctrine insists that the major combatants be targeted first. In our last fight, that was our heavy cruisers as far as Happy Hua was concerned. Now it's *Midway.* She will assume we will do the same since we now have a battleship, and that is doctrine."

"Twenty minutes to contact," Senior Watch Specialist Czilla reported.

Marphissa studied her display. The projected tracks of both formations went directly through each other at a slight angle, the sort of head-on clash that lacked finesse and led to brutal engagements. That had increasingly been the usual sort of battle in the last several decades of the war with the Alliance, as both sides lost the skills and training to try anything less direct and concentrated on trying to hit the enemy harder than the enemy hit them.

CEO Hua Boucher, believing herself to have an overwhelming advantage in firepower, would surely stick to that path, wanting nothing more than to be able to hit *Midway* with everything she had. Marphissa's problem was how to adjust her own track slightly to still give Boucher shots at *Midway*, but not too many, and also give her own cruisers and Hunter-Killers the ability to concentrate their fire on a few of Boucher's escorts.

Twist the diamond formation slightly, bend its vector a little to one side, and her escorts would pretty much bracket Hua's two heavy cruisers while *Midway* and the Syndicate battleship went by each other. "Ah, yes," Marphissa murmured, designating one Syndicate heavy cruiser, the one that had helped bombard Kane, as the target for *Gryphon* and *Manticore*, and the other enemy cruiser, the one that had been under Haris's control, as a target for *Hawk*, *Eagle*, *Sentry*, *Sentinel*, *Scout*, and *Defender.*

"Kapitan Mercia," Marphissa called. "I am sending you my final vector and formation changes just before contact so you can adjust the heading of your ship."

Mercia studied the information on her display, then nodded. "I understand, Kommodor. You are certain you will make these changes?"

"Yes. CEO Boucher will not react even if she sees them in time because they still give her a clean shot at you."

"Thank you, Kommodor," Mercia said dryly. "I appreciate the opportunity to field-test my ship's armor and shields."

"We'll be going a bit fast for the combat systems to compensate," Marphissa said. "But if the Syndicate ships stick to their vectors while we are making minor adjustments in ours, it should allow us to still have good hit probabilities while reducing their accuracy."

"I am going to be twisting *Midway* at the moment of contact, pretending that I overcompensated. The Syndicate weapons should mostly impact my side shields and armor, but they will think they got a shot at my rear quarter."

"That's going to take some very good maneuvering," Marphissa said.

Mercia smiled. "I know."

"Ten minutes to contact," Czilla reported.

"We'll talk again after the firing pass," Marphissa said, ending the call. She focused completely on her display, wanting to get the feel for the right moment to make the small adjustments in her formation and vector. Bradamont had coached her through this sort of thing, giving her tips that had supposedly been given to Bradamont by Black Jack himself. Marphissa knew that she had still screwed up the firing pass last time against CEO Boucher.

But not this time.

"All units," Marphissa said, spacing the words out and speaking clearly, "at time one four come port zero one degrees, up zero two degrees. Engage assigned targets with all available weapons."

For hours, the Syndicate ships had been very far away, just dots against the dark backdrop of space. Even in the last minute before contact, they were tiny objects because of the distance separating the two forces. Traveling at a combined velocity of over point two light speed, they were getting closer to each other at a rate of more than sixty thousand kilometers per second.

The views could be easily magnified, of course. Marphissa had a small virtual window on her display showing a clear vision of the enemy formation, seven warships seen in perfect detail across those huge distances. She could have zoomed in the image further, getting the same picture as if she were mere meters from the enemy. Space offered few obstacles to sight and none of the degradation of vision that occurred in a planetary atmosphere.

It was a mixed blessing, Marphissa thought. Being able to easily see the enemy charging at you for hours could be unnerving for those unused to the experience. And the long periods of nothing happening while the enemy charged at you could lead to a very dangerous complacency that would be shattered when those final thousands of kilometers separating you were covered in less than a second.

"One minute to contact," Czilla said.

"Make your shots count," Diaz ordered his weapons specialist. "This is for Kane."

In the last seconds before contact, Marphissa's formation shifted vector slightly as ordered, twisting and rising a little to meet the Syndicate formation at a slightly different angle. She could see *Midway* twisting in place, just as Mercia had said she would, apparently making a clumsy attempt to meet the Syndicate battleship bow to bow and failing badly.

Manticore lurched slightly as her missiles fired at the oncoming warships. Around her, *Gryphon*, *Hawk*, and *Eagle* also launched missiles.

Sensors barely had time to report that the Syndicate warships were firing missiles as well before the two formations rocketed into contact.

The enemy was there, and past, automated weapons on both sides hurling out hell lances and the metal ball bearings called grapeshot in the tiny fraction of a second when the ships were in range of each other, the weapons impacting along with the missiles fired earlier.

Marphissa hadn't felt *Manticore* lurch from any hits. She stared at her display, waiting for her warships' sensors to evaluate the results of the engagement as the two sets of warships tore away from each other.

Both of the heavy cruisers were missing from the Syndicate formation, one spinning off at an angle with its entire forward section smashed, and the other simply gone, a ball of gas and debris revealing that it had taken enough hits to cause a power-core overload.

Only a few hits from the Syndicate Hunter-Killers had struck Marphissa's escorts, everything else in the Syndicate arsenal having been aimed at *Midway.*

"They scratched my ship," Mercia complained.

"You took hits? I'm not seeing damage reports in the status feed."

"They must have missed a lot, and other hits came in at high enough angles to skip off my shields and armor. But, oh dear, I have lost half my main propulsion," Mercia reported with feigned distress.

"You didn't shut it off during the engagement?" Marphissa asked, looking at her display's review of recent events.

"No. Within seconds of the engagement, in a staggered ripple of shutdowns. As we said earlier, I wanted it to look like control failures since the Syndicate will be able to see that the exteriors of the units were not damaged. Kommodor, with my ship's reduced maneuverability, I recommend we alter vector up three five five degrees."

"All units," Marphissa called, "immediate execute, alter vector up three five five degrees. Match velocity to *Midway* and maintain your positions in formation."

The Midway diamond formation bent upward, velocity falling off as the ships fought their momentum to curve their tracks around and reverse course. The cruisers and Hunter-Killers could have made the turn in much less space than the vast distance required for the battleship to turn with half of her main propulsion units not working, but they matched their movements to the battleship, holding the same positions relative to *Midway.*

"Here she comes," Diaz said, pointing to his display.

Happy Hua's formation was turning up as well, coming back toward them. Marphissa watched, trying to look calm despite the tension she felt, as the vectors on the two formations steadied out. "It looks good. She's doing what Kapitan Mercia predicted."

"Will she keep doing it?"

"She's Syndicate through and through," Marphissa said. "Flexibility in anything but morals is not taught by the Syndicate. And she's ruthless. She sees a chance at a kill, and she's going to take it."

It took time for the formations to come back together as they swung in their huge arcs through space. "You make the call when to kill your propulsion completely," Marphissa told Mercia. "The rest of our ships will be slaved to your maneuvers, so we stay right with you."

"I understand," Mercia replied, her eyes locked on her display as she talked to Marphissa. "I will comply," she added, unconsciously using the Syndicate phrase that had been required of her for so long.

"Showing five minutes to intercept," Czilla reported.

Marphissa touched her comm controls. "*Gryphon*, *Hawk*, *Eagle*, *Sentry*, *Sentinel*, *Scout*, *Defender*, slave your maneuvering controls to *Midway.* I will not designate specific targets this time because our aspects will be changing as our formations engage. Your primary targets are the remaining enemy escorts. If you can't get a good shot at an escort, add your fire to that of *Midway* at the enemy battleship." She ended and looked at Diaz. "You, too."

"Yes, Kommodor." Diaz had his eyes fixed on his display as well.

One minute passed. Another. CEO Boucher's formation came onward steadily, tracking to pass close behind *Midway*'s stern.

"*Midway* has cut all main propulsion," Czilla said.

Manticore lurched as her automated maneuvering controls, fixed on maintaining the same position relative to the battleship, cut back her own main propulsion dramatically.

Vectors changed suddenly on the ships of Marphissa's formation, shifting wider and flatter, the projected intercept point with the Syndicate warships swinging higher to one side.

"CEO Boucher sees what's happening," Diaz said. "Her battleship is firing thrusters to bring her bow around."

The projected vectors and intercept points kept shifting rapidly, the Syndicate battleship firing its thrusters on full to try to compensate for the sudden changes in how it would encounter the *Midway*.

"All units," Marphissa ordered. "Fire when your weapons are within range."

CHAPTER TWELVE

EVERYTHING was still moving very fast, but it felt like it was happening too slowly. Marphissa watched as the Syndicate battleship, unable to counter its own momentum quickly enough, zoomed upward just past *Midway*'s bow instead of just past her stern. She did not actually see every weapon on *Midway* lash out at the stern quarter of the Syndicate battleship. It happened far too fast for human senses to register. Nor did she see her cruisers and Hunter-Killers add their fire to the barrage, or the weapons on the Syndicate warships firing back, the angle a bad one for the Syndicate battleship so that many of its weapons could not get shots off.

Manticore shuddered from a few hits, but Marphissa didn't hear any alarms going off to signify major damage.

The two formations separated more slowly this time, the Midway formation continuing to swing outward in a flat arc while the Syndicate formation angled away.

Marphissa didn't wait this time to see the results of the engagement. "All units, immediate execute, come up one two five degrees, accelerate to point one light speed." Her formation bent upward again, *Midway* lighting off all of her main propulsion again, the warships now on their backs relative to their earlier alignment, which made no difference at all to the spacecraft or their crews.

As her ships came around, she saw the results of the engagement show up on her display.

A single Hunter-Killer still accompanied the Syndicate battleship. The light cruiser was rolling off into the distance, all systems dead, one of the Hunter-Killers had blown up, and the third had broken into several pieces, which were tumbling away.

The few surviving enemy escorts must have concentrated their fire on *Manticore.* A few shots had gotten through her shields but had been weakened enough that they had failed to penetrate her armor. No other friendly warship except *Midway* had taken hits, and every shot aimed at *Midway* by the Syndicate battleship seemed to have hit her bow area, where her strongest shields and heaviest armor were placed.

Marphissa inhaled deeply as she saw the results of *Midway*'s fire on the Syndicate battleship. She had not realized until that moment that she had been holding her breath.

CEO Boucher's battleship looked as if a god's hammer had slammed into its stern quarter and stern. The battleship was trying to regain maneuvering control, but having trouble, with more than half of its main propulsion units and a lot of maneuvering thrusters destroyed.

"I wish I could have seen her face," Diaz said. "I wish I could have seen Happy Hua when she realized that *Midway* had all of her weapons operational, and they were all firing at her rear end as she waltzed past."

"Yes," Marphissa agreed. "That would have been nice. Kapitan Mercia, what's the best way to finish off the Syndicate battleship?"

"Take us past his stern again, Kommodor. If he hasn't regained maneuvering control, we can hammer him hard, and even if he does get control, he won't be able to evade us. I am happy to report that all of *Midway*'s weapons worked at high efficiency."

Marphissa brought her formation a bit farther down and angled it to port to match the wavering movements of the Syndicate battleship. The lone Syndicate Hunter-Killer still hung by the battleship, but the little warship offered the battleship no real additional protection. "They're getting the battleship straightened out," Diaz said, "but they're having a lot of trouble. The remaining main propulsion units are all pushing to one side of the center of mass, and it's taking all they can manage to keep the battleship from going into a wide spin."

"They will have an easier time controlling it if they cut back on the remaining main propulsion units, Kapitan," the maneuvering specialist offered.

"They would? Yes. I see that. But they will not because CEO Boucher will not let them." Diaz looked at Marphissa. "Am I right?"

"Very likely," she agreed. "It will be very hard to convince a Syndicate CEO that reducing thrust at a time like this is the right course of action. Boucher will think that she needs to keep her remaining thrust at maximum even though that's the wrong thing to do since it's making it harder to keep the battleship on course. We're going to come on the stern quarter opposite the one we hit last time and hammer that battleship's remaining main propulsion. They won't be able to turn his bow to face us with their main propulsion shoving them in the opposite direction, so they'll have to try turning away from us and bringing the bow all the way around the long way."

"Even if he turns away, we'll probably still get clean shots at his stern," Diaz said.

"That's what I'm counting on."

With the Syndicate battleship wavering up and toward the star, while Marphissa's flotilla closed in from behind and below, this was much more of a stern chase than the previous encounters, which reduced the relative speed of the encounter a great deal.

Kapitan Mercia called in. "We can brake velocity as we approach to get the relative speed close enough to zero that *Midway* can sit there and pound on that Syndicate bastard until he breaks."

"Not yet," Marphissa said. "Braking down our velocity like that would take more time and prolong our approach. If we give her enough time, Happy Hua may still figure out what she needs to do to get that battleship's bow around in time to meet us. I want the rest of her main propulsion taken out so she can't escape. After that, when we come back again, we'll come in slow enough to pound the hell out of that battleship for as long as it takes."

"Yes, Kommodor. Request permission to alter my own vector a little as necessary on the final approach to maximize my chances of hitting that battleship's stern hard."

"Permission granted," Marphissa said. "I will tell the other warships not to conform to your movement this time because I want to ensure that CEO Boucher's ship doesn't get good shots at any of our escorts while you're angling for a good shot from *Midway*."

Mercia paused, then nodded carefully. "I should have considered that, Kommodor."

"It's my job to consider such matters," Marphissa said. "Yours is to get that Syndicate battleship."

They overtook and tore past CEO Boucher's sadly diminished flotilla in another moment of extreme violence. This time, *Manticore* jerked badly a couple of times, and alarms sounded in the wake of the firing run.

"Happy Hua targeted us this time," Diaz said, looking furious. "She couldn't get in good shots at *Midway*, but she tried to nail us."

"How bad is it?" Marphissa asked.

"A hell-lance battery out as well as one of the missile launchers. Hull penetrations in two places. Two dead and a dozen injured."

Marphissa winced internally at the losses but kept her gaze on her display.

The Syndicate battleship's staggering attempts to swing its bow around had not come close to succeeding. *Midway* had hit its stern badly, taking out all but one of the remaining main propulsion units and badly chewing up another one of the battleship's aft quarters.

On the other hand, *Manticore* had not been the only escort hit by the Syndicate battleship's fire. *Gryphon* had taken one bad hit, *Eagle* had lost some of her main propulsion, and *Hawk* was temporarily unable to maneuver. Marphissa had deliberately kept her Hunter-Killers away from the battleship during the engagement, which was probably the only thing that had saved them from being badly damaged or destroyed.

Marphissa searched her display for the fate of the sole surviving Syndicate escort and spotted the Hunter-Killer bolting at maximum acceleration on a long, curving trajectory that would bring it to the jump point for Kiribati, far across the star system.

She made a quick check of the fuel-cell status on her own Hunter-Killers and shook her head. "We'll have to let him go," Marphissa told Diaz. "Our own Hunter-Killers don't have the fuel-cell reserves left to catch him."

"Too bad."

"Yes." She touched her comm controls. "*Midway*, you are to detach from the formation and operate independently to finish disabling and destroy the Syndicate battleship. I will keep the rest of the formation clear to avoid sustaining any more damage until the enemy battleship has been rendered safe to approach."

"It shall be done," Kapitan Mercia said, baring her teeth.

"*Gryphon*, stay with *Hawk* until *Hawk* regains maneuvering control, then both of you rejoin the formation."

"Yes, Kommodor," Kapitan Stein acknowledged, not quite hiding her relief at not being asked to once more exchange fire with a battleship.

As *Midway* began cumbersomely swinging about to reengage the enemy battleship, Marphissa began to reverse course by pivoting her remaining ships in place and starting to kill their momentum before accelerating back along the same vector in the opposite direction. Unlike *Midway*, though, she wouldn't be closing to firing range again until that enemy battleship had lost its fangs.

The Syndicate battleship no longer had the unbalanced thrust of its main propulsion shoving it to one side, but it had also lost a lot of thrusters aft. Even a ship with a lot less mass would have found it hard to maneuver under those circumstances, but a battleship faced serious trouble. And with only one main propulsion unit still working, it could not accelerate fast enough or change vectors quickly enough to have any hope of escape or evasion.

That left slugging it out with the *Midway*, and as Marphissa watched, the Syndicate battleship tried once again to swing its bow around in time to meet the latest charge.

But Kapitan Mercia had her thrusters and main propulsion still intact, so while the *Midway* remained a clumsy elephant compared to smaller warships, she was a graceful, light-footed elephant compared to the damaged enemy battleship.

Using her momentum to skate around the enemy battleship faster than it could turn, Mercia's battleship raked the enemy from one quarter to the other, destroying the last working main propulsion unit and smashing weapons, sensors, and anything else that wasn't fully protected by the battleship's armor.

CEO Boucher's battleship staggered, beginning a slow tumble under the force of the hits that its remaining thrusters strove to counter.

Having reduced her relative velocity to something nearly matching that of the Syndicate battleship, Mercia had *Midway* back in position within ten minutes and began hammering the enemy systematically, working her way up from the stern to smash section after section of the enemy warship while exposing *Midway* to only a few enemy weapons at a time.

"I've never seen it like this," Diaz said with awe as he watched the methodical destruction of the enemy battleship's weapons and remaining thrusters. "You look at a battleship and you know the weapons they carry and the defenses they have, but it isn't until you see something like this, with our battleship hurling out volley after volley that would each tear *Manticore* apart, and the other battleship soaking up all that damage and still going, that you really appreciate what terrible monsters they are."

"It's not pretty," Marphissa agreed. "If that ship hadn't done most of the damage at Kane, I might feel a little sorry for them."

"There must be a lot of snakes aboard forcing them—" Diaz began.

"I don't care," Marphissa said, her voice low and angry. "We had snakes aboard, and we did something. They're dying, but they could still do something."

They were doing something, but it consisted of attempts to continue fighting. The Syndicate battleship volleyed missiles at the *Midway*, but the range was so short that *Midway* could target the missiles with hell lances right after launch as the missiles were at a low relative velocity. The few missiles that survived failed to break through *Midway*'s shields.

Once their missiles were exhausted, the Syndicate crew tried firing bombardment projectiles at the *Midway* whenever a launcher was able to bear on her. But *Midway* was able to use her thrusters to twist out of the way of incoming rocks, adding in bursts of acceleration from her main propulsion when necessary. No launcher got more than a single bombardment projectile off before being knocked out, since they had to be visible to *Midway*'s weapons in order to fire on the battleship.

As the escorts watched the slow crushing of the Syndicate

battleship's ability to fight, *Gryphon* and *Hawk* rejoined Marphissa's formation, the light cruiser having managed to get enough thrusters working again to maneuver.

Midway had meticulously hammered about two-thirds of the hull of the enemy battleship when the enemy abruptly stopped firing.

"Hold fire," Marphissa ordered.

Mercia didn't look happy at the command. "The Syndicate battleship is still dangerous."

"I know, but if he starts firing again, you can continue reducing his defenses." Marphissa pointed to her display, where an image mostly covered with red damage markers represented the enemy ship. "If they are ready to surrender, we can use that battleship, even if only as a source of parts."

"The snakes won't surrender, Kommodor," Mercia insisted.

"I know that," Marphissa said. "The snakes on my ships didn't surrender, either. We got rid of them. If the crew on that battleship has finally had enough, they may be eliminating the snakes aboard as we speak."

"How long do you want me to wait?"

"I'll let you know." Marphissa ended the call, feeling annoyed. Mercia might have said she was ready to acknowledge Marphissa's authority when everything was going her way, but when Marphissa's orders had conflicted with Mercia's desires, there had been some obvious friction.

They waited, watching the mauled Syndicate battleship roll and tumble slowly through space. "Are we seeing any signs of what is happening inside?" Marphissa asked.

"Nothing, Kommodor," Senior Watch Specialist Czilla said. "No messages, no signs of activity, nothing being detected by our other sensors."

Another five minutes crawled by, while Marphissa tried to decide how much longer to wait before ordering Mercia to open fire again.

She felt a perverse desire to stretch out the time before such an order just to punish Mercia for being less than enthusiastically compliant, but rejected the thought. "If nothing happens in five minutes more," she told Mercia, "you are authorized to resume firing."

Mercia kept her expression and voice professionally dispassionate as she replied. "Yes, Kommodor. I will have *Midway* in position."

With just two minutes to go, activity finally occurred.

"Escape pod launch from the Syndicate battleship," Czilla reported. "Another . . . three . . . four more. They're coming out fast, lots of them."

"Get me contact with one of those pods," Marphissa ordered. "I want to know who is abandoning ship and why. Kapitan Mercia, continue holding your fire until we learn what is going on."

"I am not to target the escape pods?" Mercia asked.

"No. We do not— That is no longer policy, not where President Iceni has authority."

"O brave new world that has such people in it," Mercia said, citing the old quote usually used sarcastically. But she gave Marphissa a look that was anything but sarcastic or biting. "Sometimes I don't know whether these new policies are real until I see what President Iceni's people do when presented with opportunities to violate those policies."

"I hope you approve," Marphissa said, her tone sharper than she had intended.

"Yes, Kommodor. My apologies if earlier I did not act with sufficient respect."

She seemed sincere enough, so Marphissa waved a dismissive hand. "It takes time to adjust to new situations."

"It does indeed."

As far as the escape pods from the Syndicate battleship went, it also took a little time, a few more minutes, to gain contact with one of them while Marphissa waited with growing impatience.

"We have a pod," *Manticore*'s comm specialist announced.

"Show me," Marphissa ordered.

The virtual window that popped into existence before her showed the interior of a standard Syndicate warship escape pod, this one packed with personnel. Looking over the figures she could see, Marphissa judged that all were workers since no portions of executive or sub-CEO outfits could be seen under their survival suits. "I am Kommodor Marphissa of the Free and Independent Midway Star System. Who are you?"

The workers nearest the vid pickup looked at each other, then one middle-aged man licked his lips and answered. "Line Worker Tomas Fidor. Propulsion Section Five. Maintenance Office One. Engineering Department."

"What is happening on the battleship that you left?"

"We left . . . um . . . honored . . ."

"I am the Kommodor in command of Midway's warships in this star system," she said, hearing the snap of command enter her voice. "We are not Syndicate. I know that you left your battleship. I want to know why. Was an order given to abandon ship? Is there fighting going on inside that ship?"

Fidor nodded quickly, then shook his head. "No. I mean, yes. There was no order to abandon ship. The word was passed among the workers. There is fighting. The snakes, they are crazy. There are so many of them. A lot are dead, but we couldn't get them all."

"How many of the crew are left aboard?" Marphissa demanded. "How many snakes?"

The image fuzzed as something interfered with the signal, then cleared, showing the worker grinning nervously. "I don't know. Everyone was trying to get off. Everyone but the snakes."

"Where is CEO Boucher? Is she still alive?"

The worker's face spasmed with hate. "She is still alive. No one can get to her."

"Is CEO Boucher sealed into the bridge citadel?"

"Y-yes. No one can get in there. No one can get close."

"What about the weapons-control citadel and the engineering control citadel?" Marphissa asked.

"Weapons was abandoned. Nobody there anymore. The weapons-integration systems crashed, and the weapons couldn't fire from central control, so everyone left. Except some snakes, but they couldn't do anything."

Marphissa narrowed her eyes at the worker's image. "What about engineering?" she pressed.

"Engineering? Um . . . engineering . . ."

"I am trying to decide whether or not to board that battleship to gain possession of it," Marphissa lied. "I will be very unhappy if there is something I should know before that happens, and you do not tell me."

"I— You don't want to go aboard that unit! Just don't!"

"They've done something," Diaz said. "Before they left the battleship. Engineering specialist, are we picking up anything from the battleship?"

The engineering specialist standing watch on *Manticore*'s bridge answered immediately. "Minor fluctuations in the power core, Kapitan. That's understandable given the amount of damage the battleship has sustained. Different systems will be erratically dropping online and off-line in ways that cause core fluctuations as it copes with the variations in power demand."

"Is that the only explanation or the most likely explanation?"

The specialist did not hesitate. "The most likely, Kapitan. There is a chance it could also be early signs of instability in the core itself."

"What did you do?" Marphissa asked the worker, her voice low but commanding.

"I did nothing!"

"What is about to happen?"

The worker's expression visibly wavered with indecision.

"I can ask anyone else in any other escape pod," Marphissa said, her tone now implacable. "If you plan on living, one of my ships has to pick you up. Now, give me a straight and clear answer with no further delays."

"Y-yes, honored supervisor." The man swallowed, looking terror-struck. "There's a mechanism that the snakes installed. To cause an overload. After all the snakes in the engineering control areas died," he said, phrasing it as if the snakes had all just suddenly dropped dead of their own accord, "we modified it."

"Modified it?"

"It's on a timer. We think it will blow in about . . . what is the time now . . . about ten more minutes."

"*Ten minutes?*" Marphissa flared. "If the power core on that battleship overloads in ten minutes, a lot of your escape pods will still be within its danger radius! They can't accelerate fast enough to get clear!"

"We didn't want the snakes left aboard to have time to find out what we had done and override it!"

"Idiots," Diaz murmured, his eyes on his display. "Kommodor, our ships might be able to pick up some of the escape pods that will still be within the danger region—"

"No," Marphissa replied. "They jury-rigged something to put that self-destruct device on a timer. We don't know for certain when the power core will overload. I cannot risk any of my ships being caught by that blast." She hit her comm controls, cursing vengeance-minded workers who didn't stop to think through their plans for reprisal against their supervisors and the snakes. "All ships, this is Kommodor Marphissa. The Syndicate battleship's power core is rigged to overload in roughly ten minutes, possibly less. All units are to immediately use maximum acceleration to clear the danger radius around the battleship. Stay clear of the danger zone until I give permission to reenter it. All ships acknowledge and get moving!"

Midway was closest to the Syndicate battleship and had the farthest to go to clear the blast radius, but fortunately she was also by far the most heavily armored and shielded of the warships and thus best able to ride out the shock if it happened too quickly. Marphissa had barely finished speaking before *Midway*'s thrusters came to life on full, pivoting her to one side, the battleship's main propulsion kicking in as soon as *Midway*'s bow had swung far enough away from the enemy warship.

"All of our ships should be all right," Kapitan Diaz noted. "Five minutes less warning, and it would have been a different story."

"Are your sensors picking up definite instability indications from the battleship's power core yet?" Marphissa asked.

"Not yet," the engineering specialist answered. "Just what we had before. But, Kommodor, when we saw this snake device used at Midway, you remember the light cruiser they destroyed when it mutinied, there were no warning signs until the power core entered the last stages of overload, and those came with unusual rapidity."

"That's right." She looked at Diaz as another thought occurred to her. "How do we know those idiot workers actually set the overload device before they fled?"

"Did you see how scared they were?" Diaz answered. "They sure seemed frightened of being caught in that blast to me. Ah. All ships are clearing the danger radius, Kommodor. *Midway* is the last, and she will be beyond any danger within a minute."

"Good." Marphissa stared at her display. "See if your comm specialist can establish contact with the Syndicate battleship. I want to speak to their commander."

"Kommodor, that will be CEO Hua Boucher."

"I know. I want to speak to her," Marphissa repeated.

It took another half minute before a new virtual window appeared before Marphissa.

CEO Hua Boucher, the "Happy Hua" whose grandmotherly

appearance and pleasant demeanor had lured countless victims into deadly overconfidence or confessions, sat in the command seat on the battleship as if nothing could cause her to move from it. She had a frown creasing her usually cheerful face, but otherwise what could be seen of the bridge of the battleship had a jarring feel of the routine to it. Buried deep with the hull of the warship behind immense armor and the sheer mass of all the intervening compartments, the bridge was physically untouched by the battering which had been inflicted on the Syndicate battleship's hull. "What do you want?" Hua Boucher demanded like a disappointed elder.

Marphissa gazed back at her, marveling at how different outward appearances could be from the person inside. "I wanted to see the sort of human who could order the bombardment of Kane."

"They were traitors. They had murdered servants of the Syndicate. They had no right to expect any other fate," Hua Boucher explained, still in those disappointed tones.

"That's it?" Marphissa paused, trying to find words. "I grew up in the Syndicate. I know how horrible it is. But it is supposed to be efficient, it is supposed to be practical. Why kill all those people, why destroy so much? All you did was convince everyone in this part of space that the Syndicate cannot be trusted, that they must prepare to defend themselves against the Syndicate."

"Any other traitors will be dealt with in the same way," Hua Boucher said. From force of habit, her words came out sounding like a firm but gentle admonition.

"No," Marphissa said. "You can't keep that up any longer. You must know that. The Syndicate government on Prime must know that. Why? Why did you do something that you must have known would turn more people against you?"

"If one death does not convince traitors of their errors, then ten deaths will," Happy Hua said in her grandmotherly way. "If ten deaths do not, then a hundred will. If a hundred do not—"

Snake philosophy, laid out in the starkest possible terms. Marphissa looked away, trying to regain her composure. "You're about to die. Do you have any regrets at all?"

"Only that you did not die first." Happy Hua smiled. "But that may still happen. We may not be as easy to overcome as you think."

"We're not boarding your ship," Marphissa said.

"Kapitan," the engineering specialist said to Diaz, "we're seeing a sudden jump in power fluctuations on the battleship."

"How long do they have left?" Diaz asked.

"I estimate thirty seconds, Kapitan. No more than a minute."

Happy Hua was still gazing back at Marphissa, but with some amused puzzlement now. "Do you intend starving us out?"

"No," Marphissa said. She could see, in the background behind Hua Boucher, people suddenly rushing around on the Syndicate battleship's bridge. They no longer had any means of controlling their power core from the bridge, but their instruments could tell them what was happening. "I had no choice in this. The workers you terrorized, tortured, and murdered have had their revenge. *They* killed you. Take that thought to hell with you."

For the first time, Happy Hua looked rattled, her eyes widening. She started to turn to speak to someone at the back of the bridge.

Her image vanished.

"Overload, Kapitan," the engineering specialist said.

"We are well outside the danger region," Senior Watch Specialist Czilla said. "We will feel the shock wave, but it will have spread out too much to be a danger to us."

Diaz nodded, touching a control to speak throughout *Manticore*. "Brace for shock wave."

Manticore rocked like an oceangoing vessel hit by a large swell.

"No damage to *Manticore*, Kapitan," Czilla reported.

Diaz waved one hand in acknowledgment. "Kane is avenged, as are the crew who died aboard *Harrier*," he told Marphissa.

"And yet I have no joy," Marphissa murmured. "Only satisfaction that she will kill no more." She straightened and checked her display. The Hunter-Killer that was the sole surviving Syndicate warship in this star system was still fleeing toward the jump point for Kiribati.

Marphissa touched her comm controls. "*Midway*, you are detached to proceed at best speed to the inhabited world and provide support to our ground forces on that planet. All other ships, operate independently to recover surviving escape pods. Keep all Syndicate personnel you recover under guard until we can screen them to see if any snakes are among them.

"The space of this star system is ours. You have won it. For the people, Marphissa, out."

ICENI ate dinner in her office, seeking solitude to recover from the shock of the day's events and the stress of having dealt one-on-one with so many citizens without a single intermediary. It hadn't killed her, but it had been so different from anything in her experience that she was still trying to adjust to the mental and emotional strain of it.

"Madam President, we have received a message from the Alliance mobile forces. It is marked as a reply to your earlier message."

Iceni took a drink of wine before answering. "Send it to me. There's still no sign of Mehmet Togo?" She had wondered if he had somehow been trapped by the mobs, penned into some location from which he couldn't escape without attracting far too much attention. But if that had been the case, he should have been able to move again after the threatening mobs turned into participants in a planetwide festival that was still ongoing in many places.

"No, Madam President."

She peered at the command center supervisor. "How long have you been on duty? Didn't I speak to you this morning?"

"Yes, Madam President, you did, but we were ordered to remain on full alert until stood-down, so I have remained on duty."

Iceni barely managed not to roll her eyes in exasperation. Some senior supervisor had decided to play it as safe as possible by keeping all of the more junior personnel on full alert. "Stand down from alert status. Return to normal routine. Advise all offices of that, then you get some rest."

The supervisor smiled in sudden relief. "Thank you, Madam President. You . . . thank you."

She sighed as that window vanished and another appeared with Black Jack's message ready to play. If her supervisors started acting like those citizens in the plaza, there wouldn't be anyplace left for her to hide.

Iceni poured more wine and leaned back, determined to be as relaxed as possible while viewing Black Jack's message. If it was bad news, being tensed up wouldn't make it better. She touched the play command.

Black Jack must have sent his reply as soon as he received Iceni's message. He looked a bit stressed and worn, but given his responsibilities, that was understandable. Still, maybe someday she could give him a few pointers on managing his external appearance. Maybe at the same time he could give her pointers on dealing with masses of worshipful citizens.

"President Iceni, this is Admiral Geary," he began. "We came here only to escort the Dancers back to Midway. They are proceeding home from here on their own. We cannot remain in this star system one minute longer than absolutely necessary because of the danger that the hypernet gate may be blocked before we can leave. I don't know when any Alliance ships will be able to come through here again. Perhaps not until we figure out how to override that ability to block access to the gates. I regret that we cannot offer any assistance at this time and also that we cannot offer any suggestions as to the meaning of the message the Dancers sent you. Good luck, and may the living stars aid you. To the honor of our ancestors, Geary, out."

She sat thinking after the message had ended. She couldn't fault Black Jack for not wanting to be trapped here if the Syndicate used its trick to block access to the hypernet. Until it was learned how the Syndicate was able to do that at times and places of its choosing, and more importantly how to counteract or nullify the block, everyone had to treat the hypernet as a potential one-way street that could leave them stranded far from home.

It would be a good idea to keep as secret as possible that Black Jack had no idea when he might return with a fleet at his back. Not that Black Jack showed up very often, but the uncertainty tied with the amount of power that the ruler of the Alliance wielded surely helped discourage some parties from planning aggression against Midway Star System and its allies. The Syndicate wasn't the only problem out here.

May the living stars aid you. What exactly did that mean? She sent the query into her database, receiving a long answer about old religious beliefs and how they tied in with even older ones.

As she read, it gradually dawned on Iceni that the phrase meant that Black Jack was genuinely wishing for her success and invoking the most powerful influences he believed in to help her.

Well. That was good. That was very good.

Iceni raised her wineglass in a toast to a man who by now was somewhere nowhere in the hypernet. *You are a very good friend to have, Black Jack. Here's to what I hope will be a beautiful friendship.*

But thinking of friends and the support they could offer somehow led to thoughts of Artur Drakon and wondering whether *Midway* had reached Ulindi in time to make a difference. That took a lot of joy out of the moment.

FROM this high up, the city where the ground forces had landed didn't look too bad except for one large crater where the snake headquarters complex had once been and a big field littered with smaller craters that marked the site of the ground forces base. The base itself lay under an uneven, heavily cratered expanse that marked extensive surface-level bombardment.

Midway slid with ponderous grace into low orbit, hurling out bombardment projectiles that turned Syndicate artillery positions into more craters. A forest of hell lances danced downward from the battleship, tearing apart aerospace craft racing to hide or escape.

"Find the highest-power jamming sources," Kapitan Mercia told her bridge crew. "I want them taken out so we can speak with our ground forces."

"Bombardment?" her weapons specialist asked.

"Uh, no. Not unless they occupy isolated locations. We're not Syndicate anymore. The people . . . are safe from us." That felt very odd to say, but also very good. Mercia looked over at Bradamont, wondering if the Alliance officer was judging her, but instead Bradamont looked as if she was remembering unpleasant events. Of course. The Alliance had bombarded citizens, too. The realization that Bradamont would not be lording it over her about the Alliance's smug moral superiority in that regard (and all others) relieved Mercia, but also saddened her that such a thing had to be among their shared experiences. "Do you think humans will ever reach the point where something like Kane could not happen?" she asked Bradamont.

The Alliance officer looked back at her. "Humans seem to have too great a talent for that sort of thing. But I hope we can make such things as rare as possible."

"That's something worth working for," Mercia agreed.

"SOMETHING is going on in the Syndicate positions."

Drakon raised his head, blinking away fatigue. How many days had it been since the assault force landed? He wondered if another up patch would be a good idea but decided to put that off a little longer. "What are you seeing?"

Colonel Kai pursed his lips judiciously. "It looks like fighting."

"Fighting? *In* the Syndicate positions?"

"Yes, General. It could be a trick, of course, but to all appearances, the Syndicate troops encircling us are fighting each other at various points opposite my brigade."

"General?" Colonel Safir called in. "What Colonel Kai is talking about, I'm seeing that spreading into the parts of the Syndicate line facing me."

"Colonel Malin," Drakon called, "are we picking up anything about the activity we're seeing in the Syndicate positions?"

It took Malin a moment to answer. "General, there's still a lot of jamming, so we're not seeing any comms. Our sensors are spotting weapons fire that isn't aimed at us, though. Wait. Here's something. Watch this replay of an event that we just observed opposite sector five."

Drakon saw a small virtual window appear on his display, the image zooming on part of the Syndicate positions as a single figure in battle armor stumbled out into the open and began running at an angle, not toward the base or back into the Syndicate lines, but through the open area between them. Whoever it was had only taken a half dozen steps before weapon discharges could be seen coming from the buildings behind. The figure stumbled, tried to regain its feet, then fell and lay unmoving.

"Unfortunately," Malin said, "the lack of rank markers on the outside of the armor prevents us from knowing whether this was a worker, a supervisor, or a snake."

"Should we intervene?" Safir asked.

"It could be a trick," Kai said. "To lure us into sending troops into the open. That bit with the soldier shot down in plain sight was a bit too dramatic."

"Colonel Kai raises an important point," Malin said.

"There's a lot of weapon discharges going on out there," Safir argued. "If this is a trick, they are burning a lot of ammo and energy on it, and we've spotted other soldiers being hit inside the Syndicate positions."

Drakon zoomed in his focus from the base sensors and those on his soldiers that could see the events playing out in the Syndicate line. The command network automatically integrated all of those pictures to create a single view that showed everything that could be seen.

The open area between the outer defenses of the base and the first row of buildings had once been a flat, level expanse of pavement in some spots and grass in others, kept painfully clean and clear to avoid offering cover or concealment. Now it was littered with the remnants of expired chaff round decoys and pitted by craters of varying sizes from bombardment. The remains of the soldiers that Drakon's forces had lost assaulting the base were still out there, most of them hidden under the bodies of the much larger numbers of Syndicate ground forces who had died in repeated, futile attacks. A haze, born of the fighting, slowly dissipating chaff clouds, and the vestiges of the bombardments which had fallen on or near the open area, drifted slowly across Drakon's field of vision, partially obscuring his view.

The buildings where his own soldiers had sheltered before taking the base, and which had been occupied by Syndicate soldiers since then, were riddled with large and small holes on their first stories. Some were merely skeletons of buildings, the curtain walls within and on their exteriors having collapsed to leave bent frames standing. Rubble from the buildings had been mounded before the largest holes to provide cover and block views, and also formed into temporary, low walls across the wide streets separating blocks of the buildings to allow concealed movement behind them. The damage allowed fragmentary views of activity among the Syndicate soldiers. Drakon could get momentary glimpses of soldiers rushing through the buildings in groups of various sizes, spot weapons discharges that were not aimed at the base occupied by his own soldiers, and occasionally what looked like brief hand-to-hand encounters. But the partial views left him unable to know what he was not seeing and did not provide a complete enough picture to be sure of what he was seeing.

Finally, he shook his head. "The odds of its being a snake trick are too high. The snakes wouldn't hesitate to blow away one or a dozen soldiers to make a ruse look real. I'm also thinking that if we jump in, both sides in that fight might reunite to shoot at us."

"That could happen," Safir agreed reluctantly. "Just because they might be shooting their own officers and the snakes doesn't necessarily mean that they'd want us taking them prisoner."

"Do we have any more clues to what is going on?" Drakon asked.

Malin frowned at his display. "I've done a search for possible indications and found something. Within the last fifteen minutes, our sensors have picked up some significant ground tremors within one hundred kilometers of here, some within twenty kilometers."

Drakon called up the data. "Looks like bombardment effects. Not a big, concentrated one, but a number of different strikes on single targets. That could have something to do with what we're seeing in the Syndicate lines though I don't know where the Kommodor could have gotten her hands on more rocks."

A pulse of sound called attention to another development. "All high-powered jamming within three hundred kilometers of us has ceased," a comm specialist soldier reported. "Someone is trying to contact us on authorized frequencies. They have our recognition codes."

"Then what's the problem?" Drakon asked. "It's one of our warships, isn't it?"

"General, they identify themselves as the *Midway*."

"The *Midway*?" It took a few seconds for the meaning of that to work its way through his tired brain. "Our battleship? Where the hell did they come from? Patch them through to me."

Drakon recognized the woman gazing at him from the command seat on the battleship's bridge. He and Iceni had both had to agree on giving Mercia that command. "Kapitan Freya Mercia," she formally introduced herself. "At your service, General Drakon. Kommodor Marphissa wishes me to advise you that the Syndicate warships in this star system have been destroyed with the exception of one Hunter-Killer which is fleeing for Kiribati and unfortunately cannot be intercepted. *Midway* is here to provide whatever support you require. We have already taken out a number of long-range threats to your positions, as well as active jamming sites covering your region of the planet."

"Welcome to Ulindi, Kapitan," Drakon said, only then realizing how dry his throat was. He hastily swallowed some water, then smiled. "I don't know how the hell you got here, but it is very nice to see you."

"President Iceni sent us on after you when she received information that Ulindi might be a trap," Mercia said.

"She did?" He couldn't wait to talk to Iceni about that. "And your weapons are working?"

"As that Syndicate battleship discovered to its sorrow. Would you like us to demonstrate on the Syndicate ground forces encircling you?"

Drakon checked his views of the Syndicate positions again, where all-out warfare was apparently raging. "Not yet. I think your appearance, on top of being pushed beyond their limits, has caused substantial portions of the Syndicate ground forces to rethink their allegiance to the Syndicate."

She gave him a curious look. "Still, any that remain would be a threat."

"Possibly. Or any that remain could form the nucleus for the ground forces of an independent Ulindi. Everybody down here used to be Syndicate, Kapitan."

"Everybody up here, too. This mercy to the enemy thing is a little hard to get used to."

"There's still one set of enemies that we can't afford to offer mercy. Do you have a location on the snake alternate command center?" Drakon asked.

"If the information we were provided is accurate, we do," Mercia said.

"We need to make sure it is eliminated. Colonel— Our agent was supposed to disable the snakes' ability to detonate their buried nukes from the alternate command center, but we haven't heard from her and don't know if she succeeded."

"In a few minutes, you won't have to worry, General." Mercia turned to give the commands.

Malin was staring at Drakon. "General, if Colonel Morgan is still in or near that snake complex—"

"I know. Bran, I know." Drakon met Malin's gaze with his own. "But we can't risk everyone else on the possibility that Roh Morgan is still alive and still in or close to the snake alternate command center. If the Syndicate ground forces are falling apart, the snakes could decide to set off those nukes at any moment, or at least the nukes under this city."

Malin closed down, emotion vanishing from his face. He nodded. "That is true, General. We have no choice. It must be done as soon as possible. I know that if we did have a choice, you would act on it."

"I would." Despite everything that Morgan had done, and everything that she might yet do if still alive, she deserved that much for the services she had rendered him in the past.

SUPREME CEO Haris walked rapidly through the halls of the Internal Security Service alternate command center, moving toward the entrance of the secret bolt-hole that would let him escape to a concealed hangar where a shuttle awaited, a shuttle equipped with the latest stealth gear available to the Syndicate. Several heavily armed bodyguards walked three meters ahead of him and several more three meters behind him.

Haris wiped sweat from his brow, trying to keep from breaking into a run, trying to figure out what had happened and how it had happened. After a career spent focused on promotion, on sucking up to his superiors and frequent transfers to punch as many tickets as possible, he hadn't actually managed to acquire all that many concrete job skills. Doing the job hadn't been the point. Not for him. Doing the job got in the way of maneuvering for that next promotion.

It was a career pattern that had produced some unexpected problems when he was secretly told to proclaim himself Supreme CEO of this star system. The biggest problem, to CEO Haris's way of thinking, was that being diverted off the main ISS track meant he no longer had any promotions to vie for. That robbed him of purpose. The other problem, which Haris found annoying, was his lack of experience with the kind of day-to-day work that needed to be done when he could no longer count on someone else's doing it. His current crop of subordinates had shown a growing tendency to fall down on doing his job, despite Haris's attempts to motivate them by such measures as random arrests and executions.

In fact, he had started wondering if his superiors had chosen him for this job specifically because of his lack of effective skills other than those focused on promotion. Had they expected him to be unable to spot the ultrasecret preparations for the trap intended for Midway's forces at Ulindi?

He *had* missed them—he had known only what he was told—but how could that be his fault? Hadn't he simply been what his superiors wanted? That had always worked in the past.

Nothing had worked this time, though. The rebel ground forces had not only survived, they had wiped out Haris's own brigade and taken his ground forces base. The Syndicate division had slaughtered itself attacking the base and, according to the reports he was receiving, was now disintegrating as the workers and some of the executives mutinied. CEO Boucher's flotilla had been smashed by a battleship that the rebels weren't even supposed to have in working condition, and now that rebel battleship was in orbit and turning what was left of the visible Internal Security Service infrastructure on the planet into tangled junk.

Fine. His superiors had left him without guidance, and his subordinates had failed. He was leaving, and the subordinates and workers could have the mess created by their own failure to support him properly. Not for long, though. Once Haris reached the entrance to the bolt-hole, he would enter the detonation codes to begin the countdowns for the nuclear weapons buried under every city on this planet. He would be well clear of the surface before nuclear fires terminated every incompetent on the planet along with every enemy on the surface.

As for him, he would just consider this another transfer, an opportunity to identify new positions to vie for in other star systems. It would take some creative wording to make the events here seem like a success justifying another promotion, but that was the one job skill Haris knew very well.

The end of the corridor came into sight as Haris and his bodyguards turned a corner and passed a security checkpoint whose occupants didn't realize they would soon have the honor of sacrificing themselves to cover his escape. Another few hundred meters and—

The ceiling ahead suddenly erupted as a rectangular patch going all the way across the hall and perhaps four meters wide was outlined by a strip of fire. Haris stared, not recognizing that the cut-through represented breaching tape laid on the floor of the level above this one, breaching tape powerful enough to cut instantly through the armor in the ceiling. If he had been able to think quickly enough, he would have wondered what had happened to the guards and security sensors covering that section of the complex above him.

The section of ceiling outlined by the explosion dropped onto the bodyguards who had been walking just in front of Haris. There must have been a pinhole camera watching this corridor from above, to ensure the explosion was triggered at just the right moment.

Haris hadn't really noticed the woman standing on the segment of ceiling as it fell, riding down on the broken fragment as if it were the floor of an elevator. He hadn't noticed her wild smile, or the weapon in her hand as it fired three times, and never realized that three shots had slammed into his head before the falling portion of the armored ceiling had time to crush the leading set of bodyguards.

As his lifeless body dropped limply, Haris was also unaware of the corridor's exploding into a storm of gunfire as his surviving bodyguards at the rear poured an avalanche of fire at the assassin.

THE bombardment that *Midway* aimed at the concealed snake alternate command center fell through the sky as frightened citizens huddled and watched the fiery tracks. But the rocks did not fall on any of them. Instead, the buildings and parking lots of a drab industrial park were turned into a mass of rubble occupying the bottom of a crater. Anyone examining the crater would have found among the rubble the remnants of many things that had no place in an industrial park and would have noted that its depth implied quite a few layers of floors underground, but the people of Ulindi had a lot of other things to worry about at the moment. They couldn't spare time for yet another pile of wreckage, or for wondering who might have died in it.

CHAPTER THIRTEEN

"THE fighting in the Syndicate lines is dying down," Colonel Safir reported.

Malin nodded to Drakon. "Yes, sir. We're seeing indications that at most spots, the fighting is ending."

"Are we seeing any indications as to who won?" Drakon asked pointedly.

"No, sir. There's still fighting going on opposite sector two, and we're spotting movement of soldiers from sectors one and three converging on the areas where combat is still under way."

"That sounds like someone is in command." Drakon pointed to the comm specialist. "Try to punch a message through to the Syndicate soldiers. Use the standard frequencies and codes from before we revolted. They should be able to read those."

"What do you intend doing, General?" Safir asked.

"I intend finding out what's going on before I decide what else to do. There are times to be bold, but this isn't one of them. We're still just two brigades, and even though we've done a lot of damage to the

Syndicate forces out there, we've taken plenty of damage ourselves, and we still don't know how many soldiers they had to start with. They could still outnumber us, they could still have reserves that are heading this way right now, and for all we know, the loyalists out there finished off the soldiers who revolted."

"Our position is still tenuous," Colonel Kai agreed.

Drakon saw Malin smile at that. Kai would have felt their position was tenuous if they had ten times the numbers of the enemy and were dug into the best fortifications humanity had ever constructed.

But all Malin said was, "That could well be so."

It took the comm specialist several minutes before he turned to Drakon. "General, I've established contact with an executive third class who is willing to talk with you."

"Well, isn't that nice of the executive," Drakon grumbled. He knew he looked like someone who had been in his battle armor way too long through desperate fighting, but that was fine. Anyone whose appearance was perfect after supposedly leading troops under these conditions would very likely be a fake who wouldn't be worth talking to.

The executive third class didn't look as bad as Drakon, but she didn't look anything like fresh and perky, either. "What's a general?" she asked as her face's image appeared before Drakon.

"CEO-equivalent," Drakon said.

"Are you a CEO?"

The question came with enough heat behind it to cause Drakon to shade his reply. "I'm a general. My brigade commanders aren't sub-CEOs. They're colonels. We stopped being Syndicate a while back. We stopped acting like Syndicate a while back."

"You don't look like a CEO," the executive admitted. "Are there any snakes in there with you?"

"None that are still alive that we know of. We're still screening prisoners to see if we can spot any snake agents hidden among them."

"Prisoners?" The executive said the word as if it were totally foreign and incomprehensible to her. "You took prisoners? What, from the brigade that was supposed to hold that base?"

"A lot of them, yeah," Drakon said. "Others from one of the attacks you people launched on us. We sent out a counterattack and brought in a couple hundred, plus about forty wounded."

"You— Who are you? We were told that you were traitors trying to set up some warlord arrangement, working for a rogue CEO."

Drakon grinned. "That's what your CEO and the snakes told you? Did you believe them?"

"No." The executive grinned back, a baring of teeth that was only partly about humor. "But all that tells me is that they lied, which I already knew. It doesn't tell me who you really are."

"Fair enough," Drakon said. "We fight for the free and independent star system of Midway. The Syndicate no longer rules there. There are no snakes there."

"Then who is in charge there?"

"President Iceni. Me." Drakon felt ridiculous saying the next words, but they were increasingly true. "And the people."

"The people?" The executive laughed. "Do you think I'm that stupid?"

"No," Drakon said. "Actually, you're impressing me. What's your name?"

"Executive Third Class Gozen," the woman said, both face and voice defiant.

"Well, Executive Third Class Gozen, who's in charge out there? You?"

"I'm in charge of what's left in this part of the line."

"What about the snakes with you?"

"As of three minutes ago, there aren't any snakes with us. Except for dead ones."

Drakon nodded, smiling. "It looks like we have something in common."

"You and I might, but not the units opposite me," Gozen said. "The snakes won there. We just wiped out a last pocket of them over here and are setting up defenses on each side facing out."

"Do you want any help dealing with those units opposite you?"

Executive Gozen gazed at Drakon with a flat expression. "Look . . . General . . . I may not want any snakes shooting me for not being happy at charging into another senseless attack, but that doesn't mean I want to help you kill people in units that are part of my division. They're stuck over there, maybe some of them helped the snakes, I don't know, but others literally have guns to their heads forcing them to keep fighting. So, no, I don't want your help killing more of my comrades."

Drakon nodded again. "You seem to have quite an attitude problem, Executive Gozen."

"You're not the first person to tell me that."

"All right. You've been straightforward with me, I'll be straightforward with you. We came to Ulindi to get rid of Supreme CEO Haris. We thought he had rebelled against the Syndicate, but apparently that was part of a plan to lure us here."

Gozen shook her head. "I don't know anything about that. I haven't heard of any Haris. My unit only landed three days ago. What's a Supreme CEO?"

"Beats me," Drakon said. "Anyway, we didn't come here to conquer the place, or to die. We came here to get rid of the snakes and let the locals decide how they should run things."

"Wow. You *do* think I'm stupid."

"Executive Gozen, I don't have forever to talk to you before I make up my mind what to do. I'd advise you to listen," Drakon said. "Midway doesn't have enough ground forces and firepower to conquer and control other star systems. We can help other star systems get rid of the Syndicate and the snakes, but we can't impose our own rule. Trying to occupy and garrison Ulindi is beyond our means, but in any case, we don't want to. We had too much of that under the Syndicate.

Taking out the Syndicate here at Ulindi was a defensive move by us to remove a nearby threat. Give us credit for being able to recognize that action was in our self-interest. If you're going to stop fighting us, if you're going to stop trying to support the Syndicate, I don't care what you do as long as you don't try to set yourself up as a warlord who's a danger to nearby star systems that Midway has pledged to help defend. But I cannot allow functional, loyal Syndicate ground forces to remain active on this planet and in this star system."

Executive Gozen looked back at Drakon for a few moments before replying. "You don't have the firepower? You do know there's a battleship in orbit, right?"

"Yeah. That's ours. It's new. It wasn't supposed to be operational yet."

"It's operational."

"So I understand. It could bombard this planet until there was nothing left, but it can't control the planet or the people on it. And it's not going to stay here. It's going home with us because we need that battleship to defend Midway. So tell me, what are you going to do, Executive Gozen?"

"You're using Syndicate equipment. Have you got any good code monkeys . . . General?"

"As a matter of fact," Drakon said, "I have some of the best damned code monkeys in human-occupied space."

"Really?" Gozen grinned for real this time. "How do you know that?"

"They've told me that more times than I can count."

"I can send you a virus," Gozen said, suddenly all business. "We've been blocked from linking with anybody on the other side where the snakes are still in charge. If you can figure out how to get this virus into their network, it will identify snakes for you with a distinctive symbol on battle armor targeting displays."

"That could come in handy." Drakon said. "What's the deal? What do you want in exchange for it?"

"If you go in against them, you kill the snakes. No one else."

"What if someone else is shooting at us?"

"Look . . . just do your best. Say you'll do your best. I'll take that."

"Why?" Drakon asked.

"Because . . ." Gozen made a face. "Because you've listened to me and explained things, when the sort of commanders I've been dealing with would have long since told me to shut up and comply. And because the soldiers I've got over here are good, they're good men and women and they know their jobs and they are brave, but a lot of their friends have died, and they have been pushed past all limits, they're disorganized, exhausted, and burnt-out right now. I can't get at the snakes holding the rest of what's left of our division hostage, and I don't think I can stop them, or you, if an attack comes. That's why."

"You've been bluffing this whole time?" Drakon asked. "Seriously?"

"Yes, sir, honored CEO," Gozen said.

"Executive, I don't know what you want to do when this is all over, but if you're looking for a job and pass the security screening, I would really like to have an officer of your caliber. Now, I'll have my comm specialist bounce you a link to send that virus over, and we'll see if my people can make those snakes light up."

"You just offered me a job?" Gozen laughed. "You must be a glutton for punishment."

"You're not the first person to tell *me* that."

"All right, General. I'll tell you one other thing I'll do for you. I'll try to get word across to the soldiers still under snake control that you guys take prisoners. That ought to help both of us, right? They won't fight as hard, and more of the ones who are still alive will stay that way. Let me know before you go on the attack, so I can make sure you know where my lines are."

"Do you know where your former CEO and his command staff are?" Drakon asked.

"That I don't mind giving you," Gozen said. A coordinate appeared on Drakon's display. "That is where the exalted CEO Nassiri and his staff was in place. You will note that it is in a comfortable building a ways back from the front lines."

"And there's a bar nearby," Drakon said as his display located the building on the city map that matched the coordinates.

"Yes, sir. Convenient for the CEO, huh?" Gozen looked to one side, listening. "Got to go, General. Give me that link and remember what I asked in exchange for it."

"I don't forget that sort of thing," Drakon said just before Gozen's image disappeared.

Drakon pointed a finger at his comm specialist. "We need a link passed to that executive which can be used to download a file that will be quarantined and sent to the code apes."

"I'm on it, General."

"Sir," Malin said, a frown uncharacteristically making his feelings clear, "we should treat everything regarding any alleged Syndicate rebels with extreme caution."

"I'm aware of that," Drakon said. "Is there something in particular about Executive Gozen that concerns you?"

"She clearly impressed you, General, just as Executive Ito impressed Colonel Rogero."

"She wasn't trying to impress me," Drakon pointed out, "unlike Executive Ito, who acted like a puppy happy to find a new owner. Don't worry, Bran. If Gozen wants to join us, she'll get a full security screening. For now, I want you to contact the guards for our prisoners. Have them ask if anyone knows Executive Gozen."

Malin frowned again, this time in thought. "To confirm that Gozen is not a snake agent?"

"No. If she's that good, they wouldn't know. If we find any, I want to release one or two of them and send them back to Gozen so she'll know we really took prisoners. If we can get the former Syndicate soldiers with her to submit to us, it could save some of our own people's lives, and from what I saw of her, Gozen will be able to convince them to do what she says."

"But, General," Malin tried again, "someone with that kind of behavior toward her superiors could not possibly have survived in the Syndicate system. Unless she was a snake."

"That's a good point, and I'll want to know what kept her from being shipped off to a labor camp. Now call those guards."

"Yes, sir."

It took ten minutes for the code apes to call back. "Can you do it, Sergeant Broom?" Drakon asked.

"Yes, General. It's a nice worm. It's a beautiful worm. We just have to use a horse to get it into the Syndicate network."

"A horse?"

"A Trojan horse," Broom explained. "I hear there's a prisoner going to be released? Sent back to the ones that killed all of their snakes?"

"How did you— Never mind. Stop hacking the private command circuits."

"Yes, sir," Sergeant Broom said. "I mean, no, sir, that would be improper spying on my superiors."

"Which is exactly the sort of thing the Syndicate liked to order you to do when we were under Syndicate command. I mean it. Mess around with other systems to find vulnerabilities all you want, but if you find any more back doors into my private command circuits, I want them shut and locked. But what does releasing a prisoner to Executive Gozen's group have to do with—" Drakon smiled with sudden understanding. "We send back another prisoner?"

"To the other side, yes, sir. They don't know we talked to Executive Gozen. We say we don't know what's going on, but there are obviously two factions, and can we make a deal with you if the other guys are still hard-core Syndicate? Not really. But the prisoner we send to the snake side has a very special present hidden in their battle armor's systems, and when the snakes link with them to find out what the former prisoner can tell them, they open a path for our little friend here."

Drakon nodded. "The snake firewalls won't stop it?"

"They won't see it," Sergeant Broom said. "Nor will the security sharks guarding the network software. It will be totally stealthy thanks to its being embedded in an innocuous program that is so uninteresting nothing will notice it." He smiled and tapped his helmet where the comm link was located. "I call the program my Serge Protector."

"I see. Good." Drakon fixed the sergeant with a glare. "If I have our systems screened to see if this innocuous-seeming software is anywhere in *our* systems, I won't find anything, will I?"

"No, sir. Absolutely not. You won't find anything when you run that scan."

"Even if I ran it right now?" Drakon asked, seeing the reaction that question provoked. "Sergeant, you are valuable to me because you think and work outside the box. That's why I got you out of that Syndicate labor camp just before you were going to be shot for hacking into the wrong network."

"Yes, sir. I'll never forget your getting me out of there alive," Broom said. "You told me you needed someone who would spot things that no one else would in places that no one else would think to look, and I've been doing that."

"And you do it very well," Drakon said. "The Syndicate didn't get anywhere in our systems that I didn't want them to be before we revolted, and neither did the snakes. More importantly, they couldn't tell that there were parts of our systems that they weren't seeing. That took one hell of a good programmer to pull off. And you and your people have spotted every attempted intrusion into our systems since then. But if you wander too far outside the box, it becomes a problem for me, and that means it becomes a problem for you. I'm not going to order you to be shot like your last boss did, but I need to know you're not getting into stuff that would make both of us unhappy. Maybe when Colonel Morgan gets back, I'll have her run some checks on your work."

"Colonel Morgan? That's *really* not necessary, sir."

"I'll think about it," Drakon said. Sooner or later, word might get around that Morgan was presumed dead, but until then, fear of her would remain useful. "Right now, let's find a prisoner who meets our needs and get his systems loaded with our special delivery for the snakes."

It took about twenty more minutes to set up the whole thing, while Drakon alerted both Kai and Safir to be ready to sally out if the snake-controlled Syndicate soldiers launched attacks on the rebellious soldiers commanded by Executive Gozen. "Colonel Safir," he said, as they once again gathered for a virtual conference, "when the worm has been delivered, we're going to hit the snakes opposite your positions. They need to be priority targets. If we can take them down, resistance from the remaining Syndicate ground forces should collapse."

Colonel Malin indicated points on the display's map. "We acquired a large supply of additional chaff rounds from the stockpiles in this base. We'll be able to screen your approach to the Syndicate positions."

"Have we got enough chaff to extend the coverage for another twenty meters to each side?" Safir asked. "According to this plan, we're going in against the center of the still-loyal Syndicate troops. I don't want to catch flanking fire as we charge."

"That's a good idea," Drakon said. "Do we have enough chaff to do that?"

Malin frowned as he checked the stocks. "Yes, sir."

"Good. We'll have your flanks covered, Colonel. Penetrate the center, wipe out the snakes there, then pivot your troops to both sides and roll up the rest of the Syndicate loyalists before they can throw up internal lines of defense." He pointed to lines bisecting the rows of buildings. The Syndicate positions in the ruined buildings facing the base formed a large square, the square now divided, with about two-thirds loosely held by the recent mutineers and the remaining third along one of the sides and part of another side held by the still-loyal Syndicate soldiers, their defenses now facing both inward at Drakon's troops and cutting across the lines of the square to face the rebellious troops. "These mark the positions held by Executive Gozen's soldiers. Make sure your soldiers don't shoot at anyone on or beyond those lines."

"No problem, General, as long as they aren't shooting at us. Speaking of which, while we're rolling up these loyalists, are my people allowed to shoot at Syndicate soldiers who aren't snakes?" Safir asked.

"Yes," Drakon said. "Anybody who is shooting at them. The best information we have is that the ground forces still under snake control are not happy or highly motivated, so there's a good chance you won't encounter much resistance except from the snakes themselves. The fact that the snakes haven't tried to hit Executive Gozen's positions is a pretty clear sign that the soldiers they still control are unreliable or worn-out or both. But if they fight us, you are authorized to deal with resistance from any source."

"Good." Safir grimaced. "I've been resting my guys in shifts, but they are pretty tired, too, General. If we hit anything hard, they might stumble."

"I understand. Both sides in this fight are reeling. But we've got enough left in us for a good punch that should knock out what's left of our opponents." He indicated the virtual map again. "The remaining Syndicate forces are spread a lot thinner than we were defending this base. They've taken heavy losses, and have a lot more frontage to cover. We should have a much easier time breaking their line than they had trying to break ours."

Colonel Kai studied the plan. "What if Executive Gozen sends her soldiers after us while Colonel Safir is attacking the snakes?"

"Then you take care of them," Drakon said. "Your brigade will peel off a few units to help cover the area of the base perimeter that Colonel Safir's soldiers will be vacating during their attack, but you'll have plenty of troops left facing Gozen's positions if she tries to stab us in the back. I'll be very surprised if that happens, but your brigade is insurance if it does."

"How do we know if the worm has made it into the snake systems?" Safir asked.

"We're employing our Trojan horse prisoner for that, too. Our code apes are using him to also sneak in a linked worm that will trick the Syndicate comm systems into sending a single microburst that will alert us when the snake-targeting worm is in place. That microburst will be our signal to attack."

Safir suddenly laughed despite the fatigue lining her face. "Let's see if I have that right, General. When the worm from the apes tells us the snakes are lit up by our horse, we attack."

He couldn't help smiling. "Exactly. You might want to phrase it differently when you brief your assault force, though."

"No, sir. That's exactly how I want to tell it to them. They'll remember that, no matter how tired they are."

"General," Kai said, "would it not be wiser to simply have the *Midway* bombard those buildings held by the loyalists? We could wipe them out without any risk to us."

"That's true," Drakon said. "But the loyalists might see the bombardment coming with enough time to evacuate into the next row of buildings behind them, the ones they occupied before. If I know snakes, they've been refusing to allow any retreat by the soldiers who are still loyal to the Syndicate. But if they see a big bombardment coming down on their heads, they'll all run, and if those units get out into the city, we'll have the human resource director's own time trying to catch them."

Safir nodded. "I'd rather finish it now. Did you know that people used to say *the devil* instead of *the human resource director*?"

"What's the devil?" Kai asked.

"Something like a human resource director, I guess."

"There's another factor," Drakon said. "Executive Gozen, and the soldiers with her, don't want more of their comrades to die than necessary. Flattening those buildings in an attempt to kill everyone in them would make us look like someone who couldn't be trusted and doesn't care any more for human life than the Syndicate CEOs. Some of the survivors from this division may help form the core of a new defense force for Ulindi, and I want them to see us as trustworthy."

"And not see us as Syndicate," Colonel Kai said. "I understand. I was not aware of all of the issues that long-term planning had to take into account."

"When are we doing this, General?" Safir asked.

"As soon as you're ready. It's important to hit the snakes before they can rest too long."

Safir could be seen scanning her display, reviewing data on her soldiers. "Fifteen minutes, to brief my people, get them fully supplied for the assault, and get them in position."

Drakon nodded. "Good. Colonel Malin, prepare to release the prisoners. I want them walking toward their respective parts of the line out there in exactly fifteen minutes."

"What about the division's CEO and his staff?" Malin asked. "Do we ask *Midway* to take them out?"

"I don't know if they're still in the location they occupied before Executive Gozen's contact with them was severed. Wherever they are, once we take the rest of the Syndicate line out, I expect the CEO to stampede for safety with part of the staff. *Midway* will spot the vehicles or shuttles, and I'll decide what to do from there. All right. Let's go."

Fifteen minutes later, Drakon watched in separate virtual windows as one freed prisoner walked slowly, hands held out and open, toward the positions held by Executive Gozen's soldiers, and another freed prisoner in the same posture stepped toward the Syndicate positions still controlled by the snakes.

"It is always possible," Malin murmured to Drakon, "that the snakes will simply shoot the prisoner rather than interrogate."

"I thought of that," Drakon said. "But I think the snakes are desperate to find out more about our status, and the only way they can get that information is by talking to that prisoner we just sent them."

The prisoner who was headed for the positions controlled by the snakes clearly wasn't as confident as Drakon about the reception awaiting him. He kept stumbling over the many imperfections in the fought-over and bombarded ground, his hands held as high as he could.

Drakon saw the first freed prisoner reach Executive Gozen's positions and be brought in.

The second freed prisoner reached a spot just outside the Syndicate positions and stood there, apparently reacting to instructions.

"Stand by with the chaff rounds," Drakon said. "Colonel Safir, get ready to go."

"The snakes haven't brought the prisoner in yet, General," Malin protested.

"They're not going to," Drakon said. "I just realized what they're doing. They're going to do a remote interrogation using comm circuits, then kill him to avoid the risk that he is loaded with some kind of physical weapon." He felt sick at the thought that he had ordered the prisoner to his death that way, but until this moment had not imagined that even the snakes would be that paranoid. "They're snakes. Why the hell didn't I expect them to act like snakes?"

Malin's hands hovered over the firing commands for the chaff rounds. "General, none of us—"

"General, the microburst just came in!" the comm specialist reported.

"Fire," Drakon said to Malin. "Colonel Safir, we're launching chaff."

The chaff rounds were being fired before he finished the sentence.

The freed prisoner stumbled backward, then fell.

"They shot him just before we launched," Malin said.

"He'll be the last victim of those snakes," Drakon growled. "Safir, go when you're ready."

The chaff rounds were blooming in front of the Syndicate positions, throwing out every manner of decoy. Safir shouted "At them! For Colonel Gaiene!" then, with an ululating cry, led her assault force against the Syndicate positions.

A barrage of fire met them, the defenders firing blindly into the chaff and scoring few hits. Drakon had called up a view from Safir's armor, seeing the smoke and assorted decoys from the chaff clouds looming ahead, then Safir plunged into the chaff, and he lost the link. The only information he still had was an estimated position on her based on her last-known rate of progress.

"What's going on elsewhere, Bran?" Drakon asked, not wanting to take his attention away from Safir's assault.

"It's quiet in the sectors facing Executive Gozen's forces," Colonel Malin replied. "We haven't picked up any artillery coming in yet against Colonel Safir's attack."

"The *Midway* did a lot of damage to the Syndicate artillery," Drakon said. "Our assault should be clearing the chaff any second now."

His display flickered, updated, flickered again, then steadied. Once again, he had a clear view from Safir's battle armor in the seconds before the attack hit the Syndicate positions.

The weapons of the defenders had been ineffective while firing blindly into the chaff. With the attack clearing the chaff, the defenders had a short period in which they could use their targeting systems to fire with extreme accuracy against Safir's troops. It was the moment Drakon had dreaded. Even though the Syndicate defenders were covering more ground with fewer people, and even though the defenders were exhausted from launching attacks for days, Safir's soldiers could take a lot of casualties before reaching the Syndicate positions.

But in those few seconds, Drakon could see that most of the defenders' fire was still badly aimed. Only a small percentage of the shots hit the attackers with the accuracy expected of targeting systems, most of the rest of the enemy fire going wide. *They're not trying to hit us,* Drakon saw with relief. Had Gozen gotten word to the Syndicate soldiers that they could surrender and count on being taken prisoner? Or had the Syndicate soldiers been so badly used that they simply didn't care anymore?

Scarcely impeded by the mostly ineffectual defensive fire, Safir's soldiers crashed into the Syndicate line, in many cases literally smashing through what was left of ground-floor walls or into Syndicate soldiers who did not manage to dodge in time. To the naked eye, nothing distinguished the battle armor of regular ground forces from that of the snakes, but on the displays of Drakon's soldiers, some of the enemy symbols glowed a poisonous green instead of the usual red. The green symbols vanished so rapidly they seemed to dissolve as the attackers pressed into the Syndicate positions, wiping out the snakes in this area.

As the last snake fell, weapons swung to bear on Syndicate soldiers, who themselves aimed at Drakon's troops. For a long moment that lasted only a second or two, both sides held their fire, looking at each other.

Then Safir opened her helmet visor and yelled at the Syndicate soldiers. "We came here to kill snakes! Not you! Drop your weapons, and we'll go finish off the snakes left on this side!"

Several Syndicate soldiers threw down their weapons, then others followed in a rush. "Third Company, guard our new friends!" Safir ordered, resealing her helmet. "First and Third Battalions, wheel right and hit them! Second and Fourth Battalions, follow me to the left!"

On both sides of the breach in the Syndicate lines, the attackers ran into disorder. The snakes had ordered the troops under their control to simultaneously shift fronts and counterattack toward the breach, which in theory would have been good tactics for hitting Drakon's assault from both sides. But in practice, tired, reluctant Syndicate soldiers did not move quickly and surely, and the soldiers nearest the edges of the penetration had already begun falling back in disarray as the snakes nearest them were killed by the leading elements of the attackers. What should have been a fast change of facing and reinforcement turned into a tangled mass of soldiers who blocked each other and milled about in confusion. Snakes screamed new orders or demands to follow previous orders, adding to the chaos. Some of the snakes began firing at their own soldiers, the traditional Syndicate method to force compliance when all else failed, and many of the overwrought Syndicate troops began firing back, targeting not only the snakes but also any executives or other supervisors within reach.

Safir's attacks ran into masses of Syndicate soldiers too busy fighting each other to pay much attention to Drakon's forces. "Get the snakes!" Safir ordered, her soldiers taking up positions wherever they could get clean lines of sight and nailing snakes as fast as they could. "Split and go around this mess. Keep moving until you reach the lines held by Gozen's people and don't leave any snakes alive behind you!"

The attack split and split again, Safir's soldiers breaking into smaller groups as they pressed through the broken buildings and dodged piles of rubble or strong points of resistance. Drakon felt pride as he watched them, knowing that regular Syndicate troops could not have operated that way, using initiative, speed, and adaptability to continue their assault while overrunning or isolating the defenders they encountered. But he had trained his soldiers to think for themselves, and it paid off in fights like this.

And everywhere Safir's soldiers went, the poisonous green markers on their helmet displays that marked snakes went out like blown candles.

When the Third Battalion reached the line of defenders facing Gozen's rebellious troops and wiped out the snakes there, the defenders simply dropped their weapons and ran toward their former comrades under Gozen's command, hands held out and arms wide.

"Colonel?" a lieutenant asked. "Is it all right if they surrender to the other Syndicate ground forces?"

"The others aren't Syndicate anymore," Safir replied, her breath short from following her soldiers through the maze of shattered buildings. "Make sure they leave their weapons, though. And make sure none of them bolt into the city."

By that time, Second Battalion had reached the other side of what had been the remaining Syndicate positions, where most of the Syndicate soldiers turned on the last snakes and helped wipe them out before putting down their weapons and standing with open hands.

The soldiers of Safir's Second Battalion came to a halt, looking across a gap in the ruins at Gozen's soldiers on the other side. Drakon waited to see if anyone would do something stupid, but after sizing each other up, the two sides backed slowly out of contact.

He pulled out the scale on his display, looking for symbols of still-active Syndicate soldiers or snakes, but as he watched, the last areas of resistance ceased fighting. "Send scouts into the buildings across the street," Drakon ordered Safir. "Find out if there are any soldiers in those, and then spread your units through them to ensure none of the former Syndicate soldiers try to pull out and lose themselves in the city."

Colonel Malin had a rare smile on his face. "You did it, General. Our sensors aren't picking up any signs of resistance."

"Keep monitoring activity until we know all of the last Syndicate loyalist soldiers have been disarmed and rounded up," Drakon ordered. "I need—I need to answer this call from the *Midway*."

The contrast between the recent visions of chaotic ground fighting amid ruins and the image of the neat, well-ordered bridge of the battleship was a jarring one. "What have you got, Kapitan?"

"General Drakon." Kapitan Mercia waved to her own display. "There are two shuttles which have just lifted from a parking apron next to the location you asked us to watch. Really nice stealth jobs, but the amount of dust thrown up by all the fighting is letting us track them anyway. They are accelerating inland."

The Syndicate CEO in charge of the ground forces division which had just ceased to exist had, as expected, decided that survival was the better part of valor. "Two shuttles," Drakon said to Malin. "They must have left a lot of staff behind."

"It is a Syndicate tradition in cases like this to abandon to their fates the workers and lower-ranking executives," Malin commented.

"Kapitan Mercia," Drakon said, "can you take out those two shuttles?"

"Anytime you want," she replied. "If you want to minimize the chance of damage to whatever is below them, I can wait until they clear the city and nail them while they are over open country."

"Will you be able to track them that far?"

"There's enough dust and smoke extending out into open country for us to keep a solid track on them for about thirty kilometers from the city proper," Mercia said.

"Then nail them when they clear the city," Drakon said. "Are you seeing anything else up there that I should know about?"

"Personnel are fleeing from minor Syndicate military sites everywhere that we can see. We've stopped bombarding since I assume you will want a chance to get the abandoned equipment intact. We've identified very large numbers of what appear to be citizens in encampments outside the city you are in."

"That explains why we didn't see any civilians while we were fighting," Drakon said. "I'm surprised. I didn't expect Haris and his snakes to care how many civilians died."

"I doubt the citizens were moved out of concern for their welfare," Mercia said. "Very likely there were other reasons." She studied something intently. "Those two shuttles will be over open country in thirty seconds. Hang on."

Thirty seconds could feel like a long time when you were waiting through each one.

Mercia signaled a command. Hell-lance particle beams shot down from the battleship, spearing the two fleeing shuttles. "Both birds are dead. One down. Both down. Do you want the coordinates of the wreckage?"

"Later, if you please," Drakon said, thinking that if things had gone differently, he might have been the one in a shuttle trying to escape, the Syndicate battleship swatting him from the sky with cold efficiency.

No. He would have died, but not that way, not running. Hopefully, like Conner Gaiene, on his feet, fighting to the end.

"Colonel Kai," Drakon said, "send a company through the city to these coordinates. You should find the bulk of the Syndicate divisional staff there. Their CEO ran out on them and died. There may still be snakes among them. Round them up and see how much equipment, codes, and other useful things they will turn over to us intact."

"General," the comm specialist said, "Executive Gozen wishes to speak with you."

"Put her on."

Gozen's face appeared before Drakon. The executive looked even more weary than before, displaying no evidence of joy in the day's events. "It's over, right, General?"

"Unless the Syndicate has more hidden units on this planet," Drakon said.

"Nothing significant that I know of. They pulled in everything to hit you." She smiled wryly. "Didn't work."

"No, it didn't. Are you all right, Executive Gozen?"

"I'll survive." She gave him an intent look. "Are my workers going to be all right, General? No labor camps?"

"There are no labor camps at Midway. They were abolished, and they won't be coming back."

"That's hard to believe, but you don't have any reason to lie to me about it anymore. What will happen to them?"

"That's up to them," Drakon said. "Ulindi is going to need ground forces. I need replacements for the losses we sustained here. Or they can try to go home. I won't stop them."

Gozen's brief smile was more like a grimace. "Home. That would be a ticket straight to a Syndicate labor camp for me. Are you going to disarm us?"

"Do I need to?"

"No, sir."

"Then hang on to your weapons for now but stay within your positions. We are disarming the prisoners we took when we captured the portion of your lines the Syndicate still controlled, but we'll turn those soldiers over to you if you want."

"That would be a really nice gesture, General. I'll let my soldiers know they're going to have some real options for the first time in their lives. That's going to feel strange."

"You start to get used to it after a while," Drakon said. "Just to be all formal and everything, are you submitting yourself and the soldiers under your command to my authority?"

Gozen took a deep breath, then nodded. "Yes, sir."

"We're still sorting out things inside the base. I want you to get in touch with Colonel Malin in about half an hour. Here's his comm ID. Let him know what sort of support you need. Shelter, rations, that sort of thing. If you can tell us where other nearby stockpiles of such materiel can be found, it will help. How are you fixed for medical?"

"We can use any medical help you can provide, General," Gozen said.

"We'll get that moving."

"Thank you." Gozen's control finally cracked a little, but she straightened and nodded to him again. "It's been a long day, and I've got a lot yet to do."

"No rush. We're not going anywhere until our warships round up any of the freighters that brought us here that didn't get destroyed."

Gozen looked surprised. "You're not going to take the troop transports?"

He tried not to look surprised in turn. "What troop transports? The ones that brought you here? Those are gone."

"No. They're not. I told you we got dropped here just a short time before you showed up. Troop transports aren't the slugs that freighters are, but they weren't fast enough to clear the star system before we were told you might show up. If you had seen them, it would have ruined the trap. Plus the CEO wanted them close. They were told to park themselves with the star between them and any of your ships until they got a recall."

"The star?" Drakon said.

"Yeah. You know, that big, glowing thing up there? The star."

"Troop transports are still there?" Something else that Gozen had said registered on him. "Why did the CEO want them close?"

"From what I heard," Gozen said, "after we rolled up you guys on the ground, and the Syndicate flotilla wiped out your mobile forces, the plan was to load us up again fast and head for the star system that you came from. Us in the transports and the Syndicate flotilla as escorts. We were to hit whatever guys you'd left back there before they could even hear about what had happened to you and put an end to your revolt." She concentrated. "I think . . . I remember hearing they were to stay within ten to fifteen light-minutes from us."

Drakon stared at her as what Gozen had just told him filtered through his brain. "That was a pretty good plan." Far too good a plan. "I'll let you go now. Thank you, Executive Gozen. You've got my comm ID. Contact me directly if there are any problems."

The moment her image vanished, Drakon made another call. "Kapitan Mercia, I have some very important information that you will want to relay to Kommodor Marphissa."

Mercia blinked at him, trying to focus. There must have been some long days for the mobile forces as well. "What happened?"

"There are a bunch of Syndicate troop transports hiding behind the star, the same transports that brought the Syndicate ground forces division here. If they lifted an entire division at once, I'm guessing there will be between ten and twelve of them. They are supposed to be maintaining position within ten to fifteen light-minutes of this planet."

Mercia froze for a second, then looked impressed. "Nice. Do you want working transports or wreckage?"

"As many working troop transports as possible."

"I'm sure that the Kommodor will be happy to accommodate your request, General. She's been coming on behind me with the cruisers that got beat up fighting the Syndicate, and our Hunter-Killers, and is almost here. Do you have any idea why the troop transports haven't run for it already?"

"They had firm orders to stay near this planet, orders from that CEO whose shuttle you destroyed a short time ago. Now they're probably hoping we go away without spotting them."

"That could have happened if we'd stayed fairly close together," Mercia said. "They could have just kept changing their positions to stay behind the star relative to us as this planet we're at orbited. I'll notify the Kommodor, General."

That task done, Drakon finally sat down again, the chair creaking under the weight of his battle armor, and realized that he could finally take off his battle gear if he wanted. But first he keyed his general command circuit. "To all personnel. The fight is over but for the mopping up. Ulindi is ours. We've won. Well done. All of you. Very well done."

CHAPTER FOURTEEN

"EXECUTE Maneuver Tango Victor," Marphissa ordered her warships, then settled back to watch as all of her cruisers and Hunter-Killers accelerated away from the habitable world and toward the star Ulindi. Only the battleship *Midway* remained in orbit about the planet, an intimidating source of firepower should General Drakon need to either overawe or destroy any Syndicate holdouts.

Marphissa glanced to one side of her display, where a virtual window showed a dramatically different picture. In that view, all of her warships remained clustered near *Midway*, maintaining sedate orbits about the planet. "Confirm that the links and false feeds are stable," she told Kapitan Diaz.

Diaz waited while one of his specialists ran checks. "All stable, Kommodor. The link data and access codes the ground forces found in abandoned equipment at the Syndicate ground forces headquarters all look solid."

"Keep a close eye on it. It would be just like the snakes to plant something like that to fool us."

"Yes, Kommodor. But everything is going great," Diaz said. "Those snoop sats near the star that the Syndicate troop transports are using to keep an eye on us are showing the transports what we want them to see, thanks to that link data and those codes that let us access the sats and covertly mess with them."

"Everything was going great a few days ago," Marphissa reminded him, "right before a Syndicate battleship jumped out at us." Still, she had to admit that the operation was proceeding flawlessly. Reverse-reading the snoop sats gave her warships views of the transports that were depending on the sats to watch Marphissa's ships and stay hidden. Even though the troop transports remained behind the star relative to her warships, thanks to the snoop sats, Marphissa could see them maintaining orbits about three light-minutes on the other side of the star. The ten troop transports looked like a pod of immense whales swimming placidly through space. "We turned their snoop sats into traitor sats," she remarked.

"Kommodor?" Senior Watch Specialist Czilla asked. "Is this similar to what the enigmas did to us for so many years?"

"No one has briefed you on that?" Marphissa asked, giving Diaz a look.

Diaz shook his head. "It's not authorized. Classification Level Two, Special Circumstances."

"That's ridiculous," Marphissa said. "Who are we keeping it secret from? The Alliance told us about it, the Syndicate got the same information from CEO Boyens, and the enigmas certainly already know all about what they were doing. Someone must have classified it that way when we first learned of it and never reviewed the classification level even when things changed."

It would be half an hour before her ships got close enough to the sun to see around it and get visuals on the transports. Plenty of time to explain things to the specialists so they would understand their jobs better. She turned in her seat to look at Czilla and the other watch specialists. "What we are doing here is close to what the enigmas did to us, but not the same. We are feeding the Syndicate transports a false picture of what we are doing by using worms we inserted into the snoop sat control systems. The enigmas had placed worms into our sensor systems as well, but those worms completely blocked any detecting or sighting of enigma ships. That's why we couldn't see them at all. And the enigmas use some sort of worm that we can't copy. The Alliance can't copy them, either. They learned how to spot the enigma worms and cancel them out, but they can't make anything like them."

"That's what the Alliance told us, anyway," Diaz said, drawing mocking smiles from the specialists.

"That's what Black Jack told President Iceni," Marphissa corrected. "And Captain Bradamont told me the same."

The specialists all nodded at that news. "The Captain," Czilla said, "would not mislead us."

"No, she would not," Marphissa agreed, marveling that she could say something like that about an Alliance officer and really mean it. It was almost as amazing as the fact that to the crew of *Manticore*, Bradamont was *the Captain*.

"The sanitation routines we have to run daily in all the systems," the weapons specialist said, "are those to find the enigma tricks? We've never understood how they work since they are nothing like any security or antiviral programs we are familiar with."

"Yes," Marphissa said. "That's what they are doing. Do you want to become famous? Figure out how the enigmas do it. They code their worms using quantum-level programming."

Jaws dropped among the specialists.

"All right," Marphissa said, "keep a close eye on the links and false feeds. Every minute that we accelerate and draw closer to the star without the transports' knowing we're coming makes it less likely that the transports can have any hope of fleeing from us. But I want to nail them without any long chases," she added as she turned back to face her display.

"It's not the chases that are worrying you, is it?" Diaz asked in a low voice.

"Not nearly as much as how many snakes are on each of those transports to keep their crews in line," Marphissa said, "and whether the snakes have outfitted transports as well as warships with those devices that can cause power-core overloads on command. If those devices are on the transports, all it would take is one fanatic snake on each ship willing to give everything for the Syndicate and all we would end up with is ten balls of debris orbiting near this star."

Would all that debris have time to form a ring of wreckage about the sun before the solar winds kicked it farther out? The vision surprised and haunted her for the next few minutes as she did the only thing that she could, keep an eye on the status of her ships and on what the still-unsuspecting Syndicate transports were doing.

"Our systems estimate twenty minutes until visual contact," Czilla reported.

In a blunt reminder that estimate meant an approximate value and not a firm quantity, it actually only took eighteen minutes before *Hawk* got a direct visual on one of the troop transports. By then, Marphissa's flotilla was only four light-minutes from the transports, spreading out to pass the star close by on all sides in a maneuver formally called a High-Velocity Stellar Close Approach and Transit but informally known among warship crews as a Hot and Flat. Close by in stellar terms meant less than a light-minute, or about eighteen million kilometers. When Marphissa had been new to the mobile forces and had first heard the distance translated into kilometers, she had thought it was very large. But when skimming past the enormous uncontrolled nuclear-fusion furnace that was a star, even eighteen million kilometers seemed far too close.

"It really brings home how very small we are, doesn't it?" Kapitan Diaz murmured.

Marphissa didn't answer. She was reaching for her comm controls now that the element of surprise had been lost. "Syndicate transports, this is Kommodor Marphissa of the Free and Independent Midway Star System. We can destroy you at will. You are directed to surrender immediately. Reduce your shields to the minimum safe level for your distance from the star and refrain from changing vectors. Any attempt to flee will be met with force. Any resistance to boarding parties will result in your ships' being fired upon. Each transport is to acknowledge its surrender to me. For the people, Marphissa, out."

She gestured to the comm specialist. "Repeat that every minute for the next ten minutes."

"Yes, Kommodor."

The transports would not see *Hawk* for another four minutes, and on the heels of seeing the light cruiser not only would see Marphissa's other warships coming into view as they cleared the star but would also receive Marphissa's demand that they surrender.

What would happen then? It would depend in great part on how many snakes were on each transport and how loyal the transport crews were to the Syndicate.

"The Syndicate never sent the best to troop-transport duty," Diaz said, echoing Marphissa's thoughts. "The transports are slower, not much armor, fairly weak shields, and no weapons except some point-defense grapeshot launchers. The Syndicate figured if someone was the sort most likely to mutiny or disobey orders in some other way, having them on a troop transport made a lot more sense than having them on a warship."

"I'd heard that, too," she said.

"But it's true," Diaz said. "It's not just a rumor or a put-down of transport crews. My sister got sent to a transport, and she told me it was true."

"Your sister?" Marphissa gave him a surprised look. She vaguely recalled a reference to a sister in the mobile forces in Diaz's service files, but he had never spoken of her before.

"She died when her transport was destroyed," Diaz said, looking steadily at his display, his expression that of a man recalling something that even now he had trouble believing had happened. "She and the rest of the crew and about five hundred ground forces soldiers when an Alliance warship got through the Syndicate escorts."

"I . . . I'm sorry," Marphissa said.

Diaz looked down, then over at her, his eyes shadowed. "How many sisters and brothers do you think I have killed? I have no idea. I can't hate them, the crew of that Alliance ship. I wish they had never come near my sister's ship, but the odds are very good that they all died, too. If not in that battle, then in another soon after. And they were just doing their job. Just like me. No, I hate the Syndicate that put my sister on that transport and sent that transport to that star without enough escorts and started the war and kept the war going. But my sister told me, and would have told you, that the crews of the transports knew they were chosen because they weren't considered good enough or trustworthy enough to be on warships. It's true."

She had to look away. "Thank you . . . for informing me . . . of that important information, Kapitan."

"It's why I still fight, Kommodor."

"I understand. The Syndicate killed my brother, and even though I was able to avenge myself on the one responsible, it could not bring him back. All I can do is try to protect others."

There were about two minutes left before the Syndicate transports saw *Hawk* and received her surrender demand. Then, as the range kept closing, another three to four minutes before she would see whatever the initial reactions of the transports were.

Her warships raced past their closest point of approach to the star, bending in flat curves around its colossal mass and nuclear fires, their courses now converging on the Syndicate transports.

If any of the transports had immediately decided to surrender, she would have received their transmission by now.

"All units," Marphissa said. "Combat readiness at maximum, so the Syndicate ships will know we are ready to engage them, but no one is to fire on any of the transports until I specifically authorize each encounter. We want these transports intact if possible."

"We've got a couple of runners," Diaz noted.

Marphissa's display highlighted the same two transports, which had lit off their main propulsion at the same time as their thrusters pitched them up and over toward a vector aimed at the jump point for Kiribati. She tapped the transports, and her display immediately presented vectors which would allow fairly quick intercepts. "To the two Syndicate transports attempting to flee, you know we can intercept and destroy you without difficulty. Brake your movement immediately to remain in your current orbits."

"Incoming transmission from Syndicate Unit HTTU 458," the comm specialist announced. "We are complying with your orders and submit to your authority."

The symbol that represented Heavy Troop Transport Unit 458 was not one of those who were trying to run. "*Gryphon*, alter vector to a direct intercept on HTTU 380. *Hawk*, alter vector to a direct intercept on HTTU 743," Marphissa ordered.

"We have received surrender messages from HTTU 236, HTTU 643, and HTTU 322," the comm specialist reported.

An alarm sounded as one of the symbols on Marphissa's display vanished. "HTTU 481 has been destroyed by a power-core overload," Senior Watch Specialist Czilla said, his voice grim.

"The signature of the event matches that of the snake power-core-overload device," the engineering specialist said, her words full of impotent anger.

"How will that inspire the others?" Marphissa said to Diaz. "Fear or defiance? We'll see."

"Ten minutes until we are within weapons range of the transports," Czilla said.

"I am detecting power core shutdowns on HTTU 333 and HTTU 712," the engineering specialist announced.

"There is your answer, Kommodor. Someone is trying to preempt the snakes," Diaz said with satisfaction. "Ah, HTTU 380 is braking."

"But 743 is still trying to run," Marphissa grumbled.

"HTTU 532 has surrendered."

Hawk's commanding officer called in. "I'm almost within range of 743, Kommodor, and he's not showing any signs of slowing down."

"Try warning shots," Marphissa directed.

"Kommodor," the comm specialist reported, "HTTU 333 and HTTU 712 have surrendered but say they must restart their power cores."

"Inform all surrendered units that they must report to me the status of any snakes aboard them," Marphissa said.

"No response to warning shots," *Hawk*'s commanding officer said. "Still accelerating all out. I can stay with HTTU 743 as long as you want, Kommodor, but— There are escape pods coming off."

Marphissa watched as the transport's entire complement of escape pods shot free in a staggered volley.

"We have communications with the escape pods," *Hawk* reported. "They say the snakes on 743 have control of engineering and the bridge, that they have barricaded themselves into those compartments."

"Transports don't have citadels," Diaz said. "The snakes must have improvised something."

"That doesn't leave us any choice," Marphissa said. "*Hawk*, fire upon HTTU 743. Target main propulsion units." She glared at her display, knowing that a substantial fraction of 743's crew must be stranded aboard since there hadn't been enough escape pods for the whole crew. She wondered if the crew had selected places in the pods in a disciplined and fair process, or if there had been bloody rioting at the pod bays as men and women fought for what could well be their only chance at life.

"Kommodor," Diaz said. "From the reports from the surrendered transports, they each had three or four snakes aboard. Two transports say they took one of their snakes prisoner. The other snakes are all reported to have been killed."

"Two snakes left alive?" she asked. "That's odd."

"Maybe they weren't bad, for snakes."

"Maybe. The snakes wouldn't occasionally execute one of their own if they didn't sometimes let someone with a tiny bit of humanity through the cracks of their selection system. Have word sent back to those two transports to ensure those two snakes are heavily guarded, under constant visual watch by multiple people, and cannot access anything."

Hawk had matched velocity to HTTU 743 and swung in directly astern, slamming shots at the transport that collapsed its relatively weak rear shields and went on to impact on 743's main propulsion units.

Unable to accelerate anymore, but still moving at the same rate through space, HTTU 743 hurtled helplessly toward the distant jump point for Kiribati.

"Put a boarding party on him and find out the exact situation," Marphissa ordered.

But as *Hawk* moved in to attach a boarding tube, thrusters fired on HTTU 743, creating vector changes. "We can't get a boarding team over as long as the snakes can fire those thrusters and jerk the ship around," *Hawk*'s commanding officer reported with frustration.

"All right," Marphissa said. "Match vectors with 743 as best you can, then use your hell lances to hit his bridge. Hit him enough times to be sure nothing is left working on the bridge." Which would also mean no one was left alive on the bridge, but that didn't need to be said.

"I understand, Kommodor."

Normally, hitting a specific place on an enemy ship was simply impossible when tearing past each other at fractions of the speed of light with engagement times measured in tiny pieces of a second. Simply hitting the enemy at all was an amazing achievement under those circumstances.

But with *Hawk* positioned near the crippled transport, matching speed and direction of travel, it was like shooting at a stationary target while also sitting still. And since the HTTU 743 was a Syndicate design, *Hawk* had a perfect set of deck plans for the transport, telling the warship exactly where to find the Syndicate ship's bridge.

It took a lot to stop hell lances. The streams of extremely-high-energy particles went through most obstacles without hindrance, leaving large, neat holes in hulls, equipment, and any humans unfortunate enough to be in the way. With 743's shields down, and with only the light armor that transports boasted, *Hawk*'s hell lances could pierce right through the transport.

The light cruiser fired again and again with merciless precision, tearing holes deep into HTTU 743 and completely through the transport's bridge. Marphissa watched, trying not to feel sick at the thought of what was happening to everyone on the bridge of the transport. She managed to maintain her composure by switching her attention for brief periods to the process of her other warships' intercepting, surrounding, and matching vectors with the eight troop transports that had surrendered.

"I need to rest my hell lances," *Hawk* reported. "They're overheating."

"Understood," Marphissa said. "Try to get a boarding party over again. Give me a link to whoever leads it."

This time no thrusters fired when *Hawk* moved in close to HTTU 743 and latched a boarding tube onto the transport.

Marphissa activated the link to the head of the boarding party from *Hawk* and called up a view from that person's survival-suit helmet. She watched as breaching tape opened an access in the side of the transport where the boarding tube was attached, and as *Hawk*'s boarding party entered the transport.

"Got some dead," the officer leading the boarding party reported tersely. "Looks like they were fighting over places in the escape pods. Only here, though."

The transport was big inside, big enough to carry hundreds of ground force soldiers and their equipment. *Hawk*'s boarding party headed for the bridge to see what was left, the passageways of the transport spooky with only emergency lighting on and all atmosphere vented through damaged areas of the hull so that only the exact spot where a beam of light fell was illuminated, pitch-blackness reigning instantly beyond the margins of the beam.

Marphissa pulled herself out of her focus on that, concentrating once more on the bigger situation. "Do we send boarding parties onto all of the surrendered transports?" Diaz asked.

"No," she decided. "We'll have them go the planet, where *Midway* is waiting with all of the people in her crew to back up our boarding parties, and we'll deal with all that there. As it is, we're going to have our hands full picking up the survival pods from 743." She tapped their current orbit, then a location in orbit about the habitable planet, waiting impatiently for the second it took for the automated systems to recommend a vector. Then she had to do it again because the automated systems had assumed only the warships were going back and had used accelerations based on that. After specifying this time that all ships here were going to the planet, the maneuvering systems produced a different vector that took into account the slower acceleration of the troop transports. Having spent way too much time shepherding around freighters, which made the clumsy troop transports look like sleek greyhounds of space, Marphissa didn't waste any effort being annoyed at the extra time it would take for all of the ships to get to the planet.

"Kommodor, our landing party has established contact with surviving crew members of 743," *Hawk*'s commanding officer reported.

Marphissa glanced at the small virtual window that now showed the leader of the landing party facing a group of transport crew members in survival suits.

"All of the snakes aboard 743 are dead," *Hawk* continued. "Our fire killed everyone on the bridge, and while we were destroying the bridge, the crew members remaining aboard were able to get into the engineering control compartment and finish off the two snakes there. But they tell me the engineering controls are wrecked, and the entire main propulsion section aft was torn up when we shot out their main propulsion units."

Great. Marphissa glowered at the image of HTTU 743. *I have a big ship with no bridge and no engineering controls clumping its way toward the jump point for Kiribati.* "I need your estimate as to whether it would be worth the trouble to take that hulk in tow and get it back to the planet with us."

She could tell the question had been relayed when every surviving crew member of the transport that she could see began shaking their heads with varying degrees of violence.

"They all say no, Kommodor. I agree," *Hawk*'s commanding officer added. "From what our landing parties have seen, the 743 really is a hulk. The snakes burned out every system and circuit they could before they died, the hull structure took damage from our firing on it, and the power core is shaky because of something the snakes did to its controls."

The other issues could have gone either way, but not a power core that was less than stable. "I want that power core rigged to self-destruct. Can you take aboard all of the surviving crew members?"

"Yes, Kommodor. It will be tight, but we can do it."

"Keep them under guard until we can sort them out," Marphissa said. "Set the power core to blow a half hour after you break contact with 743."

"Only half an hour?"

"Yes. If something goes wrong, if it doesn't blow, I don't want to have to chase that ship halfway to the Kiribati jump point to catch it and make sure it is destroyed."

Marphissa scanned her display again irritably. "*Hawk* can't take aboard any of the crew members from the escape pods," she told Diaz. "She's going to be full of those who were stuck on 743."

After glowering at her display for a moment, Marphissa tapped her comm controls. "*Gryphon*, *Eagle*, detach immediately, proceed to pick up escape pods from HTTU 743. Kapitan Stein on *Gryphon* is in command until your units rejoin our flotilla."

Thirty minutes later, the remains of HTTU 743 disappeared in a flash of energy as the ship's power core overloaded. *Hawk* was returning to rejoin the flotilla, and *Gryphon* and *Eagle* were beginning to recover crew members from the escape pods, as Marphissa gave the order for the rest of the ships to head for Ulindi's habitable planet.

DEFEATS were always bad, but even victories could be messy.

This small portion of the surface of the habitable world orbiting Ulindi looked like some kind of construction site, sticking out as a dirt-shaded scar amid green fields and stands of trees. Drakon walked down the shuttle ramp and nodded to the local officials who stood nervously awaiting him. "This is it?" he asked.

"It's one of the places," a young man said, his voice trembling.

Drakon moved to the side of a fresh excavation, looking down at tumbled bodies still encrusted with the dirt that had recently covered them. The mass grave appeared to contain the remains of at least a few hundred men and women. "They look like they died a few weeks ago," Drakon said, letting his disgust be clearly heard.

"Yes, honored—I mean, yes, *General*," an older man said. "We knew there had been many arrests, that the snakes had been rounding up not only anyone they even slightly suspected but also apparently citizens at random to terrorize the rest of us into submission. But we thought they were being placed in labor camps." His voice broke on the last words.

"Do you have any idea how many?" Drakon asked.

"Our records are a mess," a woman said, sounding weary as well as sad. "The snakes detonated virtual bombs in all our databases and networks when it looked like they were going to lose. We're back to paper and pens and trying to reconstruct the data from whatever unauthorized backups saved portions of the destroyed records."

"At a guess," the young man said, "we're dealing with thousands of dead."

"How about during the fighting?" Drakon asked. "How many got hurt while my forces were fighting the Syndicate and Haris's forces?"

"Your . . . military losses . . . General?" the older man asked, puzzled. "We don't know—"

"No," Drakon said patiently. "Citizens. I understand most were evacuated from the city before we landed. How many got hurt during the fighting?"

They all looked shocked at a senior supervisor expressing concern for casualties among the workers and their families. "Not too many," someone said. "Citizens were ordered out of the city you attacked even before the snake headquarters was bombarded."

"They were afraid we would rise up and attack the Syndicate troops that were attacking you," another said. "We had no weapons, we had no leaders, we couldn't have done anything. But the snakes see enemies everywhere."

"That's funny, isn't it?" the old man said. "They saved a lot of our lives because they thought we might be enemies and so forced us to leave the city before the fighting broke out."

"Are there any leaders left among you?" Drakon asked.

The locals exchanged glances. None of them seemed eager to claim the title of leader or offer up any names. He knew why. They didn't trust him not to also round up anyone who might be a leader among the citizens. "Listen up, all of you," Drakon said as if speaking to his troops. "Neither I nor my soldiers intend staying at Ulindi. We had to get rid of Haris and the Syndicate because they were a threat to this entire region. But we aren't going to rule Ulindi. It's your star system. You need to put together a government to make decisions and plan and coordinate actions. You've had your fill of the Syndicate. One of your decisions will have to be whether you want to voluntarily align yourselves with Midway Star System. Nobody is going to be forced to join, but we're trying to set up a mutual defense arrangement to protect the local star systems from the Syndicate, from warlords, and from the enigmas."

They were staring at him again. One finally spoke. "The . . . enigmas?"

"You must have heard rumors of them even though the Syndicate did its best to keep them secret." Drakon waved toward the sky. "An alien species, intelligent and hostile. They pushed the Syndicate out of star systems like Hina and Pele, and have tried to take Midway Star System more than once."

"There have been rumors," a woman confirmed. "You know this is true?"

"They've attacked Midway Star System. I've seen their ships."

"You just came to get rid of Haris and the Syndicate?" someone else asked in a bewildered voice. "But if they are gone and you leave, who is in charge?"

"Who do you want to be in charge?" Drakon said. "I'm going to leave you all some records we have of events that have taken place recently at star systems like Taroa, Kane, and Midway. We, and by we I mean the soldiers of my ground forces and the crew members of our warships, are giving you a gift. It's a dangerous gift. We're going to let you decide who will rule you and how. We'll offer advice. We'll show you what happened elsewhere and the choices others made, and you'll see the mistakes others made."

"We . . . we need to be safe," the old man faltered. "Why did you get rid of the Syndicate just to leave us without any protection? At least they—"

Drakon pointed at the mass grave. "They did this. Look at it. Do you feel safe when you do? That's the Syndicate form of protection, where you die to keep them in power. I have no interest in killing any of you, nor do I have any interest in any of my soldiers dying to make you do what I want. I've already lost too many people here. As long as you don't threaten Midway Star System, or ally with someone who threatens us, I don't care what you do. But the decision will be yours. Figure out who you want to speak for you. We're leaving you what amounts to a reinforced brigade of ground forces, made up of the remnants of the ground forces that used to be here and those soldiers from the Syndicate division who want to stay here and help you guys defend yourselves."

"But who will be in charge of those ground forces?" a woman demanded. "Who will tell us what to do?"

Drakon paused as he was about to head back to the shuttle, turning to face them all once more. "If you want my advice, and that's all it is, advice, because I'm not going to tell you what to do, I would tell you to get together and decide which people you think can run things pretty well, who you know have looked out for the people around them and under them when they didn't have to, and even when it caused them problems, and who *don't* want the job of helping to run the planet. Put them in charge, and the minute any of them start acting like they're better than you, replace them. You know how to run things. Just like every other place in Syndicate space, you've been keeping things running despite the Syndicate bureaucracy that existed to serve itself and the Syndicate CEOs who were just out for themselves and the snakes who did their best to weed out anyone who was ethical or smart or thought for themselves. So run things. There are lots of references in the underground library that talk about ways to run a star system that aren't the Syndicate way. Whatever you decide on won't be perfect, it never is, but if you start shooting at each other, that means you're doing it wrong."

He walked toward the shuttle but stopped and pivoted to say one more thing to the citizens who were staring after him. "And if you keep the labor camps open, if you lock up people for saying the wrong thing or for disagreeing with you like the Syndicate does, then you're doing it wrong. Some of my people died to give you a chance at doing things better. A chance at freedom. Don't waste it."

As Drakon walked up the ramp and inside the shuttle, he wondered when he had become such a radical. *Freedom.* It had only been about survival and maintaining their own power when he had joined Gwen Iceni to revolt against the Syndicate.

Hadn't it?

He settled into his seat as the shuttle rose into the sky, slewed about, and headed back toward the former Syndicate base. After a few moments of watching landscape scroll by on the display before his seat, Drakon called Malin. "Anything new?"

Malin nodded, his expression shadowed. "I picked up some interesting fragments of information, General. Not long before the snake alternate command center was bombarded and destroyed, there was a lot of chatter about Supreme CEO Haris having been assassinated."

"Haris assassinated?" It would be nice to confirm the death of the former Supreme CEO who had overseen the murder of so many citizens, but . . . "Is there anything about who did it or how?"

"There are references to a lone assassin and gunfire, General. No other description."

"Do we need more?" Drakon asked. "One person who penetrated security at a snake command center and killed their CEO with a gun?"

Malin smiled grimly. "It does sound like Colonel Morgan, sir."

"What happened to her?"

"Unknown, sir. There is chatter about the assassination, a few details like the ones I mentioned, then nothing as the roof of the snake alternate command center literally fell in when *Midway*'s bombardment hit." He gave Drakon an unreadable look. "At least it narrows down our search. If Colonel Morgan was in the snake alternate command center soon before it was destroyed, she must still be nearby."

"Or in the rubble," Drakon said, deliberately being brutally direct. "Bran, if Roh made it out alive, why hasn't she contacted us?"

"You are asking me to rationalize the actions of Colonel Morgan, sir?"

He snorted a very brief laugh. "That's a good point. But why did she go after Haris? That wasn't part of her assignment here."

Malin shook his head, looking down. "I don't know, sir. Whatever reason Colonel Morgan had, it was a reason that made sense to her."

"I'm sorry, Bran."

"I'm not sure that I am, General," Malin responded, his brow furrowed as if trying to solve the puzzle of his own emotions.

"Have we run into any hitches in the mop-up operations?" Drakon asked to spare Malin from having to internally examine in any detail his relationship to Morgan.

"No, sir. The few Syndicate support units still intact are surrendering as soon as our soldiers arrive. Ulindi is still a frontier world, with only a few cities of any size and not many towns worthy of the name, so we haven't had to secure all that many locations."

"If we had faced the problem of dealing with a really large

population, we wouldn't have tried this with only two brigades," Drakon said. "Any word from the Kommodor?"

"We just received a message from her that eight of the ten Syndicate troop transports were captured. One other was destroyed by the snakes aboard it and the last sustained too much damage during its capture to be worth salvage and was scuttled."

"Scuttled? What's scuttled?"

"I believe Kommodor Marphissa picked up the term from Captain Bradamont," Malin explained. "'Scuttled' is an ancient word still used by the Alliance fleet. It means 'blown up.'"

"I suppose that's better than the official Syndicate term 'dissolution of the asset.' Eight transports is more than enough troop-carrying capacity given the ground forces we have," Drakon said, feeling a lift to his spirits. "We owe Executive Gozen a big debt for letting us know they were there."

Malin frowned again. "You do realize, General, that the snakes would consider the loss of ten troop transports as a small price to pay for getting one of their undercover agents close to you."

"You've cautioned me about Executive Gozen about a dozen times already, Colonel. I assure you that I have paid full attention to you each time," Drakon said. "Especially given what I learned not long ago about secrets my closest aides were keeping from me."

Malin had the good grace to openly flinch. "I understand, General. I just feel a duty to—"

"That's fine. I don't mind your watching Executive Gozen. If you find anything, any solid grounds for identifying her as a possible snake agent, I want to know it."

"Yes, sir." Malin hesitated. "Executive Gozen has asked to meet with you."

"Patch her through. I have time to talk to her on the way back."

"In person, sir."

He thought about that, then nodded. "That's probably a good idea.

I can evaluate her better face-to-face than through a comm link. I've been thinking I should take a personal look at her soldiers, as well."

Malin nodded resignedly. "Yes, sir. How many escorts, sir?"

"Just a couple. No battle armor. I want guards on hand if someone lunges at me, but I shouldn't need more."

"General, you do need more—"

"No. This is about my being so confident of my authority and my strength that I don't need a swarm of bodyguards. I need to impress these soldiers, Bran, so none of them start thinking they can get away with anything. But I don't want to impress them as being like a Syndicate CEO, and a lot of bodyguards would show them exactly that image."

"Yes, sir."

It was amazing how much emotion the normally impassive Malin could pack into two short words.

"EXECUTIVE Third Class Gozen," she said, standing at attention and saluting.

Drakon returned the salute with enough care to show that he respected the person who had rendered it. "You look like hell," Drakon said.

Gozen had put aside her battle armor, its surface scarred from the recent fighting, and stood in her working uniform, which was considerably the worse for the days it had been worn under armor and through combat. She had smudges on visible skin, and her short hair was grimy and matted from being continuously under a battle armor helmet for days. Her eyes were shaded by fatigue and her lips badly chapped.

She looked surprised at his words, then grinned. "I feel like hell, sir. I don't want you to think I'm hiding anything."

"Let's walk." Drakon strode alongside Gozen as she led him

through the nearest portions of the ruined buildings that had been part of the Syndicate positions. The buildings were packed with surrendered Syndicate soldiers who gazed back at him with sullenness, or resignation, or hope, or curiosity. He stopped to talk to some of them, getting a feeling for their mood that couldn't be conveyed by reading reports or watching vids.

Drakon stopped before one old soldier who was sitting hunched over, staring at nothing. "Weren't you at Chandrahas?"

Startled, the soldier looked up, then leaped to his feet as he realized who Drakon was. "Devon Dupree, Combat Systems Worker First Class, Heavy Weapons, Fifth Company—"

He broke off as Drakon made a chopping gesture. "You don't need to recite that. Were you at Chandrahas? About ten years ago?"

"Yes, honored CEO," the soldier replied, rigidly at attention, looking straight ahead.

"Sit down," Drakon ordered. The man sat. "Now, relax. You were with the . . . Three Hundred Seventh Division then, weren't you? You were one of the soldiers who held a position for six hours against heavy Alliance attacks."

The old soldier blinked at Drakon in surprise. "Yes, honored—"

"I'm not a CEO. Not anymore. Damn," Drakon continued in an admiring tone. "You guys did an amazing job. I thought you were being given early discharge and retirement as a reward for the heroism."

"Yes, they told us that," the soldier said, looking at Drakon in dawning wonder. "And then a month later, when we got out of the hospital and the news vid crews had left, they told us we had done such good jobs that we were too valuable to lose. We were sent back to our unit. You're CEO Drakon?"

"I used to be CEO Drakon."

"You'd just taken over the Hundred Sixteenth Division back then, hadn't you?"

"That's right." Drakon waved back toward the base. "That's who you were fighting, two brigades of what was the Hundred Sixteenth."

"Well, damn, no wonder we got beat." Dupree shook his head. "That's weird. I don't feel so bad now, knowing who we were fighting."

Drakon sat down next to the old soldier, aware of all of the nearby soldiers watching and listening. "What are your plans?"

"Try to survive, I guess," the old soldier answered. "The usual."

"Ulindi can use someone like you. So can I."

"That's for real? Why?"

"Because I got sick of seeing soldiers like you treated the way you were."

Specialist Dupree nodded back at Drakon, his eyes serious and searching. "Your workers always fought really hard for you. I can't stay at Ulindi, though. It's got some rough memories now. And the Syndicate is out even if I wanted to go to a star they still controlled. I killed two snakes myself. Young fools who didn't think an old worker like me was anyone to worry about. You're going back to Midway? I've never been there."

"There's a lot of water," Drakon said.

"Good beer?"

"We're a major trading junction because of the hypernet gate and all of our jump points. We get a lot of good beer."

The old soldier smiled broadly and sat straight. "If you've got any interest, uh . . ."

"General," Drakon said. "I dropped the CEO as fast as I could."

"Yes, sir. General. If you'd take me, I'll join you."

Drakon reached out and clapped the man on the shoulder. "One of the soldiers who held the point at Chandrahas? I'll always have room for the likes of you. And, heavy weapons, you said? We could use a veteran heavy-weapons specialist." He stood up, looking around at the crowd watching silently. "You've been told the choice is yours, and it is. This isn't the sort of trick the Syndicate pulled. Just before I met

Executive Gozen, I was told that our mobile forces have captured the troop transports that brought you here. We'll use one or more of those transports to take anyone who wants to a star where they can get a lift back to Syndicate space. Or you can stay here and see what kind of star system can be built at Ulindi free of the Syndicate. Or you can ride those transports with my people and join us at Midway. It's your call."

He spent another hour that he couldn't really spare walking among the defeated Syndicate soldiers, then back into the open area where the fighting had raged. "Give us some room," Drakon told his two guards, who had not been needed and now faded back until they were ten meters away. He turned to face Gozen. "What about you, Executive Gozen?"

CHAPTER FIFTEEN

INSTEAD of answering his question, Executive Gozen looked steadily at him before asking her own. "Did you really know that guy from Chandrahas?"

"Yeah." Drakon smiled crookedly. "He's a bit older now, but so am I."

"But remembering his face? After ten years?"

Drakon shook his head, looking down at the scarred pavement. "He should have been dead. All of them should have. But six of them survived and held out until we got to them. You don't forget the face of someone who does something like that." He looked back up at her. "You've got some good soldiers there. Right now, they're beaten. Give them a week, and I wouldn't want to tangle with them again."

She bent one corner of her mouth up. "Thank you."

"Yeah. Good soldiers. But—I hope you won't take this wrong," Drakon said. "But I expected the Syndicate to send ground forces against us who were considered absolutely reliable."

Gozen smiled without any trace of humor. "We were absolutely reliable. By which I mean as reliable as any ground forces except for vipers," she said, naming the fanatical snake special forces. "We had a lot of people who believed in the Syndicate and wanted to help save it."

"You weren't one of those people," Drakon said, making it a statement, not a question.

"No, sir." Gozen looked to one side, her expression somber. "No, sir," she repeated. "I wasn't one of the hard-core loyalists. We had a good number of them, though. But they sent us against your positions, head-on assault after head-on assault. Shots and shrapnel don't care what anybody's politics are, but the enthusiastic workers and execs, the ones who really believed and really wanted to win another one for the Syndicate, they pushed to the front during the attacks and they pushed farther forward during the attacks and they took longer to fall back during the attacks. That would have been great if you guys had cracked. They would have been the ones forming the penetrator while the rest of us provided the mass behind them. But you didn't break anywhere. You had too many people at each point and too much firepower and you were dug in at the base and you were just plain tough. So instead, the enthusiastic ones died a lot faster than the people who were less enthusiastic."

Gozen looked outward to where the largest craters marred the open field. "Of course, the rocks your mobile forces dropped didn't care who they killed, either, and they cut the units in that attack off at the knees. But that left the enthusiastic people isolated in front of your positions, so that bunch got wiped out. Bottom line, after enough attacks, what was left weren't very hard-core."

She waved one hand across the field. "The hard-core, the true believers, the really loyal, are lying out there. They gave it their all. And when they were gone, the rest of us asked ourselves why the hell we were doing this."

"I see." Drakon looked out at the dead still lying out in the open area even though teams were moving methodically through it, recovering the bodies. "The Syndicate did have a good weapon in your unit, but they broke that weapon."

"Yeah," Gozen said. "Like any other Syndicate unit these days, we had rot at the heart, and beyond that, people who would do their jobs out of fear or not wanting to let down their comrades, and then an outer shell that made us look strong." She tilted her chin toward the piles of dead. "That was our shell. The rest of us wouldn't have broken against the Alliance, no matter what. We would have held to the end, for our families and our homes. But we knew you guys were just doing what a lot of us had already thought about, and we knew you couldn't threaten our homes. The only people who can do that now are the Syndicate and their snakes."

"Not quite," Drakon said. "There are other dangers out there. There are a lot of tough fights left to fight."

"Are you always this encouraging?"

He smiled at her. "Tell me something. How did you make it this far? Why were you still an Executive Third Class instead of an inmate at a labor camp?"

"Why do you ask?" Gozen said, feigning surprise.

"That attitude thing," Drakon replied dryly.

"There is that," Gozen admitted. "The truth is I wasn't going to last much longer. I'm good at what I do, I'm a damned good soldier, and I get the job done, and my workers respected me, and didn't try to undermine me because I tried to look out for them. But I only survived long enough to get here because I had a strong patron, the sub-CEO in charge of my brigade. He was my uncle. And he had something on the CEO running the division. I don't know what. Some potential source of blackmail that gave him leverage."

Drakon couldn't stop himself before his eyes went to the field of dead.

"No," Gozen said. "He's not out there." She inhaled heavily, then sighed. "Just before we came here, something slipped. I don't know what. We were told we had a new CEO for the division, and when I tried to check with my uncle I found out our sub-CEO had been replaced overnight as well. Before the day was out I was called in and told that my uncle had been arrested for crimes against the Syndicate, and the snakes had their eyes on me. I had the choices of performing heroically on this mission, which might save my butt for a while longer, or dying heroically, which would be relatively painless, or going to join my uncle, though it wasn't specified whether I'd be joining him in a labor camp or in death."

"A Syndicate motivational talk," Drakon said.

"Exactly. That and a few other abrupt changes of command within the division and the addition of a lot of extra snakes to look over the shoulders of everyone was supposed to ensure that we were in the best possible shape to take you guys out." Gozen laughed bitterly. "It had the opposite effect, of course. We moved slower against you than we would have if the bosses hadn't just been changed and the snakes hadn't been questioning every action before they approved it. You would have been taken out before you attacked and took the base if our effectiveness hadn't been hurt so much by those changes."

"The Syndicate undercut its own efforts," Drakon said. "Nothing new there. So, what are you going to do now, Executive Gozen?" he asked again.

She gestured back toward her positions. "Make sure those guys are all right."

"You'd be in the running to be in charge of ground forces for Ulindi," Drakon pointed out.

"Don't want that, sir. Not ready for it. I can handle small units well, but I was frozen out of a lot of the staff work. My uncle wanted to keep my profile low, and the other sub-CEOs wanted me to go away."

"You could get that experience with me," Drakon said. "If you pass the security screening."

"Huh." She eyed him. "General, just to be clear on one point, I don't think I'm some big prize, and I've never really understood male preferences in women, but if you're thinking I'd be the sort of protégé whose duties include satisfying your physical needs and stroking your ego, that's not my thing."

Drakon shook his head. "That's not my thing, either. I don't put that kind of pressure on my subordinates, and I have firm policies against it. I know, so does the Syndicate. But I'm serious about it." Which was one of the reasons his failure to control himself that one night with Morgan stung so badly. No matter how drunk he had been, he should have restrained himself, should have successfully resisted her attempts. "You can ask my people about it. They'll tell you."

"Fair enough, General." Gozen jerked her head toward her positions. "But those men and women come first. I can't leave or take another job until I know they're all right." She blinked back tears. "And, I've got to tell you, General, I don't know . . . We lost a lot of people. We lost too many."

"We lost too many as well," Drakon said. "Even one would have been too many."

"Yeah." She rubbed her eyes irritably. "I don't know if I can keep doing this."

"I wish I knew another way," Drakon said, his voice low. "I do it because it's the only way I know of to stop the kind of people who sent you to Ulindi, who killed your uncle, who filled the mass graves here with bodies, who bombarded the helpless people at Kane, and have done so many other things to hurt and control and take."

She looked back him, her eyes red. "If I stopped, they wouldn't. Same old. And I owe it to Uncle Jurgen, who kept me alive this long even if he couldn't save himself. I'm going to need happy pills to keep going, though," Gozen said, using the common slang term for the medications and therapies used to help soldiers cope with post-traumatic stress.

"Welcome to the club," Drakon said.

"I was already a member." She nodded to Drakon. "By my rough estimate, about half of the surviving soldiers from my division will be interested in staying at Ulindi to help defend this star system and build new lives here, especially if they can figure out ways to get family members out here. About a quarter will want to head back to the Syndicate. And about a quarter will be interested in your offers to join you guys."

"Which fraction do you fit into?" Drakon asked.

"I've always wondered what it would be like to work for somebody who cared about their workers," Gozen said. "And what it would be like to fight for something I wanted to win instead of fighting just because I was afraid of someone else's winning. But I probably can't do anything about my attitude."

"Are you always this encouraging?" Drakon asked.

She grinned at him. "You've got an attitude, too, don't you, General?"

"So I've been told."

"All right. You want my kind of headache, you got it."

"I, along with *Manticore* and our other cruisers and Hunter-Killers, will remain here to escort the transports, but I have to send *Midway* back to . . . Midway," Marphissa told Drakon. All of her ships were once more orbiting Ulindi. "They need her there in case the Syndicate tries another attack."

"Or the enigmas," Drakon said. "I understand, Kommodor. Please inform Kapitan Mercia that the ground forces are extremely grateful for the support of her ship. Of course we're also extremely grateful for the support your other units gave us. It's no exaggeration to say that we probably would have been overwhelmed without that bombardment you tossed off at just the right time."

Marphissa smiled. "We were happy to provide that support,

General. I'm just glad that President Iceni shared that code phrase with you. If you hadn't tacked that onto the end of the text message asking for assistance, I wouldn't have known whom to target with the bombardment."

"That code phrase." Drakon looked at her, his expression suddenly guarded. "The one from President Iceni."

"Yes," Marphissa said, wondering at Drakon's reaction.

"I'm glad the code phrase made a difference," Drakon said.

Uncertain what was going on, she changed the topic. "Do you have an updated estimate when we can begin loading your ground forces onto our new troop transports?"

"They're not exactly new, Kommodor," Drakon said, appearing relaxed again. "More like previously owned. Not that I'm not happy to have them."

"Considering that four of the freighters that brought you here were destroyed and six others kept running until they jumped for another star system, you ought to be extremely happy," Marphissa said. "I'm not sure how we would have gotten your people home without the transports. We can load as many people on six troop transports as it took all twenty modified freighters to carry."

"How confident are you about the crews of those transports?"

"We took off some from each transport and replaced them with some of ours. There are no grounds for worries there, General. So, that estimate?" Marphissa pressed, wondering why Drakon had avoided answering the question.

He made a face, then looked straight at her. "We promised to take any of the surrendered ground forces who wanted that back to a star system where they could find rides to Syndicate space."

Oh. So that was it. "How many?" Marphissa asked.

"Four hundred sixty two. A lot less than expected, actually."

"One transport can handle that." Marphissa pondered the problem. "I am reluctant to send any ships on to Kiribati. That is entirely too likely to have some sort of ambush waiting in case some of us had tried to flee that way to escape the Syndicate flotilla. But if we bring that batch of Syndicate loyalists with us back to Midway, we can have the transport carrying them continue on to Iwa. From Iwa, they can find rides into Syndicate space. Not easily, but they can do it, which satisfies your promise to them without risking our ships in a trip to other Syndicate-controlled stars that we know less about than Iwa and that are farther away. I have no desire to stick my ships into a hornet's nest in Syndicate space, General."

"Iwa." Drakon thought about it, rubbing his chin, then nodded. "That's reasonable. We can start loading those guys as soon as you're ready."

"We acquired some extra shuttles along with the transports," Marphissa pointed out.

"Major Barnes has already informed me of that and of her intentions to requisition a few of those shuttles to replace losses during our assault here. I'll get the load plan finalized and start sending the loyalists up. Which transport?"

Marphissa frowned at her display. "HTTU 458."

"Transport 458," Drakon repeated. "Are you planning on giving the transports names, too?"

"That will be up to President Iceni, General."

"I do have some input, you know," Drakon said, a bit of an edge entering his voice again.

"Of course, General," Marphissa said. She wasn't about to get into the middle of a debate between Drakon and President Iceni. Especially when she was certain that Drakon was just the most senior of Iceni's subordinates and not her equal, despite what courtesies the president had offered to him. Not that she had any problem with the general. Not after the way he had handled the crises that had erupted at Ulindi in space and on the ground. But that didn't make him President

Iceni's other half, no matter what rumors said about their private relationship.

NINE days later, Drakon stood on the bridge of HTTU 322, watching as the entire flotilla left orbit about Ulindi's inhabited world and accelerated toward the jump point for Midway. He felt a trace of guilt as he watched the planet receding behind them. Ulindi had the beginnings of ground forces in a unit cobbled together from reliable men and women who had once been part of Haris's brigade or of the Syndicate division. It had no warships, though, and no government. The Syndicate was gone, Supreme CEO Haris and his snakes were gone, but what was to replace them was still up in the air, with vigorous debates under way on almost every street corner about how Ulindi should be run. Drakon felt his job was half-done.

But the brutality of the snakes in the last weeks of Haris's rule and the mass deaths they had inflicted had served to cool the hottest tempers. There had been no sign in the street debates that the various groups were interested in taking up arms. *Enough* seemed to be the motto of Ulindi these days, and perhaps that was not a bad basis for forming a government.

Drakon kept his eyes on the planet, wishing that he or Malin had been able to locate any trace of Morgan. They had turned up plenty of reports of what she had been up to on the planet, along with a casualty list she had caused that would have been impressive for anyone less deadly than Morgan. As it was, Drakon had marveled at her restraint.

And wondered if she had indeed died in the snake alternate command center. It would take a lot more excavating and DNA sampling before the answer to that would be known, and he simply could not remain in Ulindi for that long.

Nor was Morgan the only soldier that he had lost at Ulindi. The new recruits from what had been the Syndicate division had more than filled out the losses, but there was a difference between adding personnel and replacing the individuals who were gone.

They were bringing Conner Gaiene's remains back with them, but Conner's mischievous grin would not be seen again.

The flotilla looked a lot bigger now, having gained eight troop transports. The Kommodor had described the troop transports as looking like whales to her, which was a fair description of their general size and shape. As Drakon watched the depiction of the flotilla on this ship's display, the escorting warships resembled very large sharks and other predators swimming all around the whalelike transports.

The commanding officer of HTTU 322, a harried-appearing man named Mack, gave Drakon an appraising look. "How are your accommodations, honored—I mean, uh, General?"

"Comfortable," Drakon replied. Transport executives were notorious for looking down on the ground forces they hauled from star to star, but once Drakon had reached sub-CEO, then CEO status, he had seen dramatic improvements in the way he was treated. These transport crews, who had only recently thrown off the Syndicate yoke, were still following those old patterns, and to them, Drakon was a CEO in all but name.

Mack leaned back in his seat, looking around the transport's bridge, which was small for the size of the ship. "It feels different without them around. The snakes. The unit, every unit I served on, always felt like a prison, and they were the guards." He glanced at Drakon as if trying to judge his reaction to the words. "I've got family still in Syndicate space, but when your mobile forces came swooping in, I knew it was act or die, and dead I couldn't help my family."

"There are a lot of holes in the Syndicate security perimeter these days," Drakon said. "Holes that families can slip through. And a lot of room in the star systems around here."

One of the women on watch on the bridge, a senior executive

whose expression seemed fixed in a state of sullen unhappiness, looked at Drakon with a spark of hope in her eyes. "I've heard of Kane. How is Kane?"

"It has a good planet," Drakon said, "and a lot of room." He took a deep breath. "Especially since the Syndicate bombarded it. Most of those who lived there are dead. Most of what had been built there is ruin. But the planet remains good, and Kane needs those willing to help rebuild it."

"But if the Syndicate comes back—"

Drakon shook his head. "Did you see the Syndicate battleship that was in this star system? The one that was destroyed? It was that warship, and the CEO commanding it, who bombarded Kane. Neither that warship nor that CEO will be bombarding any more planets."

"Who are you people?" Mack asked. "The snakes told us you were just rebellious CEOs out for yourselves. I've seen enough and heard enough to know you're not that, but I'm still trying to figure out what you are."

"We are the people who are going to stand up to and stop the Syndicate," Drakon said. "Just as we did here." He took a last look at the planet. "I'll be in sick bay."

An HTTU had pretty decent medical facilities. Nothing to equal those on a battleship or a well-equipped ground facility, but adequate for dealing with casualties among the ground forces the ship had brought to the battlefield. Drakon reached the entrance to the first of the medical bays and stopped, looking into the brightly lit compartment where rows of bunks were topped by long, rounded devices resembling ancient mummy cases. Many of the cases were open at the top end, showing the faces of men or women relaxed in deep sleep. Other cases were completely sealed, only the steady green readouts on them betraying the presence of the badly injured soldiers confined within.

Two medical personnel were seated on opposite sides of a desk talking in low voices to each other. One noticed Drakon and both stood up, their movements betraying fatigue.

"How is everything?" Drakon asked.

"No problems that aren't being fixed," a woman with weary eyes told him. He recognized her as belonging to the medical team attached to Kai's brigade. "They're all in rec sleep, General," she added, using the common term for a deep form of sedation that hastened healing.

"Thank you, Doc. I know medical hasn't had much chance to rest." Drakon looked at the man with her. "I don't know you."

He nodded nervously before answering. "Worker Gundar Castillon, Medical Specialist, Field Treatment, uh . . ." The man faltered as he realized that he couldn't recite a work-unit assignment.

Drakon smiled reassuringly. At least, he hoped it was a reassuring smile. He had been told that when he was really tired, his attempts at reassurance could look a little demonic. "A medic. Were you with the Syndicate division?"

"Yes, honored—I mean, yes, sir."

"We want him in our med team, General," the doctor said. "He pitched right in on the surface. Just started doing everything he could because he was there and saw some soldiers who needed help."

"I don't see why he can't be part of your med team, then," Drakon said, gesturing toward the chairs the two had vacated. "Sit down." They took their seats again, the doctor gratefully and the new medic a bit stiffly, as if expecting Drakon to yank him back to attention at any moment. "Consider the unit assignment approved. How much longer have you got on duty?"

The doctor yawned. "Thank you, General. Another hour, sir. Then eight off."

"Good." Drakon leaned against the nearest bulkhead, wanting to sit down as well but afraid he would have too much trouble getting up again if he did. He looked down the rows of sleeping soldiers again. "You guys do miracles."

The doctor quirked a smile. "General, if I could do miracles, I'd be about forty light-years from here in a soft bed with someone to keep me warm."

"Would you? Or would you be where you were needed?"

"That's not a fair question, General," the doctor protested. She rubbed her eyes with one hand. "I admit it's going to be nice to rest for a while. This was a rough one."

"They're all rough ones for the ones who get hit," Drakon said. "Thanks for fixing up all the soldiers that can be saved."

"You know, General, if you didn't break them in the first place, we wouldn't have to try to fix them."

The new medic looked horrified, as if expecting Drakon to shoot the doctor on the spot.

But he nodded to her. "If I knew a way to never break another, I'd use it. But life isn't that simple."

"No," the doctor agreed. "I guess not. Sometimes I wonder why I keep trying, though." She waved one hand to indicate the rows of bunks. "I fix them, they go out, sometimes they come back, sometimes their next hurt is so bad nothing can save them. It's like shoveling sand. We break our backs to save them, but how much difference do we really make?"

Drakon met her eyes. "Let me tell you something I sometimes wonder. I sometimes wonder about the human race, about our seemingly limitless capacity to inflict death and destruction on each other. I wonder if there's any reason to keep trying to make anything better, to try to save anything, when someone else is just going to come along and kick over whatever I built."

He nodded again, this time toward the sleeping wounded. "But then I see people like you, giving their all to save others. The medics, like you, Specialist Castillon, braving enemy fire to do all they can for someone who got hit. And it makes me realize that the human race has some good in it. That there are people who work at least as hard to save others as some other people work to destroy. That's why I keep trying."

The doctor smiled tiredly. "You're welcome."

Drakon looked at the medic. "Are you all taken care of? A place to sleep, eating arrangements set up?"

"Not yet, General," the medic said.

"If you run into any trouble," Drakon said, "have your team leader"—he pointed at the doctor—"contact me about it."

The doctor smiled again, watching Drakon closely. "If you don't mind my saying so, General, I'm diagnosing you as being almost as tired as I am. You're sort of wavering on your feet even though you're leaning on that wall."

"You don't have to prescribe bed rest," Drakon said. "I'm on my way." He straightened, looking at the injured soldiers again, thinking of those who hadn't made it this far. "Why can't we save them all? Couldn't we replace anything they needed?"

"Up to a point," the doctor said. "A few centuries back, they started running into something odd." She sighed, her eyes closing as if she didn't want to look upon history. "Medical science had progressed to the point where we could replace anything as it failed with some sort of device. Cloned parts worked fine. But stuff we made, artificial parts, started causing problems if they made up too much of a person. We can build a cyborg, but they're unstable, especially if we've built them from someone who got blown apart in combat and put back together. There are lots of theories, most of them built around the idea that the artificial parts create some cumulative impact on the nervous system, so once you pass a certain threshold, a certain percentage of the body that was built instead of grown, the cyborg becomes untreatably psychotic and either goes into a coma or goes berserk."

"That's not just a rumor?" Drakon said. "I've seen that plot used in a lot of horror vids, but I didn't know it was based on reality."

"It's real," the doctor said. She opened her eyes and gazed at

Drakon. "You know what else is real? They found out if someone had been hit badly enough, if they had been medically dead long enough before being revived, then when they brought them back, something was missing. It was like those cyborgs were just robots with human programming. Something that made them actually human was gone. We've never figured out what that something is. That's why we don't try to bring them all back. Even the Syndicate got scared by that."

It took him several seconds to reply. "Good reason." The old "rest in peace" saying took on new meaning for him as he considered what the doctor had said. Didn't someone like Conner Gaiene deserve that chance to rest even if what was left of him could have been brought back to life? Or, rather, back to some form of life that would be a sorry way to repay someone who had been a friend and comrade for so long. "Thanks for the nightmare fodder."

"It's what doctors do to laypeople who listen to our shop talk."

"I keep forgetting that." Drakon waved a farewell, then made his way to his stateroom. He couldn't recall the last time he had been able to get an adequate amount of rest, but it was definitely before they had arrived at Ulindi.

Despite that, he still needed a down patch to calm his mind enough to sleep, and finally dropped off, haunted by visions of battle.

"WELCOME back." Iceni tried to put genuine feeling into the words, but in reply received a tense look from Drakon.

"You missed me that much?" he asked.

"It got a bit hectic here," she said, waving him to a chair. "Not as bad as it did for you at Ulindi, but bad."

"Colonel Rogero has already briefed me," Drakon said as he sat down. "We all dodged the bullet this time."

"Our enemies spun a much wider and cleverer net than we realized," Iceni said, clasping her hands on her desk before her as she sized up Drakon's mood. "And we may have thought we were cleverer than we actually are."

"It's hard to outsmart an opponent who knows what cards you hold," Drakon said, his voice flat. "As I'm sure your Kommodor has briefed you, the Syndicate knew a lot about our plans."

So that was the source of Drakon's tension. Was he going to accuse her of betrayal? Did he believe that she had betrayed him? "Yes," Iceni said, keeping her own voice serious but free of tension. "They apparently had many details, including very specific information about the timing of our planned attack."

"They not only had that information," Drakon said, "they based their plans on having that information. The entire trap was constructed assuming that they would be able to time the arrival of their reinforcements to just before we arrived, and to have CEO Boucher's flotilla show up just early enough to conceal itself behind a gas giant. That information couldn't have been provided by someone who watched us depart. They couldn't have gotten the information to Ulindi in time."

Drakon had hunched forward, tapping his forefinger forcefully on her desk to emphasize his words. "The Syndicate source must have known our date of departure as soon as you and I had settled on it. Anyone could have seen the preparations, but no one could have known when we would actually get moving for the jump to Ulindi because that exact time depended on a lot of factors and a joint decision by you and me. Given the time needed to get that information to the Syndicate at Ulindi and wherever else their forces were, and the time needed to land those Syndicate soldiers and get their flotilla in place, there simply wasn't enough time for them to do it unless that date was dispatched to them within a day of when we made the final decision."

She let frost enter her voice. "Are you implying something about me?"

He frowned, momentarily puzzled by the question. "You? No. That . . . never occurred to me."

Either he was a much better actor than Drakon had previously shown, or the words were sincere. But Iceni still felt angry and defensive. "Then what are you saying?"

"That someone very close to you or me must have fed that information to the Syndicate."

"Who on your staff knew the exact date of departure that early?" Iceni demanded, trying to keep Drakon on the defensive.

"Colonel Malin, Colonel Kai, Colonel Gaiene."

"*Not* Colonel Morgan?"

"How could she have known? She was already at Ulindi when we made the decision, and had been there for weeks."

Iceni managed to stifle her disappointment. The momentary hope that Morgan could be a prime suspect in the trap was running headlong into simple questions of time and space that definitely eliminated her as a suspect. "But the information she sent us was woefully incomplete," Iceni pointed out.

"It was," Drakon agreed, some defensiveness entering his voice. "The files we captured when the Syndicate staff abandoned the divisional headquarters confirmed that CEO Haris himself wasn't even in the loop on the trap. He, and Ulindi, were dangled as bait for us. We didn't guess that the Syndicate would completely cut Haris out of their plans, but then we didn't guess that Haris was really still working for the Syndicate."

"It should have been obvious," Iceni said, her voice sharp, seeing Drakon's defensive glower deepen. "Oh, I'm not pointing the finger at you for that, General. I share plenty of the blame. Haris supposedly made himself independent from the Syndicate but took along the entire snake apparatus at Ulindi? All of it intact?"

"A charismatic leader could have done that," Drakon said. "Do you want to know what the files we captured said about the Syndicate source at Midway?"

Iceni tried not to stiffen, wondering what bomb Drakon was about to drop. "What did they say?"

"Nothing."

It was her turn to glower. "Did you really want to see how I would react to the implication that those files contained important information?"

Drakon closed his eyes, speaking slowly but still with force. "I was at Ulindi, pinned between two enemy forces, knowing that the odds greatly favored my entire force's being wiped out, and knowing that I had led them there."

Iceni leaned toward him, letting each of her words drop like a hammer. "Do you actually believe that I would have set you up that way? That I would have conspired to destroy not only you but two-thirds of the professional ground forces available to this star system? Do you think I am that *stupid*?" Because, she realized, that was what was bothering her the most. She could be ruthless. She could double-deal. But weaken her own future prospects by that much overkill? "If I wanted you dead, I would have killed you and kept all of those valuable ground forces soldiers. Do you really think I am that *incompetent*?"

He had opened his eyes and was staring at her, then abruptly laughed. "Oh, hell, you think I suspect you? You personally? Why the hell would you have sent the battleship to save the day if the whole trap had been your idea to begin with? No, I don't think you're stupid or incompetent, but I think someone close to us is playing both of us and wanted *me* dead."

She eyed him, thinking. "Yes. The plan would have led to your death. As well as the deaths of Colonels Kai, Gaiene, and Malin. Only Colonel Rogero of your senior staff would have survived." Her mind whirled down new paths as it considered possible scenarios. "He would have replaced you, General. Colonel Rogero would have been the senior ground forces officer, commander of the only loyal professional soldiers left to me. He could have faked that assassination attempt aimed at him."

Drakon, instead of getting defensive again, just shook his head. "For security reasons, I didn't tell Rogero the departure date. He didn't need to know it."

"He could have learned what it was. He must have sources. It would have been as simple as chatting with Gaiene when he was drunk."

"That's true." Drakon finally sat back again, watching her. "But I can't believe it. Donal Rogero. If he could so cold-bloodedly plot to murder me and two-thirds of the others in the division, along with Conner Gaiene, who was his friend, then he's so good at being a snake that I don't know how I survived this long."

She grimaced, then nodded. "You're right. Especially since he could have very easily died when he exposed himself to the crowds along with his soldiers. That action would make no sense if he intended to survive as your successor." Iceni took a deep breath. "Which leads us back to my side of the table."

"I am confident that Kommodor Marphissa is loyal," Drakon said.

"As am I. Not all of the former Reserve Flotilla members have been fully screened, but none of them had access to the departure information early enough to have alerted the Syndicate."

"Who does that leave?" he asked.

Iceni tapped her desk surface lightly to cover up the turmoil inside her. "My personal assistant."

"There isn't anyone else?" Drakon said, startled.

"Not on my end. We kept it to those who needed to know until the ships actually started moving," Iceni said.

"Where is your assistant?" He looked around, his hands moving in ways that she knew must be readying the hidden weapons and defenses built into his uniform.

"I don't know." She met his surprised gaze with her own level look. "Mehmet Togo disappeared shortly before the mobs took to the streets. I have not been able to find out anything regarding him since that time."

Drakon twisted his mouth, looking into the distance. "Your Togo struck me as someone who would be pretty hard to take out."

"Extremely hard. If someone did eliminate him, they must be a very dangerous threat."

"If?" Drakon asked. "You think he may have chosen to go into hiding?"

"I don't know." She indicated her desk. "I've taken the precaution of resetting every password and access that Togo knew. I've also reset the passwords and accesses that Togo was not supposed to have known."

"If he gave that information to the Syndicate—"

"I know!" Iceni calmed herself. "But he can't be loyal to the Syndicate. If that were so, he would have tipped them off before we revolted. Neither one of us would have survived. And, if he wanted only you dead, all Togo had to do was pass word of *your* plans to the late and unlamented CEO Hardrad early enough that my own involvement could have been covered up." She chewed her lip, gazing worriedly at Drakon. "Togo knows a great deal. There are means available to extract information from even those capable of withstanding standard interrogation methods."

"If he's not choosing to give that information freely," Drakon said. "But those means of forcibly extracting information that you're talking about don't leave anything recognizably human behind."

"I know that. I also know that they are not foolproof, and can sometimes destroy the information they seek, and so even the Syndicate rarely employed them. But I can't disregard the possibility. Perhaps Togo betrayed me for reasons I don't know. Or perhaps the information he carried was harvested. I don't know. I am bending every effort to locate him."

"Colonel Rogero didn't mention being involved in that."

"I haven't asked the ground forces to assist," Iceni said, waving a cutting gesture of denial with one hand. "It seemed to be a purely internal matter."

"It might have been until we learned someone fed the Syndicate information," Drakon said. "I would like to inform my staff. Your assistant knows a lot of my secrets, too, secrets that I shared with your office."

"Damn." Iceni slapped her forehead. "Codes. Togo would have been able to gain access to some of your codes as well. Yes. Yes. Tell your workers so they can take the necessary steps to protect your data and networks."

Drakon frowned downward, then back at her. "If your assistant did have a deal with the Syndicate, they were going to betray him. The Syndicate plan included a quick follow-on attack here. Wipe us out at Ulindi, then bring all of those soldiers and CEO Boucher's flotilla here to hit you before you had any warning."

She inhaled deeply, taking in that information. "CEO Boucher would not have shown any mercy to me or anyone else no matter what deal Togo might have made. Togo was involved in enough executive actions to know that the Syndicate has a history of making many promises to turncoats, publicly hailing them, then privately eliminating them to ensure that they could never turn their coats again. Though we still don't know that he betrayed me. Why disappear if he was certain that you would die at Ulindi?"

"I hope you won't mind my remaining suspicious," Drakon said with obvious sarcasm. "Speaking of secrets being spilled, how did you find out about the trap at Ulindi? All Freya and Bradamont knew was that you had received some highly credible information."

"CEO Boyens told me." She saw the immediate skepticism in him. "It was a matter of self-interest."

Drakon snorted. "That makes it plausible. I wish Boyens had coughed up that information before I left."

"I made it clear to him how disappointed I was," Iceni said.

"Is he dead? Or just wishing he was?"

"Neither. Yet."

"I might want to have a personal talk with him about it," Drakon said. "His little game of withholding information almost cost us everything."

"You don't have to emphasize that to me." She looked down at her hands. "Until *Midway* came back with the news of your survival, of your victory, I spent some time coming up with imaginative means of making Boyens regret not speaking earlier. But here you are. Still in one piece. Coming home with more soldiers than you left with, and more ships than you left with. You really are amazing, you know."

Drakon sat back, giving her an enigmatic look. "If you really believe that, perhaps you'll explain something else that I'm curious about."

"Oh? What's that?"

"I had some time to talk to your Kommodor." Drakon cocked his head to one side, still gazing at Iceni. "She said she got a text from my command that told her we had taken the base, and needed some help with the Syndicate troops attacking us from the outside. But there's one thing about that message that I don't understand. Kommodor Marphissa said she knew the message was authentic, and not a Syndicate trick, because of a code phrase it contained. A code phrase that she said President Iceni had provided to a few trusted people to use in emergencies." Drakon leaned forward, his elbows resting on his knees as he looked at Iceni. "Your Kommodor thought I was the one who had sent the message with the special code phrase in it. Only, I didn't."

Iceni managed not to reveal her feelings. *Damn. This is going to be awkward. And right after I protested against him suspecting me of anything.* "Really? Who did?"

"I don't know. But I'd like to know."

She sighed and held up both hands in mock surrender. "Colonel Malin. It must have been him. I had, purely as an emergency measure, given him one of the code phrases."

"Why Colonel Malin instead of me?" Drakon asked. He sounded and looked curious, not angry, but that meant nothing. When he really wanted to, the man could hide his true feelings as well as any CEO.

"I could lie—" Iceni began.

"I wish you wouldn't."

That had come out with more force than Drakon had probably intended, Iceni thought. "—but I'll tell you the truth," she continued smoothly. "I wanted a backup. I knew that Kommodor Marphissa would accept something that she knew was from you. But you were going into battle. Something might have happened to you. I wanted Colonel Malin to have a means of letting the Kommodor know that he could be trusted."

Drakon studied her, looking perplexed. "You trust Colonel Malin? When did that happen?"

"Over time," Iceni replied with a shrug.

"Even after you found out he was Morgan's son and had kept that information from me?"

"Yes."

"I'll be honest with you. I don't know what the hell to think of that."

Iceni met his eyes. She didn't have to pretend to be speaking the truth as she continued. "Artur, I felt confident that Colonel Malin would not betray you. If Colonel Rogero had been going along, I would have given him the code phrase, but he stayed here. It was about ensuring that Kommodor Marphissa would know when a critical message was authentic, and it worked as intended. Without that code phrase, she could not have learned the situation on the ground in time to intervene as she did."

Blowing out a long breath, Drakon sat back again, his eyes hard. "I would have preferred knowing. As it is, even though it indeed worked very well, it feels like a measure taken not as insurance for me but insurance against me."

"That's not true." Iceni surprised herself with the heat of her reply. "It was not based on any fear of you, or distrust of you. But I thought if you knew Colonel Malin had the code phrase, it would cause you to distrust him, or anyone else with such a phrase."

Drakon nodded. "That's probably right. I know you didn't trust Conner Gaiene."

She looked away, distressed. "I am very sorry that he died, Artur. He was not my favorite man, but his death ennobled him."

"Conner was always that noble man inside. He had just gotten very good at hiding it," Drakon said, his voice heavy. "You and Colonel Kai haven't interacted much, that I know of—"

"We haven't," Iceni said.

"So it makes sense that you would have entrusted Malin with that code phrase." He looked straight at her again. "But I would very much not want to have that sort of thing happen again without my knowledge."

She could tell that Colonel Malin would have some pointed questions directed at him when Drakon got back to his headquarters. If Drakon stopped trusting Malin at all, it would greatly lessen his effectiveness as a source of information for her. "I should also tell you that Colonel Malin thought you were already aware of the arrangement."

Drakon paused, searching her face. "You misled him as well?"

"That's what we do, isn't it?" She had been hoping for more openness with Drakon, for a lowering of barriers, but he obviously had plenty of defenses up, so she could scarcely afford to lower hers. "But I will not take such actions again."

He took several seconds to answer, then spoke with care. "There are forces working to keep us distrustful of each other. We can't afford to let them succeed."

"Forces?" Iceni asked. "Do you mean the Syndicate?"

"Certainly the Syndicate. Divide and conquer is an old CEO tactic. But maybe your assistant Togo as well. And maybe . . ." He gave her a look that carried an admission of his own failure. "Maybe that's part of what Colonel Morgan wanted."

Iceni's smile was hard and cold. "I don't know about you, but I hate being yanked around on anyone's strings."

"I never cared for it, either."

"Then let's move forward," she said. "We can't lose sight of the fact that we did win both here and at Ulindi."

He nodded to her. "Or the fact that we won at Ulindi because you sent the battleship there."

"Oh, hell, Artur, that battleship could have done nothing but avenge you if you hadn't saved yourself and your soldiers." She looked back at the star display. "Speaking of being yanked around, have you been told the message the Dancers sent to us?"

"Colonel Rogero passed it on," Drakon said. "*Watch the different stars*. Do we have any idea what that means?"

"I talked to our astrophysicists," Iceni said, "and according to them, all stars are different. No two stars are identical."

"Why would the Dancers tell us to watch all stars? And if they wanted us to do that, why wouldn't they say *watch all the stars*? What is it the Dancers expect us to do?"

Iceni smiled humorlessly, leaning back in her seat. "Or, what is it the Dancers are trying to manipulate us into doing? I get the impression that the Alliance is taking the Dancers at their words, as if they are completely sincere, truthful, and guileless."

Drakon raised both eyebrows. "Seriously?"

"Yes. Whereas you and I know that no one, no matter their

external shape, is completely sincere, truthful, and guileless. The Dancers have an agenda. They want us to do certain things, which may be to our benefit, or may be to the benefit of the Dancers."

"They did save this planet," Drakon pointed out.

"Agreed. Which would give them every right to express their wishes openly to us because we owe them payment for that debt. Instead, they offer vague warnings."

Drakon shook his head, looking stubborn. "That doesn't make sense. It's hard enough to make people do what you want when you directly tell them what you want. Trying to manipulate them with vague statements is likely to make them do the opposite of what you want."

"Maybe the Dancers don't realize that. Maybe they're using a tactic that works with Dancers."

"Maybe." Drakon eyed the star display, rubbing his chin as he thought. "Let's assume that for whatever reason, the Dancers think that message is useful. Different stars. All right. I spent a lot of time in the Syndicate ground forces as opposed to the government or industry branches. To me, watch is a cautionary word. It means you're looking for danger, or guarding something."

She sat forward. "Then the Dancers would be telling us to guard or be on guard somewhere? That's nothing we don't already know."

"Somewhere *different*," Drakon said. "Which would mean not the usual places, or the places we're already doing that."

Iceni indicated the star display. "We've had a couple of enigma ships show up at the jump point from Pele while you were gone. They appear, turn, and jump back to Pele."

"Scouts," Drakon said. "We saw one right after we got back."

"Yes. Keeping an eye on us and what we're doing. The first one showed up while there were only a few cruisers and Hunter-Killers here, plus our battle cruiser *Pele*. That worried me that the enigmas would launch an attack as soon as possible, having seen our relative weakness. But the second enigma ship showed up after you and the *Midway* had returned."

"So they saw we have some teeth," Drakon said. "But the Dancers must have known we are already watching the jump point from Pele. That can't be what they were talking about." He paused. "A warning to watch different stars. It has to be related to the enigmas, not the Syndicate. The only place we know of that the enigmas can access human space is through Pele, then here at Midway. Were the Dancers telling us to worry about the enigmas being able to reach other stars? Different stars than Midway?"

Iceni gave him a startled look. "That is plausible. Black Jack gave us some star charts showing enigma territory." Inwardly cursing Togo's absence, which meant he wasn't here to do this, Iceni played with the display's controls until it zoomed out and framed a wide region of space. "There. This is the picture Black Jack's fleet put together from actually traversing part of enigma space and from what they could get out of the Dancers."

Drakon studied the star chart, shaking his head. "If that chart is complete, then Pele is all the enigmas can reach for a long way using jump drives. They could go scores of light-years up, down, right, or left and find other access points to human-occupied space, if there's nothing blocking them from going those directions, but nothing else near here. And it also matches our experience since the Syndicate boundaries got pushed back from Pele. The only place that has shown evidence of enigma activity since then is here at Midway."

What had she been told about jump drives? Iceni frowned, thinking, then nodded. "Captain Bradamont told me something, confirming what I had seen in a Syndicate intelligence report. Do you remember when Black Jack's fleet hit Sancere?"

"Not really. That was a big Syndicate shipbuilding star system, right?"

"Yes," Iceni confirmed. "The thing is, Black Jack's fleet shouldn't have been able to reach Sancere from the star system where they entered jump space. But he knew some tricks, from the old days, that allowed the range of the jump drives to be extended a bit. The Syndicate had guessed that was what he had done, and Bradamont confirmed it for me."

Drakon gazed at the star display again, plainly reevaluating his earlier assessment. "If the enigmas can jump farther than we think, far enough to access human space from other stars, why haven't they done it already?"

"Maybe they're trying to figure out how to do it. But how would the Dancers have learned of that?" She glared at the glittering stars on the display in frustration. "Every question we have just leads to more questions."

"One thing I do know," Drakon said. "Speaking in military terms. When you hit an obstacle, there are two approaches you can try. The first is to keep hitting it, trying to break through it. That happens a lot. The other approach is to go around it, to try to find some way of bypassing the obstacle. I don't care how enigmas or Dancers think. Those are basic realities. The enigmas have tried going through Midway twice, and they've been thrown back twice. That's another reality. So, either they keep trying to push into human space through Midway, or they try to find a way around us."

"A different star?" Iceni chewed her lower lip as she looked at the star display. "It doesn't help much, does it? If we don't have a range to work with, any human star could potentially be within range of the enigma jump drives. Which ones are the different ones that we're supposed to watch?"

"Maybe the astrophysicists can give us some clues," Drakon suggested.

"Maybe they can. I'll tell them to get together with our best jump-drive technicians." Iceni smiled. "It will drive them crazy. Theoretical physicists hate dealing with engineers."

"And vice versa," Drakon pointed out.

Iceni sighed. "There's been something I've been avoiding asking, but since we brought up the subject of crazy . . ."

He didn't need her to specify what she meant. "I don't know whether or not Colonel Morgan is dead," Drakon said bluntly, his voice harsh. "But, as of when I left Ulindi, she had not contacted any of our people or been found by anyone, and there were a lot of ways she could have died. Odds are, what's left of her is buried in the rubble of the snake alternate command center."

Drakon shrugged before continuing. "If she didn't die there, well, planets are big places, and that planet has a lot of smashed buildings and craters and rubble now. They'll still be finding remains of people in the wreckage a century from now."

As much as she did not want to feel any sympathy for Drakon where Morgan was concerned, Iceni could see how his shrug was an unsuccessful attempt to cover up his own distress. "I know she served you well, but she also betrayed you. If she died in the line of duty, that may have been the best possible outcome."

"Yes. If she died," Drakon agreed, nodding heavily.

"You think she might still be alive?"

"Until I see a body, I will not be sure. Morgan could be almost superhuman at times."

"And you are no longer concerned about the child, who by this time might already have been born?"

Drakon sat looking at nothing for several seconds before replying. "Either Morgan's fail-safe plans took effect, and the girl is already dead as well, or what Morgan told me about provisions being made was true, and the girl has been allowed to survive Morgan's death. That will give me time to find her."

He focused on Iceni. "That makes one more person we need to find, but it seems to me the priority is to find your former assistant."

"We do not *know* he acted against us," Iceni repeated. "He may be pursuing whoever did pass that information to the Syndicate."

Drakon let his skepticism show. "I'm sure that's what he will say. If he shows up at your door. You changed all your codes, so he shouldn't be able to get through that door."

Iceni shook her head. "If Togo wants to get somewhere, he'll do it. The tougher the defense, the longer he will take to get through, but he will succeed." She lightly tapped one sleeve of her jacket, the one from which Drakon had once seen a weapon appear with startling swiftness. "If necessary, I can defend myself, and I will shoot to kill, but my chances against him, if he has turned, are not nearly as good as I would like."

"Do you need extra security?" Drakon asked. "I can send over some people and some equipment."

"Me?" Iceni laughed. "Need extra protection? I'm invincible, General Drakon. The people idolize me."

"I saw the vids," Drakon said. "You did look invincible." It was hard to tell how he felt about that.

"You didn't see me once I got back inside this office," Iceni said. She let her defenses slip. There was quite literally no one else with whom she could share this. "I am frightened, Artur."

He sat straighter, alarmed in a way that gratified her. "Of what?"

"Them. The people. Not in the Syndicate way. I am frightened of what they will do for me, what I can ask of them. You weren't there, Artur. You didn't feel it." Iceni ran both hands through her hair. "I got back into this office when it was over, and I swear I could hear the gods laughing at me. Have you ever held a weapon so dangerous that you were afraid to use it?"

"It really felt like that?" Drakon asked.

"Yes. I know that I can do some very big things now, Artur. But that means I can make some very big mistakes." She closed her eyes, seeing the vast crowd again in her memory. "We've been worried about giving them more freedom, enough freedom, enough rights, that they wouldn't revolt against us."

"Yes," Drakon said. "The last elections should have kept them quieter longer than this."

"No!" She opened her eyes and glared at him. "They didn't want more freedom from me. They wanted a leader. They wanted safety and security and surety. I could have reinstituted all sorts of Syndicate rules then and there, and they would have cheered me."

Drakon just stared at her. "You're sure of that?"

"Positive. They will do what I ask, but I still can't force them. Does that make any sense? It's true. Let's lay this out. You must know from what Colonel Rogero told you that the ground forces can no longer be used to enforce our rule."

"Yes," Drakon agreed. "Which means I can't launch a coup against you."

She lowered her hands and deepened her glare. "That wasn't my point. I still consider this a partnership."

"Even though you no longer have to consider it a partnership?" Drakon smiled thinly. "Thanks. It's been trending this way for a while. I've seen it. To the citizens, and to the mobile forces, you're the one in charge. I'm your senior assistant."

"You are my partner," Iceni insisted.

"Not to the citizens. And you were just talking about how much power they have given you."

"It's not like I could order my warships to bombard the planet! I'm not talking about coercion! Don't you understand that?"

"Yes, I do." Drakon shrugged again. "It's called leadership. Real leadership. It's why my division followed me here and why they followed me when we moved against the Syndicate. You've built something stronger than that with the citizens, and," he continued, "you earned it. That was an incredibly gutsy move, facing that crowd with nothing between you and them but whatever defenses were worked into your suit."

"My suit's defenses wouldn't have accomplished anything against that many people except making them angrier," Iceni said. "Thank you. *You* understand what it took for me to do that."

"And you surely understand how it feels to know your co-ruler could get rid of you and not fear any backlash or other trouble."

She tried to hold her temper in check, because she did know how that would feel. "If you think I could dispose of you and not have a lot of trouble from the likes of Colonel Rogero, you are seriously mistaken. I will admit that because I came up through the Syndicate system, just as you did, I could not help but realize the option existed for me to simplify the ruling arrangements in this star system. But," she added, letting her voice harden, "I hope you realize that I am capable of seeing where such an action would lead. It would take me right back into the Syndicate system no matter what name I gave it. I do not want that legacy, Artur Drakon. I also do not want to spend however much life I have left swatting down anyone who might threaten my control of this star system."

"I don't want to be pushed aside," Drakon said, "but I won't threaten what you have. I will not pull down the stars in an attempt to lessen your authority."

She did not answer at once, trying to think through the right thing to say. "Do you understand that I am not attempting to lessen your authority?"

This time he took a moment to answer. "Actually, you did. That bit with the people. The mob that worshipped you. That was all about you." Drakon held up a restraining hand as Iceni began to respond, hot words ready to fly. "But. You didn't have any choice. You had to make it all about you. I can see that. I'm unhappy, but I can't fault you. You did what you had to do, and I think you understand as well as I do that you and I could destroy this star system very effectively if we started really trying to undercut each other."

"Yes," Iceni said, keeping her answer short to avoid saying something angry and wrong, wanting to disagree but unable to find grounds for doing that.

"Let's talk about what stirred the people up," Drakon suggested. "Snake agents must have been involved, but I can't shake the feeling that there are other parties playing in this game."

"I have the same feeling," Iceni said. "If . . . if Mehmet Togo is working his own agenda, he could be one of those parties."

"Could be," Drakon agreed. "One of them, but not all of them."

"Not even close. You already said it. We have to stand together. Any division between us will offer leverage to those wanting to pry apart this star system."

He smiled crookedly. "We'd better not stand too close. There are already rumors about you and me." Before she could comment on that, Drakon went on. "I've brought back a lot of new people, as did your Kommodor. We need those people, but, obviously, they represent potential danger. As I've been reminded repeatedly lately, the snakes would pay almost any price to get someone close enough to you or me."

"Agreed," Iceni said, grateful that Drakon's transition to the new recruits meant that she didn't have to discuss the rumors about her and Drakon with the man himself. "We finally have plenty of crew members for all of our warships. But our security screening processes are overloaded. How confident are you of the loyalty of the soldiers you acquired at Ulindi?"

"Fairly confident," he said. "For some of them, extremely confident. But they are all getting screened."

She blew out a breath in exasperation. "Eventually, they will all get screened. The new soldiers you recruited, the crew members from the transports, and the survivors from some of the Syndicate ships destroyed at Ulindi."

"Your Kommodor didn't want any of the crew members who survived the destruction of CEO Boucher's battleship. I agreed with her."

"So do I," Iceni said. "Even if they were reliable, they helped destroy much of Kane. We don't need any trace of that legacy among our crews."

"Even if snake agents are among our new people," Drakon said, "they shouldn't sabotage our defense against the enigmas if a larger force shows up based on what the enigma scouts reported. And we took out a lot of Syndicate power at Ulindi. The ground forces, the flotilla, all of the snakes there, and Ulindi itself, which won't be able to serve as a Syndicate base without being conquered by the Syndicate again."

"You're saying our primary external worry in the near future is the enigmas?" Iceni fell back in her seat, gazing at the ceiling. "We can't forget about or underestimate the Syndicate. That almost caused total disaster for us at Ulindi. And there are other concerns. We've received information about warlords in other sectors."

"We've been worrying about nearby warlords for a while. Is this information about threats anywhere close to us?" Drakon asked.

She lowered her gaze back to him. "Close enough. Moorea might be threatened. Or it might already be part of someone else's sphere of influence."

"Moorea? Should we have sent *Pele* and the transport to Iwa?"

"If there are problems at Moorea, if Moorea has shifted from the Syndicate to some warlord's dominion, *Pele* might be able to learn something about it while she's at Iwa," Iceni said. "I told Kapitan Kontos to find out all he can. If he doesn't learn anything there, I might consider sending a heavy cruiser on to Moorea on a scouting mission."

Drakon nodded with a rueful expression. "Trying to preempt trouble at Ulindi nearly got us wiped out, but I still think trying to spot and deal with problems before they hit us is a good policy."

She sat forward, her eyes intent. "Then we need to spot and deal with the internal problems as well. Whatever our enemies are planning in this star system, they will never assume that you and I are working together as closely as possible."

"I agree," he said. "But, Gwen, can we do it? Can two people raised and trained as Syndicate CEOs actually work together without constantly keeping their guards up against each other? Especially when we have things like that trap at Ulindi to worry about? If it wasn't your assistant Togo who tipped off the Syndicate, then we have someone still close to us who is working against us."

"And if it was Togo, he will remain a serious threat until eliminated. Do you believe that I am working against you?"

He gazed back at her. "No."

Did he mean it? "No matter what our subordinates do, if you and I do not figure out how to work without any suspicions between us, Artur Drakon, the next trap set for us will not fail."